A New World

A New World

A Novel

Robert M. Keane

RESOURCE *Publications* · Eugene, Oregon

A NEW WORLD
A Novel

Resource Publications
An Imprint of Wipf and Stock Publishers
199 W. 8th Ave., Suite 3
Eugene, OR 97401

www.wipfandstock.com

PAPERBACK ISBN: 978-1-5326-5372-8
HARDCOVER ISBN: 978-1-5326-5373-5
EBOOK ISBN: 978-1-5326-5374-2

Manufactured in the U.S.A.   07/05/18

PART I

Chapter 1

The Meaghers lived on Brush Avenue in Riverdale, a neighborhood of tree-lined streets in the Northwest section of the Bronx. When the father and the son got home they walked up the path single-file to their two-story brick home. The father, walking ahead, was a tall, large-shouldered Irishman, still handsome at fifty-nine, with black hair and blue eyes. The son, nineteen, was very nearly a physical copy of the father, without the wrinkles around the eyes or the thickening at the waist.

Florence heard the door open, and stuck her head out of the kitchen. "Oh, you're home." She was Mr. Meagher's daughter, the woman of the house, for the mother had been dead for nineteen years.

Mr. Meagher passed through the foyer into the living room, then the dining room, and then into the kitchen, where he opened an upper cabinet and took down a bottle of Old Overholt whiskey. Florence watched him pour out two ounces and drink it down. She was surprised. He almost never drank except at parties.

"Daddy, do you mind if we eat early?"

"Why so?"

"I have so much to do this afternoon."

"It's alright with me."

The father, son and daughter sat down to the table in the dining room, a room dark even now in mid-afternoon in the month of May. Florence gave her brother James a series of orders. "There's a big order at the A&P that has to be picked up. I shopped this morning but I didn't bring it all. And the bathroom has to be done. And this week it has to be done right."

James gave her a sour look. She was four years his senior, a big girl, heavy at the breasts and hips. She had the family blue eyes in a pretty face.

"You always wait until he's in the area before you issue commands," Jim accused.

Her father cut her short. "We'll say grace first." He stood up. "Bless us, O Lord, for these and all thy gifts which we have received from thy bounty through Jesus Christ, our Lord" —he hit hard on the "Our" and "Lord"—"Amen."

"—and the order has to be picked up tonight," continued Florence.

James didn't answer. The father also remained silent. Florence looked at them both. "What's the matter?" James still didn't answer.

"He came out to the brewery to me," said the father, "to tell me he's been thrown out of college."

Her eyes went wide. "What?"

James said in a voice loud with exasperation, "I told you, Pop. I haven't been thrown out of school. I've been suspended for two weeks. Two weeks."

The father turned on him angrily. "Don't you raise your voice at me, you pup. Whether it's two weeks, or however long it is, they don't want you."

"A lot of guys get suspended. You don't have to make such a big deal over it."

"Big deal? Big deal is it? You talk as if it was an honor they gave you. Sure, maybe I've been mistaken. Maybe it was an honor they gave you, and me thinking you were in disgrace."

James threw down his fork, pushed the chair back and started for the other room.

"Sit down there!" the father thundered, his arm pointing to the chair.

James stopped. "I don't want to eat."

"Sit down there."

"I don't feel like eating."

"Sit down there! You'll get up when we're all finished."

James sat down again.

"What happened?" Florence asked.

Mr. Meagher answered, "He's been put down for theft."

James answered, "I borrowed one of the reference books from the library."

Mr. Meagher: "He stole it."

James: "I brought it back already." He turned to the father. "And it wasn't stealing."

"What does suspended mean?" Florence asked.

"It doesn't mean anything really," said James. "I don't go to class for two weeks."

"The priest wants to see me tomorrow," said the father.

"What priest?" Florence asked.

"The dean," said James. "Father Phelan."

Florence started to cry.

"What are you crying for?" the father asked.

She wouldn't reply. She covered her face and continued to sniffle.

"What's wrong?"

"Nothing." She was still sniffling.

"Well, your bladder is very close to your eyes if you're crying and there's no reason."

"Everything's going wrong," she wailed.

"How does it affect you?" the father asked.

"How does it affect me?" Her eyes were big. "Ralph is coming with his family tomorrow and everything's in a mess. The house is a wreck. The food is still in the store. Nobody wants to do anything to help. And James is suspended from school. And now you won't even be here tomorrow. The whole thing is going to be a. . .a. . .fiasco."

"Won't I be back for dinner?"

"Well, Ralph will hear about it. And his family will hear about it."

"Why should they hear about it?" Mr. Meagher asked.

"Even if they don't hear about it," she continued, tears still flowing, "everything is going wrong. Aunt Nora wants to cook the turkey. I tried to tell her I don't need her help, but she's so bossy, you can't tell her anything. And she cooks her turkeys so dry. She'll just ruin it. I don't see why Nora has to come tomorrow at all."

"Don't they have dinner with us every Sunday?" asked the father.

"Couldn't they miss one?"

"Don't they want to meet the boy and his family too? And why not? Your Aunt Nora has been good to you."

"I'm sure Ralph's mother and father will be delighted to meet Aunt Nora and Uncle Arthur," she continued. "Especially if Arthur is high, which he will be, because he hasn't come home yet this weekend. I hope he stays high, wherever he is, God forgive me."

Mr. Meagher was exasperated. "If you don't want Nora to do the cooking, then tell her you don't want her to do the cooking."

"You tell her that," said Florence. "I can't."

"If she can cook every other Sunday," said the father, "I see no reason why she can't cook tomorrow."

"Fine, fine," said Florence in a strained voice, throwing out her hand dramatically, "we'll let Aunt Nora do the cooking and Ralph and I and his mother and father will go out to a restaurant."

Mr. Meagher smashed his fist down on the table so that the dishes jumped. "Will you stop talking horse shit."

Florence pushed back her chair, stood up and walked out of the room. "Come back here," the father roared. But the command went unheeded. She went up the stairs to her bedroom.

Mr. Meagher got up. "Goddammit," he said, "a man can't have a meal in peace." He clumped out through the kitchen and out the back door of the house.

Jim was left alone at the table. He started to laugh.

Florence leaned over the banister. "Where's he gone?" she asked.

"To Nora's."

"Oh hell," said Florence. "She'll get mad now. What are you laughing at, anyway? Sometimes I think you're crazy."

"The two dragons will have a fight in the backyard," said Jim.

Mr. Meagher crossed the backyard to a neighboring house where the Connollys lived. He found Nora Connolly, his sister, peeling potatoes in the kitchen. The glistening white spuds were all around her. A stout, large-breasted woman, she had a round, freckled face with a pug nose stuck incongruously in the middle of it. Her cotton stockings were knotted in ugly lumps above her knees, and she was wearing an old green housecoat. She asked, "Harry, what are you all upset about?"

"Don't cook tomorrow." Realizing how loudly he had spoken, he softened his voice. "Florence wants to cook, so let her do the cooking."

Nora pursed her lips and said, "What do I want to be doing the cooking for if she wants to do it? Tell her go right ahead. The best of luck to her."

Mr. Meagher nodded his head, satisfied.

"She doesn't know the first thing about cooking a turkey," said Nora, cutting a half inch into the meat of the potato. "And I was thinking she wanted to make an impression on the young man and his family, but she thinks she knows it all, so the best of luck to her."

"Good," said Harry. "Where's Arthur? He's off again?"

"Old Nora will be good enough for every other Sunday. Indeed 'n' I don't feel a bit bad about it. It will be a pleasure to just sit down and eat. That is, if we're welcome at all."

"You're welcome of course," said Harry, annoyed.

"I could have made good brown gravy with giblets in it, and potato dressing, and—."

"Enough of that. Where's Arthur?"

"Who knows where he is? Wherever there's a bum in town with a nickel in his pocket looking for a carousing, that's where he is."

"He hasn't called?"

"He wouldn't remember the number if he could reach the phone."

"He'll be in," said Harry.

"He always makes it home," said Nora. "'Tis God's blessing for me."

"I have to finish my dinner," said Harry.

He went back to his own dining room and sat to the table again. Thinking Florence was up in her room—she was out of sight, looking out the window in the living room—he yelled up to the second story, "I told Nora you'd be doing the cooking, and she says that's all right. So that's the end of it. We'll have no more of it."

Jim wanted to break out laughing at the incongruity of the father yelling upstairs to Florence when she was actually only eight feet away, but his father was in a dangerous mood, so he choked off the laugh. The two went on eating in silence. The father seemed to be lost in thought. At length he looked up and asked Jim, "Who is this Ralph?"

Jim couldn't hold it anymore. He burst out laughing. Florence bolted into the dining room and cried "Daddy!" in a shocked voice. "You don't even know who he is?"

"I thought you were in your room," said Mr. Meagher, flustered.

Florence said, "You know who he is. He's the lawyer. You told me one night that you liked him."

"I know well enough who he is," said the father.

Jim was laughing like a fool.

"What in hell are you laughing at?" the father demanded.

Jim challenged him. "What does Ralph look like?"

"Never mind what he looks like," the father stormed.

Florence was near tears again. "We've been steady for almost four months. I thought you liked him, Daddy. You know who he is, don't you?"

"Well, there's a lot of them come in and out."

Florence charged on. "He's the one who's the assistant district attorney. Remember you said that was a good job for a fellow who was starting in law?"

"Certainly I remember."

"He talks about you all the time, Daddy. In fact, he wants to go out and see you at the brewery."

Mr. Meagher had grown white in the face. But this time it wasn't in anger. He pressed his hand against his midsection, and bent forward.

"Are you all right?" Florence asked.

He didn't answer for a moment or two, then said, "Get me a glass of milk."

Florence got the glass of milk. Mr. Meagher took it and got up from the table. He sat down in the living room and switched on the television. A wrestling match was on. He watched the program in silence. He still had his hand pressed against his stomach. His face was drained of blood.

Florence quietly cleared the dishes from the table.

"I'll go for the groceries," said Jim.

"Good," said Florence. "Curley is minding them at the counter."

Chapter 2

Jim found a beautiful afternoon outside. The sun had sunk only low enough to mellow the greens of the trees and the lawn. He looked over to the wooden-shingled house next door. There was a girl sitting on the porch, her feet propped against the railing, reading a book. It was Geraldine South, or Jill, as she was called. Her twin brother, Jack, was Jim's classmate at Fordham.

"Hey, Jill, you want to go for a ride?"

"Sure."

He waited with a pleasant feeling of proprietorship as she came across the lawn.

She climbed into the Meaghers' car.

"Well, hi," she said. It seemed to Jim that the whole front seat was suddenly filled with bare leg. She had shorts on, and her bare legs had fine, subtle lines, not muscular at all. It took a moment for the shock and pleasure of it all to wear off. But then the accustomed ways of thinking took hold: after all, it was only Jill. She was wearing a sweater; it emphasized that, at nineteen, she was still as flat-chested as most of the girls were at fourteen. And no one had ever called her a beauty. She was so much Jack's twin it hurt her appearance. They had the same Roman nose, which fitted into Jack's face but was too large for hers.

"What are you reading," he asked, as they drove down Brush Avenue.

"*Pickwick Papers.*" She held up the book.

"You're on a Dickens kick?"

"He's terrific," she said.

"He's corny."

She turned sideways in the seat to face him, and doubled her legs under her. "How can you say that?"

"He is."

"His novels have more, more. . .sweep than anything that's being written now," said Jill.

"You go for that 'You bounder, I'll tweak your nose' stuff, and all the rest of it?"

"I just finished reading that," she said, excitedly.

She opened the book and read aloud:

"And allow me to say, sir, said the irascible Doctor Payne, that if I had been Tappleton or if I had been Slammer, I would have pulled your nose, sir, and the nose of every man in this company."

She gave out with a loud, rippling laugh. "Didn't think that was funny when you read it?"

"It's been years since I read it," said Jim. "We read that in high school, didn't we?"

"I read it every year," said Jill. "He was a great man. I would love to have known him."

"I guess so," said Jim. The he remembered an item from a class lecture. "He didn't get along with his wife, did he?"

"He was a genius," said Jill. "But his wife didn't develop at all."

"It's funny though," said Jim. "You'd think with all that he knew about human nature, he'd know how to pick a wife."

"Sex is irrational," she replied airily.

"Look at Thackeray, too," said Jim.

"I don't know anything about him," said Jill.

"His wife was in an asylum."

"Is that right?" she asked.

"Sure."

"Well I bet you could find a lot of examples of writers who get happily married too."

"Sure. Uncle Arthur," said Jim. They both laughed, though Jill tried to stop. She felt mean, laughing at Arthur.

At the store, Curley had the two boxes waiting. He packed groceries at the checkout counter, a beefy youth with a sleepy smile. Jim suspected that he had a crush on Florence, and figured she made quite practical use of his affections by assigning him to guard her groceries.

Jim went into the store proper to get some more items; then he had to wait at the checkout line. Idly he studied the different types of razor blades offered for sale on the back of the register. Then his eye caught Jill. She was looking at the pocket-book rack stretched across the front of the store. She leaned backwards to see the top titles, and occasionally would pull one off the shelf and thumb through it. She looked clean-limbed and pretty from the back. Her natural blonde hair was another characteristic she shared with Jack.

As he watched her, the thought struck Jim that, if his sister Florence had come to the store with a guy, she would have made a big production of walking up and down the aisles with him, oohing and aahing over everything. But not Jill. If she'd rather stay up front and look over the pocket books, that's what she'd do. She was always on the level. Even in conversation. He reflected on what she said of Thackeray: "I don't know anything about him." If that were Florence, she would have made some comment about *Vanity Fair*, which she hadn't read, and the man would have gone rushing into a discussion of Thackeray, only to discover five minutes later that she didn't know anything more than the one fact about *Vanity Fair*.

When he got checked through the line, he went over to Jill and ran his fingernail across the back of her knee. She jumped, and turned, and asked, "What are you up to?"

"I was just admiring your legs."

She half-smiled.

"They're all right," he said, "But you know me, Jill: I don't go much for that cheap physical stuff."

"Not much," she said, her mouth tightening quickly.

He loaded the groceries into the car and they went to the Peppermint Stick for a soda. The ice cream parlor had red and white striped walls, and round marble tables with wire chairs, and the sodas served had two scoops of rich ice cream and were heaped with whipped cream. Each part of the soda had its own delight: the first pull on the straw brought the sweet liquid; then the whipped cream could be eaten away on one side of the hill, until the chocolate syrup and the ice cream were exposed; then the two scoops of ice cream could be patiently carved until the bottom of the glass was reached, where there was a full inch of residue of chocolate syrup.

"How's school?" asked Jim.

"All right." She went to Fordham also, but to the School of Education downtown, which was co-ed. No women were admitted as students on the main Bronx campus.

She probably knows about the suspension, Jim thought. Jack did, and he would have told her.

"I've been suspended you know."

"Jack told me. I think it's ridiculous. Over an old book! If they suspended everybody who hooked a book out of the library they wouldn't have any students left. Downtown, some of the boys go in and cut the pages right out of the reference books with razor blades. He must be a crank, that Phelan."

As she talked on with the sympathy he expected, Jim wanted to tell her more. He wanted to tell her the whole story, for Father Phelan had done more than suspend him. The priest had told him there was a "smoothness and cleverness" in his character that was "not fitting." What it amounted to, Jim had concluded bitterly, was he had called him a sneak. It was the capstone to his increasing load of doubts about himself. "You're not worth a shit," as his father had put it graphically in his rage in the car that morning. There were so many doubts, so many fears that he wanted to talk about. He almost started. But he didn't have the courage.

"What are you going to do now?" Jill asked.

"Take it easy for two weeks," Jim replied. "What the heck. Don't pass up a vacation."

"Will you be back in school in time for the Freshman Prom?"

He thought for a moment. "Yeah. I guess so."

She hoped he'd follow up on the subject, but he let it drop. He was probably taking Eva anyway.

Chapter 3

Jill came back to the house with Jim. When Mr. Meagher heard her voice, he left the television set and came out to greet her. "Ah, Jill," he said. She went right to him, and kissed his cheek as she always did, and he grinned.

"You're a high blossom," he told her, "from a sweet tree."

Jill loved it. She loved him too. And he'd do anything for her. Just the opposite of his attitude toward Eva. The father wouldn't give Eva the time of day from an armful of watches. The Polock. She wasn't even Polish, but he had decided she looked Polish.

"What have you got against the Polish?" Jim had asked him one time.

"You'd starve to death with them," the father said. "When I was new in this country, I went out once with a Polock, and she brought me to the house, and opened the ice-box, and sure there wasn't a damn thing on the five shelves, but an apple, and that with hair growing on it."

That was the origin of his favorite name for Eva: Hairy Apple.

Jim grabbed his baseball glove and went off to a ballgame in the park, leaving his father with Jill. As he walked along the street, punching his fist into the pocket to soften the leather, he wondered how his father ever got around to asking out a Polish girl in the first place. He must certainly have been a different man in those days. And what would his father have been like on a date? Jim couldn't even imagine it. For the girl it must have been like going out with a grizzly bear. But no, he would have been tender, as he was with Jill. He was so many contradictions, that man.

Chapter 4

When Jill left the Meaghers', she walked across to her own yard in a happy mood. The ride with Jim had been fun; a talk with Florence had been interesting; and the visit with Mr. Meagher, who showered affection on her, made her tranquil. She went to the lilacs along the fence and inhaled long and deeply: they had been in bloom three days. It was lilac time at South's, she thought to herself, and tried to remember what song it was that that line was trying to bring to mind. She went up to the porch and decided to indulge herself in her favorite pastime: just to think for a while.

By nature she was reflective. Her father called her "the greatest thinker ever wore skirts." Jack teased her too, and told her she was in another world. But she had to. And she made very satisfying discoveries too, even if they took her a long time. When she finally had a whole situation analyzed, the actual event would be way in the past. A boy would say something on a date that she wouldn't quite understand, and she would not pursue it at the moment because it wouldn't be that important. But still she wouldn't forget. She would tuck it in the grab-bag in her mind. It might not be until months later that it would suddenly dawn: "*That's* what he meant!" Then she'd be happy.

Today she had two items for her grab-bag: Jim running his finger across the back of her leg in the A&P, and Florence's panic over Ralph's visit.

She rested her sneakers on the rail of the porch, and smiled when she thought about Jim. She remembered the party after graduation from Saint Margaret's Elementary School when they were fourteen. At the party her brother Jack turned out the lights in the living room, and the whole group played Flashlight, Spin-the-Bottle, and Post-Office. Jack was the star since he was the best-looking of the boys, and easily the most aggressive. Jill had to sit against the wall, and watch the girls throw things at Jack, and squeal and act silly. But when it came Jim Meagher's turn to pick someone to go to the post office, he had picked her, and she was delighted. When the two of them had shut the door to the group, she stood with her heart almost stopped, and closed her eyes and waited for the kiss. She got a cruel disappointment, for it turned out he had no courage at all. He backed and slid along the wall away from her. He looked ill. There was nothing to do but wait. After a minute, Jack hammered on the door and demanded, "What's going on in there?"

He tried to open the door but Jill used all her strength to hold the knob against him. Finally Jim said in a small voice from up the hallway, "We'd better go back in, Jill." As he passed her to enter the living room, he gave her a quick kiss and then ran. Jill smiled more when she remembered how wild with suspicion Jack was. "You didn't have to take so long."

He even got sore at Jim, having made the natural error of projecting what *he* would have done behind the door. Jim of course was delighted to be suspected; he walked around the room like a rooster. It was all very funny.

The other situation in the grab-bag, the dinner Florence was giving for Ralph and his family, was not so funny. It disturbed Jill to see anyone to get as upset as Florence was. She had actually called Jill "Mary" when Jill was leaving the house. Several times during the conversation it was clear she wasn't paying attention to what was being said at all. But Jill knew what was most disturbing about the situation: it was so calculating. Florence was on a campaign to get Ralph, and the campaign was at a critical stage, the meeting of the families.

Well, the families had to get together at some stage of the romance, didn't they? Yes. But they didn't have to get together before an engagement. For Florence to take this step before a ring was given was to force the issue. It was a critical moment in Florence's campaign; hence her panic. The problem was that Florence *was* on a campaign. She was like Jill's girlfriend, Nancy McGann. Nancy went to nursing school, and picked out a medical student the first week she was there. For two years she refused dates with any of the other medical students so as not to give even the appearance of being entangled with anyone else. In the end, she got him. She told the story to Jill in the afterglow of her victory. Jill was shocked. She said, as cautiously as she could, that she had always had the idea that in Providence her man would come along. Nancy had stiffened and replied, "God helps those who help themselves."

Jill suspected her own attitude was somewhat romanticized and silly. How would two people get together unless someone did some planning? But still, she couldn't shake the idea that her own attitude in the end made more sense. Perhaps, she thought, it was because we know so little about another person that we have to trust in God that we won't make an absurd choice.

She was hard on Florence, she knew. Florence would be a good wife. On Saturday mornings, when Florence decided to bake, she baked for everybody, and the Connollys and the Souths and the other neighbors got a cake as well as the Meaghers. She had a good heart.

Yet Jill liked Jim better, for all that he was as thoughtless and kiddish and harum-scarum at nineteen as he had been at nine. He seemed sometimes to deliberately try to get Florence and Mr. Meagher upset. He seemed to do it almost from malice. Maybe he was striking back because the father—and perhaps Florence too—was sitting too hard on him, was too critical of him. Of course, all the Irish fathers were alike, Jill thought. If the son or daughter brought home a "99" grade on the report card, the father didn't praise the high mark: he wanted rather to know why it wasn't a hundred. It was the same in the South household. But there was more there in that relationship between Mr. Meagher and Jim. Mr. Meagher had been a youngest child. Had he been sat on too hard by a father and older children? In that case, the sins of the father weren't being visited on the son, so much as the sins of the grandfather were. Wasn't that great? And where did it all begin? Back in the mists of some Celtic dawn? And where would it end? In some American twilight?

In any event, Florence would be married: Jill had no doubt that she was going to get Ralph. The question was, was he worth getting? He seemed very mild to handle someone as domineering as Florence could be. But that was a question that would be answered only by the years.

Florence would be married, and Nancy McGann was getting married, and Tootsy Vesh had a baby already, and how many others? A lot. How about herself? The old fear: was she pretty enough to get married? It was the fear that made her arrange the bathroom mirrors so that she could almost get a profile, and she always had the hope that the nose would be a little shorter, and the chin more feminine and rounded. She did have nice legs though. Jim said that. She knew it anyway. She held her legs up. Boys did like her. They seemed to, anyhow. But she hadn't gone out in two months. So? How many girls had dates all the time?

Why wasn't Jim taking her out if he thought she had such great legs? There could be a lot of reasons. Maybe it was just because she was next door. Maybe he was afraid to get involved because the families were so close. But Eva lived only two blocks away. That was pretty close too. What secret did Eva have? She was cute all right. But no personality. Nobody knew anything about her, really, because she never said anything. "Like a tomb," as Tootsy Vesh said.

Maybe Eva was letting him take liberties with her, Jill thought. Maybe she wasn't as sweet and innocent as she looked. Jill sat straight up. That was mean, she said to herself. Catty. Most likely untrue.

Maybe Jim went out with Eva instead of her because Eva wasn't a cold fish, worrying all the time.

That's me, thought Jill. Worry. Worry. Worry.

Bob Pinelli, who was the last boy to take her out with any regularity, undoubtedly thought she was a cold fish. They went dancing, and in the slow number when he held her too close ("that Italian blood," she could hear her aunt saying), she fended him off. In the end she sat him down, worrying that perhaps she was inciting him, which would be a serious sin. At the same time she was thinking: Am I crazy? I finally find a guy I can get excited and I'm fighting with him?

Oh, face facts, Jill thought. She didn't really like Bob Pinelli. He always had his comb too handy. And he was forever squatting down before gum machine mirrors in the subway to admire himself. And he scented himself. Like a rose. And as for getting him excited, a female cat could get him excited. Worst of all, he had no sense of humor. If a girl didn't want to go along with him, he could at least have made a joke out of it. But Pinelli got angry, made comments about her being a cold fish, asked, "Are you a nun?" and went on in that vein.

Later on that night in her bed, Jill framed the answer that hadn't come to her at the dance. "It may come as a surprise to you, Mr. Pinelli, but the question of religion *is* central."

Pinelli wouldn't have known what she was talking about, but it was true nevertheless. The question of religion didn't seem to trouble her parents. They had the good, old-fashioned, unquestioning kind of faith. They were—as the students sometimes put it sarcastically— of the pay, pray, and obey generation. True, they didn't have any college degrees on the wall, and the only books in the houses of the first-generation Irish immigrants were of the odd-lot variety to be found in the living room bookcase, but then they didn't have to worry whether Bertrand Russell was right in calling the earth an orb spinning heedlessly through a mindless universe, or if the French Existentialists were right in demanding that man learn to live without God because there wasn't anybody up there. Jill had to worry about that. That was the gift of education that the Irish worshiped.

One thing was sure. If Bertrand Russell was right, then girls like Eva were right; there was no need to bother. Why scruple if the world were after all a jungle? But Jill hadn't come to any such conclusion, and hoped she never would.

Chapter 5

Jim left the ballgame after several hours and headed home. He had to make another stop at the store for Florence. He got in about 7 in the evening and went up to do the bathroom. Florence was on her knees, scrubbing the tub. She had certainly heard him coming up the stairs, but she gave him no acknowledgment.

"I told you I'd do it," he said.

"You don't have to bother now."

"I said I'd do it and I'll do it."

"When? Monday?"

"I had to stop at the store for you."

"Oh I'm sure it took you all this time to stop at the store."

"I bought the poultry seasoning. It's downstairs."

"How much was it?"

"Twenty-nine cents."

She went to her bedroom, and came out and gave him a quarter and four pennies.

"Thanks. I have at least twenty-nine cents for tonight now, anyway." He gave her a pleasing little smile.

She was stone-faced. "It's not my worry if you have no money." She went down the stairs.

Florence had been scrubbing at the brown stain formed by the constant drip of water from the tap. He powdered on cleanser and scrubbed at the remaining brown section until his arm was sore. He still couldn't get it as white as the section she had done. He rinsed with tap water, powdered on another layer of cleanser, and went back to scrubbing. How did she ever get it so white? She was as strong as a horse. Heaven help poor Ralph, he thought.

Already tired, he sat back on the mat and lit a cigarette. A cockroach came out from behind the adjoining wall and Jim sent him spinning down the drain with water from the tap. He could of course stay at Eva's for the evening and watch television, and then he wouldn't need any money. But that was awkward. Her father never left the living room.

Maybe Cricket. He went to the bedroom and pulled the bureau out from the wall that separated the Meagher house from the attached Connolly house. He got on his knees and put his mouth to the hole drilled in the baseboard. "Hey Cricket."

He got an answer right away. "What?"

"What are you doing?"

"I'm in the rack."

"You got any money?"

"Yeah."

"Great." Cricket, Nora's older son, worked sometimes after school as a copy boy at *The Mirror,* where his father was a deskman. He'd probably gotten a paycheck. "How much?"

"A nickel," said Cricket.

Jim was silent. Then he said softly, "You bastard." He could hear Cricket giggling. "How about Harold? Does he have any money?"

"Nah."

"Why don't you come over?" Jim asked. The bathroom would go easier with someone to talk to.

"Okay. In a minute."

Back in the bathroom, Jim spied the diary. Florence had left it out again, on the small table, with the clasp hanging loose. Putting the seat cover down over the toilet, he sat down and paged through it to see what was new with Florence's private life. It was a disappointment: she hadn't entered anything for two weeks. He skipped back to the entry in January where she had given him a slam. It always gave him an odd feeling to be reading about himself.

> Furious at J. at dinner. He can be so cruel.
> Wanted to know how old Ralph was. I told
> him, 33. He said parents will turn out to be
> nice to me because they probably want to get rid of him.
> He really hurt. A professional man shouldn't marry
> before thirty.

The best entry in the book was the one for the following Wednesday:

> Hi/ Dinner at Luchow's with R. He was

delighted when I told him Mr. Haskings
was nice all day when I made believe I
liked him. He said psychology teaches a
lot. I guess so. I wish I went to college.
Dinner terrific. Chateaubriand (sp?) Blue
cheese salad. Wond. coffee. R. decides he
will not go skiing now, wants to go out Sat.
night. Told him I didn't think so. On the
Central he asked me for Sunday. I said I
wasn't sure. He sulked the whole ride.
Very jealous. Said that four out of five
times I turn him down, which isn't true.
We go out almost every weekend. He
asked me if he should call anymore since
it just made him frustrated and resentful to be
refused. I told him he was acting like an ass.
But we made it up at the door. Show Boy
Friend. Very funny. Daddy mad when I got
home. J. ate at Nora's but Daddy said she
fries everything. R. is certainly acting very
Silly. Is ten years too much difference?

Jim could picture the scene of Florence calling Ralph an ass, and he laughed out loud. There was another entry somewhere where Florence had written: "Ralph has beautiful hands." He looked for that one, but he couldn't find it.

Jim heard Cricket downstairs. Florence was questioning him and he heard her say: "Jim has to do the bathroom, Edward."

Jim ran to the hallway and yelled down, "He's not going to bother me."

"Well, make sure you do it right," she shouted back.

Cricket came up. He was a slight youth, a full head shorter than Jim, with a mischievous face. He had a receding chin, and his eyeglasses were thick as the bottoms of milk bottles. He had brought his trick smoking pipe with him. It had a stem two feet long, patched with adhesive tape where it had snapped in the middle. This was only one of his oddities. Back in his room he had a goat-skin wine bag, a leopard-skin vest, and a white woolen cap with an elongated top that hung over his shoulder and had a white pom-pom sewed to it.

"Take a look at this," said Jim, handing him the diary, open to the entry describing the fight with Ralph. Cricket read it and then hunched his shoulders and squinted his eyes and let go with his staccato giggly laugh.

"Isn't that something?" Jim asked, grinning broadly. "She calls the guy an ass. And he's back for more." He threw the book on the table.

"What do you want money for?" Cricket asked.

"I'm supposed to go out with Eva."

Florence came up to find out what was going on. She stood in the doorway, and spied the diary, and rushed over and grabbed it from the table.

"Have you been reading this?"

"You know I wouldn't do a thing like that, Flo."

She looked at them both suspiciously. Cricket gave it away with a giggle.

"That's terrible," said Florence. "It's not even honorable."

"What, Flo?"

She went to her room to put the book away. She came back and she looked at the two of them, not saying anything right away. "You read it, didn't you?"

"Read what?"

"Aren't you ashamed?"

"Ashamed of what?"

"Ashamed to read something personal like that?"

"I thought you were like Anne Frank: you wanted everybody to read it. You leave it around all the time."

"You're so witty." She swung around to go downstairs.

"Hey, Flo."

"What?"

"Can you lend me a couple of bucks for tonight?"

"No."

"Thanks a lot," he called after her.

"You're welcome."

Jim came back to the bathroom. He had finished the sink. Now there was only the commode left, the most distasteful part of the job. He turned his back so he wouldn't have to look at it, and took the brush and gave a few fast sweeps around the inside of the bowl, then flushed. "That's that."

"What are you going to do for money?" Cricket asked.

"Change bottles, I guess."

They went downstairs. Florence was hammering a carpet in the back-yard. Jim found seven nickel bottles and ten three-cent milk bottles. "I'll see if there's any in your kitchen," he said to Cricket.

Florence stopped them as they crossed the backyard. "Did you finish?"

"Yes."

"How about the downstairs bathroom?"

Jim paused.

"That one has to be done too," said Florence firmly.

"I have to change some bottles so I can go out tonight."

"Honest to heaven," she complained. "You made such a fuss over a half-hour's work." She went upstairs. Jim waited to see what she was going to do. She came down again, and handed him two dollars. She had on her face the treat-me-as-cruel-as-you-will-I-can-return-only-goodness look.

"No matter what anybody says, Flo, you're all right."

"Finish the other bathroom."

"Okay."

"And make a good impression tomorrow." She had changed to an earnest tone. "You can be nice when you want to be."

"I will. Don't worry. We'll really roll out the mat."

"And when Ralph comes tonight, talk to him for a while, will you?"

"Okay."

"No one ever pays any attention to him," said Florence.

"Where's Daddy gone?"

"He said he was going for a walk. I think he's probably gone to see Dr. Ferry. He's not feeling well at all."

At this news of his father, Jim felt guilty. He went in quietly and worked for a few minutes on the downstairs bathroom, while Cricket watched and sucked on the two-feet-long smoking pipe. Then they went next door to the Connollys. As soon as they opened the door, Jim spotted five ginger ale bottles under the sink. Twenty-five cents. "Aunt Nora, do you mind if I change the bottles?"

"Help yourself. And sit down and have some tea and soda bread."

"Sure."

Aunt Nora looked at her son. "Your father is still among the missing."

Cricket didn't reply.

Nora's eyes blazed. "He's a God's curse on me, that man. The whelp of a skunk. He couldn't put a dime in a telephone box to tell me he's all right, but he's got a dollar down for every thirsty bum in the bar wherever he is. If I had the strength of a man, I'd grab him by the two legs and drag him out to the street and beat the head off him, the little rat blaggard."

It was awkward. "He'll be in soon, Aunt Nora."

"When?"

"He's been good for a while."

"Stop it! The latest is that he's leaving the church. He announced that the other night. 'Call up the rectory,' I told him. 'They'll have a party when they get the news.'"

Jim burst out laughing, and sprayed tea. Cricket made a high-pitched radio noise, as he did often. Down in the basement, Harold, Cricket's little brother, was sawing away on the violin.

"I've got to get off," said Jim. "That was good. Thanks."

Nora asked Cricket, "Where are you going?"

"Just to knock around."

"Be in early. I have enough to worry about."

"Okay, Ma."

Nora asked Jim, "How are preparations coming for the young man and his family?"

"Fine. Place looks great."

Nora grunted.

Chapter 6

In front of the house Jim and Cricket met Ralph Spaulding, Florence's boyfriend, coming up the adjoining path.

"What do you say, fellows!" he greeted.

They escorted him into the living room. "Hey Flo," Jim yelled upstairs, "Ralph is here."

"Be right downnnnnnn," Florence responded. Her voice had a little silver tinkle in it.

Ralph was big, well-built, with a way of holding one shoulder higher than the other. He would have been handsome had his hair not receded far back on his head. Amiable in temperament, he wanted to please. He gave the impression of being a loose-jointed friendly dog, and if given half a chance, would come and give a lick. Jim and Cricket discussed him frequently; neither could picture him as an assistant district attorney.

Jim got four cans of beer from the refrigerator. He bit the opener into them and got the satisfying spurt of air and foam. He reflected that this was going to be his brother-in-law. One way or another, they would be seeing each other for the rest of their lives. It was a funny thought. He brought the cans in and passed them around. If Florence were down, he would have had to bring glasses in too.

Ralph went through all the formalities. He enquired how Mr. Meagher was, then how school was, and then he discussed the weather. Cricket eyed him warily; he was even hostile. The fact was, Ralph was too polite to him and made him suspicious.

Ralph started to talk about his work, and that was more interesting. Jim went out for a second round of beers. Ralph was a two-beer man. Florence once had a boyfriend who drank a six-pack while he waited. Then when Florence got down, there was another delay while the guy went to the can. Mr. Meagher couldn't stand him. He didn't care about the beer—he got that cheap enough—but the boy felt obliged to talk the whole time he was drinking, and Harry had no stomach for interminable conversations. Harry would just get up and walk out of the house.

Another boyfriend wouldn't take beer at all. He would stand in front of the mirror to smooth down any stray hairs, adjust his tie, and fix his shirt sleeve lengths so that they showed just the proper amount beyond the sleeve of his suit. While this was going on, Cricket would do an imitation of him a few feet away. He would also do the imitation at other times. It was so good, Florence dropped the boyfriend.

While Jim was opening the second round of beers in the kitchen, he suddenly heard Cricket asking Ralph to get up and stand next to the wall. Jim hurried in. He knew what was coming. It was a gag they pulled on the boyfriends, but this time—for the first time—he didn't want it, out of loyalty to Florence, for Ralph was quite obviously not just another boyfriend.

"Stand with your back against the wall," said Cricket.

"Like this?" Ralph pressed himself against the wall.

"Yeah. Now bend forward." Ralph bent from the waist.

"Now put the sole of your left shoe against the wall."

Ralph obliged. "Hey, you were right, Crick. This isn't so easy."

"The hard part's coming," said Cricket. 'Leap one step forward on your right foot but keep the sole of your left shoe back against the wall."

Ralph took the hop forward. He was so enthusiastic and compliant, Jim found it painful to watch.

"How am I doing, Crick?" Ralph was bent forward with his left leg up in the air behind him.

"Great," said Cricket. "Now bark."

Cricket hunched his shoulders and came out with his crazy giggle. Ralph was really embarrassed. He got red. He laughed a bit.

"You really trapped me there. Heh heh." He sat on the couch. He tried to laugh another little bit.

Cricket was in hysterics. The act had never worked so well. In fact, Cricket figured he had such a prize victim, there was no point in stopping. "You want to try another exercise?"

"I had enough for a while," said Ralph. "Let Jim do this one."

So Jim did it. He knew it was the Miss America act, of course. Cricket looked at Jim as if he had lost his mind. He couldn't see any point in doing it with someone who knew the gag. But Jim insisted, so Cricket followed through with a shrug.

"Get up on your toes," Cricket ordered. Jim got up on his toes.

"Hold your arms out full length to the side." Jim complied.

"Focus your eyes on that corner of the ceiling." Jim did it.

"Now take fifteen quick steps and make them as short as you can." When Jim was coming across the floor with the ballerina steps, Cricket yelled out the punch line: "Here she comes! Miss America!"

Ralph got a big kick out of it. It took the pressure off him.

Florence came down the stairs. She beamed. Jim could see it on her face: Ralph cutting up with the boys. "Well, you three are certainly having a grand time for yourselves."

She looked great, Jim thought. Her hair was in an upsweep, and she was cloaked with the autumn colors: chestnut hair, yellow dress, beige coat on her arm. Her eyes were alive, and the way she immediately looked across the room to Ralph and opened out in a smile, as if there were no one else there, it was obvious she was hung on him. As for Ralph, as soon as she appeared, he jumped to his feet. He put her coat on her. And with a lot of little giggling and small talk, the two of them left.

Chapter 7

By three o'clock in the morning, Florence was home from her date, had put up her hair, and was asleep. Jim was home from the movies, and was also asleep. Only Harry Meagher was still awake. He had spent four sleepless hours in bed. He got up and went downstairs. He had the doctor's report on his mind. And the trouble at work. And Florence and the boy coming for dinner. And James.

Sure it was no wonder a man couldn't sleep.

He poured himself a glass of milk in the kitchen and came back to the living room and sat in his chair and drank it. He looked around. There wasn't a lace doily on a chair arm that wasn't pinned right. What would he do when Florence was gone? She had done a grand job on the house. He got up and opened the door of the downstairs bathroom to see what kind of a job James had done to help her. There were stains still on the sink, and rings in the toilet. A half-assed job, as usual. Goddam kid, there wasn't a thing he could be depended on to do right. Harry got a newspaper and spread it on the bathroom floor and, even though it was the middle of the night, got down on his knees and washed the toilet himself.

He avoided looking up at the tile job, which always annoyed him. The tile setter had started from the end instead of from the middle, so that the top of the last tile laid was a full inch higher than the first. Harry had a professional eye: his first job in the States had been setting tile. For almost three years he had tiled a room a day, thinking of the one in Ireland the whole while. Phyllis, tramp that she turned out to be.

He finished the job, and took up the newspaper. He went to the refrigerator and poured another glass of milk and put it in the pot to heat. It was supposed to make a person sleep, the warm milk. A lot of old horse shit: it never worked. He took the Old Overholt bottle down and poured some of that into the milk. Back in his chair, he held the milk glass in his hand and stared at it, swishing the milk so that it made shifting half moons on the sides of the glass.

Slow down, the doctor said. Sure, easy to say. The son was about to be thrown out of school, and the daughter was looking to get married, and the brother-in-law was drinking himself to death, and the two families were depending on him, and he was supposed to sit in the chair and slow down.

Cracked doctor.

And more trouble at work. Collins from personnel said there was talk the new brewery manager would be a quality-control man from Chicago. Don't talk nonsense to me, Harry had told him. They'd never pick a man who hadn't come up the technical side. But sure, there might be truth in the story. They'd cheat him out of the plant managership in the end, Harry thought. They didn't want him anyway. He was too old. He gave them thirty years and they'd give him the thanks of a shoe in the ass out the door. He was almost sixty and what did he know of the new things coming along? They were talking about a line that would move a thousand cans a minute, and plastic packers, and self-opening cans, and throwaway bottles and what more? Sure, didn't Schwartz change the labeler arm yesterday without even consulting him? The bastard, he wouldn't try that again. Ah, but things were slipping. They'd pass him by. They'd pass him by. The last disappointment.

Suddenly a scene of his childhood came to his mind. Toppy.

"Who gets Toppy today?"

Am I drunk, thought Harry, that I'm thinking about Toppy after fifty years?

When he was a boy in Ireland, and his father had his afternoon egg, he would crack the top off and cry: who gets Toppy today? Sean would elbow Harry out of the way, and grab the top of the egg. For Sean was older and stronger. Or was then.

His mind stayed in Ireland. Phyllis elbowed her way into his memories. He was eighteen and running with her across the checkerboard fields that contoured the hills of Kerry. I'm going to go to America and I'll come back and I'll have the biggest hat and the whitest teeth of any Yank ever came home. Do, she cried, do. She came down to Queenstown to see him off, and she was the last he saw, standing there with the black curls blowing across her white forehead, waving, while the band played "Come Back to Erin," and ahead the mouth of the harbor leading out to the open sea, and he gripped the upper rail and cried, his teeth drawing blood from his lower lip.

He worked for almost the three years tiling a room a day, and he finally made it home. The whole trip back on the ship he thought of her.

He had come up the hilly path and saw her riding the milk cans to the market. She saw him and stopped and paled. He ran to her.

"Phyllis! Phyllis!" he called, running.

But she hung back; she turned her face away as he approached.

He took her hand. Did she have a ring on?

"Jesus, is that a ring?"

"T'is."

"Whose ring is that?"

"Joe Houlihan."

"Are you married to Joe Houlihan?"

"I am."

An eternity passed. He had no words. He wanted to give her a cuff across the face. Finally he blurted out the only thing that came to mind.

"Goddam ye!"

She answered right back, tartly, her face now red.

"Was I to wait forever?"

She climbed down from the cart and sat by the side of the road and wept.

"Could you not have written a letter?" she asked bitterly, angrily.

Such crap and nonsense, he thought.

"And I that had no schooling?" he asked. "Was I going to be sending letters in the handwriting of a child, to be laughed at?"

And so that was the welcome in Ireland.

He came back to the States, and he went to school at night, and he got the job in the brewery, and he worked his way, in fifteen years, to Maintenance Superintendent. He built a home in Riverdale and banked money when all he knew were starving in the city. But he had no family, and no happiness. He cursed the one in Ireland, and he cursed God, and he cursed whoever the unfortunate woman was who happened to be with him when the black mood came on him.

Finally, his own misery drove him to his knees. He went one Saturday night to the church.

In the dark of the confessional box, he mumbled out the words.

"It's been fifteen years."

The priest led him down through all of it. When all was said, Mr. Meagher heard the words half-remembered from so many years before.

"*Dominus noster Jesus Christus te absolvat; et ego auctoritate ipsius te absolvo ab omni vinculo excommunicationis et interdicti in quantum possum et tu indiges.*"

The priest paused.

"*Deinde, ego te absolvo a peccatis tuis in nomine Patris, et Filii. . .*"

Harry made the sign of the cross out of memory.

"*et Spiritus Sancti. Amen.*"

Then Harry went out to the pew outside the confessional, and looked up to the Blessed Sacrament, and asked for a wife.

Two weeks later she was waiting for him outside of Sunday Mass. Con Aiken introduced her. Mary McInerny. She was a year over from the old country, and was working for the telephone company. At first he wasn't sure she was speaking to him, for she had a wall eye. But he knew that this was her, the wife he had asked for.

He courted her. There were those who wanted to make a hare out of him because of her eye. "Sure," said Finn Dolan, "You won't know whether she's looking at you or across the street." He had grabbed Dolan by the throat and thrust him against the wall so that he'd have no more breath to make jokes about her. And sure, it turned out in the end, she was worth two of the one in Ireland. A clean, good woman and a hard worker, she made him laugh in the house, he who had never laughed.

Then God saw fit to take her. When James was born, and she was up and about again, they went to a picnic in Fort Tryon Park at the beginning of the trolley line.

In the heat of the afternoon, she drank a glass of water. Later that night, Mary complained she felt nauseous. She got up that night and vomited. Neither of them paid it too much attention at the time, and the next day she said she felt a bit better.

Three days later she was dead of cholera.

Perhaps the best thing would have been for him to find another mother for the children. He went back to the church and asked again. But another Mary McInerney did not come. So he raised them himself, with the help of his sister Nora.

What kind of a job had he done? The boy was stealing. That's what it was. Cut it five ways and put jam on it: it still came down to theft. He'd like to take him by the shoulders and shake him. If a man wasn't as good as his word, he wasn't worth a damn.

Harry drank the glass of milk and whiskey and got up, and went out to the back to see if Nora's kitchen light was on. It was. She was sitting in the kitchen, a long face on her.

"He's not in yet?" Harry asked.

"He's not. What are you doing up?"

Harry didn't answer; he looked at the piece of soda bread she had in her hand, a layer of butter on it.

There was a time, Harry thought, when his sister had been so beautiful the reporter from the *Irish Record* called her: "the prettiest lass ever came out of Kerry." God save the day the reporter ever laid eyes on her: for it was Arthur Connolly. She still had the article upstairs. Michael Murray had been mad for her, but she wouldn't give him a look. She wanted Arthur and she got him. He didn't bring home ten checks in a year, while Michael Murray was building the government buildings now in Washington. There wasn't a sawhorse on the street down there, they said, that didn't have his name on it.

Ah, but how could you blame Arthur, Harry thought. He didn't want to get married. She dragged him to the altar. He stumbled on the altar step, and whimpered during the service. The priest got through the ceremony and dashed for the sacristy, and shut the door, and laughed so loud he could be heard above the wedding march. Arthur was no man for a family, but Nora had to have her way.

"He'll be in soon," said Harry.

Nora grunted, but didn't say anything. Harry went back home and went upstairs. He hung his pants neatly. He put his shoes in trees. He knelt down at the bedside, and put his face in his hands.

Why were there so many disappointments? He had worked hard and seemed to have got so little. He had plowed at eleven years of age a straight line, a man's work.

He prayed that Florence's young man might turn out all right.

He prayed that Jim might find a good, homely girl who would love him, like Jill next door.

He prayed that he'd be able to look Mary in the face when the time came, and be able to tell her that it had turned out all right.

Chapter 8

Jim Meagher awoke Sunday morning at seven o'clock with a headache. He got up and pulled the shade, and lay down again for another five minutes, but he couldn't sleep, so he put his shoes on and a sweatshirt over his pajamas and went downstairs. There was orange juice in a plastic container in the refrigerator, and he finished that, tilting it back on his head. He wanted to make coffee, but he knew there would be no chance of sleep after that, so he made tea. With a lot of milk and sugar, it tasted good.

He thought about Eva, and he went over the pros and cons of a plan he had been thinking about the night before: to invite her to that night's party. He had about made up his mind to do it, in spite of his father. He wondered if it would be a good tactic to tell the father ahead of time, but he was doubtful. The father was liable to get mad, and this was no morning to alienate him, with the visit to Father Phelan in prospect.

He noticed how clean the kitchen was. The linoleum was spotless and the refrigerator shone like mother-of-pearl. Ralph was getting the full twenty-one-gun salute. There was even a basket of flowers on the table, with a red velvet ribbon around the base. Jim leaned close to read the tag: "pink and white sweetheart roses, babies' breath and coxcomb."

Florence padded down the stairs. Jim was surprised. She could usually sleep forever, cuddled up in a ball, especially on Sunday morning. She came into the kitchen wearing pajamas and her quilt-patterned housecoat. She had all kinds of metal in her hair. She looked at him in sleepy-eyed surprise: "What are you doing up?"

He asked her the same question and she replied that she couldn't sleep.

"Where did you get this thing?" he asked, pointing to the flower basket.

"I bought it."

"How much?"

"Ten dollars."

She wasn't awake yet or she wouldn't have told him the price. "You're out of your mind," he cried. "You know that?"

"It's a centerpiece for the table. Don't you think it's pretty?"

"For ten bucks it should be."

"The babies' breath is starting to die," she said drowsily, fussing around in the basket.

"You want some tea?" he asked.

"Didn't you make coffee?"

"No. I'm going back to bed."

He poured her a cup of tea. She came to life as she drank it. "What did you do last night?" she asked.

"Went to the movies with Eva. I was thinking about asking her over this evening. That would be all right, wouldn't it?"

"Of course." She paused, then said, "Jimmy?"

She wanted something; it was in her voice. "What?"

"You know that piece you used to play on the piano?"

"'Danny Boy'?"

"Yes. That one. Would you teach me it?"

"Teach you 'Danny Boy'?"

"Yes."

"Are you kidding?"

"Not the whole thing. Just a few notes."

She got up and went to the piano in the living room. "Come on," she called.

"It's only a quarter after seven."

"Just a few notes."

"No. Daddy's sleeping."

"Just a few notes. You don't have to play it loud. Hold the pedal down."

She pestered him until finally he got up and went in to the piano.

"Play the right hand," she said. He played the first dozen notes with one finger. She had her mouth pursed in absorption.

"Again."

Then she tried the first few notes.

"It's Ralph's favorite song."

"You can't learn how to play the piano in five minutes."

"Just show me those first couple of notes again."

Jim played it again.

The father roared from the bedroom. "What in *hell* is going on down there?"

Florence flipped the wooden cover over the keys.

"It's nothing, Daddy. I was just trying something. Go back to sleep."

"Go to bed," he roared.

"Okay. I am."

The two of them went back to the kitchen. "What a stupid idea," said Jim. Today of all days he didn't want to aggravate the father.

They could hear him coming down the stairs. "Oh hell," said Florence. "He's up now." She went to the living room to meet him.

"You don't have to get up Daddy. It's only twenty after seven."

"I don't know how a person is supposed to sleep when you're thumping the piano down here. Are you gone cracked?"

"I was just practicing something," she explained, following him into the kitchen. He had on the pants of one of his good blue suits and a pajama top. His gray-black hair was tousled.

"It's a hell of an hour to be practicing something."

He saw Jim. "Are you up too?" He went to the stove. "Is there no coffee made?"

"No," said Jim.

"What are you drinking?"

"Tea."

"You couldn't make a pot of coffee?"

Jim got up from the chair. "I'll make it now."

"I'll make it myself," said the father. "Sit down." He measured out the coffee and water, and put the pot on to boil. Then he sat at the table with the two children. "There's neither one of you can make coffee as good as your father, anyway."

"What time will you be back from Fordham today?" Florence asked him.

Jim gave her a look: she would have to bring it up.

"When I can," said the father. "About three, I suppose."

"They're coming around that time," said Florence, "so don't delay."

"What would I delay for?"

"How do you like the centerpiece?"

Harry looked at the flowers. "It's all right," he said. "The whole house looks grand. You did hard work."

Florence beamed. "You're going to like them, Daddy. I know you will."

"I don't know of any reason why not."

"We'll have fun. We can have some people in this evening. Jim is having Eva."

There were often times Jim wanted to strangle Florence, and this was another one. If he hired a sound truck and announced his business up and down the avenue, it wouldn't be half as effective as telling Florence. The father got his hackles up right away at the mention of Eva. "The Polack?"

"She's not a Polack, Dad," said Jim. "Her mother and father are Hungarian-born Americans, and she's an American-born American."

The father made a noise with his mouth. "Were you out with her again last night?"

"Yes, I was."

"Have you intentions of marrying this girl?"

Jim was startled. "Who? Eva?"

"If you're going out with her every week, certainly she has expectations."

"We don't go out every week."

"Well it's damn near to every week if it's not every week."

"It's not anything serious."

"Indeed 'n' I hope it's not anything serious. You haven't your school finished yet. You haven't a tosser in your pocket. Is there any sense in courting a girl?"

"What do you mean, courting?" Jim forced a laugh. "We're just friends."

The father made a guttural noise that was the equivalent of "horse shit," but he didn't say it.

"You're making a big thing out of nothing," said Jim.

"I'm just warning you for your own good."

Jim stood up to leave. "Is it all right if I have her in this evening? I mean, you won't take that for a formal engagement, I hope, if she comes this evening?"

"Have her in if you want," the father replied. "She'll be glad enough of something to eat, I suppose."

"She doesn't need anything to eat," Jim retorted. "They eat better than we do."

"Sure."

Jim left the kitchen before they could get started on the Hairy Apple again. Was there anywhere a more pig-headed man?

Jim got to his room and nestled under the covers again. His resting spot was still warm, and it felt good. But he couldn't sleep; he didn't have any peace of mind. In a way, he had been looking forward to his act of revolt when he would bring Eva into the house. Now that it was all set, the father had taken all the pleasure out of it with his talk of expectations and marriage. Maybe she did have expectations of marriage. Why shouldn't she? He'd make a good husband too. He imagined himself married to Eva. He could almost see her in the bed with him. He fell into a half-sleep, and he dreamt that he and Eva had their wedding night. It was a delightful dream.

But then the dream continued. Eva was standing in the front hallway of the Meagher home with her belly pushing out a maternity dress, and Mr. Meagher was standing beside her livid with rage. Jim, backed up against the wall, had chains around his arms and legs, and the father was shouting, "You gave her expectations! You gave her expectations!"

A huge, shapeless monster was suddenly descending on him, swallowing him.

He felt himself plunging off a precipice.

He fell down into hell, into the eternal fires.

He screamed.

Florence ran into the bedroom, and Jim suddenly became aware that he was lying on the floor beside the bed, tangled in the bedclothes.

"Jim! Jim! What's the matter with you? You're white as a sheet!"

She helped him untangle the bedclothes, and he got loose, and stood up and sat on the bed. "I'm all right."

She bent over and looked into his face. She felt his forehead for a temperature. "Are you worried about school? God, you're in a sweat."

"I'm all right."

"What's the matter? Tell me."

"There's nothing the matter."

"Are you sure?"

"Yes, I'm sure."

"You're not getting a grippe?"

"Oh, stop it, will you? I'm all right. Let me get dressed."

She left. He dressed and went to Mass. Sitting in church, he felt a heavy load of guilt. He had added a new betrayal. The dream wasn't difficult to interpret: as soon as he had gotten Eva pregnant, he couldn't get away from her fast enough. Good, kind, sweet Eva.

Yesterday, when everything was going wrong—Phelan called him a sneak, his father told him he wasn't worth a shit, Florence told him there was something wrong with him—he went to Eva and she had bound up the wounds, and he betrayed her now too.

It was just a dream. But it wasn't just a dream. It was him. His stomach was bouncing.

He left Mass, chastened, resolved to do good things.

Florence was waiting for him at home. "Jimmy? Would you do me a favor?"

"What?"

She was hesitant even to ask. "It's a trip all the way downtown."

"For what?"

"I forgot the cranberry sauce."

"Okay."

He was so compliant, she couldn't believe it. "Do you feel all right?"

"Yeah, I'm all right."

"I'll make breakfast for you."

He sat at the kitchen table and pulled the sports section out of the *Times*.

His father always bought the *Times* on Sunday before he went to Mass. It was the thickest paper on the newsstand, and therefore obviously worth the money. Florence fried Canadian bacon, chicken livers, blood pudding, slices of tomato dipped in batter, and two eggs. She was a great cook. Amid a constant stream of conversation, he tried to read Arthur Daley's sports column. "You don't mind if Ralph is bartender today, do you?" she asked.

"Huh?"

"You don't mind if Ralph is bartender?"

"No. Of course not. What do I care?"

"It will make him feel good," she said. "And it will give him something to do."

She poured two cups of coffee and brought one to Jim, and sat opposite him to drink the other. He continued to read the paper, and nodded automatically as she talked.

"It's not that he's that way, really. It's his mother. He says that she influenced his sense of himself. She's very fearful. She put all kinds of restrictions on him when he was growing up. She wouldn't let him go to the pool when the other kids went, because she was afraid he would get some kind of a germ. And she didn't want him to drive. And things like that. He says she practically destroyed his self-concept. He needs a lot of reassurance. You like him, don't you, Jim?"

"Huh?"

"You like him, don't you?"

"Yeah, he's a nice guy."

"He's kind. Sometimes lawyers are shrewd and hard, but he's not that way. He's got brains too. He presents his own cases, and that's very unusual. Usually the younger ones just help the older ones in court. But he presents his own. And he wins. He just needs someone to tell him all the time that he's good. To give him confidence."

She brought over the plate of food, and Jim put the paper down. "It's a terrific position for a young lawyer," she continued. "Like Ralph says, he can go in a hundred different directions. Dewey was District Attorney in New York, you know."

"Yeah, it's a good job," said Jim, opening the yolks of the eggs with the prongs of the fork.

"I hope everything goes all right today."

"You're really sweating this dinner, aren't you?"

"They're not as easy to land when they're over thirty."

Jim looked at her in surprise. It was such a naked declaration, especially for Florence.

"The mother will be watching like a hawk today," Florence went on, "And she can ruin me before I ever have a chance."

"What is she? A real dragon?"

"She doesn't want to lose her baby."

"At thirty-three he's not exactly a baby."

"Well, you know. Talk to her today, will you?"

"Who? The mother?"

"Be nice to her," said Florence.

"Yeah, all right."

"I'm worried about Daddy," she said.

"Don't worry. He'll be a big hit."

"If the mother annoys him, he's liable to tell her off."

"Don't worry," said Jim. "He'll be a big hit."

"Do you think so?"

"Sure. He appeals to the masochist in women."

"What does that mean?"

"I'm only kidding. He goes over big with the women, though. You'll see."

"I'm worrying about Arthur," she went on. "If he comes in high, I don't know what I'll do."

"I'll keep an eye open," said Jim. "And steer him out if I have to."

"You will?" she said, encouraging him.

"Yes."

Chapter 9

Jim had to go all the way down to a store on East 70th Street for the cranberry sauce. Heaven only knew how Florence ever found it. It was the Frenchy kind of place that she loved. Probably the only grocery store in New York with a carpet out on the sidewalk. He couldn't take the car either, because his father would be taking it to Fordham to see Father Phelan. He had to go all the way downtown on the subway. By the time he got to 42nd Street and shuttled over to the East Side, and then took the Lexington Avenue train uptown, he had lost his good resolutions and cursed Florence.

The cranberry sauce was three dollars for a pint. It was unbelievable, Jim thought. The clerk gave him the jar to examine before it was wrapped. Jim read the label: "A piquant mixture of whole berries, spices, fresh orange juices, fresh orange rind, and an occasional raisin." The clerk was smiling expectantly. Jim shrugged and handed it back, and the clerk wrapped it, carefully, as if it were a bottle of perfume.

By the time he got home, the family car was gone from the driveway, so his father had left for the interview with Father Phelan. Harry might be getting the word already about his sneak of a son.

Thank God for Ralph and his parents. His father could hardly say much until tomorrow, and with a little skillful dodging Jim knew he could avoid him until the evening when he would get home from work. By that time the edge would be off his anger. Even old Harry couldn't stay in a rage for two days, Jim thought. He'd be boiling at first though. Jim felt an involuntary tremble at the thought.

Mints were set out in the candy dishes in the living room, and nuts, and spice drops. The plastic cover was off the couch. Even the glass cover had been removed from the coffee table, something done only for events of the first magnitude.

Aunt Nora was talking in the kitchen about Arthur, and the gist of the story was that Arthur had finally returned. "He came in at the dawn," said Nora, "And didn't he come into the room to wake me. 'Pee wee, where did you put the bottle? I'm awful dry.' 'The bottle's down the sink,' I told him. 'And divil a bit more you'll get, you dirty skunk.' The stink of his breath was all over me. I don't know what to do with him. God knows what will happen in the end."

Florence was pale as she listened. Both the women were dressed for the occasion. Florence had on a blue dress with a decorative half-round white apron. She looked pretty. She was cutting hors d'oeuvres that she had made by rolling bread slices and soft cheese into a cylinder shape. Aunt Nora had on a dress of yards of flowered rayon stretched over the stays of her corset. Her hair was done, and the top of her head was massed with little brown-gray curls. The turkey in the oven made crackling noises, and gave off fragrant odors. Jim noticed Nora had her nails painted.

He put the jar of cranberries on the table, aware that Aunt Nora with her insatiable curiosity would investigate it. Florence immediately put the jar on top of the refrigerator, without comment. "What's that?" asked Nora.

"Oh, just cranberries," said Florence.

"Show it here."

So Florence had to bring it over. Jim felt a malicious joy; the price was marked on the label. This would be good.

He watched Aunt Nora hold the jar out at arm's length to read the label. "Honest to Jesus," she cried. "Is that three dollars?"

Florence abandoned diplomacy; she snatched it out of Nora's hand.

"Is that three dollars for a jar of cranberries?" Nora asked again.

"It's a special kind," Florence said. There was a snap of annoyance in her voice.

"Did I ever hear the like? Three dollars for cranberries that can be had in the A&P for twenty-nine cents!"

"You can't buy this kind for twenty-nine cents."

"I'm telling you, my dears," said Nora. "This will be a dinner for the duke."

"Cranberries set off a meal," said Florence.

"Whatever you like, sweetheart," cried Nora. "Whatever you like."

Florence was clipping off the hors d'oeuvres with a vengeance.

"What time are they due?" asked Jim.

"Very soon," said Florence. She glanced at the clock.

"You help your sister this afternoon," said Aunt Nora to Jim. Then she gave him a series of instructions. He didn't bother to answer, since the comments were being made for Florence's benefit anyway. He took one of the round little sandwiches. It was good, especially with the olive at the center. He took another.

"Don't eat too many," said Florence.

"You don't want to be filling up on that old crap," Aunt Nora advised. "Wait for the good turkey. And why is your father having to go over to the school for you today?"

"One of the priests wants to see him."

"Edward says you're in trouble."

Big-mouthed Cricket, Jim thought.

"It's nothing to worry about," said Jim. He got out of the kitchen before there were any more questions.

The dining-room table was set with gleaming china. The goblets with the gold rims were out. When these saw service, Jim was not told to help with the dishwashing. It was no penalty. The flowers were at the center. Even the tablecloth, a good Irish linen one, was set out so that it fell in perfect folds at the corners. The silver setting was the most elaborate he'd ever seen. There were three forks, two knives, two spoons and a butter knife at each place. Where, Jim wondered, would she get all the courses?

Florence came in from the kitchen and rolled her eyes up in an expressive gesture of annoyance at Aunt Nora. She formed the words with her lips to Jim: "I wish she'd go home."

Nora followed her in. She looked over the table setting. "Isn't it lovely? Sure any boy who looked at that table would know he was getting an uncommon girl."

Florence worried about the seating arrangement. "It's much too crowded," she said. There were twelve places set: Harry, Florence herself, Jim; Ralph, his mother, father, and aunt; Aunt Nora, Arthur, Cricket, Harold. Uncle Arthur, of course, was a doubtful guest, but a place had to be left.

"Why don't you get Harold to play the violin during the meal?" Jim suggested.

Nora brightened. "That wouldn't be a bad idea," she said.

"No," said Florence decisively. "I have Mantovani dinner music." She continued to ponder the seating arrangement, talking to herself. "Daddy goes at the end; then the first two places will be me on one side and Ralph's mother at the other side; then Ralph next to me, then his father next to his mother."

"Oh no," said Nora. "You want Ralph sitting opposite you and not next to you. He can see your eyes then."

"He should be sitting next to me, shouldn't he?"

"Of course not," said Nora, "Your eyes are like stars today. You want him to be looking into them."

"Jim, shouldn't he be sitting next to me?"

"Why don't you put him at the end near the door," Jim suggested. "Then if anyone wants any extra gravy or anything, he can run out and get it."

"Be serious, will you!" cried Florence. She was near tears.

Nora was rearranging the place cards.

"Aunt Nora, would you please leave those alone!"

Nora looked up angrily. Florence saw the sudden flush in Nora's face. She tried to tone down what she had said and to explain. "I thought it over for a long time before arranging them that way."

"Suit yourself, girl. Suit yourself," Nora said in a tone that showed she was seriously ruffled.

"Take it easy," said Jim to Florence.

"They'll be here any minute," said Florence, "And my father's not even here to welcome them. I might as well be an orphan."

"Aw, come on."

"Why don't you lay down for a minute?" suggested Nora.

"How can I lay down when they're coming!"

There was a noise at the back door.

"That's them!" cried Florence.

"Are they coming in the back door?" asked Nora, startled.

"That's not them," said Jim.

It was Jill. "I brought a cheese dip for your dinner, Florence," she announced.

Florence came over to look.

"Wow," Jill said when she saw the table. She had a white dress on, with rosebuds at the waist.

"They're going to be here any minute," said Florence. She took the foil off Jill's dish. "I'll put it in the living room on the table."

"It would be better to put it in the refrigerator until they come," said Jill.

"You're right," said Florence. She reversed direction and headed for the kitchen. "I'm so confused. My father won't even be here when they come. What will I tell them?"

Jill thought for a moment. "Just tell them he went to see one of the priests," she said. "He'll probably be back before they come."

"I hope not," thought Jim.

Jill and Florence made a check to see if anything had been forgotten. Sure enough, something had: extra ice. "I'll go get some," said Jim. He was glad to get out of the house.

Chapter 10

Jim was on his way through the living room to go out the front door when he heard the crunch of car tires on the gravel in the driveway. He hurried to the window and parted the curtain. It was Ralph's car. He dashed to the kitchen. "It's them," he cried. "They're here."

"Oh God," said Florence softly.

"I'd better leave," said Jill.

"Stay," said Florence, casting about for support.

"No, I'll come in later," she said and she went out the back.

Nora suddenly sang, "I love you," in a high, crooning brogue.

Florence walked with measured, deliberate steps to the living room, and then to the foyer, and stood at the front door. Nora followed. Jim was third in line.

The bell rang.

Jim felt his heart would stop at the energy in the room.

Florence wouldn't answer the first ring. She let the seconds tick by until there was a second ring; then she reached for the knob.

The door swung open. Ralph was in front, a big smile on his face.

"Hi ya!"

He swung his head forward to kiss her; she swung her head forward at the same time.

They cracked heads, forehead on forehead, nose on nose.

They reeled from the impact.

"I'm sorry," he cried. He had horror on his face. Florence laughed gaily, as if it were the most delightful thing that had happened to her all day. She held her nose. "How silly," she said.

"How stupid of me," he said.

They both paused. Florence looked at him expectantly.

"My folks," said Ralph. He leaped to the side to let his parents come forward. He slammed his back against the door and the door hit the wall with a heavy thud.

"I want you to meet my folks."

"Ralph, I've met your parents already."

"Of course," he replied.

Florence took the mother's hand. "Mrs. Spaulding," she said softly.

"You're all welcome," Nora cried from the rear.

Florence kissed Mrs. Spaulding. She looked to Jim to be a pleasant-enough middle-aged woman. In answer to the greetings, she widened her eyes, and fluted her mouth and said, "Oh, oh."

Florence turned to the father. "Mr. Spaulding." She put one hand under his, and another over, and got him in a sandwich grip to kiss him.

"You're all welcome!" cried Aunt Nora from the back.

Mr. Spaulding, tall and thin, stepped inside the doorway, and gave everyone a lopsided grin. He had a question-mark frame, stooped at the shoulders.

Florence had the aunt now. "Aunt Anita." As she was embraced and kissed, Aunt Anita tried to look inoffensive. She was a gray-haired woman, with a grin-and-bear-it smile.

"You're all welcome," boomed Aunt Nora.

Florence, Jim and Nora back-pedaled slowly into the living room. The Spauldings came forward. Everyone was talking.

Aunt Nora was introduced. "You're welcome," she cried.

It was Jim's turn. Florence took his arm. "This is my brother, Jim."

"Well," said Ralph's mother. "Well," she repeated. Her mouth was in the fluted position as she said it. Each time she spoke she widened her eyes.

"Ralph told us about you," she said to Jim. "He says you look just like your father."

Jim stammered an incoherent answer. The reference to the father was a cue for the Spauldings to look around for the father.

Florence got a panicky look. "Dad should be back soon. He said he was going to be here at three. He should be back, shouldn't he, Jim?"

So she had thrown the hot potato to him. "I think so." There was an awkward moment. Jim cast about for something to say in excuse for his father's absence, anything. "He probably stopped in at church."

Florence seized at it. "Yes, he probably stopped in church."

Mrs. Spaulding looked puzzled.

Jim elaborated. "He probably went to a novena."

He said this before he realized what he was saying. There was an element of truth in his father stopping in church, for he often did on a Sunday afternoon, to sit in the pew and look up at the tabernacle. But the idea of his going to a novena, with the elderly ladies, was impossible.

"Isn't that nice?" said Aunt Anita. "I make the novena of the Holy Souls every Tuesday night."

"Ralph, why don't we have a drink?" cried Florence.

"Swell," said Ralph.

Jim felt awful. He went to the kitchen ahead of Ralph. Then he went to the backyard. He had destroyed the whole occasion. The father should have been there at the door. What must they think?

He went next door to the Connollys. He was still caught in the panic of the arrival scene. He wasn't sure what he was doing. But he had a vague idea that, if he could do something about Uncle Arthur, then perhaps the situation wouldn't be so bad for the rest of the afternoon. He would check on Uncle Arthur.

Anyway, he just had to get away for a few minutes.

Chapter 11

"They're here," said Jim to Cricket in the Connollys' living room. Cricket was watching the Yankees game.

"I saw them from the window," said Cricket. "I hate old ladies."

"You're coming, aren't you?"

"Do we have a choice?"

"No."

"I'll wait a while," said Cricket.

Jim found Harold on the screened-off porch in front, working on his stamp books. He was slim-figured, and small, like his father, though he didn't have his father's fragile good looks. He was even a bit monkey-faced, with a long stretch of skin from his nose to his mouth. In his manner, he was supercilious, and obnoxious, or so it seemed to Jim. "Are you coming over to the dinner?"

"Oh yes. I've heard that we're supposed to have a festive belt-loosening this afternoon."

"Are you coming?"

"I don't know," said Harold, pondering his answer, as if the world were waiting.

"Don't put yourself out," said Jim. He thought to himself: they come to dinner every Sunday; today it's a big deal.

"I'll see," said Harold.

Jim restrained himself from telling Harold what a pain-in-the-ass he thought he was. He went upstairs to locate Uncle Arthur. He found him in his bed, his legs stretched to both corners, his pants still on, along with an undershirt. He looked small as he slept there in the big bed. Doll-like. Looking at him at first, a person would take him for a theatrical figure: his coloring was dramatic, silver hair, florid complexion; his features were delicate, almost childlike, with finely arched nostrils at the end of a small nose, and a fragile weak chin. He was inclined, in fact, toward the theater. He wrote publicity for the Riverdale Playhouse, and years before he had tried some plays. He claimed a producer had stolen the best of them. But he had made his living in the newspaper business, working all over the country before he married Nora, and was settled now as a rewrite man for the *New York Mirror*.

Jim felt sorry for him. He was breathing heavily. He looked so haggard. He had always a beaten look about him, except when he had a few drinks, then he became a pixie, with a beaming smile and a fey humor. When he was in that humor, Nora became "PeeWee." But once he started drinking, he could never stop, and fairly soon he would just become stupid with alcohol. Jim liked him; he had told Arthur at length of his ambition to be an actor, and maybe write plays, too, and Arthur had encouraged him.

Arthur suddenly opened his eyes halfway, and sat up in the bed, resting on his right elbow. He pressed his free hand to the top of his head and moaned. He peered in Jim's direction with half-seeing eyes, eyes that were hidden behind the slits of his eyelids. He gave a quick jerky motion and sat up straight.

"Jim?"

"Yes. How are you, Uncle Arthur?"

Arthur lay back. "I thought they had me back in Knickerbocker."

Jim laughed. Arthur had given him detailed descriptions of his stays in Knickerbocker, the Harlem hospital where cops often dropped off unfortunates in need of detox. With his gift for mimicry, he had taken off the doctors, nurses, and orderlies until Jim had felt he was at the scene himself.

"Where's Nora?" Arthur asked.

"She's over at our house."

"There's something going on today?" He tried to recall.

Jim debated: should he tell him. No. "A dinner," he said, without elaboration.

Arthur gave Jim a wave of dismissal. "Go away now and let me die in peace." He shut his eyes.

"Do you want me to call a priest?" Jim asked, with a grin, remembering what Nora had told him about Arthur leaving the church.

Arthur got up on his elbows. "Get out," he shouted and fell back, "with your talk of priests."

"How come you're leaving the Church?"

"Who told you that?"

"The pastor."

Arthur was interested. "You're joking?"

"Yes, I am," Jim agreed.

"You little fartface. Get out."

Jim laughed. "Maybe he'll talk you into taking the pledge."

"I'm taking no pledge."

"You're not keeping any, anyway."

"Damn straight."

"Why don't you join AA?"

"Why don't you get out of here. Bad as the father with religion, and priests and the like. A grown man and they lead him around like he was a sheep."

"Nobody leads him around. He's too pig-headed."

"On his knees every morning at Mass," said Arthur in disgust. "For what?"

"Because he loves God, I guess." Jim was surprised to hear a sincere answer coming from his own mouth.

"Go over to the closet, and unzip the clothes bag, and get me the bottle."

Jim did as he was told but he couldn't find the bottle. Arthur then looked himself, to no avail.

"I think she dumped it out," Jim said.

"No," said Arthur. "She has it hid."

He looked around the room, checking under the bed, behind the radiator, and in the clothes hamper.

"Maybe she hid it in another room," said Jim.

"She wouldn't go far with it," said Arthur.

He pulled the drape aside at the window and there was the bottle. Arthur uncorked it, tilted the bottle back on his head and took a slug of whiskey. Jim had watched many of his relatives drink a shot as though they were taking medicine, making a face as they swallowed. But not his Uncle Arthur. Arthur loved the taste; he swished it around in his mouth before swallowing.

Sitting again on the bed, the bottle beside him, Arthur sighed and said, "Ah, shit," softly, not with anger, but just for something to say. Then he sighed again, looking at the floor.

"Big head?"

"I must have spent the whole fuckin' night on the subway," said Arthur. "I'm sore all over." He reached his hand over his shoulder to knead his back muscles. "I remember some big cop giving me a hard time. They pull them out of the trees and teach them how to use a nightstick and then they make them subway cops."

Arthur looked up, and gave an impish grin. "Do you know what the best racket in the world is?" he asked. "Those guys who beg in the subway. Did you ever see them?"

Jim had, of course; but he stayed quiet, waiting for Arthur's imitation of one of them—sure to be good.

"I have to get a hat," said Arthur. "They always have a hat on." He went to the closet and put a hat on, turning back the front brim. "They always have the brim turned up." He went to the door of the room. "What's that instrument they play?" He held one hand chest high, and the other waist high, and moved his fingers.

"Trombone?" Jim asked.

"That's it," said Arthur. "Okay, now you make a subway noise, and I'll go outside and come in."

Jim tried to imitate the sound of a subway train, going clickety-click, clickety-click, while making a throat noise, and at the same time banging his hand rhythmically against the bed board.

Arthur went out. When he reappeared at the door, he had dark glasses on; his mouth was shut, but held in such a widespread position it seemed he had a stirrer from cheek to cheek within; he was fingering the imaginary trombone; and all the while his feet were shuffling back and forth in the motion necessary to keep one's balance in the subway.

It was so good an imitation, Jim screamed laughing. Arthur shuffled across the room, lurching, dipping, almost falling. He pretended a rider had his legs in the aisle, and cursed out the inconsiderate man. Jim laughed so hard his breath came in gasps, and he got the pain in his side. "Stop," he said. "Please stop."

Arthur took his fingers from the trombone to shake an imaginary tin cup with trembling fingers. He then lifted the dark glasses to see how much he had got. He cursed out the riders. Then he resumed his shuffle up the aisle.

Arthur took off the glasses and hat and took a slug of whiskey. He sat on the bed. "It's a good living, walking up and down the subway."

"You have a great talent," Jim said to Arthur.

"That's what they told me down at the paper," said Arthur, "the last time they refused me a raise."

"You should have become a comedian."

"If I could become something now," said Arthur, "I'd be a playwright like George Bernard Shaw."

"Is he that good?"

"A laugh in every line," said Arthur. "And not all jokes, either. The man knew what he was talking about. Did you ever hear what he said about getting married?"

"What?"

"Let me read it to you." Arthur went to the bookcase and brought back a green-bound volume of Shaw's plays.

He walked back and forth beside the bed as he read aloud. Then he turned to Jim. "That part where he calls a woman seeking a husband the most dangerous of all beasts of prey? Where he says that marriage is a trap?" Arthur stabbed the book with his finger. "There it is! In black and white!"

Jim laughed, thinking of Florence. "What play is that?"

"*Man and Superman,*" Arthur replied. "Listen to this too. It's Don Jooan talking to the girl who wanted to marry him." Arthur read out a long passage where Don Juan accused a woman of learning to play the spinet to trick her suitors into thinking their married life would be full of melodies.

Jim gasped with recognition. "That's Florence!"

"That's every woman," said Arthur. "Later on—on the same page— Shaw says she forgets about the music after the marriage. That she tosses away the bait once she has the bird in the net. Let me tell you, that's the God-honest truth. Does this man know what he's talking about, or does he know what he's talking about?"

"This morning," said Jim, "Florence wanted to learn how to play 'Danny Boy' on the piano so she could play it for Ralph when he came to dinner this afternoon."

"Sure, they're all the same," said Arthur. "So, she's having the boy and his parents."

"Yes," said Jim weakly. He hadn't intended to refresh Arthur's memory.

"I'll be over. I'll warn the poor boy what he's getting into."

"Florence has her good points."

Arthur took a slug of whiskey. "They're all just grand until they get their hooks into you."

Arthur's speech was already beginning to slur. The bottle was half gone. "It might not be a good time," said Jim, "to say something this afternoon."

"When are they coming?"

"Not for a good while yet."

Arthur corked the bottle. "I'll get some rest first. You'll call me, eh?"

Jim agreed, knowing that he wouldn't.

Arthur fell asleep. Jim sat there, and worried.

Arthur would wake again. He was coming to the dinner. What could Jim do?

Tie him to the bed?

Hide his shoes?

That was it! Hide the shoes.

He gathered all of Arthur's shoes and carried them downstairs with him as he left.

Chapter 12

Jim went in the back door of his own house to find Ralph mixing drinks in the kitchen. Ralph was more nervous than Florence, if that were possible. He kept whistling "Don't Fence Me In," obviously unconscious of the irony. He was mixing the Manhattans with such gusto that he was smashing the ice cubes against the side of the shaker. Jim wished that Florence was making the Manhattans. She just had the touch. Anyone else could start with the same bourbon, and vermouth, and lemon, but it just wouldn't come out the same way.

"How do you like it, Jim? Two to one?"

"Two to one, two and a half to one."

"Coming up."

"How's work, Ralph?"

"Great. Great."

They always talked the same conversation: his work or Jim's school activities. The trouble was: there was no common experience.

Ralph was pouring now, and making a mess of it, splashing good liquor all over the sideboard. "Hey we're short a glass," he said.

"Up there in the closet."

"I don't see any."

"Maybe down below."

Ralph stooped down. Jim was about to cry out a warning about the open closet door above his head, but there was no time. Ralph was moving with ultra-accelerated nervous gestures. He swung his head up and smashed the closet full force. His knees buckled, and Jim had to steady him. When he sat down in the chair, his face had a disoriented expression, and it was not until long moments had passed that he came out of it. He looked up at the closet door.

"Son of a bitch," he muttered. Jim laughed. Ralph put his hand to his head to see if there was any blood. There wasn't. But there was a lump, and it showed clearly on Ralph's half-bald head.

"Son of a bitch," he said again. Jim laughed again. Amiable old Ralph had a spark of profanity in him after all.

Florence was in transit to the kitchen. Her voice sang out: "What happened to the drinks?" Ralph forgot his injuries; he leaped up and grabbed the tray and headed in.

Jim stayed in the kitchen and waited for Ralph to come back. Suddenly, he heard his father's voice in the living room. He was back from Fordham.

Jim had a Manhattan in his hand and he gulped the whole drink. He thought of running out the back door. Maybe the best tactic would be to go right in the living room and hide in the crowd. He listened to the voices. The women were laughing. His father's tone was jovial and good humored. He heard his father and Ralph coming back to the kitchen. When they came in, his father had his arm around Ralph's shoulder. Was it possible he hadn't been able to find Father Phelan?

Without wiping the smile from his face, the father said to Jim, "I'll see you later."

He'd found Father Phelan all right.

"Can I fix you a drink, sir?" Ralph asked Mr. Meagher.

"I can get it myself," said the father. He took down the Old Overholt, and poured himself a shot, and in one swift arm movement threw it right down. He followed it with a long slug from a can of beer. "Well, how you doing, Ralph boy?"

"Fine, sir. Gee, that dining room table really looks inviting."

"Florence," said Mr. Meagher, "is a great girl."

"She sure is, sir."

"Call me Harry." He threw out a jab. It caught Ralph in the shoulder and jolted him. Jim had to muffle a laugh with his hand. Ralph was really taking a beating in the kitchen.

Harry poured another shot and sent it following the first one. When he wanted to drink he could hold a milk can of whiskey, or a twelve-pack of beer. Jim had never seen him drunk. He put the shot glass down, and looked Ralph over.

"What are you drinking, Ralph boy?"

"I'm fine, sir. I mean Harry."

"What have you got there, those goddamn Manhattans. That's all they drink around here. High society. Here. Have a ball." He poured the shot of whiskey before Ralph could protest, and handed it over. Ralph held it, turning it slowly in his fingers, looking at it. Then he drank it down in the accepted style, one swoop. His Adam's apple did an inch leap.

"Here. Have another one."

Ralph took it as if it were his medicine. He drank it down. Harry watched carefully. Then he apparently decided the round was over, because he didn't pour another one.

"You're a lawyer, eh, Ralph?"

"Yes, sir."

"One of the D.A.'s boys, eh?"

"Yes, sir. I mean, Harry."

"What do you think of this business down in Washington, trying to hang McCarthy?"

Ralph hesitated.

Harry caught the pocket of opposition right away, and he went in after it.

"That whole State Department is full of pinkos and Reds. Don't you read the papers? Read Pegler. He's got the goods on them."

"It's a complicated business," said Ralph.

"Nothing complicated about it," snapped Harry. "A bunch of commies. Just get rid of them. That's what Senator McCarthy's doing. They don't like it."

Ralph looked distressed.

"It's about time," said Harry. "They need someone to go in there and clean up the whole mess."

"Sometimes you wonder if the end justifies the means," said Ralph, picking his words and smiling as he said them.

"What are you talking about, the end justifies the means? They're trying to undermine the country, aren't they?"

"Well—."

"Aren't they?"

"I was thinking of civil liberties."

"Don't talk nonsense, boy. Down the D.A.'s office they're not worried about civil liberties. They get a crook, they put him in jail."

"Well—."

"Don't they?" Harry had his forefinger up against Ralph's chest.

Ralph swallowed. "If we come out and say a man's guilty before it's proven in a fair trial, they'll put us in jail."

Jim was rooting for Ralph. Thatta boy, he thought, give it to him; don't take any crap from him; that's the only way you'll ever handle him.

"If they're commies, get rid of them. Send them back to Russia where they belong," said Harry.

Florence came flying out to the kitchen. She stopped at the doorway and looked around with big eyes. "I see the boys are gathering in the kitchen already."

"We're talking," said Harry.

"The ladies are calling for you, Daddy."

"Crap," said Harry, annoyed at the interruption. But Florence wouldn't let the discussion go on. She said to Ralph, "Would you mix another batch of drinks?" Then she steered her father to the door. He went reluctantly. Before he started inside, he turned to Ralph and said, "I got to talk to you, boy." Then Florence, more or less tugging him, took him inside.

Ralph, standing by the sideboard, had worry lines on his forehead, in addition to the bump. "I guess I said the wrong thing to your father."

"I should have warned you," said Jim. "Senator McCarthy's big around here."

"Your father is sore, I think."

"Don't worry about it," said Jim. "It's better not to take any guff off him."

Chapter 13

Ralph went to the living room; Jim couldn't face the prospect for the moment; he stayed in the kitchen. After a few minutes, Florence came out. ""How's Arthur?" she asked. "Did you check?"

"He's sleeping."

"I hope he stays that way."

"He won't be over," said Jim, confidently. "I hid all his shoes in the basement."

"Good," she said, after pausing and looking at him for a moment. Then she started making a batch of Manhattans.

"This is awful," Jim said, holding up Ralph's Manhattan.

Her eyes grew wide. "Don't say anything."

Ralph came into the kitchen. She put down the measuring glass, and said to him immediately, "Here, hon, you do it."

"Trying to steal my job."

She kissed him on the cheek and said, "Never."

He beamed. Jim was fascinated, watching them. Ralph was rather simple. He had just one thought: Florence. But Florence, like a general, balanced fifteen items in her mind at once: Arthur, the guests, the turkey, Ralph, the drinks, her father, Jim, Cricket and Harold, and so on.

Ralph measured vermouth into the drink mix, while Florence looked at the turkey in the oven. "You may know how to cook a turkey," Ralph said, "but it takes a man to make a drink."

She turned and smiled at him.

Aunt Nora came out, also to check the turkey. "You're a lovely young man," she said to Ralph, "and you have a lovely family."

With that, Jim went out to the backyard. He sat on the chaise lounge and stretched one leg out, and let the other hang down. I wonder how long, he thought, it took Aunt Nora to master the art of giving a compliment so that it sounded like an insult.

He looked up at the blue sky between the green leaves. He listened to a bird sing. The lawn was cool and green. So nice. Better than cantankerous fathers, and silly aunts, and scheming sisters, and drunken uncles, and slaphappy fiancés, and fluttering ladies, and perverse cousins.

A screen door cracked shut in the next yard. Jill was hurrying over. She still had on the Sunday white dress, but she sat down on the grass anyway. "How's it going?" she asked, breathlessly.

"It's so bad I had to take time out."

"What a sociable thing you are."

"It really is a pain. Florence is putting on a performance. I can't take all three acts at once."

Jill didn't answer. He was glad she didn't agree. He just wanted someone to listen.

"The best will be the dinner. Uncle Arthur is upstairs over there getting piss-eyed—" It had slipped out. He wouldn't want to offend her. But she wasn't offended. So he let it go. "I had to hide his shoes to keep him away."

"Then there's Ralph. I can't figure him out for beans. Florence says jump and all he wants to know is 'How high?'"

"That's old," said Jill.

"Well."

"You're too harsh," she said. "He's in love with her. The essence of love is wanting to consent. Someday you'll realize it too. If you ever fall in love."

"I don't even see how Florence has any sex appeal."

"That's because she's your sister."

"I'm a man."

"You're accustomed to her. Oh, stop being so mean, Jim."

"She never stops scheming."

Jill got up. "I like Florence, and you're not fair. I'm sorry I came over."

"I'm sorry. I guess I just don't like myself."

She sat down again. "What are they doing?"

"Getting drunk."

She made a face.

"Mrs. Spaulding keeps going, 'ooooh, ooooh' and every time she makes that noise, she looks like she's kissing a lemon."

Jill laughed in spite of herself.

"Ralph is getting the crap knocked out of him. He banged his head on the kitchen cupboard—."

Jill made an "Oh" of sympathy.

"—And then my father gave him a straight arm that almost decked him."

"Why?"

"Ah, my father is on the McCarthy kick. People are plotting against the country, the same people who are plotting against him. The Irish conspiracy mentality."

Jill had a distressed look. "McCarthy's not all bad."

"He's a madman."

"Anyway, your father is nice."

"He's a pig-headed old man."

Jill got up.

"Come back, will you?"

But she wouldn't. She went into her house again.

He got up and took a walk along Brush Avenue. He couldn't figure the world out, and he couldn't figure himself out; and he liked neither. His stomach was bothering him.

Chapter 14

When Jim got back to the house, the whole group was gathered in the living room. The hors d'oeuvres plates were empty, but apparently dinner was not yet ready. There were three separate conversations going on.

Aunt Anita was talking to Mr. Meagher: they were sitting together on the couch. Jim sympathized with her, for the father was a hard man to talk to when he got into one of his withdrawn moods, as he had now. His face was grim—probably, Jim thought, he was gathering more arguments to defend Senator McCarthy. Jim pulled up a chair next to the couch. He got there just in time to hear Aunt Anita say to Harry, "I make the novena of the Holy Souls every Tuesday night."

Harry turned and looked at her with a startled expression. Then he grunted. That was all the answer he gave. From the expression on his face Jim could read his unarticulated answer: "Cracked old woman."

Aunt Anita refused to give up. "What novena do you make?"

"Wha?"

"What novena do you make?"

"I make no novena."

Jim interrupted before she'd reveal his lie. "What part of Westchester do you live in?" he asked Aunt Anita. She was glad enough to turn away from Mr. Meagher and talk to Jim about her neighborhood.

Aunt Nora had Mr. Spaulding's ear. He sat there with his gray hair and his lopsided smile, very urbane-looking and genial—at the same time, however, there was something frozen about the genial smile. Aunt Nora waved her finger in his face, and told him, "When cabbage gets up to fifteen cents a pound, there's something wrong somewhere."

Florence was talking to Mrs. Spaulding. Having left the lesser game to others, she was taking care of the big game herself. She told the story of her

Caribbean sailing cruise, a year ago the previous winter, where she met an actual French-born Frenchman. Mrs. Spaulding listened, her eyes widening at the appropriate intervals, occasionally fluting her mouth and going "oooh," to let Florence know she was listening, though she kept watching everything else that was going on in the room.

Florence left to go to the kitchen. Every eye watched her leave, hoping it was a sign that food was coming. Cricket and Harold arrived, coming through the kitchen and dining room, and standing at the living room door. Nora introduced them: "My Edward" and "My Harold." The two of them immediately went back into the dining room and Jim followed them out.

"It looks like a swinging party," said Cricket.

"Real gasser," said Jim. "How are you, Harold? Good you were able to come."

"I'm fine," said Harold, adjusting his vest.

They stood for a moment, shifting from foot to foot.

"What happens now?" Cricket asked.

"We eat soon. I'm going to put you next to the old aunt. Maybe she'll tell you about her sex life."

Cricket hunched his shoulders and gave his crazy giggle.

Jim wished he could stay with the two of them, and mock the dinner. He would love to have stepped outside the whole affair, and laughed. But he couldn't. Somehow, through conditions not of his making, he was involved. So he went out to the kitchen, and asked Florence if he could serve a drink, or something.

"No," said Florence. "We're ready." She was taking the shrimp cocktail cups from the refrigerator, and setting them on a silver tray. The pink shrimp had been slit across their midriffs so they'd hang tantalizingly on the rim of the cup. The red sauce was in a smaller cup in the middle of each serving, nestled into the shaved ice.

Suddenly she produced a bell, a little silver thing that she gripped by means of the clapper within. "Go to the door of the living room," she said, "and ring this, and announce dinner."

"You're kidding?"

"No."

"Ah, shit," he said. "I'm not going to ring that thing."

"Don't," she said. "Don't bother."

She rang it herself, and gave the glad tidings of food, and in a moment everyone was in the dining room. She ran back to the kitchen to bring in the tray of shrimp. In that brief interval, Aunt Nora took care of the seating arrangement.

She lined herself, and Cricket, and Harold along one side of the table, and left an empty space for Uncle Arthur. There was nothing left for the Spauldings to do but ignore the cards, and take the other side of the table. Jim and Florence were also to sit on the other side with the Spauldings. Mr. Meagher took the place of honor and Mr. Spaulding took the end place at the other end of the table. Then Aunt Nora sat down, and the others followed, so that when Florence arrived with the tray of shrimp, the seating arrangement was accomplished, and Nora sat there with a stubborn, impassive look on her face, and refused to look at Florence, who glared at her.

Jim watched the two spots of red form in Florence's cheeks. She was really in a blaze. But Jim knew, and Nora, of course, knew, that Florence would do nothing to destroy appearances. The seating arrangement had to be left the way it was.

"Where is Arthur?" asked Aunt Nora.

This turned Florence's look from anger to alarm.

"He should be here," said Nora.

"There's no sense bothering the poor man," said Florence.

"Harold," said Nora, leaning forward, "go see where your father is."

Harold got up obediently, and started out.

"Bring your fiddle back," said Nora. "Maybe you can play a few tunes for the people."

"There's no need—," Florence cried, but Harold was already out the door. Florence immediately went over and turned on the hi-fi, and the Mantovani melody floated through the dining room.

The way the eating arrangement had worked out, there were five on Jim's side of the table: Mrs. Spaulding, Aunt Anita, himself, Florence, and Ralph. He had the obligation of talking to Aunt Anita. She had already exhausted the subject of her home surroundings so he didn't know what to say to her. He smiled at her each time she turned and smiled at him. He seized at the opportunity presented by Harold's leaving: "Harold plays the violin very well."

"Oh," said Aunt Anita, smiling.

Jim didn't know what more to say.

Mrs. Spaulding looked over the table from her point at the end of the table near her husband. "Isn't it just lovely?" she said across the table to Cricket. "Isn't it just beautiful?"

Cricket looked up from his plate, and peered across at her from behind his milk-bottle lenses; he didn't answer at all.

"We'll eat," said Mr. Meagher firmly, "but we'll say grace first." He stood up and made the thanks, while all bowed their heads.

He sat down again. Everyone got set to pick up a shrimp, when Florence cried, "The toast first!" She rushed out to the kitchen for the champagne; Ralph followed her out.

Each person stared hungrily at the shrimp in front of him, but waited. The conversation ceased altogether. They listened to Florence and Ralph bustle about the kitchen. The opening of the champagne in the kitchen took an interminable time. "Have they gone to buy it?" Mr. Meagher asked impatiently.

"Florence!" he called to the kitchen.

"Coming right in," answered Florence.

The whomp of a champagne cork was heard. Then Florence gave a stifled cry. They heard her say in the kitchen, "Are you all right?"

Jim went out to the kitchen. Ralph had both hands over his mouth. He had apparently been hit with the cork.

"What's going on?" Mr. Meagher cried from the dining room.

Florence turned in the direction of the dining room and called, with a smile on her face, "We're coming right in"; then the smile turned to concern as she asked Ralph, "Are you sure you're all right?"

"I guess so." He was testing his left front tooth with his index finger. "I think it's a little bit loose."

"Oh God," cried Florence. She was near tears.

"It's all right honey," said Ralph. "It'll tighten up again."

"We'll go right to the dentist," she said.

"That's not necessary," said Ralph. "It's fine." But Jim could see that his lip was already getting fat.

"Are you sure?"

"Positive."

The entered the dining room. "You'll never guess what happened," said Florence to the group. "The champagne cork flew out and hit Ralph."

Mrs. Spaulding's eyes went wide. Both Florence and Ralph went to reassure her. "It's nothing. I'm fine," said Ralph.

"You're sure," said the mother.

"I'm fine," he repeated.

The champagne was poured. "A toast!" Jim said.

Cricket looked across at Jim with a smirk on his face and said, "Yeah. Let's hear it for Florence and Ralph."

"You should give the toast, Dad," said Jim.

Everyone looked to Mr. Meagher. He took the champagne glass— fragile in his powerful hand—and held it, while he paused for thought. Finally, he said gruffly, "Good luck."

They all made sounds of approval, and drank.

Harold came in with his violin.

"Oh, Harold is back," Aunt Nora proclaimed. "Where's your father?"

"He's getting up."

Jim got into a panic. How could Arthur come without shoes?

Harold stood there, fiddle in one hand, bow in the other, and waited for his cue.

"There's really no need for Harold to interrupt his dinner by playing now," Florence said to Aunt Nora. "I'll just play the dinner music for now."

"Don't you want him to play?" asked Aunt Nora.

"It's not that I don't want him to play," said Florence evenly. "It's just that I want him to have his dinner."

"Wouldn't the guests like to hear some violin music?" asked Nora.

Both Mrs. Spaulding and Aunt Anita had inscrutable smiles. Mr. Spaulding was looking longingly at the shrimp.

Mr. Meagher settled it. "Play one tune, then leave us to get on with the meal."

Harold raised the fiddle under his chin, and began to pluck strings looking for the right pitch. It was meant to be background music for the dinner, but suddenly it had become a concert, so everyone had to sit with hands in lap and look at the shrimp and wait for the recital to be ended. Harold drew the bow once across the strings in a test run, and drew an awful cat-yawling from the instrument. Florence sat herself in a chair, put her hands in her lap, and looked up at Harold, and beamed, actually beamed, as if she had planned the whole thing herself.

Jim looked at Nora, who had a satisfied air. She was such a blockhead of a woman, he thought. She couldn't step into the background for one day.

Harold played "The Last Rose of Summer." He could play well, but he was nervous, and there were screechy overtones, and an occasional rumbling low note. Once there was a nerve-jarring flat.

During the concert the two Spaulding women nodded their heads in time with the music. Mr. Spaulding studied Harold with a puzzled expression. Cricket looked at Jim and rolled his eyes in agony. Jim just wanted to get away from the table. If Arthur was going to come to the dinner, Jim had to give him his shoes back. But it would seem such an obvious thing if he were to get up now in the middle of the violin concert. Mrs. Spaulding leaned across the table to Cricket, and said in a low voice, "I bet you're musical too." Cricket stared at her.

"The Last Rose of Summer" was finally coming to the end of its span. Harold was on the last line. Just at that moment, the screen door in the kitchen opened and shut.

Jim straightened. Florence looked up. Aunt Nora turned warily in the direction of the door. They all had the same thought: Uncle Arthur.

Harold put down the violin from his chin. The group at the table, with the exception of Mr. Meagher, clapped politely. Mr. Spaulding grabbed a shrimp. The others picked up their forks. Suddenly, from the kitchen, there was a moaning sound. The moaning sound rose and fell, and rose again. Undoubtedly it was Uncle Arthur. Jim got up from his chair. The moaning got louder. Florence gasped.

Uncle Arthur appeared in the doorway. He had on the dark glasses, and the brim of his hat was turned up. He was still making the moaning sound, and it was intended to be the sound of a saxophone, for he was working the imaginary keys. He was barefoot.

"Jesus, Mary and holy Saint Joseph," cried Nora. Florence gripped Ralph's arm like a vise, to keep herself from fainting. Mr. Meagher pushed his chair back and cried, "What in hell—" Mrs. Spaulding's eyes were the size of saucers as she stared at him. Aunt Anita had a frightened look. Mr. Spaulding was bewildered.

Even though his audience didn't react with laughter, Arthur tried to bring the act off. He lurched around the table in his subway motion. He even went through the routine of going around the man who had his legs in the aisle.

Jim frantically clapped. He told all the group: "It's a blind man begging in the subway. Isn't it terrific? You have to imitate the subway noise!" Jim tried his best to make a subway noise. He banged his own plate up and down in rhythm, and then moved the shrimp cup off Aunt Anita's plate, and rattled her plate on the table also. He concentrated especially on Mr. Spaulding. "It's a blind man begging in the subway," he repeated. Mr. Spaulding, bewildered, tried to understand. "A blind man?" he asked Jim.

"A blind man in the subway," said Jim. "An imitation." Jim laughed, and tried to laugh some more. Please laugh, he said to himself.

Mr. Spaulding, realizing what was expected of him, laughed. Florence took it up. "Uncle Arthur is always doing imitations," she cried. She joined Jim and Mr. Spaulding in laughter. She poked Ralph, and he laughed with all his strength. But Mrs. Spaulding and Aunt Anita were aghast. They stared with horrified fascination as Uncle Arthur went shuffling by them. When Uncle Arthur reached Mr. Meagher, Mr. Meagher barked at him, "You're a goddamn lunatic."

"Sit down," Aunt Nora commanded him.

"Oh no," said Florence. "We're enjoying it."

Uncle Arthur took off the dark glasses, and broke into a laugh himself. "I'm pleased to meet you all," he said. He was high, Jim could see, but his speech was still clear.

Mr. Spaulding stood up and extended his hand. "I'm Fred Spaulding."

"Good to meet you," said Uncle Arthur. "I'm Art Connolly."

Then he was introduced to the women. Aunt Anita never took her eyes from his bare feet. Finally, he took his place next to Nora. Ralph jumped up and got him a glass of champagne.

"That was very entertaining," said Mr. Spaulding to Arthur. Jim looked sharply at Mr. Spaulding. He seemed to be sincere. And maybe he was. Perhaps anything was better than the stilted formality that had paralyzed the previous part of the afternoon, even one of Uncle Arthur's wacky performances.

Florence began to recover. She sensed that perhaps the damage wasn't irreparable. And, anyway, the bare feet were at least no longer visible. Except to Aunt Anita who leaned back in her chair for a surreptitious peek under the table.

"We've always told Uncle Arthur that he should be a comedian," said Florence. "Whenever we have any kind of a family affair, he loves to put on a show." She came around the table and put her arm around Uncle Arthur.

"Have some shrimp," she told him, eager to get something into his stomach. Arthur, however, seemed to be more interested in the champagne. He finished one glass, and held up the empty glass for Ralph to refill it.

Before he drank the second glass, Arthur held it up in a toast to Ralph. "Good luck to you, son." He added under his breath, "You'll need it." Then he asked in a loud voice, "What do you do for a living?"

"I'm a lawyer," said Ralph.

"It's kind of a family tradition," said Mr. Spaulding.

"Are you a lawyer too?"

"Yes," said Mr. Spaulding.

"Two of them," exclaimed Arthur. "Count the silver tonight."

The father and son both laughed. "Tell your story about lawyers, Dad," prompted Ralph.

"It's an old one," said Mr. Spaulding.

"Give it to us," said Arthur.

"It's a story I heard from a judge years ago," said Mr. Spaulding as he settled himself comfortably, pushing himself back in the chair and crossing his knee.

"I think it's cute. It seems there was a dispute between Saint Peter and the Devil over who owned some land up there. They argued, but they couldn't reach any agreement. Finally the Devil offered a compromise. 'We'll bring the whole thing to court,' he said. 'And we'll accept the decision.' 'But you're sure to lose,' Saint Peter told the Devil. 'Why?' asked the Devil. 'Because,' said Saint Peter, 'we've got right on our side.' 'You may have right on your side,' said the Devil, 'but down where I come from, we've got all the good lawyers.'"

Mr. Spaulding sat back and gave a hearty laugh at his own story.

Florence went out to the kitchen, and Aunt Nora followed her. Mr. Meagher went to carve the turkey. For those at the table, Florence rushed out with another bottle of champagne.

"Did you hear the story of Pat and Mike, and the time they went to a wake?" cried Arthur.

Mr. Meagher, had he been in the room, wouldn't have approved of a Pat and Mike story. "Demeaning to the Irish," he would have said.

Arthur launched into the story. "Pat and Mike were going to Mike Dugan's wake. They had stopped and had a few after work, so they had trouble finding the funeral home."

Florence and Aunt Nora could be heard arguing in the kitchen. Then the guests could hear the low rumble of Harry's voice, undoubtedly trying to reconcile the two women.

"They finally reached a piano factory and stood in front of the open door," Arthur continued. "Pat says to Mike, 'This is the place. You go in; I'll wait outside.' So Mike walks into the piano factory, and he sees the brown wood of the piano, and he thinks that's the casket so he kneels down and says a prayer."

Aunt Anita and Mrs. Spaulding both had their ears cocked to hear what was going on in the kitchen. Uncle Arthur got up out of his chair and acted out the joke. He even knelt down in front of the piano to demonstrate. When he got up, he staggered a few steps.

"When Mike came out again into the street," said Arthur, "Pat asked him, 'How did poor Dugan look?' 'Well,' said Mike, 'I never knew Dugan in life, but one thing I'll say about that man. He had a lovely set of fine, white teeth.'"

Mr. Spaulding enjoyed the joke; he laughed heartily. The women joined in, to be polite. Arthur grinned, pleased at a good audience. The only one who didn't laugh was Ralph. As soon as he heard the punch line about the fine, white teeth, he gingerly touched his own front tooth with his index finger. Mrs. Spaulding noticed this and she quickly asked, "Are you sure that tooth is all right dear?"

"Yes, mother," said Ralph. He immediately put his hand down, and turned on a smile.

Aunt Nora came in. Blood was pounding behind her cheeks and in her temples, and her eyes flashed fire. She paused before sitting down, torn between the urge to air her grievances against Florence and the instinct to keep the family dispute private. Arthur, who was still up and moving about, gave her a full-handed slap on her backside. "PeeWee, darling," he said.

"Shut up," she snapped at him. Then she said in a more audible tone to the group, "I don't know what time we'll be eating. The potatoes are being put back in the skins at the moment."

Florence heard her comments in the kitchen, and rushed to the door. As she talked she looked significantly at Nora. "I'm mashing the potatoes with sour cream and putting them back in the jackets. I hope that's the way everybody likes their baked potatoes."

"I love them that way dear," said Mrs. Spaulding.

"Delightful," said Aunt Anita.

"Personally," said Nora, "I don't think there's anything can top mashed potatoes with lots of good butter beat into them."

"As long as everyone likes them with sour cream, that's enough for me," said Florence. She returned to the kitchen.

When Nora sat down, she looked at Arthur stumbling around, and murmured, "For Christ's sake, sit down!"

Jim could feel himself getting angry. He hated it when Nora ordered Arthur about as if he were some kind of misbehaving family pet. Though, to tell the truth, Arthur was near helpless. He barely made it to the chair.

Mr. Meagher came in with the platter of turkey. The white meat was succulent, and the legs of the bird were crisp with roasted brown skin. Steam rose from the whole platter. "Let ye all eat now," he said.

Florence followed with the platter of potatoes. Whatever had been done to the baked potatoes, they were again wrapped in silver foil. The Spauldings went into ecstatic praise when they tasted the potatoes. Nora took this as an affront. She informed the group that an even better way to have potatoes with turkey was to stuff the potatoes inside the turkey.

Aunt Anita liked the cranberry sauce, and, in her timid voice, she said so. She put wind again in Florence's sails. Florence went into a delighted explanation of how she had first discovered this special cranberry sauce when she had dinner at a friend's house.

"You'll just have to tell us where to get it," said Mrs. Spaulding.

The women, engrossed in talking about food, found much to talk about, for the dishes came fast now; sweet potatoes baked in casserole with candy sauce and marshmallow, string beans with nuts, cauliflower with cream sauce, turnip, and broccoli with butter sauce. For Jim the best part of the meal was the gravy—rich, brown, filled with mushrooms and giblets—a specialty of Nora's.

Mr. Meagher, with his bad stomach, ate sparingly, and soon he put down his utensils to wait for the chocolate cake and ice cream and coffee and liqueurs. He watched Ralph warily.

Finally he asked, "Did you watch the McCarthy hearings on television?"

Florence leaped in. "No politics," she cried cheerily.

"I'm just asking the boy a question."

"No politics."

"Sure, can't we talk?"

"Oh Dad," said Florence. "You and McCarthy."

Mr. Meagher decided to ignore her. He again spoke to Ralph. "If you watched those hearings, they'd have showed you all the Communists in the government."

Ralph had a mouthful of food. He put his hand up to his mouth as he tried to swallow more quickly. Suddenly his eyes grew wide with alarm, and his face turned white. He opened his mouth and touched the gum. "The tooth!" he cried. "It's gone."

This announcement threw the whole group into consternation. Florence screamed. Mrs. Spaulding rushed to her son. Ralph opened his mouth. Sure enough, there was a gap. "I must have swallowed it," he cried.

Cricket took a fit of giggling. He covered his mouth with both hands, and tried to muffle the noise.

Florence had her fingers on Ralph's lips. "How awful," she said.

"His lovely teeth," moaned Mrs. Spaulding.

"I haven't any of my teeth," said Uncle Arthur. "But nobody's taking any notice."

With that he took out his upper and lower plates.

"We have to go to the dentist," said Florence.

"Is there any sense in going to the dentist now?" asked Mr. Meagher. "The tooth is out."

"He has to go to the dentist," said Florence. "I'll call Doctor Friedman." She dashed into the living room.

Mrs. Spaulding was hysterical, weeping and wailing and waving her arms. Mr. Meagher looked at her for a moment. For lack of a better response, he commanded her, "Shut up."

She was stunned at the command. But she followed it.

Aunt Anita sat watching everything that was going on. Cricket still had his face covered. Harold looked on with a faintly disapproving air. Ralph's face was entirely drained of blood, and every few seconds he put his finger to his gum, hoping he might find a tooth. Uncle Arthur was still displaying his false teeth.

"Get him home," Mr. Meagher told Nora, indicating Arthur. Nora and the boys got Arthur and took him out the back door and across the yard home.

"Doctor Friedman says to come over," said Florence as she dashed into the dining room.

"Shouldn't he go to his own dentist?" Mr. Meagher asked.

"I'd rather," said Ralph.

"That's right," said Mr. Spaulding. "We'll get him to his own dentist."

"Come on, dear," said Mrs. Spaulding, taking Ralph's arm.

The whole group, including Florence, went out the front door. The Spauldings and Aunt Anita climbed into the car. As they drove off, Ralph gave Florence a grotesque, gapped smile from the back seat.

Florence came back into the house. "He's going to have a false tooth," she said. "And he had such lovely teeth." She broke into weeping.

Chapter 15

Eventually Florence stopped crying. As she wiped away tears, she said quietly, without theatrics, "I've lost him."

"Don't worry about it," said Mr. Meagher.

"No." she said. "He's gone."

"You're young and pretty. There'll be another one," said Mr. Meagher.

"No. No."

"Oh, don't take the whole thing as the end of the world. Sure, you'll find yourself another fellow with a full set of teeth."

Jim smiled despite himself. He knew his father didn't go in for witty nuances, and meant this as a factual statement, but it was brutal as it came out, and Florence recoiled. It also opened up the tear ducts again.

Eventually, she quieted. Silence came over the three of them. Mr. Meagher cleared his throat, and Jim could tell from his softened tone that this time he was trying to be more diplomatic. "Maybe, when all is said and done, we were trying to put up a bit of a bluff, eh?"

"What do you mean?" Florence asked.

"Maybe, without being rough, we should have kept things more simple."

"I just wanted everything to be nice," wailed Florence. "And Arthur, and Nora and Harold ruined it, ruined it all. I hate them."

"Such crap and nonsense," exploded the father. "It's not your aunt and uncle, and cousins that are on trial in this house, but them that came here today."

Florence turned and went to her room.

This left Jim in a situation that he wanted to avoid at all costs: he was left alone with his father. Jim edged toward the door. "I'd better go see Eva, and tell her the party is off."

"I saw your Father Phelan."

Jim stopped and waited.

"He told me you were dishonest, and a sneak, and a thief, and a lot more."

Jim said nothing.

"It was all a lot of horse shit," said Mr. Meagher. "You're none of those things and I told him so. I did tell him that you were the laziest boy that God ever put the breath of life into."

"And what did he say?"

"He said you go to school tomorrow."

"The suspension is off?"

"To what purpose was a suspension? To give a heedless boy a chance to waste two more weeks? T'was I being punished, who earned the tuition that's sending you there, for a chance at an education, a chance that I never got."

"Thanks, Dad."

"You're nineteen," he said. "Talking isn't doing any good at this stage. You'll be what you will. You understand?"

"Yes."

Mr. Meagher put on his hat and left the house. Jim went to the window and watched him until he was out of sight on Brush Avenue, walking in the direction of Saint Margaret's.

Chapter 16

Jim felt sorry for Florence during the following week. She was very low, keeping to herself, sitting in her room most of the evening when she got home from work.

Then on Thursday Ralph called, and Florence became exuberant again. Ralph also became the main topic of conversation again.

On Saturday morning, while Jim and his father and Florence were having breakfast, Florence was wrapping toast in wax paper and filling a thermos of coffee.

"Where are you taking the toast and coffee?" Mr. Meagher asked.

"I'm going to meet Ralph in the city. He never eats breakfast, so I thought I'd bring him something."

"Are you going to set up housekeeping on the New York Central?" Jim inquired.

"It's just something for his breakfast."

"If you're going to have breakfast with him," Jim said, "why don't you wear your curlers and house dress? Give him a preview of what married breakfast is going to be like."

"Nobody said anything about getting married," Florence replied. But she wasn't at all angry at this mention, so Jim assumed that things had at least reached the discussion stage.

"Has he got a new tooth?" Jim asked.

"Yes."

It didn't matter, thought Jim, whether he got a new tooth or not. If Ralph was going to get married, he wasn't going to be doing much smiling anyway.

An automobile horn blew outside. It was Jack South, Jill's twin brother, and Jim got up immediately.

"Where are you off to?" Mr. Meagher asked.

"Field Day over at school. Jack is driving me over."

Chapter 17

Jim Meagher and Jack South stood on the football field, Jack holding a kite string, peering into the distance, trying to locate the kite. It was way out over the East Bronx, only a dot in the sky, and Jack had to study the sky before he could even see it. Just one other contestant on the field had a kite out as far, and that was Vinnie Carbone, a classmate, whose nickname was "The Chief." Vinnie was already proclaiming victory to a group of youths around him.

Red Harrigan came by, holding a clipboard. He was Freshman class president.

"Are you judging it?" Jack asked.

"Yes," said Red. "Which one is yours and which is the Chief's?"

"The one farthest out is mine," said Jack.

Red studied the sky in the direction where Jack's string pointed. "I can't see it."

"It's way out," said Jack. "You see that smokestack? Look above it. You can hardly see it."

Red continued to look. Then he said, "I see it. Wow, that's really out."

Vinnie Carbone watched them. Suddenly he shouted, "Hey, he's showing you my kite!"

Jack started to laugh. "I'm showing him mine," he shouted back.

Vinnie, red in the face, cried, "That one over the smokestack is mine."

"Follow the string," Jack answered. "Follow the string." A dozen of the spectators peered into the distance, trying to locate the kites. "Yours is near it, but mine is farther out."

"Your ass," Vinnie shouted.

"I'm not flying my ass today, Vinnie," Jack replied placidly. "I'm flying my kite."

"He's cheating," said Vinnie.

Red went to listen to Vinnie's case. Jack followed, keeping a hold on his string.

Red told each of them to pull their strings. Jack pulled, then Vinnie. Neither movement seemed to affect the dots in the far-off sky. Vinnie then appealed to the spectators, and tried to win his argument by witnesses.

As Vinnie's head was turned, Jim Meagher took out a pocket knife, and reached up and cut Vinnie's string.

When the string went limp in his hand, Vinnie screamed. Jim ran. Vinnie raced after him, yelling as Jim laughed.

"Both kites are disqualified," said Red, moving on to the other contestants. Vinnie stopped chasing Jim, and pursued Red, protesting that he couldn't be disqualified since he had already won. He pointed frantically to the section of the sky where his kite had been flying a few minutes before. He called others as witnesses to buttress his case. Red, the politician, tried to placate him.

Jim went across the field to see what the girl contestants looked like. Three girls from Molloy College on Long Island were trying to launch a kite with a tail of tied-together pieces of cloth such as girls used to put up their hair. Jim ran the kite across the field for them. It rose ten feet or so, then nose-dived, and hit the ground so hard that the main stick of balsa wood snapped.

"Be sure to come back next year," Jim told them.

"It's broken." One of the three looked like she was going to cry.

Jim didn't have a chance to console her, for out of the corner of his eye he could see Vinnie running across the field after him again. He took off, and Vinnie chased him a full circuit of the football field. "You're going to pay for that kite, Meagher."

"It was an accident, Vinnie."

"Your ass," Vinnie cried, enraged. He took up the pursuit again. But eventually he got winded and gave up, and went off to watch the other kites.

Jim sought out Red Harrigan. Red had plans to work a construction job during the summer to build himself up for football in September, especially his arm for passing. He had approached Jim about it. Jim had decided he wanted to do it also. He wanted to build himself up; but he also had another reason: he wanted to become a workman, powerful and strong like his father, an intellectual but not just a pantywaist scholar.

"Hi, Red."

"Meagher. You still up for the job?"

"Looking forward to it, if it's still there," Jim answered.

"It's all set," said Red. "We start the first Monday in June."

Chapter 18

Jack South decided not to wait for the judging. He had promised to be home for dinner, so he went to get his car. He walked across the campus whistling. He stopped briefly at his room in Hughes Hall. He was one of the few New York City boys who wasn't a day-hop, but lived on campus. This had come about through a scholarship for room, board, and tuition from the Holy Name Society of the New York City Police Department. Jack had won it in a competitive examination, to his father's delight. In that same year his father had been promoted to Precinct Captain, but of the two events he seemed more pleased at Jack's scholarship, perhaps because it was so unexpected. The family hopes had been placed on Jill. Actually, she might have done better in the exam, and lost out to better competitors in the girls' division. However it came about, the result was the only thing that was credited, and Jack had won in the men's division.

He loved life on campus. At home, his mother, a nervous woman, had surrounded the children with her fears. If he came in late, she would be waiting up, a hundred worry lines on her forehead. There was none of that at school. The restrictions of the dormitory were more impersonal, and there were ways to get around them. He kept his room neat, and that was so unusual the proctors assumed he was keeping the other rules too. Also, the priests liked him, for his good disposition and extraordinary smile, which he used to good effect.

Of the nine months on campus, life had never been more pleasant than now in May. The fears of Freshman year were past. The anxieties of Sophomore year were yet to come. It was the time to relax. And Jack was relaxing. He was a ringleader in the uproar in Hughes Hall that had announced the Spring. At nine o'clock each night, the building erupted with lion roars, each man hanging out his window trying to outdo the man in the window next to him in ferociousness and volume. The roars carried across the green quadrangle to the nuns' residence, where sister students prepared for graduate degrees. The younger nuns laughed at it; they even waited for nine o'clock—MGM hour, as the boys called it. But the older nuns complained to Father Phelan. The priest was already immersed in the search for the statue of Father Del Prado, University Founder, missing from its pedestal for two weeks. A postcard had arrived from Japan during the week, addressed to Father Phelan, with the message: "Having a wonderful time. Wish you were here. Father Del Prado." Father Phelan had retaliated by handing out numerous suspensions, even for offenses that wouldn't have ordinarily been punished so heavily.

In his room, Jack changed his clothes, ran a comb through his blond hair at the mirror, and then went down to the car. It took him only half an hour to get to the house on Brush Avenue. Jill was sitting on the porch.

Jack got out of the car and brought with him the football that was usually resting in the front seat. "Mom home?"

"She's shopping," said Jill. "What have you been doing?"

"Just hacking around over in school. Hey, Birdie, come on, throw me a couple." He held out the football.

"No. I can't."

"Come on," he insisted. "You don't have to throw it far."

"No."

He pleaded until she finally came down to the lawn. He bent over the ball to hike it. "After I give it to you, count to five," he ordered. "Then hit me with it right here"—he pointed to his stomach—"The old Chuck Conerly special."

He hiked the ball and went tearing across the lawn. She bobbled the ball. When she finally threw it, it wobbled ten yards up the lawn and bounced on the ground. Jack was disgusted.

"What do you call that?" He came back to give some lessons. "Get your fingers on the laces. This way. See. You get a grip that way. Then just whip it. Right out in front."

She tried again. The ball went a little way, and started to die again. But this time he had only gone out about five yards, and he scooped the ball up before it hit the ground. With a whoop of joy he went dashing up the lawn for his own private touchdown. He came trotting back happily, and announced, "Gifford saves the day with another spectacular catch." He got set to hike the ball again.

"I don't want to," she said. "It hurts when you throw it that way."

"You want to go out for one?" he offered. "Go on."

She was hesitant. "Throw it easy."

She went running up the lawn, hoping she wouldn't miss it and look silly. She stole a glance across the street to see if any of the Dolans were watching. She glanced ahead at the Meaghers' to see if anyone was looking out the window. Suddenly the ball was bouncing past her.

Jack laughed hilariously. He sat on the porch step and slapped his thigh. She turned around and walked back, her feelings much bruised. She didn't retrieve the ball.

"You're in a fashion show," he said. "You never even looked at the ball."

"You could have told me you were going to throw it." She sat on the porch. "I don't feel like playing anymore."

"Ah, come on, Birdie. Just throw me one more."

"No."

"Just one?"

"No. You're too smart."

He laughed again. "I'm sorry," he said. "You really looked good when you were going out for that one. No kidding. You really looked good."

"I have *no* desire to be a football player."

He sat on the porch, throwing the football around, restless as always.

"Did they find the statue yet?" she asked.

"Nope."

"Do you know where it is?"

"Sure."

She waited for him to continue but he wouldn't. "Don't you get suspended."

He laughed.

"I was talking to Jim," she said.

"He wasn't worried?"

"He didn't seem to be."

"Half the school is suspended," said Jack. "Phelan is going off his nut."

He went in to watch a football game on the television; she followed him in. "Have you got a date tonight?" she asked.

"Naw. What are you doing?"

"I don't know," she said. "I'll probably go to the movies with Peggy."

Later she asked, "Aren't you going out at all?"

"I'll probably go to Feeney's," he said.

"What's Feeney's like?"

"Just a bar."

"Can you dance?"

"Yea. To the juke."

"Who's going to be there?"

"Red. Some of the other guys I guess."

"How is Red?"

"He's fine. Jill, I'm trying to watch the game."

"Oh. Okay."

Later she asked, "Is Jim going?"

"Huh?"

"Is Jim going?"

"Is Jim going where?"

"To *Feeney's*."

"No. He has a date."

"Is he still going with Eva?"

"Yea."

"She's very nice," said Jill.

"Yea. I guess so. I never talked to her that much. Little on the heavy side."

Later again, she asked, "Do many girls go stag to Feeney's?"

"Huh? Not too many."

He wouldn't take the hint. He didn't want any family observers on the scene.

"How come you didn't get a date for tonight?" she asked.

"I got one tomorrow."

"With who?"

"Noogie."

"Noogie? Who's Noogie?"

"Evelyn Nugent."

"Noogie?" Jill screwed up her nose. "Noogie?"

"Everybody calls her that," said Jack. He'd let it slip unawares.

"I never heard anybody call her that. Noogie?"

He watched the game intently.

"Does she like you to call her that?" asked Jill. "I'll bet she calls you Southie. No. Jackie. Jackie and Noogie."

"I'm trying to watch the game, Jill."

"Oh, I think that's nice. Jackie and Noogie."

"Get off my back."

Jill laughed. Despite himself, Jack grinned.

Mrs. South came in. She was carrying groceries and some smaller, flatter packages of the Woolworth's type. Her face gave indications that twenty years before she was a beauty. She had a kindly expression, but the lines branching out from her eyes were many and deep. Jack got up and kissed her. "I'm glad you're home," she said. Then she announced, "There's a letter from Charles."

"From Charles!" both cried.

"He's fine," the mother replied. "He's well. You can read it for your-selves." She dropped her packages in a chair and searched in her purse for the letter.

"He saw Cardinal Spellman. The Cardinal said Mass for all of them for Christmas. Charley even received communion from him."

"Cardinal Spellman, eh?" said Jack. "And still no more fighting?"

"He says it's over now," said Mrs. South, with satisfaction. "Here it is."

Jack grabbed it out of her hand, and started to read. Jill read it over his shoulder. It was a one-sheet fold-over airmail letter. "He's in Seoul," said Jack.

"Yes, he wants to get to Japan, now," said the mother, going out to the kitchen with her packages. "Thank God he's all right."

"He thinks he'll make captain," said Jack.

"I read that already," said Jill. "Turn over."

The mother came in again. "Thank God and His holy mother he'll be home soon and safe."

Jack was finished. "He doesn't say anything about what the fighting was like." He was disappointed.

Jill took the letter to a corner to read the whole thing again.

"When your father comes in," said Mrs. South, "We'll say a rosary to thank God that he's safe." She sat down in a chair. She was a little winded from the shopping. She was getting stout. Suddenly she started to cry. Jill dropped the letter and ran to her, and Jack also.

"He's all right," said Jack. "Come on, Ma. He's all right."

"Sure they'll be killing each other over there again yet," said the mother. "It's in the papers this morning."

"That's nothing," said Jill. "It's over."

"He's not up on the line," said Jack. "He's in Seoul. That's way back."

"God knows where he is today," she said. She was shaking with sob-bing. "It's a desperate place, that Korea."

"Charley can take care of himself," said Jack.

"Sure he wouldn't tell us if there was anything wrong," said the mother. "He might be in a hospital."

Jill forced a laugh. "Mother, if that isn't ridiculous."

"Stop being silly, Ma," said Jack.

"I suppose I am silly," she said. "But I won't believe he's all right until he's home."

"He'll be home before the summer," said Jill.

"Sure," Jack added.

"Please God," said the mother. She got up and went out to the kitchen again.

The father got home half an hour later. He was wearing the blue serge uniform of the New York Police Department and up on his breast was a round gold Captain's badge. He took off his jacket and sat right down in his chair to read the letter. The two children watched him while he read it. When he was finished, he folded it over and on his face was the satisfaction of a father pleased with the eldest son. "He's going to be a Captain."

"It's great, isn't it?" said Jack.

"A good soldier," said the father. "A good soldier." He got up from the chair and went to the head of the stairs and turned and said, "He's the spit of me."

The two children hooted him. He put an expression on his face that was a pretense of offense. "Wasn't I an army officer at the age of twenty-one?"

"Oh, the I.R.A.," said Jill.

"What do you mean 'Oh, the I.R.A.'"

"That was a pitchfork war," said Jill. She could give the father the most outrageous insults and he would only laugh. On the other hand, if Jack tried anything like the same raillery, the father would take offense. Part of the reason was that it wasn't Charley but Jack who was the spitting image of the father. They both had the same brown mischievous eyes, and same high foreheads, and eventually Jack would be as bald as the father too. They were so alike they almost competed.

"Well, by golly," said the father, forgetting that he had started up the stairs, and coming back into the room, "I wish I was nineteen again so that I could be young enough to scoff at the army that brought the British Empire to its knees, and has been an inspiration for men fighting for freedom from that day until this."

The two children clapped.

With the father it was hard to tell if he was serious, from his face anyway.

"Sure, everything is a joke to this generation. I saw the best friends I had lying in pools of blood dying from bullet wounds, and now I'm hearing thirty years later it was a pitchfork war."

"That's what Uncle Nicky calls it," said Jack.

"Nick would know," said Mr. South. "He was a grand fighter. He was what you might call nowadays a sniper. He never came out of the hayloft from 1916 til 1922."

"There were more men shot in one day in Korea," said Jill, "than were shot in all the Irish wars."

The father was sitting down now. "England had Ireland by the throat for a thousand years," he said. "Then all of a sudden in 1921 they said to the

Irish: 'You're free.' Not because there were any British soldiers being shot in Ireland mind you. T'was merely an act of kindness from an enlarged heart."

"What was your rank?" Jack asked.

"I guess you might say I was a kind of commandant in my own territory."

"What's that equivalent to in our army?" Jack asked.

"Well, I. . .I guess you might say it's a colonel."

"What did you have to do?"

"Drill the men. And lead them when the fighting came."

"Did you have guns?"

"Not at first. We got them after."

Mrs. South came in. "We'll say the rosary for Charles now, that he come home safe."

"After dinner, Ma'am," said Mr. South.

"Dinner will be another quarter hour yet," she said.

"Sit down, Ma'am," said Mr. South, "and tell them about the brigade we organized in Drumgannon."

"Haven't they heard all that old gaff already?" the mother asked.

"Your mother and I were a courtin' couple then," said Mr. South. "And sometimes we'd have to go for three months without the sight of each other."

"How come?" asked Jack.

Jill answered him. "They had a dowry system. Daddy had to go away to earn the cows to buy Mommy."

"Geraldine!" said Mrs. South, "that's not funny at all."

"She has the story backwards," said the father, lighting his pipe. "T'was I that was offered the cows."

"What cows?" demanded Mrs. South.

"Didn't your father offer me six cows the night we got engaged?" asked Mr. South.

"He did no such thing," said the mother.

Mr. South blew a cloud of smoke reflectively up in the air. "Will I ever forget how happy the old divil was that night?"

"There was nothing about any cows," said the mother.

"I turned him down," said Mr. South. "I said, 'She's a grand girl. There's no cows needed.'"

"Charles! You're making all this up."

"Did you get engaged during the troubles?" Jack asked.

"The sixteenth of July, 1919," said Mr. South. "There was many a girl's heart in Drumgannon cracked in half that night."

"There's never been anything lacking to your opinion of yourself," said Mrs. South.

"The next night," said Mr. South, "I went on the run. I lived in the fields and the barns. I'd go for a whole day sometimes without a bite to eat or a drop to drink, and I'd think it was a Christmas feast if I was able to crawl out into the fields to get a squirt from a goat's teat."

"Charles!"

"Sure, it's true."

"They were after you, eh?" Jack prompted.

"They had my name."

Suddenly the mother got serious. "The Black and Tans would come," she said to Jack, "and there had to be a list of every man in the house posted on the door, and if one of the men was missing, there was liable to be a shooting."

"Didn't you get to see each other at all?" Jill asked.

"I'd sneak back when I could," said the father. "Molly, who did I bring back with me one time?"

"Mick Collins," said Molly South, and she smiled at the memory.

"Who was he?" Jill asked.

"He was the military leader of the rebellion." This information came from Jack.

"He was the next man to De Valera in Ireland," said the father.

"He was the handsomest man I ever saw," said Mrs South. "With black curly hair."

"Well, he wasn't bad looking," conceded Mr. South.

"He was grand," said the mother.

"Many's a time we had an old wrestle, the two of us," said the father. "And when I'd throw him, he'd get off the floor and say 'Charles South. You're the only man who can beat me in Ireland.'"

"That's a lot of old cod," said the mother. "He's making it up."

"You got it wrong, Daddy," said Jill. "He got off the floor and said 'Charles South, You're the greatest thrower in Ireland.'"

The two children howled and the father cocked his head and gave them a wry smile.

"Why don't you tell them the truth?" said Mrs. South in annoyance to her husband.

"Because there wasn't any Drumgannon Brigade," said Jill.

"There was," said the mother to Jill.

"How come it's not mentioned in any of the books?" asked Jack. "Like *My Fight for Irish Freedom* by Dan Breen. How come your name isn't mentioned Dad?"

"Because," said Jill, "he didn't tell anybody about it. He didn't want his memorial to be written in words of empty praise, but engraved in the hearts of his countrymen. Like Robert Emmet."

"There's truth in that," conceded the father. "Sure there's farmhouses in Ireland today where, if you mention the name of Charles South, the people will bow their heads in reverence."

"Will you for the love of God stop it," cried the mother.

After dinner they said the rosary, kneeling into the chairs in the living room. Then they split up and each went his own way. The father set up the poker table downstairs. He was having some of the boys in. Mrs. South went out to play bingo. She passed Jack as he washed his car in the yard and, after urging him to be in early, and to be careful driving, she told him: "I don't feel a bit lucky." Jill did the dishes and went to her room and played the phonograph. Jack could hear the music: the Toreador March from "Carmen."

His car was a fourteen-year-old Chevrolet coupe inherited from Charley. The brush strokes of a hand-paint job were clearly visible on the black finish. The name was stenciled on the driver's door: the Black Seducer.

He cleaned the inside too with a whisk broom. What to do for the evening? Well, Feeney's. But Feeney's wouldn't liven up until late. It wasn't even dark yet. And there was spring in the air. He wished now he had a date. He could go to one of the girls' colleges and maybe get some action going. It seemed like a good plan. He decided on Mercy College. He put on the white wool sweater with the blue "F" in front and took off, making a satisfying racket with the car muffler as he raced up the street. He heard the Pied Piper music of a Good Humor truck, and he searched out the truck and bought an ice cream cone. He was still licking it when he reached the college. On his left as he went in the gate, he read the plaque: "Dedicated to Our Lady of Mercy. Founded 1950."

He went up the winding driveway at 25 miles an hour, too fast to navigate the turns easily. Suddenly he was forced to hit the brakes hard, for a procession of girls was coming along the path. They had a banner stretched out in front of them; it read: D'ARCY. He beeped the horn. The girls waved.

He stuck his head out the window and shouted, "Yeah, D'Arcy!"

The girls responded enthusiastically, "Yeah, D'Arcy!"

"Are you a friend of D'Arcy's?" they asked him.

"Sure."

"He's a friend of D'Arcy's," they passed the word back.

Jack gave another yell for D'Arcy. The girls cheered; they gathered around the car.

"Are you going to the nominations?" they asked.

"Sure."

"He's going to the nominations!"

"Yeah, D'Arcy!"

"Yeah, D'Arcy!" Jack licked his cone and laughed. It was silly as hell, but why not?

"Can we use your car?"

"Sure. Hop in. Yeah, D'Arcy."

The girls piled in. Three of them managed to get into the front seat. Three more discovered the rumble seat. "It has a rumble seat!" Two perched on the front fenders and hung the sign across the radiator. There were more on the running boards.

Jack counted them. Altogether he had ten of them. "Yeah, D'Arcy."

The girl in the seat next to him asked Jack, "Are you from Fordham?" Jack had to yell to make his answer heard. "Yes."

"He's from Fordham!"

"He's from Fordham."

"Are there more fellows coming?"

"Sure," said Jack.

"There are more fellows coming!"

He got the car turned around. The shock absorbers were all the way down. The girls were making a racket. He gunned the motor so the muffler roared; this caused more excitement. The girl next to him kept beeping the horn. There was also a musical horn hung on the driver's window, and the girl on the running board squeezed the rubber ball to keep it sounding.

They moved up the path at five miles an hour. "Yeah, D'Arcy!" he yelled again. Whoever the hell D'Arcy was.

There was one serious girl in the front seat. She seemed to be memorizing some notes. Jack leaned over and asked her, "Are you D'Arcy?"

"No." She had a surprised look.

Jack straightened up. He'd better not ask any more questions.

The girl on the running board had spotted the name. "The Black Seducer," she called out.

"Yeah, the Black Seducer!"

"Yeah, the Black Seducer."

The car rolled across the athletic field. They came to a bandstand with red, white, and blue bunting around it. A crowd of girls was gathered in front. Jack stopped the car near the edge of the crowd. The girls piled out and he went with them. He looked around to see if there were any other men on the field; there were perhaps a dozen, but they were widely scattered. The girls chanted: "D'Arcy! D'Arcy! D'Arcy!"

From across the field came the chant: "Constance! Constance! Constance!"

Still another group cried: "Marilyn! Marilyn! Marilyn!"

A nun went to the microphone on the bandstand. "We'll have the nominating speeches, please."

D'Arcy's group made way for the girl who had been studying her notes in the front seat of Jack's car. She went to the bandstand and up the stairs to the microphone. She had a clear high voice when she spoke:

> "Who embodies the generosity, know-how, and
> spirit of total dedication which is demanded by
> the office of Student Council delegate?"

She paused, then cried out, "D'Arcy Donovan!" The cheering section around Jack erupted with screams, and leaps and hurrahs. Jack yelled. "Louder. Louder," he was told. He yelled as loud as he could.

> "We have in D'Arcy a thinking candidate,
> a person whose every act as a student councilor
> has been determined by her devotion to the
> student welfare."

"Yeah," the girls cried.

"House committee, vice-chairman Freshman year."

"Yeah."

"Class vice-president, Freshman year."

"Yeah!"

"Class president, her Sophomore year."

"Yeah!"

"Member of the Athletic Association."

"Yeah!"

"Children of Mary."

"Yeah!"

"NFCCS delegate."

"Yeah!"

"Lay apostolate work in the South."

"Yeah!"

"Her influence is soft, yet forceful."

"Yeah!"

"Her mind is quick to decide, yet slow to condemn."

"Yeah!"

"Her schedule is crowded yet there is always time for the individual."

"Yeah!"

"Feminine, modest, kind."

"Yeah!"

Jack couldn't wait to see D'Arcy. She sounded like the greatest thing since Helen of Troy.

He kept searching around the bandstand to see when she'd appear. The nominating speech was coming to a close. "I give you"—the speaker paused—"D'Arcy Donovan!"

The girls screamed. A girl walked up the steps of the platform and embraced the girl who had nominated her. She got rousing cheers. She walked to the microphone and waited for quiet.

Jack was disappointed. He was hoping she'd be a real beauty, a Venus de Milo. Instead she looked like any other college girl. She had a sweater and skirt on, and the skirt was the wrap-around kind, with an oversize decorative safety pin in the front. In height, she was medium-tall, and full-figured. She was full-faced, as well, even round-faced, especially now, for she was laughing. Her hair was dark and fell in big curls, almost to the shoulder. Actually she was all right, thought Jack; he was only disappointed because she had been built up too much.

She grinned as she raised her arms to get silence. He started to like her more. She looked like she was full of fun.

Suddenly he was in a trap. The girl who was standing next to him pointed to him and shouted up to D'Arcy: "D'Arcy, your friend is here."

D'Arcy looked at Jack, perplexed.

"Your friend, D'Arcy!" A whole group of them were pointing to him now. Some of the crowd was turning.

He panicked. He ducked to the ground and pretended he was looking for something he had dropped. But that was a mistake; he was down at eye-level in a forest of girls' legs: the sudden fear came to him they'd think he was trying to get away with something, so he jumped up again.

The girls had made him the focus of the group. He had to brazen it through. He waved his arm and called, "Hi, D'Arcy."

She waved back, a spontaneous reaction. The girls were pleased.

D'Arcy spoke. "Thank you for the nomination. If you vote for me, and I hope you will, I'll do my best."

Just a few more minutes and she was done. She left the microphone to a renewed round of applause. She came down the stairs and headed through the crowd to the girls who had come with Jack. They made way so that there was a corridor right to where Jack was standing; even the girls next to him moved away so that she could stand beside him.

She came up to him hesitantly, but she didn't have a chance to say anything, for the next nominating speech had begun, and she had to give attention for decorum's sake. At the first round of applause, she asked him with a curious look, "Who are you?"

He gave her an engaging smile and shrugged his shoulders. "I don't know how I get into these things. Honestly, I just drove in the gate and your girlfriends climbed into the car."

"Did you come to meet somebody?"

"Naw. Just knocking around."

She smiled.

He went to work to make his impression, as he would have with any girl. He got her laughing. When the speeches were over he brought her to the car and showed her the D'Arcy banner draped across the radiator. She walked around to the side and she saw the name, The Black Seducer, and she really laughed then.

"Can I drive you somewhere?" he offered.

"Would you want to stop in at the tea house for a while?" she asked in turn.

"What's the tea house?"

"A spot on campus for an informal date or something like that."

"Sure."

At the tea house, Jack talked away. He told her about Feeney's. "It's a place where the guys from Fordham hang out in Kingsbridge."

D'Arcy listened. She didn't have a date and she was hoping he'd ask her. She'd like to go down to the city, especially to a place she had never been. And when Jack told her what a real dive Feeney's was, that completed the enchantment.

"Would you like to go?" he asked her.

"Sure," she replied, her eyes glowing.

So they agreed: he'd be back in two hours to give her time to get ready.

Chapter 19

Red Harrigan lived around the corner from Feeney's in a neighborhood that had more bars than grocery stores.

In the Harrigan apartment, Red was stretched out on the couch listening to a tape recording of Irish songs by John McCormack. His friend, Tom Power, was sitting opposite in a chair, watching impatiently. Out in the kitchen his mother was entertaining a woman neighbor over tea.

"What do you have to go to Feeney's for?" Tom asked. He was a pudgy, Irish-faced youth, with a powerful body and short legs that he had twisted over the side of the chair.

Red didn't even hear him. His craggy face was set in peaceful lines as he stared at the ceiling and listened to "Sweet Vale of Avoca." McCormack hit a high note, and Red held up his finger for Tom's attention.

"We stay around there and drink and I get stuck on the rounds," said Tom. "South is drinking scotch and sodas and I'm supposed to pay for them."

"Don't buy a round," said Red. "We'll work it on a kitty."

"Then you're telling me later I'm cheap."

"You are. Listen to this one now. Notice how his voice changes. He couldn't hit the high notes anymore when he got old." McCormack sang "Kerry Dancers."

"Why don't we go to a dance?" asked Tom.

"Where?"

"I don't know. We'll check around."

"We'd have to get dressed up then," said Red. "Anyway, last week you didn't even dance."

"I'll call up Sacred Heart School," said Tom. "See if there's anything doing."

Tom made the call. While he was on the telephone, Dolly, the six-year-old, came in. She was the seventh of the eight children. Red was the oldest. She sat next to Red on the couch and he put his arm around her. "Did you have a good time at the zoo?"

"We saw bears," said Dolly. She had on a flowered print dress that was bunched tight at her chest and flared out all the way down. "One of them scared Mommy."

"No dance," said Tom.

"Dolly went to the zoo today," said Red.

"Oh yeah?" said Tom with no real interest. He had his own problems. "Show Tom your ballet step."

Dolly covered her mouth with both hands and giggled.

"No showing off now. Come on. Show Tom your ballet step."

She got up and did a pirouette, making the dress billow out, obviously pleasing herself with the effect.

"That's good," Tom said absently.

"Do you want to see another one?"

"I thought you had to wear those funny shoes to do ballet."

"No!" said Dolly. "It's not that kind of ballet." She got giggly and ran over to Red and hid her face in his shoulder.

"Don't get silly now," said Red. "Show Tom how you can recite now. Go on."

Dolly stepped to the middle of the floor. "K-i-s-s-i-n-g," she spelled out. "First comes love, then comes marriage, then comes Tom with a baby carriage." She was overcome with giggles and ran right out of the room.

Red laughed.

"What kind of a thing is that to teach a kid?" asked Tom.

"I didn't teach her," said Red. "She came out with it herself last night."

"She doesn't know what it means, does she?"

"Of course not," said Red.

Red yelled, "Come on in here, Dolly."

"No!" Dolly called back from the kitchen.

He went out after her. She was in the ironing board closet. He opened it and asked her, "What, are you getting shy?"

"Leave her alone," said Mrs. Harrigan from the kitchen. "She's playing coy." The mother was a red-haired, bright-eyed woman, still slim for her age.

"How are you, Mrs. Dunphy?" Red asked the neighbor guest, who still had her hat on.

"There's no use complaining," she sighed.

"What happened to dessert?" Red asked the mother.

"There's cake in the refrigerator. What am I supposed to do? Serve you?"

Red brought the chocolate-iced cake to the table, and cut a slab out of it.

"Bring a piece to Tom, too," the mother said.

Red cut another piece. "I hear you got scared by the bears."

"Honest to God," said the mother, "that zoo is a crazy place. There was some old crackpot and wasn't he feeding the bears pieces of fig? When he'd give the bear a piece, he'd say, 'Now don't be greedy, one treat apiece.'" Mrs. Harrigan let out a whoop of laughter. Even Mrs. Dunphy smiled. Dolly jumped around the kitchen with excitement. "Sometimes I wonder," the mother went on, "who should be behind the bars."

Red started in with the pieces of cake, but she stopped him. "Can't you eat those out here?"

"We'll be careful."

"You shouldn't be eating in the living room."

"Don't worry."

"Here, take two plates. Honest to heaven, he's going to bring the boy in a piece of cake in his fist." She took out the plates. "My onchik."

Tom swung his legs up when Red appeared. "Hey! Anything to drink?"

"Hey, Ma. Anything to drink?"

"I'll add some water to the tea," she called back.

Red went out to get the tea. He could hear Peggy and Bart squabbling in the back bedroom. Peggy came up the hallway. She was fourteen, fourth in line, after Red, Mary, and Larry. She had an angry look on her face.

"What's the matter?" Red asked.

"Bart won't let me study." Bart, eleven, came after Peggy in the family lineup.

Peggy went into the living room and sat opposite Tom. This annoyed Red, for now the boys wouldn't be able to talk. She pushed her lower lip out in a pouty shyness, which made her look almost sullen. She stretched her legs, so Tom could see them—they already had fine lines. At another time, under better circumstances, Red would have admitted she gave promise of real beauty: she had a fair complexion and gold-blonde hair. Her figure was just starting to fill.

She opened her school workbook on her lap. "How do you spell 'pretty,'" she asked Tom.

"P-r-i-t-t-y," said Tom, between mouthfuls.

"It's p-r-e-t-t-y," she said.

"If you know, what are you asking me for?"

Red asked her, "What are you sitting out here for?"

"Bart won't let me work."

"There's three bedrooms. Go to one of the others."

"What's a coordinate conjunction?" she asked Tom.

"They're the ones like 'and' and 'but,'" Tom replied.

"A coordinate conjunction," Peggy read from the book, "is a connective between two independent clauses."

"That's what I said, 'and' and 'but.'"

"Beat it, will you, Peggy," said Red. He turned to Tom. "She's going through a difficult time. Don't ask her for explanations, though, because she won't give one."

Peggy, offended, closed the book with elaborate formality, laid it down, and walked out with her head held up. She went to her bedroom and turned on a blast of rock and roll music on the phonograph. Mrs. Harrigan called, "Peggy, we're not deaf, you know." The machine cut off altogether.

The youngest of the children, Tim, four years old, was awakened by the music, and he toddled up the hallway and stood in the door of the living room, a forelock of hair hanging in his eyes, a huge grin on his face.

"Hello Timmy," said Red fondly. "Say hello to Tom."

Timmy walked over to Tom, watched him for a moment, then said, "Give me all your money."

Red roared laughing.

Tom jerked his thumb at Tim. "What's up with this one?"

Red got up and gathered Tim in his arms and brought him to the couch. "Now didn't I tell you not to say that to people?" He started to laugh again.

"Are we going to play with kids all night?" asked Tom, exasperated.

"I'll put him back to bed. I'll be ready in a minute."

After he put Tim back to bed, Red went to his own room, where he found Bart examining baseball cards. "You stop bothering Peggy."

"Who's bothering Peggy?"

"Don't talk to me like that. I'll give you a shot in the head."

"Hey, Bill?"

"Yes?"

"Take it easy on me, eh?"

Red turned away as he pulled on his sweater, so Bart wouldn't see him smile. He was a fresh kid, but he was usually funny.

"Did you carry packages in the A&P today?" Red asked him.

"I had to play ball."

"Did you pitch?"

"Yeah."

"Yes. Not yeah."

"Yes."

"What'd you do?"

"Shutout."

"All right, here." Red gave him a dime.

"Gee," said Bart, with mocking, big dove eyes. "You're a sport, you know that?"

Red took a swipe at him, but Bart ducked easily out of the way. From a safe distance, Bart flexed his shoulders, and said, "Watch yourself. I got a trigger temper."

Red laughed.

He went to the bathroom and knocked. "Dolly?"

"Don't come in," she shouted.

"You're taking a bath?"

"Yes."

"Pull the curtain over. I have to go out."

He waited. "All right," she said.

He went in and brushed his teeth, while Dolly thrashed around behind the curtain. He debated whether to shave. Dolly appeared. She had red, wet curls on her forehead, and her eyelashes were gathered in wet sheaths over her blue eyes. She had a big smile on her face. The shower curtain was drawn across her neck and shoulders. The six-year-old siren.

"Get down there. You're going to slip."

"I won't."

"Get the rubber mat then."

"Okay."

Red decided to shave. When Dolly reappeared, she put her face up near him. He planted a small ball of lather from the can on the end of her nose. She squinted, but didn't bother to take it off.

As he shaved, he had trouble with the razor. It pulled, though he had changed the blade only that morning.

Dolly went into her K-i-s-s-i-n-g chant. He stopped shaving as he laughed. "Where did you learn that?"

"I don't know. Mary was shaving with your razor today."

"She was?"

"She was shaving her legs."

"Dammit," he said. "You didn't hear that."

"Yes I did. You said a curse."

"That's because I'm mad. You tell Mary next time you see her doing that that she shouldn't."

He changed the blade.

"Why don't you use the electric razor like Daddy?" she asked.

"It doesn't go deep enough."

"Daddy uses it."

"Daddy has a different kind of beard."

"Why?"

"His isn't as heavy."

"It isn't?"

"No. His is easier to cut. That's the way his beard is."

"Why?"

"Because the electric razor has little blades that go around and cut Daddy's beard good enough but they don't cut my beard good enough."

"Why?"

"I haven't got time now, Dolly. I have to go out." He rinsed his face.

"Bye," she said.

"Bye, Dolly. Hurry and finish now."

He went to the living room. Peggy was sitting opposite Tom again. "I don't want you playing that tape recorder, Peggy. I'd better wind it up."

"I like McCormack too, you know," said Peggy.

"If you press the wrong button, you're liable to erase the whole thing."

"I guess I don't have any rights around here at all." She started to cry as she marched out of the room.

"I don't play your records, do I?" Red called after her.

"And you won't, either," she yelled from the door of the girls' room.

Red went to the hallway. "It took me a whole year to get this tape together. You want me to leave it around now so you can press one wrong button and erase the whole thing?"

"I don't care what you do with your lousy old tape," Peggy shouted.

The mother came out. "What's all the yelling about?"

"She wants to play the tape recorder."

"I don't want to play the tape recorder. I didn't say anything about playing the tape recorder. I wouldn't play your stinky old tape recorder if you asked me to."

"Are you fighting over that again?" cried the mother.

"She presses the wrong button, she'll erase the whole tape. It took me a whole year—."

"Put the tape away."

"That's what I'm going to do." He went to his room. As he passed Peggy's door, she muttered, "You stingy, mean thing."

"It's my tape," he replied in a loud voice.

"It's his tape," said the mother. "Let him do with it what he wants."

Peggy slammed the door. "Don't you slam that door!" the mother cried. Peggy opened it again.

When Red came by, Peggy taunted him from the shelter of the doorway: "Willie, Willie, Willie, Willie."

"Don't you call me that."

She pulled her ears and stuck her tongue out, and made a humming
noise.

Red yelled to his mother. "Come here, Ma. Come here. Look what she's
doing."

"For God's sake," said the mother, coming down the hallway.

"I'll give you a slap," said Red to Peggy.

When the mother reached the doorway, Peggy changed her expression
to a Madonna look, beatific and peaceful.

"She had her tongue out," said Red.

Peggy raised her eyebrows ever so slightly, questioning if such a thing
were even possible.

"How old are you?" the mother asked Red.

"It was her doing. She should get a slap."

"If there's any slapping to be done, I'll do it," said the mother. "Go on
out now."

Red went to the living room to get Tom, and then the two boys went
to the front door.

"Where are you off to?" the mother called.

"Feeney's, I guess."

"I don't want you hanging around that dirty old bar. Your father will
have a fit."

"That's where all the guys are going to be."

"I don't see why you can't find some other place to meet."

Red paused. She didn't say any more. "I'll see you later."

"Be careful," she called.

Chapter 20

When they got to the bar, Tom took a stool and Red stood next to him. Hoppy, the bartender, came to them. He had one useless leg, and the boys had given him the nickname when he owned the candy store up the street. He had lost out in the candy-store business because his store had been too dirty even for the unfinicky children: it had been rumored that roaches had been found in the malted milk cans.

"Wha'd'ya say, Hop?"

"How are you fellers?"

"The usual."

He got Red a beer, and Tom a ginger ale.

"Nobody here tonight," said Hoppy as he wiped the grill. He took more pains with the bar than he had the candy store. Red and Tom looked around. There were a dozen boys at the bar, and over to the other side of the tavern there were three tables of girls. Some of the boys wore Corsair jackets. It was the street gang to which Red and Tom had belonged. Hoppy had been their candy-store concessionaire, and sold them "loosies"—unpackaged cigarettes—at two for three cents. The Corsairs made the transition with him from the candy store to the bar.

They looked over to the girls. One table had a group of nurses from the hospital nearby. Both Red and Tom could tell they were nurses: it was something about them, perhaps only that they were obviously a cut above the neighborhood girls. Another table did have neighborhood girls, chewing gum, angling their heads back to check their upsweeps in the bar mirror. The third table had a group of Irish girls, with the red cheeks and the curly hairdos, "greenhorns," as they were called. One of them looked very pretty to Red.

"Look at the brunette," he said to Tom.

"Greenhorn."

"Cute though."

"I don't like greenhorns," said Tom.

"What were your mother and father but greenhorns?" Red asked.

"That's the trouble with greenhorns," said Tom. "They all look like your mother and father thirty years ago."

"What's wrong with that?"

"I don't want to bother with any girl who looks like my parents thirty years ago."

Red threw back his head and laughed. "What a hell of a thing to say."

Tom didn't laugh. He was serious.

They were quiet for a few minutes, sipping their drinks.

"I'm going to go over and check out that greenhorn," Red said.

"Wait a minute," said Tom.

Something in the tone of Tom's voice was out of the ordinary; Red turned and looked at him. "Why?"

"I want to tell you something."

Red waited.

"I'm thinking of going into pre-med next September."

"You are?"

"It's not definite yet."

"Be a doctor?"

"What do you think?" Tom asked.

"It's great. It's great."

"I don't know if I'm smart enough. Do you think I'm smart enough?"

"Sure you are."

"Do you think it's a good idea?"

"Well, sure it's a good idea."

"It's not easy to get into medical school."

"It can't be that hard either."

"You don't think it's a silly idea?"

"Of course not. It's great."

"I'm not that type though. You know?"

"What do you mean? You'd be a great doctor."

"You think so?"

"Sure. How long have you been thinking of it?"

"A while. A year."

"It's great."

"I hope it works out."

"Hey, this calls for a celebration," said Red. "Let me buy you a drink."

"Okay."

"You're not kidding, are you?"

"No, I'm serious. I should have started this year."

Red called for Hoppy. Tom had a double bourbon. He drank so rarely that it hit him right away, and he started laughing.

Jesse Rosenbaum came in. Tom touched Red's arm. "Don't tell him."

"I won't."

Jesse had a sharp outfit on: a double-breasted glen-plaid suit, a midnight-blue shirt, a powder-blue tie.

"You're looking good, Jesse," said Red.

"I got a date."

"Who?" asked Tom.

"You don't know her."

"What's her name?"

"She's not from the neighborhood."

"Where's she from?"

"Bronx."

"You don't want to say what neighborhood?" Tom laughed.

"She got a lot of money?" Red asked. Jesse's goal in romance was common knowledge.

"She's loaded."

"What does her father do?" asked Tom.

"He's a bookie."

"A gangster?" asked Red pointedly.

"What do I care?"

When Jesse talked, he wouldn't look at his listener. He watched the floor.

"South coming?" Jesse asked. Jack South was popular with the neighborhood gang. He always had a stock of jokes.

"He's supposed to."

"He's probably out cattin'," said Jesse.

"Yes," said Red. "He mentioned something about going out with a girl from the Bronx whose father's a bookie."

Jesse's answer was obscene.

"Is your girlfriend Jewish?" Tom asked.

"Shiksa."

"Jesse's got more sense than to chase Jewish girls," said Red.

"Don't kid yourself," said Jesse. "Jewish girls got the money."

Maynard McNeely came in. When Jesse saw him, he grimaced, and said, "Here comes crap-on-wheels." Maynard had a mustache, and sideburns, and a black-leather jacket.

Red, genial with everyone, asked, "What have you been doing with yourself, Maynard?"

"Down in Philly." As he answered, McNeely studied himself in the bar mirror. "I'm heading down to Mexico."

"What are you going to do down there?"

"Shoot some cats."

"Cats?"

"Mountain lions."

"Crap," said Jesse.

McNeely had gotten a whiskey. He drank it in one gulp, flicked his tongue over the bottom of his mustache, looked at himself in the bar mirror, then turned to Jesse and asked, "Something bothering you, Rosenbaum?" He ended the question with his mouth open, and he left it open, inquiringly.

"Your eyes are turning brown," said Jesse.

"You don't believe I'm going to Mexico?"

"No, I don't."

"You'll find out."

"Like last summer," said Jesse, "You were making three hundred a week on construction."

"I was."

"Bull. I saw you around the neighborhood."

"I didn't work every day."

"You didn't work any day."

"I'll write you when I get to Mexico."

"Save your money, go see a doctor, you're crazy."

McNeely lunged for him. Red pushed them apart. Jesse had his fists cocked; he would probably have won. McNeely allowed himself to be pushed away. Jesse straightened the lapels of his suit and re-knotted his tie. "Hands off the merchandise."

"You're looking for trouble," said McNeely. "You're going to find it."

"Get out of here." Jesse articulated with scorn.

Three more boys from Fordham arrived, among them Cricket Connolly. Cricket had his two-foot-long pipe.

Junior Casey came in. As soon as Cricket saw him, he went into his crazy giggle. Casey was wearing his father's trainman's uniform, as he always did. He father was an oiler on the New York Central. Casey had been wearing the blue overalls and the blue shirt—off the clothesline, un-pressed — for years, and nobody had taken notice of it, until Cricket discovered him and made him a celebrity. Cricket was fascinated by the outfit; he talked about Casey all the time, even at school. Now whenever anybody looked at Casey, it was with a laugh. The whole business made Red uncomfortable.

Junior had been in his class in parochial school in the neighborhood, and Red liked him. He was a simple sort, but a good guy. Junior was puzzled at his sudden fame. He stood in front of the group and asked, "What's up? What's the matter?" Everyone laughed the louder. He smiled a silly, puzzled smile.

It wasn't just Casey they made fun of. It seemed to Red that when his classmates, Cricket and Meagher and South and some of the other boys, discovered Feeney's, they put the whole cast of neighborhood characters in a new light. Actually, of course, Red had to concede, many of them *were* odd. It was ridiculous that someone should walk around all the time in his father's work uniform. But still. It seemed to Red the Riverdale boys had the idea they were from a better world, and had the right to come down and laugh at the characters on Broadway.

One time, in the newspaper office at school, Red had said as much. He couldn't persuade Meagher and South to go downtown that night. They wanted to go to Feeney's. He accused them of wanting to go to laugh at the guys. They were surprised. They protested—and they meant it — they really thought the place was entertaining. Red felt bad going home on the subway that night. The whole thing suddenly reversed itself in his mind: perhaps it wasn't so much that they were making a mockery of the neighborhood as he was ashamed of the neighborhood. Maybe they didn't look down on the dirty streets so much as he looked up to the green lawns.

Red left the bar to go to the men's room. When he came out he asked the brunette greenhorn to dance to the record on the jukebox. He sat down next to her afterward and asked her her name.

"Kathleen."

"What's your job, Kathleen?"

"I just started it Monday. In an advertising place if you don't mind. A bunch of old slavers. If you had eight arms and eight legs to do what they wanted, they'd think you were born short. Jews, you know."

"Are you a secretary?"

"That and ten other jobs. I have two bosses. One of them comes in at nine. A little creep. I could step on him. He's dictating letters until noontime as fast as he can get them out of his mouth. Then there's hardly a break for lunch before the other one comes in, an old one, and he's giving orders like the grand duke. He gives me fifteen jobs to do and I don't know how I'm going to be doing them if I'm typing letters from the other one in the morning. The phone is ringing the whole day, with five buttons lit all the time, and I'm answering one and yelling in another. If it keeps up the same Monday I'll go in and tell the two of them to take the job and stick it."

"Just leave the office," said Red. "Take a coffee break."

"Will you stop it! Leave the office! The old man's hanging around the door watching me like I was a thief, for fear I'll blow my nose on his time. The tight old creep. He'd skin a flea for the hide of it."

Just then Red happened to look over to the bar. Jack South had arrived with a girl. Red was sure from the first look she was a girl the like of which he had never seen in Feeney's before. Jack shook hands, slapped backs, laughed. The girl hung back. She had a red coat and a small red hat. The way she stood with such stylish lines to her clothes and figure, it seemed to Red she could just have stepped out of an expensive dress store window. The clothes and cut of her would have set her apart from the world of Feeney's: but there was more. She had a regal quality in her stance, her expression as she looked around, her eyes as she took in everything. A queenliness. After studying the boys at the bar, her eyes moved from table to table; she took in each person, and for a moment, her gaze was on Red too. He felt it through his body. Her gaze passed on to the next table, but he continued to stare at her, unaware that his mouth was hanging open. Kathleen stopped talking and looked at him. "Is there anything wrong?"

"Huh? Oh, excuse me. You were saying. . ."

"I don't know that it mattered what I was saying," she replied.

In less than a minute, Red excused himself from Kathleen and headed to the bar. He sized up the situation as he approached: it struck him that what was going on was crazy. Somewhere Jack had discovered this girl in red, who was obviously somebody special, and brought her to Feeney's. But he wasn't five minutes in the place, and already he had forgotten about her. He was at the center of the bar, and was telling jokes to a whole group of boys. The boys were howling. The girl in red was left with Cricket and Tom Power.

D'Arcy saw Red coming toward her and at first she didn't know how to react. She was startled at the size of him, six feet four inches, and the obvious physical power that showed in the thick wrists hanging out from the green sweater, and the hands like hams. She looked at the red hair, and the red face and big ears and the red eyebrows meeting above the long nose, and the slightly crooked brown-toothed smile, and she was repulsed and fascinated at the same time. He was wearing soiled old clothes, and she decided he was a workman who had stopped in, and had taken a few drinks too many and was coming over to make a pass. She didn't return his smile.

Red did have a drunken feeling as he got closer and closer to her, an uplifting akin to the surge of joy that came in the movie house when the skirling of bagpipes announced the arrival of the rescuing army. He wanted to keep looking at her face, the big eyes, the spots of color in her cheeks, the mouth, well-formed, though even in the flush of emotion he noticed a blemish, a shadowing of her upper lip, for her hair was dark.

"Hi. I'm a friend of Jack's. Bill Harrigan. Everyone he calls me Red."

"Oh. Hello."

"It's nice to meet you."

"It's nice to meet you too."

He couldn't think of something to say.

"Do you go to Fordham?" she asked.

"I'm in Jack's class."

"Oh. I'm D'Arcy. D'Arcy Donovan."

"Hi, D'Arcy."

Why the hell didn't I get dressed up, Red thought. He looked down at his khaki trousers: they were bagged out at the knees, and they were soiled, and the old green sweater had moth holes, and he was wearing the old sneakers. Hell.

A fragile gold cross was twinkling at her neck. She was fragile-looking herself. Fragile and pretty. With the kind of face, he thought, that a person just wanted to look at and look at.

Jack South came breezing back. He had a drink in his hand already. "Hey, D'Arcy. Did ya meet Red here?"

"We just met."

"Come on," said Jack. "I want you to meet some of the other guys."

"All right." She smiled. The smile was an added perfection.

"Hey," said Jack to D'Arcy. "You and Red got a lot in common."

"We do?" she asked.

"Sure. He's class president." He said to Red then, "This gal's a real politician. You should've heard the buildup she got today at Mercy."

D'Arcy grinned. "I wish it were all true."

"Are you running for office?" Red asked.

"Student Council."

"I hope you win."

"Thank you."

Jack brought her then to introduce her to Jesse and other boys from the neighborhood. Red watched her. He looked at Jack too, and especially at how Jack was dressed. He had a suit on, a gray one, neat and clean. His shirt was blue and a small bit of the shirt showed at the cuffs of the suit, just enough, just right. His tie was yellow-and-blue-striped and it was just right too. His shoes were polished and he had a handkerchief at his breast pocket. His hat was tilted back on his head. I got to buy some clothes, said Red to himself. I got to buy some clothes.

Red turned to Tom. "She's beautiful, isn't she?"

"I hope she stays down there," said Tom Power. "I don't want to be buying her drinks."

"Is that all you're worried about?"

"She probably drinks Scotch."

"Relax."

"I thought we were going to work it on a kitty," said Tom.

"You don't have to buy her drinks. Jack brought her. He'll buy them."

"Somehow I always get stuck," said Tom.

"Relax."

"Whenever I get involved with South, it always costs me money."

Jack and D'Arcy came back. In a few minutes, Jesse called Jack aside, and soon Jack was back in the middle of the boys, telling jokes. They didn't want D'Arcy; she would have been a damper on the jokes. When Tom Power saw the way things were going, he went to the other end of the bar. Cricket also drifted away. Red and D'Arcy were left; Red was very pleased with the arrangement. D'Arcy made it easy for him to talk too. She gave cues; asked about his family, his plans. He told her eagerly about his hopes for law school. She seemed interested. But occasionally when there was a burst of laughter from the group of boys she would turn and look sharply at Jack, who was at the center of the circle.

Jack got high. Jesse bought him a double scotch. Even though Jack was telling most of the stories, he was the one who laughed loudest at the punch lines, slapping his leg.

Red would have been just as pleased if Jack never came back. But he could see that D'Arcy was getting uncomfortable. Increasingly the two of them looked at Jack. Their conversation began to lag. Eventually Jack went to the men's room. Red assumed that when Jack came out he would return to D'Arcy. He was astounded, however, to see him come out of the men's room, a happy grin on his face, and sit down next to Kathleen the greenhorn.

D'Arcy's eyes were flashing.

Red went to talk to him. He couldn't even get his attention at first, Jack was so engrossed in impressing Kathleen. "You've got a little bit of the old country in your voice," he was telling her.

"I'm from Ireland."

"My father," said Jack, "was in the I.R.A., commandant of the Drumgannon Brigade." He was slurring his words.

"Where was that?" Kathleen asked.

"Cork. They were pretty famous."

"What does your father do now?" she asked.

"He's a captain in the Police Department."

"A captain makes a lot of money, I guess."

"He does all right. You know he was a friend of Mick Collins?"

"Is that right?"

"Sure. He wrestled with him." Jack put his arm around her waist.

"I don't care to wrestle myself," she said as she pushed the arm down.

Jack grinned. "Let me buy you a drink," he said.

"I don't mind. You seem to be more generous than some of the other fellows around here." She looked at Red. Red was tapping Jack on the shoulder.

"I only do it for the pretty girls," Jack told her.

"Some of the boys don't seem to care whether the girl has a mouth on her or not."

"I care," he said, and he moved his lips close to her.

"I'm talking about a drink. I don't know what you're talking about."

Jack squeezed her waist. "Kathleen, ever since I first saw you I've had this mad desire."

"What's that?" she asked, eyeing him suspiciously.

"To kiss you."

"You try it," she replied, "and I'll split your skull open."

The whoop of Jack's laughter carried all over the tavern. Red shook him by the shoulder. "Jack."

"What do you say, Red?"

"D'Arcy."

"D'Arcy?" Red could see the moment of incomprehension on Jack's face. Then Jack woke up. He looked past Red to where she was standing at the bar.

"How you doing, D'Arce?"

He didn't get so much as a finger reaction to his wave.

"Is she mad?" Jack asked Red.

"I think so."

"Oh hell," said Jack, getting up and walking back to the bar with Red. "It's going to be a cold ride home."

Chapter 21

When Jim Meagher went out on Saturday nights, usually to a movie, Eva showed no interest in going anywhere else afterwards, except to the soda shop and then home. On many occasions Jim tried to persuade her to stop at Feeney's to meet with the group that late in the evening included some dating couples. But she wouldn't.

Of course Florence wouldn't have gone into Feeney's either. She would have been appalled at the very idea of a young woman standing at a bar. But in Eva's case it didn't seem to be so much a matter of decorum as timidity. She paled when Jim even mentioned it. Jim tried again this Saturday night, but Eva shook her head no. Jim felt annoyance. He wanted to show her off. He also wanted her to participate in the laughter and the banter, and the camaraderie of Feeney's. By refusing to go ever, it was as if she were passing a negative judgment on the whole group.

"You're sure?" he asked her. "Just for half an hour? Just to meet with Red and Jack South and the gang?"

"I have to get up early," she said.

So he took her home and caught the subway to Feeney's himself. He loved the place. He liked the smell of the beer and the pretzels, and the blare of the jukebox, and the laughter and the jokes.

Inside the door, Jim saw Hoppy the bartender incessantly polishing the beer runoff. The group standing at the rail were mostly men. Over to the side were two tables with women, and two small tables with couples on dates.

He spotted Red at the near end of the bar. He was talking to a girl Jim didn't know.

Jim gave Red a wave and walked down to the end of the bar where Jack South was entertaining Jesse Rosenbaum, Cricket and others with one joke after another.

"A beer, Hop," Jim ordered, and listened to Jack.

"This farmer," said Jack, "was driving around in a cart with a dog pulling the cart. The farmer was whipping the hell out of the dog to make him go faster. Another farmer came along, and said to the farmer in the cart, 'That's the cruelest thing I've ever seen! As long as you're going to be that mean, why don't you smack your poor dog across the balls with your whip?'

'No,' said the farmer in the cart. 'That's his passing gear.'"

The whoop of laughter caused heads to turn toward the merry group. Jim saw Red Harrigan and the girl turn and look at Jack. The girl was no doubt Jack's date, and Jack was keeping her at a distance because she would have inhibited his telling of his repertoire of farmer jokes. Nor would Jack have worried about the girl; he never had any trouble getting dates. Not with his blond good looks.

Jim greeted the group of young men, and then picked up his beer, and walked to where Red and the young woman were standing.

"Hey Jim. This is D'Arcy Donovan. She's from Mercy College." Red was very excited, and animated and attentive. Jack could see immediately that Red was taken with D'Arcy Donovan, if Jack South wasn't.

The three of them talked. Red and Jim told her of their plans to do construction work. She said that she and her girlfriend would be working for the summer as waitresses in the Buckingham Hotel at Mallard Lake, a resort on the New Jersey shore. Red and Jim and any of the other boys who were interested should come down some weekend, and they could get a group of the waitresses together. She gave Red the telephone number of the waitresses' residence. It was a very casual thing, very simple and informal, she added.

"We'd love to," Red blurted out.

"Once we've been working a while and have some money," Jim cautioned.

"Soon," Red said with some excitement.

Chapter 22

Soon after Jack and D'Arcy left, Red left Feeney's also. He went home to the apartment. His mother was ironing in the kitchen. He cut a piece off the chocolate cake and made some tea. She sat down with him. "Hey, you know what, Ma?"

"What?"

"Tom Power's going to be a doctor."

She smiled slightly. "Is that so?"

"He told me tonight in Feeney's."

"Sure, there's a lot of doctors come out of Feeney's."

"No. It's serious. He's switching to pre-med."

"When's this going to happen?"

"September. Don't laugh. He might be good."

"I wouldn't let him treat my cat."

"Well, you don't judge a guy by what he is now. It's what he *can* be."

"I hope he's successful," she said.

"He's just pig-headed enough to make it," said Red thoughtfully.

"Maybe I should encourage the romance," said the mother.

"What romance?"

"Peggy."

"Peggy?" he asked.

"She has a terrible crush on him."

"Peggy?"

"Didn't you know that, you big dope?"

"Are you kidding?"

"Why do you think she acts like a half-simp whenever he's in the house?"

"She's just a kid."

"She doesn't think that," said the mother. "And you make it worse. She's trying to make an impression on him, and you treat her like she was Dolly's age."

"I do not."

"She says you do."

"It's silly," said Red. "He's not interested in her."

"Of course he's not," said the mother. "And when she finally realizes that, she'll get over it. But you could treat her nicer in the meanwhile."

"She drives me nuts hanging around."

"Give her the slip then. But do it quietly."

Red started to grin. "Do you really think she's stuck on him?"

"I know she is," said the mother. "You can't get her out of the house if she thinks he's coming. And she told me as much tonight."

"That's hot."

"If you say a word," said the mother, "I'll get mad."

"I won't."

"Who was at Feeney's?"

"The usual. You know, Ma, I met a really nice girl tonight."

"At Feeney's?"

"Jack South brought her."

"Oh."

"He's a funny guy. You know? He brought this girl and she was really special, and he didn't pay any attention to her at all."

"What was she like?"

"Nice. Pretty. And real nice clothes. She had a red coat on, and a red hat. You could see she really had class. She's going to be president of the Student Council too."

"Where does she go to school?"

"Mercy"

"Is Jack interested in her? He must be if he brought her."

"They just met today. It's hard to tell with Jack. He was in the chute tonight anyway."

"One thing I'll say about that boy," said Mrs. Harrigan. "Whenever he's been in this house, he's been very clean and neat. He carries a comb and he uses it. You could do with some of his habits."

Red didn't answer.

"That dirty green thing you've got on," she said. "It must have walked across the bedroom and leaped on your back."

Red still kept silence. The mother noticed. It was the first time she got no back-talk in a lecture on cleanliness.

"I think maybe I'll get a new suit."

"Fine," she said. "You can go to Klein's during the week."

"It's all right?"

"Of course. It would make me happy."

He was silent and meditative.

"Are you going to ask this girl out?"

"I was wondering. If I asked Jack, I don't think he'd mind."

"What's her name?"

"D'Arcy Donovan."

"D'Arcy?" The mother had a smile.

"It's a nice name, isn't it?"

"Well, yes. It's a bit rich for my blood."

"She is rich."

"She said that?"

"No, but she lives in Pelham Manor. Nobody lives there unless they have pots of dough."

The mother didn't say anything.

"I don't know. Do you think I could ask her out?"

"The cat can look the king in the eye. It's America."

Chapter 23

Year-end examinations came and went, and then it was summer and they were free. Jim Meagher and Red Harrigan took the bus to the construction job Red had arranged for them both on a Monday morning at a building site in Yonkers, just north of the Bronx.

Red was assigned as a carpenter's apprentice, and Jim was put with a group of men who were laying cement. He was told to take off his sneakers and put on heavy work boots for walking in the wet cement. Then, for two and a half hours, Jim did nothing; the cement mixers were late in arriving. He sat with the other workmen and gloried in being part of a tough-looking, heavy-bearded crew such as he had often watched from the sidewalk on construction jobs. Frequently during the delay, the foreman came over and lectured them: "When those trucks get here, I want you guys to move because those sons-of-bitches get fourteen cents for every minute of overtime in getting that cement out, you got that?"

Finally, the first truck arrived and backed in, the heavy tires chewing into the ground as the men talked the driver into position. Then the trough was pulled out, and the truck trembled as the huge mixer began to turn. The men lined up with the wheelbarrows; Jim the third in line. "Okay!" the foreman yelled. "Go! Move!" The first barrow was filled and the workman steadied it, and then pushed it along the runway.

The second workman was slow in getting his barrow up under the trough, and some of the wet cement slid off the end of the trough on to the ground. "Get that son of a bitch up here!" the foreman yelled at the workman. Jim resolved that he wouldn't make that mistake and he got his barrow so close that he was nudging the backside of the man filling the barrow in front of him.

Then Jim was up under the trough, and the truckman pulled the hook, and the wet cement slid down the run and plopped heavily into the barrow, twenty-five, fifty, seventy-five, perhaps a hundred pounds of it before the deep-bellied barrow was full. "Get that son of a bitch moving!" the foreman shouted at Jim.

Jim tightened his hands on the two wooden handles, and lifted, and with his whole body tried to push the barrow forward. Suddenly the barrow was over on its side and the cement was sloshing out in an ever-widening circle on the ground. "Get it up dammit!" the foreman screamed. Jim got the barrow righted with a strength born of fear, but it tipped over in the other direction, and spilled the rest of the cement on the other side. "Dammit to hell!" the foreman screamed. "Get out of here. Get that goddamn kid out of the line!" The foreman grabbed the barrow himself and pushed it up the runway.

Jim stood to the side and hung his head. The rest of the men in line had a doubly difficult time in pushing their barrows out, because the wet cement turned the dirt runway into a quagmire, and eventually the truck was held on overtime. Periodically, the foreman would turn around and swear at Jim.

Before the second truck arrived, the foreman banished him to a dirt pile. Here Jim worked with two powerful black men. In his shame and fear and desire to redeem himself, he shoveled dirt as fast as he could. The worker next to him watched him for a minute and then said quietly, "Take it easy there, boy. Take it easy."

So Jim slowed down. He had to in any event; his arms were already aching.

"Move it!" the foreman screamed from above. So Jim sped up again. He kept glancing at the workman next to him.

"Take it easy there, boy," the workman kept repeating softly.

From above, the foreman kept bellowing, "Take a full shovel. Move it!"

The foreman moved away and the workman took a step toward Jim, and Jim leaped away. "You not holding that shovel right," the workman told him. And you working your foot wrong. You get the front of your foot into that shovel, and don't you be pushing down with your arch. You goin' hurt yourself."

"Thanks a lot," said Jim, and the workman gave him a wide smile.

"And take it easy boy. When we finish this here pile, there's only goin' be a 'nother one."

"Okay."

They worked only another hour until lunch, but it seemed to Jim the noon whistle would never come. His whole body ached. He sought out Red to eat his lunch with him. Red hadn't even stopped at noon. Jim found him hammering nails into two-by-fours, having a good time, bantering with the carpenters, and obviously doing his work competently.

When the whistle ended the lunch period, Jim got up to go back to the dirt pile and stepped on a nail that was imbedded in a board. He felt the sharp pain and pulled his foot up, but the board came with his boot. Then the board fell back to the ground and he could see the blood on the end of the nail. He took off his boot and the sweat sock, but there was only a small puncture mark, and after the first sharp pain, the hurt lessened so he went back on the dirt pile. He told the black worker next to him what had happened. "Do you think it's serious?"

"Man," said the workman. "They ain't no thinking involved. If that there nail went in deep enough, you going to be so sore an hour from now, you going to know about it."

That was the way it turned out. The infection took root, and in an hour the foot was pulsing. Jim finally was impelled to go and tell the foreman, who sent him on with a curse to the trailer office at the side of the lot. He was sent to a doctor's office across the street, and the doctor cleaned the wound, gave him a tetanus shot, told him to take sulfa capsules every four hours, soak the wound in hot water with Epsom salts, and sent him home from the job.

At home that night, Harry came up to the room where Jim was in bed, one foot out in the soaking solution. He told his father the story, omitting the earlier details about the spilled wheelbarrow, but emphasizing that the doctor's bill would be taken care of by workmen's compensation.

Mr. Meagher shook his head. "The whole thing was foolish from the beginning. You're not fit for hard work." He didn't say it sarcastically, just matter-of-factly. Somehow that made it worse.

In the following days, Jim feared that his father might decide to bring Jim back to work in the brewery, as he had the previous summer. The prospect filled Jim with alarm; things had not gone well working alongside his father. He could vividly recall, as he lay in bed, the yeasty smell of the brew hops and grain and the warm odor like fresh-baked buns. He could hear the high whine of metal on metal from the machinists' area and, over all, the collective roar of the assembly lines that poured out bottles and cans at the rate of four and five hundred units a minute.

He remembered one day in particular. A telephone was sounding, not with the familiar ring of the home telephone, but with a bellow almost as deep and vibrant as a foghorn: it was the only sound that would carry over the din of the bottling plant. Jim opened the office door that was lettered with his father's name and title of Superintendent of Maintenance. His father was out somewhere in the plant. Jim went to the drafting board and looked up at the nude calendar picture. Just as he reached it, his father came in the door, and Jim looked quickly away. Had his father seen him? He had. Mr. Meagher walked to the wall, pulled the calendar down, tore it in half and threw it in the trash basket. "They got nothin' to do around here all day but look at some girl's tits."

"What do you want me to do, Dad?"

"You finished those time cards?"

"All done."

"Check them," the father ordered.

"They're all right," said Jim. He was annoyed.

"Let me have them then."

As Jim gathered the time cards on the other desk, he could hear his father chomping hard on his gum, one of his nervous mannerisms at work. He also had a number one pencil in his hand, and he was going over the letters of a handwritten memo in front of him. Four, five, six times he over-lined the strokes of the letters until the characters were black and thick.

Jim turned over the cards. His father had gotten only to the third one when he found a number uncircled. He circled it with a vicious swipe of his pencil. "I thought they were all right," he said.

"There's a mistake?" asked Jim, looking down over his father's shoulder.

"Damned right there's a mistake."

"I didn't see that one."

"How about this one?" His father turned and held up another card which had a number uncircled.

"I missed it, I guess."

"You guess?"

"Everybody makes mistakes."

"How can you miss two numbers in five cards?"

Jim didn't answer.

"Are you all right?" his father asked sarcastically.

"I'm all right."

"You're sure you're all right?"

"I told you. I'm all right."

"If you're going to get cocky with me, I'll tell you something. I don't know what else you can do, but when it comes to checking cards, you aren't worth a shit."

Such was life with his father at the plant.

The foot healed in two days. On Friday, Red brought Jim his check for a day's pay.

"Let's go down to the shore, to Mallard Lake," Red suggested. "I want to see that D'Arcy Donovan."

Jim was ready and out the door almost before Red had finished the suggestion.

Chapter 24

In front of the bandstand, the college students were dancing. Whooping and hollering from sheer exuberance, they kept time to the Dixieland music. Some wore sneakers. Some were barefoot. All the girls and most of the boys wore Bermuda shorts and other beach attire, for the club was only a half-mile from the Atlantic Ocean. A keg of beer ran out at the bar, and when the bartender hammered in the cork on a new one, there was a loud thump and a whistling of escaping air. Boys stopped dancing and roared approval; the girls added their shrill cheers and clapped delightedly.

Jim Meagher was sitting with his back against the bar. His legs were wrapped around the steel legs of the bar stool, and he was bouncing his body and weaving his shoulders to the music. The music was pleasing; he loved Dixieland, and it was a good band.

Standing next to him was Red Harrigan. They were waiting for two girls, and Red fretted because the girls were late, and he had made the arrangement. He glanced frequently over to the door. Jim was completely engrossed in a drum solo that was just now reaching its peak.

"There they are!" shouted Red, standing upright and waving to the girls amidst the throng at the door. One girl, D'Arcy, waved back, and gave a helpless shrug that she had to wait at the door in line to show her identification rather than join them immediately. The delay gave Jim a chance to study the girl next to her, the girl who was to be his date. His first impression was that she was very pretty. She had black, curly hair, cut just short of her shoulders, and her complexion seemed very fair in contrast. She was standing on her tiptoes, looking through the smoke and dim light at himself and Red. Her straight stance accentuated the slimness of her body and legs, and the fullness of her bosom. She was dressed in white shorts and a white blouse, and a red pullover sweater so that only the collar of the blouse showed.

Red started toward the girls. Jim should have followed but suddenly he lost his courage. He drank half the glass of beer that was resting on the bar. Red came back.

"That's them. Come on."

Jim followed as Red threaded his way through the crowd. They reached the girls and D'Arcy made the introductions. Her friend's name was Alaco Armstrong and, like D'Arcy, she was a waitress for the summer at the resort hotel. Jim was struck by the name. It was pretty. He smiled. Alaco returned the smile, and blushed. Jim saw the color rising in her face, and suddenly he got back all his confidence.

Red found a table and they sat down and talked for a few minutes, and then Red asked D'Arcy to dance, and Jim did the same with Alaco.

Alaco had been quiet at the table. When they reached the dance floor, she remained quiet. But the silence was not awkward. She was very calm. She had an almost tangible air of peace, Jim thought. She smiled at him. She had fine, white teeth, and her blue eyes were in the smile. Jim couldn't stop looking at her. Her coloring was marvelous: raven hair, and blue eyes, and fair skin, and then the white blouse and the red sweater. He was caught up in her smile and grinned at her. He had to fight the impolite desire to study her body as well as her face. He could see the reaction among the youths at the bar to the full bosom and rounded hips, and slender graceful legs.

She was quick on the dance floor. She came in lightly when he drew her, and whirled out prettily when he propelled her with his hand.

They were only dancing a few minutes when the band slowed the tempo from the Dixieland to a rare slow number. It was the saxophone solo. The couples danced close and Jim held her tight with his arm and her hair brushed against his face and gave a clean fragrance of perfume. They danced slowly halfway around the floor. Suddenly she drew away. He looked at her in surprise. Her composure was gone. Her face was again flushed. They continued dancing, though she would not come so close. Jim, sure now that he could affect her, grew exuberant. When they went back to the triple-time music, he delighted in watching her bounce and turn and spin, and he let out war whoops of joy which were in no way unusual in the general uproar.

They danced until long after midnight, until the room was smoky and sticky and hot. Alaco had long since taken off her sweater. Jim was sweating profusely, and he was especially conscious of it dancing.

"It's awfully hot in here," he said.

"Mmmm," she agreed. She looked up. "Your face is all wet. Have you a handkerchief?"

He was about to say "Yes," then he remembered that the handkerchief he had in his pocket was soiled so he said, "No."

"Use mine," she said, and she brought out a small handkerchief from the pocket of her shorts. She rubbed it across his forehead.

"Thanks," he said. He could smell the scent of perfume on the handkerchief. "Thank you very much."

"Do you want to get some air?" he asked.

"Sure."

They went back to the table, and Alaco knotted the red sweater over her shoulders. They said goodbye to Red and D'Arcy.

When they got outside, the night air was a shock. The temperature had dropped to the seventies. Exhilarated, they ran hand-in-hand across the parking lot. When they reached Red's car, a beat-up convertible coupe he had borrowed for the evening, he let go of her hand and for sheer joy he made a running jump and vaulted over the trunk into the seat. Alaco ran around and climbed in beside him. They drove down to the beach, singing together a Dixieland song.

They went far up the beach after parking the car. They played the game of the sand birds, racing out after the waves as the ocean pulled back to open a temporary track of hard wet sand, and then racing in again as the next wave crested and ran up the beach after them.

When they stopped to rest, his trousers were wet to the knees, and her beach shoes were streaked with wet sand. They sat with their arms around each other's waist and looked out over the ocean. The blue-black sky was interspersed with gray lines of clouds, and stretched out into immense distances.

On an impulse he pinched her on the backside.

She jumped. "Stop that," she said. She added, with half a smile, "You lech."

He laughed and the sound rang out on the beach. She turned her head and looked at him with a kind of feline smile. "I don't know anything about you," she said.

"I don't know anything about you either," he answered.

"You and Red just finished freshman year?" she asked.

"Yes."

"Tell me something about you," he said.

She shrugged. "I just finished my first year at Marymount."

"I went to dances there," he said.

"I never remember seeing you."

"I didn't go much," he explained. "I didn't have much time during my first year. Anyway, I didn't like them very much."

"They're stiff," she agreed.

"We used to stop in a bar and get tanked up before we went in."

"Oh."

"How come you got that name 'Alaco?'"

"It was my grandmother's name in Ireland. It's after the French saint, Margaret Mary Alacoque."

"It's a funny name," he said. "Nice though."

"A fellow asked me once if I was named after the Aluminum Company of America. You know, ALCOA."

He laughed.

They watched the ocean. She talked quietly. "I love the ocean. It's so majestic. I like it best of anything this summer. A lot of times at night we bring cheese and crackers from the dining room of the hotel, and the boys bring wine and we build a fire on the beach. I like to go off by myself and just stand and listen to it."

She paused, and continued.

"And sometimes I can't take my eyes off it. I come down here before work, sometimes, to watch it at the dawn. It's so clean and wild. And you don't have to think about anything when you're by the ocean. There's so much to it that you just have to think about ocean."

She paused again.

"Except that it makes you think of God," she said, and continued.

"When we first came down in June we had a storm here and waves were right up to the boardwalk there. I was standing up there in the rain. The thunder was crashing, and you could see the lightning bolts out there in the water, all jagged like, and blue, and some of them weren't far out at all. I guess it was a crazy thing to stay outside. But I wasn't afraid. Really. I wasn't a bit afraid at all. All I could think of was, 'God, how powerful you are.'"

She stopped. In the sudden quiet, Jim felt called upon to say something. "What do you major in?" he asked.

"I have to pick a major this fall. I think I'll pick history."

"That's a good one."

"What do you plan to major in?" she asked.

"English."

"I like English too," she said.

Jim had been looking at his watch. "You know what time it is?"

"What time?"

"Two thirty."

"I don't care. I'm having a good time," she said.

"You have to get up to serve breakfast, don't you?"

"It's early yet."

"What time do you have to get up?" he asked her.

"Six thirty."

"When are you going to sleep?" he asked.

"Between meals tomorrow."

She was looking at him intently.

"You should cut the hairs in your nose," she said. "They look ugly."

He laughed at the irrelevance of this. "I'm sorry."

"If you don't cut them," she said "I'll cut them myself."

"Oh really," he said. "When?"

"Tomorrow night."

"How do you know I'll take you out tomorrow night?" he teased.

"You will," she said.

"Pretty sure of yourself, aren't you?"

"Uh huh. I never went out with a boy who didn't ask me out again."

"Maybe I can't go out tomorrow night."

"Really?" She was concerned.

"I'm only kidding."

"Good." She started sifting sand down his back, inside the collar.

"Cut that out, will you?" He grabbed her hand.

"Where are you going to take me?" she asked.

"Down to watch the submarine races."

She put a disgusted look on her face. "Are you going to start that corny line? I must have heard that twenty times this summer. 'You wanna go to the ocean and sit in my car with me and watch submarine races?' Ha ha ha. Men are so conceited. They all think they're original. And they all say the same thing."

"Men are conceited? How about you? 'The boys always call me up a second time.'"

"That's not conceit," she replied. "That's just true."

"Oh boy," he said.

She was still sifting sand down the back of his shirt.

"Cut it out will you?"

She got up on her knees. "Come on. Let's run. Are you a good runner? You want to have a race?"

"I know where you want to go tomorrow night," he said.

"Where?" She sat back on her thighs and looked at him inquisitively.

"The Buckingham." This was the hotel where she worked.

"Mmm," she agreed, her eyes lighting.

"You'd like to be there for a dance, wouldn't you?"

"Oh wouldn't I! You should see the dresses they wear."

"Someday I'm going to take you."

"You will?"

"I'll have a lot of money someday."

"Is that what you want?"

He hesitated. "It seems like the best thing now." He leaned toward her impulsively. "Do you know what I want, Alaco? I want the whole world. Do you want the whole world?"

She grew serious and thoughtful. "Yes, I do."

"You do?"

"Yes I do."

He was growing excited. He shifted his position. "Ever since I was a kid," he said, "I felt like I was born to be a great man. You don't think that's wrong, do you? I mean, presumptuous or arrogant, or kind of a nutty thing to think, do you?"

"No I don't."

"I want to have everything," he told her. "I want to have lots of money, and power, and I want men to look up to me. Did you ever feel like that?"

"Yes. But I don't know if I'd want money or stuff like that so much—."

"Oh, I don't mean that so much."

"Do you know what I want?" she said, leaning forward herself now. "I want to be so happy that I can leap from mountaintop to mountaintop."

"Yes, yes," he agreed quickly.

"I want to be so much in love that it just fills me altogether. So that I'll be just singing all day long, just for being happy."

"Yes, yes," he said. He was up on his knees in his excitement. "But you know what scares me, Alaco? I don't know where I'm going. Sometimes I think 'Well, suppose I did have all the money in the world.' I don't think I'd be happy even then."

Jim's words were spilling out of him now.

"One time when I was a kid I had a dollar that nobody knew about, and I bought a whole layer cake, because that's what I always wanted to do, eat a whole cake all by myself, and I took it in the house when nobody was home and I ate it, but it wasn't anything like I thought it was going to be. I mean it wasn't anything so great. I get scared that maybe everything will turn out like that."

He was looking at her so intently that it was hard for her to hold the gaze of his eyes, and she looked down. She traced her finger in the sand. "Saint Theresa says that if we want to be happy we have to work for the things that last forever, trying to please God every day without anybody knowing it, and then we won't be famous, but we'll have glory forever."

He didn't say anything in answer, but looked out for a long time to the ocean. She watched his face. Finally she turned and rested against him. He put his arms tighter around her waist, and they intertwined their fingers.

They both watched the ocean, the cresting of the waves, and the tumbling of the water, and the rush of the surf up the beach and out again.

"We shouldn't be so serious," he said.

"No."

They lapsed into silence. Her body was warm against his own, and he could feel each breath she took. Her hair was a soft cushion against his cheek. He suddenly realized she was crying. "Alaco, is anything wrong?"

She shook her head no.

"Turn around to me. Is anything the matter?"

She turned her head part ways and she had tears in her eyes. But she was smiling at the same time. She shook her head no.

"What's the matter?"

"I'm just happy."

"Crying because you're happy? Talk about clichés."

"I'm crying," she said, not serious, "because I'll always remember this night. You don't understand that now, but you will."

"What?"

She freed her fingers and ran her hand across her eyes. "I'm just being silly." She got up to her feet. "Come on. I'll race you down the beach."

She danced a few steps away, grinning at him. By the time Jim scrambled to his feet and set off in pursuit she was running full speed with a ten-yard head start. He was just starting to close the gap when they were both halted by the sound of a whistle from the boardwalk. They turned in the direction of the sound. They could see a police car, identified by the flashing red light on its roof. A searchlight came on which picked out first Alaco, then Jim. A burly figure stood beside the car.

"Get up here, you two," the man barked. The voice, bass and resonant, easily carried over the noise of the surf. The two of them obeyed the command and trudged across the sand to the boardwalk. Jim took her hand.

"A policeman," Alaco said softly.

"We're not doing anything wrong."

"The beaches are closed after nine o'clock," she said.

When they got close, the policeman ordered, "Get over here!" He turned the light on them, so that they both turned their faces away.

"You're blinding us," said Jim.

The policeman turned the light down. He was a stocky man, about fifty years old. His face was contorted in anger. "What are you doing down there?"

"We were just walking," said Jim.

"What kind of a town do you think we're running here?" the policeman demanded.

"We were just walking."

"I saw you running after her."

"We were having a race," said Alaco.

"A race," he repeated disdainfully. "You think I don't know what you were up to?"

The insinuation caused Jim's face to go white.

"What are you trying to say?"

"You think you're the first kids I've caught trying to screw on my beach?" the cop retorted.

"You watch what you accuse us of," Jim said angrily.

"Get up here," the policeman ordered. The two stepped up on the boardwalk. "You got no home to go to?"

"We have a home to go to," Jim answered, "but there's no law against walking."

"You watch your mouth, or I'll run you ass over heels into jail."

"You watch *your* mouth. You should learn how to talk when a woman's around."

"Jim, stop," Alaco pleaded, pulling at his hand.

"You wise guy, I'll lay you out on that boardwalk. I don't care who you are," the policeman said.

"You lay a hand on me and you'll be sorry." Jim clenched his fists. The policeman took a step forward.

"Jim, please," Alaco pleaded.

The policeman was red-faced with anger. "You come down here for the weekend, and you don't care what you do. Well, there's decent people who do care. I put one wise guy like you in jail already tonight, and I'll fix you too."

"Honestly, officer," said Alaco, in tears. "We were up at the Village Barn, and we were just taking a walk down the beach."

"Beach is closed."

"I know. We only went down for a little while. We're going now."

"Don't plead with him," said Jim to Alaco.

"How old are you?" the policeman demanded of Alaco.

"Eighteen."

He pointed at Jim. "How old are you?"

"Nineteen."

"What's your name?"

"Kelly," said Jim.

"Full name?"

"Robert Kelly."

"What the hell are you telling me? She's been calling you Jim. Let me see your driver's license."

Jim produced it. The policeman copied the correct name. When he finished he looked up and said, "Lying little punk," and handed back the license. "Where are you staying?"

"The Buckingham."

He wrote the information in his pad. He turned to Alaco. "Your name?"

She hesitated. "Armstrong. Alaco Armstrong."

"Where are you staying?"

"114 Salem."

"All right. Get moving."

Jim stood still. Alaco pulled at his hand.

"Get moving," the policeman repeated.

"There's no law against standing on the boardwalk," said Jim.

The policeman stared at him angrily. "I'll be back along here in five minutes. If you're still here I'll run you in." He turned and strode to the police car and drove off.

Jim couldn't stop his legs from trembling. "I'm staying right here," he said to Alaco.

"He'll arrest you."

"I don't care. No one ever talked to me like that."

"He must be one of the temporary policemen here for the summer," said Alaco. "The regular ones are very nice. They let us stay on the beach after hours."

"He was a creep," said Jim. "He had a dirty mind."

"We can report him tomorrow. They'd never let anyone stay if they knew he said things like that."

"I can see why guys hate cops."

"My father's a policeman," she said.

"I don't mean it that way."

"I know you don't. But he was a psycho and you shouldn't let it get you all upset." She pulled at his hand. "Come on now."

"I'm staying right here. Let him come back."

"Please, Jim. For my sake." She tugged at his hand and he yielded and they started walking slowly.

"I'm sorry you had to hear something like that," he said.

"Oh stop it. You must think I'm an awful innocent."

"I wish you hadn't heard it."

"Honestly, men must think women live in glass cages. You're more of an innocent than I am."

"I am not."

"Yes you are," she repeated.

It was a good distance to the waitress' residence. On the way his anger subsided. They walked together in silence.

At her residence, she said a quick "g'night" and bounded up the steps of the house and went in.

Jim felt disappointed. He'd thought she'd kiss him good night. They'd hit it off so well together. He had the feeling from the first that this was the girl he wanted to marry.

It was the policeman's fault. He'd soured the evening.

Jim walked slowly up to the boardwalk and sat on the bench and smoked a cigarette. Then he walked back to Red's car. On the drive to the bungalow where the boys were staying he passed the spot where they had met the policeman. He felt a sick sensation again in his stomach. He was glad when he was past the spot.

At the bungalow, Red was half-asleep in his cot, but he awoke when Jim came in.

"How's your girlfriend?" Red asked.

"Good."

"Man, she was a real looker," said Red. "I was going to forget about D'Arcy and chase her instead."

"We were having a great evening," said Jim, "until a cop ruined it." He told Red the story.

"It doesn't matter," said Red. "She's going in the convent. That's what D'Arcy says."

"What?" Jim asked. His stomach lurched.

"That's what D'Arcy says," Red repeated. "The convent."

Jim was silent for while. This can't be true, he thought.

"Hell she's going in the convent!" Jim protested.

But it was true, and he knew it was true as soon as the words came out of Red's mouth. Just then, everything clicked into place.

Chapter 25

Red Harrigan went home from Mallard Lake to the city on Sunday night. The four had gone out again on Saturday night, but there had been no mention of Alaco's plans for the convent, or even that Red had mentioned it. Jim was happy to leave the question in the air.

Jim stayed on. He had no job to go back to. He knew the foreman at the construction site didn't want him back. He could find a job on the shore, and be near Alaco.

On Monday morning he tried several of the hotels on the Shore Road. In one of the smaller hotels, called the Churchill, he got a job as a dishwasher. Then he walked to the Buckingham Hotel, to tell Alaco.

The Buckingham Hotel dominated Mallard Lake, a magnificent hotel sparkling with a new coat of white paint in the June sunlight. On the ocean side Jim could see the blue waves of the Atlantic rolling into the immaculately kept beach. Where the sand ended, green lawn extended all the way up to the hotel. On the land side of the hotel, the main entrance had a candy-striped awning, and beneath it several men of college age in gold-braided uniforms were opening doors of limousines and ushering guests into the lobby.

As Jim entered the lobby, men and women were exiting the dining room after breakfast. Jim watched a man in white duck pants and a sport jacket light a cigar and stroll over to the stock ticker giving the market reports from Wall Street. Women in brief-skirted white outfits were going out to play tennis, or crossing the lobby in bathing suits or terry cloth robes to go swimming.

He walked to the door of the dining room. The morning sun shone in the floor-to-ceiling windows and caught the crystal goblets in rainbows of color. College-aged waitresses were standing smartly at their stations in pink uniforms with white aprons gathered behind in oversized bows.

The maitre d' was talking to guests who were leaving, and Jim quickly slid past him and into the dining room proper. He saw D'Arcy Donovan carrying a tray of dishes, her arm muscles caught in tight little knots near her shoulders, and she looked at him questioningly.

Then he saw Alaco. She was down at the end of the dining room and she was laughing. With her was a college-age young man in kitchen whites sitting in a dining room chair turned around so that the back was against his chest. Otherwise her tables were empty and she was cleaning up. Jim started up the aisle, his apprehension increased by the presence of the young man. He was jealous already. She's the most beautiful girl on the shore, he said to himself, why wouldn't she have guys after her?

When Alaco saw him, she was startled at first, and then gave him a big greeting. "You stayed on!"

"Yes. How are you?"

The young man in the chair was introduced. His name was Mark Hall, and he was a student at the University of Pennsylvania. He was working as a cook for the summer, and that made Jim feel inferior in his new position as dishwasher.

They had been laughing about an offer from one of Alaco's table guests to name a thoroughbred horse "Alaco" in her honor. She pealed laughing again as she told the story to Jim. "When men start associating me with horses," she said, "it's time to start thinking diet."

But it wasn't true, of course. With her buxom long-legged figure set off by the pink and white uniform, she looked beautiful and was anything but fat.

Mark Hall was commenting on the horse naming. "The medieval philosophers used to say that for an object to possess real beauty it had to have three things: proportion of parts, pleasing color, and magnitude. They wouldn't have thought a woman beautiful without magnitude."

"I can do without the magnitude, thank you," Alaco replied.

Mark had to leave then for the kitchen. "Is he a philosophy major?" Jim asked, very much impressed at someone who could talk about philosophy in an ordinary conversation.

"Yes," said Alaco. "He's very bright."

D'Arcy came to the station and she asked the questions that Alaco hadn't. "What are you doing here?"

"I got a job in the Churchill Hotel."

"Did Red stay too?"

"No, he has a construction job."

"Weren't you working together?"

"I got fired." Now what did she have to bring that up for?

When D'Arcy left, Alaco asked him why he got fired.

He told her the whole story of his one day in construction. She was alarmed at first about the foot, but when she discovered it was nothing, she was amused at the whole affair.

She started putting out the luncheon dishes on her tables. "Are you just going to sit there, or are you going to help?" she asked, with a smile.

He was delighted to help.

Chapter 26

The months of June and July were wonderfully happy for Jim and Alaco both. Jim would work his shift at the Churchill and then come to Alaco's hotel and help her finish setting the dishes for dinner. There was always laughter in the dining room. When the guests were gone, she would carry her tray down the aisle with a do-si-do step, and when she had set the tray down on the catch-stand she would do a cheerleader's leap. Jim never tired of watching her.

The staff did zany tricks. They printed up a fake dinner menu where in between *Roast Loin of Pork, Sauce Robert, Baby Carrots Bonne Femme,* and *Baked Chicken Saute, Grilled Banana Mango Chutney,* there had been *Underarm Press of Ground Sirloin, Creamed Camel Vomit.* The menu never reached the guests—it was caught by the maitre d'—but the college students had a good time speculating about how many guests would actually have ordered the dish. It was silly, but typical of the spirit of the summer.

That first morning when Jim had come in the Buckingham entrance looking for Alaco, he had envied the guests for the luxury of their lives. But he discovered that the student workers had more. They had all the advantages of the hotel, without the worries. They played tennis on the grass courts when the hotel guests weren't using them. They swam on the beach. They sunned themselves on the employee veranda. In the evening, they had beach parties, and sang, or rode out in old cars, singing and yelping, whooping and hollering to the dance hall outside the town proper where rock bands blew their minds with deafening steel guitar music, and girls flush-cheeked with health gyrated their bodies to the drumbeats.

The dishwashing job at the Churchill Hotel was for Jim an interval between his hours with Alaco. But it was not unpleasant. There were two old cooks, Henry and Nick, working at the hotel. They were retired, but worked for the summer months to stretch out their pensions.

Henry, a kindly-faced man of seventy, broke Jim in the morning he started, demonstrating how to work the dishwashing machine. "How much are they paying you for the summer?" Henry asked.

"Five hundred."

"They need a third cook. If you learn how to do the backup work, you might have a chance for it."

"How much does that pay?"

"Seven-fifty."

Jim decided immediately to try for it. Besides the extra money, Jim had the incentive that it would make him an equal of Mark Hall, the Ivy League philosopher cook. If Mark had made his way to cook, then Jim would do it too.

Jim followed Henry around the kitchen and watched his every move. In addition to washing the dishes, he made salads and sliced tomatoes and grated carrots, and made cole slaw.

"You're doing great, son," he told Jim repeatedly. He was a very paternal man, kind not only to Jim but also to the waitresses and the suppliers who came in during the morning, and even the garbage men. Jim also noticed that, as soon as the breakfast rush was over, he took time to call his wife, just to say "Good morning," and ask her how she was, and tell her everything that had happened to him since he left the house before dawn.

Then he would motion Jim over to the flour room to have a cup of coffee. They were sitting there one morning on the bins of pancake flour—Jim loved that pungent sweet smell—when Jim told Henry about Alaco, and what a wondrous summer he was having, swimming with her in the afternoon, going out with her in the evening.

Then Henry told Jim about his life. "I was a heavy drinker one time. But I stopped. My wife asked me to. You sweat a lot in this business and you lose your appetite, and as soon as you finish a shift you want to go out and have a few drinks, so you need to watch that."

It surprised Jim that Henry didn't put any great stock into going to college. Even though Jim told him that he would be returning to college in September, Henry kept emphasizing the importance of becoming a cook. "I will never forget the day I got my hat," Henry told him. "The chef called me in after breakfast—this was 1918, September 12th—and said, 'Hank—that's what he called me, Hank—Hank, I'm giving you the white hat.'" Henry smiled in reminiscence. "It was the greatest day of my life."

The weeks of June went by, and it was July. Jim loved the routine of the kitchen, a well-defined world with a kindly father overseeing everything.

Jim loved it especially in the early morning. He walked to work from the employee residence, along the boardwalk, clutching his collar tips together against the dawn winds off the Atlantic, looking askance at those blue-cold waves rolling in and smashing white as ice against the jetties and the rocks. At the kitchen, Henry would have all the stoves going, with the oven doors open, and it would be as warm as his smile as he listened to what Jim and Alaco had done the night before, and the red of the fires would be dancing against the floor tiles and the walls. Henry would have sweet rolls baked already, but he wouldn't let Jim have one until Jim had bacon and eggs and oatmeal and orange juice. "You're going to be one of those cooks that *eats*," he said.

Then Jim punched the buttons that started the dishwasher, and sang and whistled as he dreamed of his girl, at the same time wiping the scraps off the late supper plates from the night before into the food disposal. He liked the sound of the disposal unit as it whined and roared when the garbage hit it. At the top of his lungs, he sang, "I'm in Love With a Beautiful Girl," making himself louder even than the disposal unit. He clustered the half-empty water glasses by thrusting five fingers into them, enjoying the clammy wet sensation, and racking them five at a time to go through the washer to meet the whooshing rush of hot water.

This only took a few minutes, then he went up next to Henry to watch him fry eggs. Henry fried them two-at-a-time in butter, in shallow eight-inch pans. To get the "over easy" eggs that nearly everybody wanted, the eggs had to be gently flipped. Henry, with a lifetime of practice, did it with ease. Jim had a difficult time getting the knack. "Don't worry about it," said Henry. "The hotel can afford a few eggs if you learn how to do it right." Then Henry taught Jim how to protect the frying pans. Rather than let Jim wash them, Henry polished them himself with fine steel wool, because the slightest imperfection on the surface of the pan would cause the white of the egg to stick, or the yolk to break.

Jim grew so fond of Henry, he really wasn't prepared for Nick, the other cook, when he took a morning shift. Henry had Jim trained to run the clean plates back through the hot rinse so they would be warm for breakfast. But Nick gave him no chance to touch the plates. Nick wasn't interested in breakfast. At five in the morning he started making cheesecakes.

Henry was a big man with a big belly that made his apron project out like a maternity dress. But Nick was a little man. There was a door into one of the storerooms that was only six feet high, and Henry had to stoop to get in there, and Jim cracked his head half a dozen times before he got the habit of stooping, but Nick could walk right through with his chef's hat on.

He had a heavy beard and his face always had a dark look. His teeth were brown-rimmed, and his eyes were intensely black.

Nick kept Jim running to get the ingredients for his cheesecakes. Jim watched him carefully and made note even of the measurements he used: two-and-a-half pounds of cream cheese, eight eggs, vanilla, a pound dipper of sugar, and lemon juice. Nick mixed the batch, poured it into a cake pan and stuck it in the oven.

"How long do you leave it in the oven?" Jim asked.

Nick turned, gave Jim a long look, and snarled, "I had to pay for my lessons."

Henry came back on the next morning, and, when Jim told him the story, Henry bellowed laughing. He made Jim repeat the story several times he enjoyed it so much. Then, however, he advised Jim: "The hell with him. Watch him anyway. Learn all you can. He's a good man. He was a hotel chef. You can learn a lot from a man like that. Do you see? The more you know in this business, the more you're worth and the more you get paid."

So Jim stuck on Nick's heels too. It was a trial. When the waffles stuck, when the pancakes crumpled, when the oatmeal burned, Jim got the blame, though it was often Nick's fault. He was too busy with his dinner preparations to give much attention to breakfast.

After breakfast, Nick made pies. Jim watched him mix the shortening and flour. "Is that all you need to make the crust?" Nick didn't even answer. But Jim had to admit the pies were good. And Henry was honest enough to tell Jim that he didn't know how to make pies and cakes that well. "What the hell have I been all my life," he said, "Just a hash house cook."

Nick had no such modest opinion of his own talents. He would turn to Jim suddenly and say, "I've worked with the very best." He made it clear it was a great comedown for him to be working in a resort hotel. "Before I retired, I wouldn't even walk into a kitchen like this."

For Jim, the worst thing about Nick was that he put doubts in Jim's mind about Henry. Jim was grating the carrots one morning. Nick stood nearby and watched with those glittering black eyes. He made Jim so nervous that Jim grated his finger.

"Who told you to do that?" Nick asked.

"What?"

"The cabbage and the carrots."

"Henry. If I learn the backup he thinks I have a chance for third cook." Jim said this though he had long since given up hope for the promotion. It was too far along in the summer.

A smile crossed Nick's face, exposing his brown teeth. "He's got you doing his work, eh?"

"I just help him out."

But Nick had planted the doubt: was Henry using Jim just to get his work done? No, said Jim to himself. It was an innocent cooperation that benefitted both. But Nick was such a blight he could tarnish any situation. Jim resolved to steer clear of him.

As a result, after a while Jim didn't help Nick with breakfast anymore. He stayed over at the side of the kitchen to watch, and drink a cup of coffee. One morning the waitresses were in a cranky mood. There had been an employee dance the night before. They pushed for their orders. Big Henry was able to handle these situations easily with his air of paternal benevolence. He would just kid the waitresses along. But Nick got flustered. When Jim saw that he was answering their barbs and letting them get under his skin, he felt a malicious joy.

Nick was having trouble with the eggs especially. He had so much trouble with the eggs sticking that he picked the pans up off the stove and ordered Jim to wash them. When Jim brought the pans back, the eggs continued to stick. Nick apparently didn't know that the pans should be cleaned with fine steel wool. He had never had to learn that sort of thing. Jim wanted to laugh as the little cook swore and cursed. When Jim looked at the waitresses and they rolled up their eyes in disgust, it made him feel great.

When Nick had thrown out about a dozen eggs, and the egg he was cooking was turning black at the edges, he threw the pan on the counter in a fury, and started cooking the eggs on the grill.

When the breakfast cooking was over, Nick came back to the dishwasher and watched Jim. He puffed on his cigarette, which was wet from the perspiration trickling down around his mouth.

"You want to be a cook?"

"Yes," Jim replied, warily.

"How are you on eggs?"

"All right."

"Let me see you fry one."

"Sure." Jim put a lot of bluster in his voice, but he was nervous as he turned off the dishwasher and headed for the cooking area. Nick was really the head cook, with seniority over Henry. He might even have the authority to make Jim third cook right then and there.

Jim took one of the pans and scoured it with steel wool. He lit a burner with a low light, plopped some butter in the pan, melted it until it had become a full round circle, then broke the egg into the pan. Nick didn't say a word. He just watched. Jim waited while the clear portion of the egg whitened at the edges. When he thought the moment had come, he tried the deft flip that he had seen Henry do a thousand times. "Over easy," he had said, "and right back again. All you want to do is put a coating on the yolk." But the egg didn't slide to the edge of the pan as it did for Henry. In fact, the egg didn't move from its center position in the pan. Then Jim lost confidence and flipped much more vigorously than he should have. The egg sailed out of the pan and dropped down between the wooden slats on the floor.

Little Nick laughed and laughed and laughed, showing his brown teeth back to his molars. He called the waitresses and busboys to the stove area to tell them what had happened.

Jim looked at the egg carton. It would have been a simple matter to pick up one of the eggs and let Nick have it right between the eyes. But that would be the end of the job, and he would have no excuse then to stay down at the shore and be with Alaco. So he clenched his fists and left the cooking area, and went back to the dishwasher. For fully a half hour he could hear Nick breaking out into laughter and telling more and more people the story. He didn't mention anything about the eggs Nick himself had wasted.

Later on in the morning, Nick came back again to the dishwashing area. He said to Jim, "I never had to do any fry cooking. I was a head chef. I always had a couple of fry cooks under me to do that kind of work."

Apparently he felt he still had to justify himself for wasting a dozen eggs.

"What kind of place did you work in?" Jim asked.

"The *Place Concorde* in New York City."

When Jim heard the name he was impressed in spite of himself.

"If you want to cook, you got to have a specialty," Nick said. "A lot of people can cook. But if you want to be valuable in this business, you got to have a specialty that only you can do."

"Like cheesecakes?"

"If you want to be a pastry cook, cheesecakes are all right."

"Why didn't you let me watch you?"

"You never let another cook watch you," he said. "When I was working in my first hotel, the head chef had a specialty of short ribs in his own special type tomato sauce. It was his feature. He wouldn't let anyone watch him make it. He waited until everybody had gone home from the kitchen, then he made his sauce. And prepared his meat. But I found out how he made it."

"How?"

"I drilled a hole in the ceiling and watched him from upstairs."

Nick walked away. Then he turned and said, "If you want to be good in this business, you don't give anybody a break."

Jim repeated the conversation to Henry the next morning. Henry thought about it for a while. "Maybe he's right," said Henry. "What the hell, I never got anywhere in this business. I've been just a fry cook all my life. He's been a hotel chef. He made big money."

"Money isn't everything."

"Money isn't everything," agreed Henry. "But it sure don't hurt. No sir. It sure don't hurt." He walked over to the side wall then to call his wife, for it was nine o'clock.

Jim smiled at the old cook. Most people paid lip service to a decent goal, and pursued a crass one. Henry gave lip service to the crass one, and acted decently. The kind old man, Jim realized, was a large part of his happiness in this golden summer.

Jim was impressed especially at the devotion of the old man to his wife of fifty years. The kindly cook made marriage a very special ideal.

Chapter 27

By mid-August, Jim and Alaco were inseparable. Jim begrudged every minute he had to spend apart from her. For her part, she seemed exuberantly happy. The convent had never been mentioned again, apart from what D'Arcy had told Red that first weekend on the shore and Red had relayed to Jim. Jim wasn't even sure if Red remembered telling him.

Jim decided as it came close to the final weeks of the summer that he didn't want to lead his life apart from Alaco. That decision entailed some very practical steps that he had to take.

He called his Uncle Arthur at the newspaper where he worked in New York, and asked if he could meet him in New York City the next day. Arthur agreed, though puzzled. Jim put off the questions until the meeting. Henry gave Jim the day off, seeming to know what was needed.

They sat in the White Rose Bar on Third Avenue, the short older man and the nephew with his tanned face in sharp contrast to the other patrons of the bar. Arthur ordered a shot of the well whiskey and drank it right down, and then looked at the bartender and pointed his finger at it: again. Jim wondered how Arthur could ever work a shift with all the whiskey he drank, but that had been a family mystery for years. "What's up?" Arthur asked.

"I'm going to get married."

Arthur was chagrined, even appalled. "What would you want to do that for? What a ruin of your happiness."

"Alaco is different than what you think of women, Uncle Arthur," Jim laughed.

"I thought you were having a good summer."

"I am." He told Arthur about their courtship and the hotel and the good times. But it was coming to the end of the summer, and he didn't want to leave Alaco.

"So that means marriage, doesn't it?" Jim said.

"But you've got to finish college," Arthur protested. "What will your father say?"

Jim didn't answer. His father would be enraged. But that would be later.

"Did you ask this girl yet?"

"Not yet. That's what I wanted to see you about. I've got to have a job when I ask her, to have any chance at all. Can you help me get a job in the newspaper business?"

"Your father could get you a job in the brewery in five minutes, if it's a job you need."

"I thought about that. And if that's the only way, I will ask him. But I'd rather not."

"Do you mean a copyboy job?"

"I mean a reporter's job."

"You don't have any experience."

"I'll learn fast."

Arthur thought for a while. He took out a piece of paper and wrote a man's name on it. "This fellow," he said to Jim, "is the head of bureaus for the wire service."

Jim thanked his uncle profusely and hurried over to the wire service main office on 42nd Street. Arthur's friend gave him a kind welcome but gruffly asked Jim what experience he had.

Jim had none. "At Fordham. . .," he hesitated.

"You're a Fordham man?" Arthur's friend asked excitedly. "You should have said. My son went to Fordham. A priest now."

"I just finished my first year," Jim said. "An English major."

The man looked at him for a long while. "There's an opening in the Newark bureau if you're willing to go over there."

Jim went to the Port Authority bus terminal, took the 118 bus to Newark, and then a taxicab to the wire service bureau there. While he waited in the office to see the bureau manager he watched the newsmen hammering away on their typewriters, and listened to the incessant ringing of the telephones, and watched the news machines ticking away with reports from all over the world, and he was entranced.

With the recommendation of the head of bureaus, the Newark bureau manager agreed to give Jim a chance. Jim left the office feeling like a character out of *The Front Page*. He immediately called Alaco, and told her he was starting a job with the wire service and he would see her as soon as he had a day off. Then he rented a room in a boarding house in Newark near the office. He went to the library, took out half a dozen books on news writing, brought them to the furnished room, and studied them endlessly.

For the first week on the job, Jim wasn't allowed to touch a typewriter. He rolled news reports, and ran coffee, and began to see himself himself as a newspaperman, imitating their work routines and admiring their style.

At the same time, he missed Alaco. When the weekend came, he had to physically force himself to go back to the furnished room and practice news stories, and not take the train down to the shore.

He also felt guilty that he had not told his father what was happening. So far as his father knew, he was still down at the shore. But his father would never consent to the newspaper career. His father had long ago formed his opinion of newspaper reporters from Arthur, and he wouldn't change.

On Tuesday of the second week, the bureau manager handed him the telephone and told him to take the facts of a story and write it up. It was an ordinary enough story—the death of a prominent businessman. He wrote the story, and turned it in. The bureau manager read it quickly, blocking out the paragraphs, inverting one of the sentences, cutting out a few words, and then initialed it. He handed it back to Jim. "Send it out."

Jim brought the story to the teletypist. In a few minutes, his first story was going out on the wire, no name credit of course—it wasn't important enough—but it was his first story. He had a wonderful feeling. He rushed out to the men's room.

It wouldn't do, Jim thought, to have tears in your eyes in a tough-talking newspaper office.

Chapter 28

On Thursday night, Jim called Alaco from Newark from the office before he left work. She was on her way to the dining room, so they could only talk for a few seconds, but they agreed to get together Friday night.

All day Friday, Jim was so nervous he couldn't eat. When he finished work, he caught the train to the shore. He got there at 6:30. Alaco wouldn't be finished and dressed until nine, so he had plenty of time to waste at Greentree's boarding house, where many of the men from Fordham stayed.

As he walked in Greentree's yard, he looked to see what cars were there. He saw Vinnie Carbone's green Mercury, and Danny Morrissey's red Ford. During the summer, a dozen young men had been coming down, including Jim's cousin Cricket, and Jack South, and Tom Power, and of course Red Harrigan.

Red was talking to old Clarence Greentree, the landlord, at the front door. Red was in charge of arrangements, and collected from the men at the end of each weekend, a dollar a night apiece. They stayed over the garage in one large room, which the men had nicknamed "The Ballroom."

Jim was glad to be back. He had had a bed for most of the summer in the employee residence near the hotel where he had worked, but often enough he had paid the dollar to stay here, for the laughs. And that's what he needed for the next few hours, some laughs, to take his mind off things. Was he really going to ask a girl tonight to marry him?

Clarence pumped his hand vigorously. "How are you, boy?" He clapped Jim on the back. "You're just in time." He winked. "I was down on the beach today." He lifted his hand dramatically. "Full of chippies." Clarence was seventy-two but he still had young dreams. "I wish I was a young feller again." He poked Jim on the shoulder. "You fellows are going to have a big weekend."

Red had been teasing Clarence, and he continued now. "Clarence was just telling me," he said to Jim, "How well the ladies are treating him." There were many elderly ladies staying at the boarding house, widows who rented out their Mallard Lake homes for the summer. So Greentree's had an improbable clientele of elderly ladies and college men. The assemblage at Greentree's was even more incongruous tonight, thought Jim: as the old joke went, the home of the almost wed and the nearly dead.

Clarence wheeled on Red. "Don't you be wise, redhead."

"You told me they follow you around," Red said, innocently.

"They follow me around from the time I get up in the morning until I go to bed at night," said Clarence. "I have to sit in the bathroom and pull the shades down to get a moment's peace. Even last night—eleven o'clock—I'm sitting out on the porch, getting some air, and Mrs. Horton comes down. 'There's somebody under my bed,' she says. So I go up two flights of stairs and what do I find? Nothing. She *wishes* there was somebody under her bed."

"Where did you disappear to?" Red asked Jim.

"I've been working up in Newark, in a reporter's job. At the wire service."

"I wouldn't give you a nickel for that Newark," said Clarence. "I wouldn't live there if they made me the mayor. The only place worse is Jersey City. Even the cops are scared there. I wouldn't give you a nickel for New York either, if you want to know the truth. I'm not talking about the way it was back in 1915, when it was a clean town. I drove Ella into New York in 1915 and you wouldn't believe—."

They had to stop Clarence before he went into a monologue. "Well, Clarence," said Red, "I guess we better get over to the ballroom and catch a shower before the other guys get down."

"You don't want to listen to an old man. It's all right. You fellows have a good time. And come in quiet." He punched them each in turn on the shoulder, and then he went in the house.

"So you're back," Red said to Jim. "D'Arcy says Alaco was upset. You can't see a girl day and night all summer and then just disappear. Want to tell me why you vanished?" They walked toward the ballroom.

Jim wanted to tell Red the whole story but he couldn't. What would Jim say? "I've been working for two weeks, so now I'm going to get married"? Jim knew it would sound ridiculous.

"South has been trying to move in on you. The Chief too. Even Winston has been hanging around the Buckingham dining room." "Winston" was their nickname for Tom Power.

"I'll see Alaco tonight," said Jim. "How's D'Arcy?"

"She's fine," said Red.

Jim stopped walking. Red stopped also and looked at him quizzically. "Do you think Alaco likes me?" Jim asked.

"She probably does," said Red. "There's no accounting for taste."

"I mean seriously. Be serious."

"Honestly, I think she's crazy about you," said Red. "I wish D'Arcy looked at me the way Alaco looks at you. Why do you have to ask?"

Then it was possible, Jim thought. It was possible she would say yes. Happiness undreamed of was indeed within reach. It was possible.

Just then Cricket Connolly drove up to the house. Jim went to his cousin to find out if there was any news from home.

"Everything's fine," said Cricket, not much interested in home. "Help me get this stuff inside." Cricket took a bag of ice cubes from the car and gave them to Jim to carry. He himself carried a shopping bag filled with cans of beer. They passed Mrs. Horton and another elderly lady, sitting out on lawn chairs. They were wispy women with gentle smiles. Mrs. Horton nodded in greeting and, as the two young men passed, she said, "Here come the boys with more groceries."

Behind Cricket and Jim, Red was carrying a cooler full of beer. As he passed Mrs. Horton, she leaned over to him as if to share a secret. "I know somebody who's going to go on a picnic this weekend."

The three young men quickened their step to get into the garage before they'd start laughing. When the door was shut, Cricket broke into his half-squealing laugh that he delivered with his shoulders hunched up, his eyes squinted. "Here come the boys with more groceries," he mimicked, and he was off laughing again. "Maybe we should invite them in for a beer."

While Jim was shaving at the sink at the end of the room, Vinnie Carbone came back from the shower, and started slapping aftershave lotion on his body.

"What the hell are you slapping on yourself, Chief?" Cricket asked, from his perch atop the beer cooler.

"That's man-smell, twerp."

Jim watched Cricket through the mirror, and at the word "twerp" he saw him move. Cricket hated to be reminded of his small size or boyish face, and Vinnie was aware of that.

"Man-smell!" said Cricket disdainfully. "You smell like a gardenia."

Vinnie moved into a boxing stance. "You looking for a mouthful of teeth?"

Cricket held up his hands and shook them. "I'm scared, Vinnie. No kidding. You scared me."

"You should be scared," said Vinnie, walking away with his customary exaggerated swivel movement.

"Why don't you put some up your ass?" said Cricket. "That's where you need it."

"I'll slap some in your mouth," said Vinnie. "It will be the same difference." He gave a loud horselaugh of triumph at this bon mot.

It was the same argument every weekend.

Jack South and Tom Power arrived. They were both working in downtown Manhattan for the summer, and had come to the shore on the "party train," the five-thirty Friday night train out of Pennsylvania Station. They were raucous, both of them, having made a good part of the trip in the bar car. Indeed, most of the 5:30 Friday night train was a bar car.

Jim was almost dressed for the evening. Jack came down to Jim's end of the barrack room, and said, "Come on outside, I want to talk to you. Let me get some drinks first. You want scotch or beer?"

"A beer."

"I'm having scotch myself," said Jack.

Jim went outside and waited. Jack came out with two beers. He was dressed in a summer striped seersucker suit, with a Panama hat and, as always, had a happy expression on his face.

"The scotch is missing," Jack said. "Clarence must have found the hide again. That old bastard, he's not only horny, he's thirsty."

"Speaking of horny—."

"That's what I wanted to talk to you about, Jimbo. Is the romance still on with you and this unbelievable quail that works up in the Buckingham dining room?"

"Yes, it is."

"That's all I wanted to know," said Jack.

"I heard you've been on the prowl there."

"Well, I will admit, I made a few trips to investigate."

Jim started to laugh. It was impossible to be annoyed with Jack South.

"The Chief is after this. . . what's-her-name? Alaco? He's after her too. He's been around there. He thinks if he goes up there smelling like a skunk-in-heat, she's going to fall for him."

"She's a nice girl, isn't she?"

"Beautiful face," said Jack. "A body that won't stop; smart, and she goes to Mass every morning. What else does one look for?"

"How do you know she goes to Mass every morning?"

"I stayed on a few days last week and saw her there. That's where the guys make a mistake. They hang around the bars. The good-looking quail are in church."

"Red says D'Arcy told him that Alaco is going in the convent."

Jack made a hand motion of dismissal. "Don't pay any attention to that. They're all going in the convent. Jill was going in the convent too. Until some guy gets interested in her."

They talked for a few minutes more. Then Jack got up. "I've got to go in and defend myself against Tom Power. Old Winston will be telling everybody he had to pay for my scotches."

After Jack went inside, Jim started toward the waitresses' residence. He thought about what Jack had told him. Perhaps the most interesting item that Jack had revealed was that he was going to Mass on weekday mornings. Of all people: Jack South.

Chapter 29

It was shortly after midnight, and Jim and Alaco were walking on the beach. He looked at her in silence. In the long look was the question he had waited long to be answered. That he had waited June, July, and August for.

He gathered himself. "Alaco, did you wonder why I left? Why I ran off and got a job all of a sudden?"

"I had an idea," she said, "that you felt like you needed to prove something, or get ready for something, or—."

"Alaco, there's something more serious I want to ask you."

"Wait, Jim," she said. "Don't. There's something I have to tell you first."

She gathered herself. "Jim, this is going to be hard for you to understand."

"I knew it," he said, and his shoulders slumped, and his whole body sagged. "I knew it."

"Knew what?"

"What you're about to tell me."

"Two weeks from today I'll be a postulant," she said. "You knew that, didn't you?"

He nodded yes. "Red told me the very first night." He looked so listless and beaten that he didn't seem to have full capacity to respond. It frightened her.

They walked a little more in silence.

"The whole summer was a last little fling, eh?" he said.

She stopped. She had tears in her eyes. "If you think that, then you don't know me at all." She started to cry.

He took her back to the waitresses' residence. They paused outside in silence.

"Jim," she hesitated, then finally spoke. "I don't know what else to say."

"You don't have to say anything more, Alaco. It's all understood."

Alaco went inside. Then Jim went down to the beach and wept.

It was nearly five in the morning when Jim walked back to Greentree's. The sky was already pearl gray with the dawn, and behind him as he walked the sun was tracking a red path across the ocean.

Red Harrigan was sitting outside the garage where the men stayed. "I've been waiting for you," he said. "Come on. Let's get a nightcap at The Harbor." The Harbor Inn was the last bar to close on the shore.

Jim got in the car with Red and they drove back down the street he had just walked. "You look like you've been through it," said Red.

Jim sat in silence.

"I was going to take D'Arcy to The Harbor," said Red, "but when she got back to the waitresses' residence to get a sweater, she found Alaco all broken up."

Jim nodded.

"She was crying," said Red.

Jim nodded again.

"I guess it's over, eh?"

"She's going into the convent," said Jim.

At the Harbor, they ordered two beers at the bar, which was crowded with young people drinking Bloody Marys and Ramos Fizzes. Red talked quietly. About the summer, and about Alaco, and about how there was nothing to be done if a girl went in the convent.

Just after six o'clock, Red said, "She's going into New York on the early train. D'Arcy was going to drive her to the station." The early train for the shore was the 6:05.

Jim went outside the bar and looked over to the train tracks. The train was in sight, coming up from the south. It roared past, too quickly for anyone to be recognized in any of the passenger car windows. Then it was gone.

The only sound was the low moan of the train whistle fading away in the distance.

D'Arcy arrived a minute later, driving her car into the parking lot of the The Harbor. Jim realized then that Red and D'Arcy had planned to occupy him while Alaco left. But it would have been what Alaco wanted. She was no person to be manipulated.

"Why did she leave so quickly?" Jim asked.

"Because," said D'Arcy, looking at him with her deep sad eyes, "she would have married you if she had stayed."

Chapter 30

R ed and Jim got back to Greentree's at 6:30.
Jim was surprised that while it felt to him like the world had ended, no one else felt the same way. The weekend party in the ballroom was only in its twelfth hour. Vinnie Carbone and two others were playing stud poker. Jack South was leading a group baiting Tom Power.

"I can't believe you did it," Jack said, shaking his head. When Jack saw Red he yelled, "Winston gave his high school ring to a waitress last night, on the first date."

"It wasn't the first time I met her," Tom said, indignantly.

"Which waitress?" someone asked.

"Connie. That Connie Corcoran. The redhead."

"Oh, I know her. They call her 'Connie the Ring Collector.'"

"After Labor Day she melts them all down into gold bars."

"Like hell!" Tom cried, and they laughed and laughed.

"You never get them back, Tom."

"She probably has the rings on a string over her bed. She plays with them at night, like an abacus."

Then they started on Vinnie Carbone. "Vinnie, where did you get that girl you had in the Beacon?"

"None of your business."

"She was no kid."

"She was no kid all right. She was a full-grown goat."

"A toast, men. To Winston who got engaged last night."

"Bullshit," cried Tom Power.

"A song, a song."

"Sing 'Long Ago and Far Away,'" said Vinnie.

"Kid has a razor wit."

145

Down at the end of the ballroom, twelve cots away, a stout youth named Danny Morrisey, nicknamed Popeye for reasons no one remembered, sat up and yelled, "When the hell are you all going to shut up and let us get some sleep?"

"Take it easy on us, Popeye."

"Popeye is frustrated. He needs a woman."

"Me frustrated!" cried Morrisey angrily. "You're the ones who are frustrated. You're not content to come down and rest for a weekend. No, you've got to yell and scream for twenty-four hours! You can't lie on the beach and relax. You've got to run around and bounce basketballs. Or if you're not bouncing basketballs, you got to run up to the bar and drink. Beer! Beer! Beer! You're big men when you're drunk. Then you got to sing songs and keep everybody awake at night."

"Hear! Hear!"

"Let's have it again for the West Coast audience!"

"Somebody put a cork in his mouth."

"In his ass."

Popeye stood up on the cot. "Makes me sick! Then you got to play kissing games. You don't know what it's all about. You haven't passed high school yet. If a real woman came up to you, you wouldn't know what to do."

"Give us a few pointers there, Popeye."

It was the last thing Jim heard before he fell off to sleep.

PART II

Chapter 31

December 1959

D	The night before he got his final papers to be mustered out of the Navy, Lieutenant Junior Grade James Meagher teamed up with Lt. J.G. Charles Bonanno, or "Cholly Bananas" as he was called, and the two of them went to the U.S. Grant Hotel in San Diego and got smashed.

After nine months in the South China Sea aboard the U.S.S. Barry, they were finally back in port.

They got back to the base at three o'clock in the morning and they laughed until five. They promised they'd get together again when the first of them got married. At noon that day, Cholly got a flight home to his state of Washington ("I'm going back to my father's apple orchards," he said), and Jim Meagher started the trek to New York.

He wasn't going straight home. Cricket Connolly was stationed at Camp Pendleton up the coast, and he wanted to stop and see him first, so he caught the Santa Fe train up to San Clemente. On the way—it was an hour's ride, and pretty, along the water—he counted his traveler's checks; $650 worth. They included his last pay check and money due for leave not taken. It was the most money he'd ever had in his pocket.

Cricket had told him on the telephone the night before that he was living off base, in a house on the edge of a bluff in San Clemente, which adjoined Pendleton. Jim was to get off the train and walk up the railroad track for a tenth of a mile, until he came to a red-and-white house up on the bluff, then he was to climb the trail up the bluff and he'd be there. Leave it to Cricket to find someplace crazy.

Looking at the ocean through the train window, Jim thought it was unbelievable weather for December. *The San Diego Union*, which he had in his hand, called it Santa Ana conditions, which meant that the prevailing wind was blowing from the desert rather than from the ocean. The temperature was near 90, and he could see surfers riding their boards in on the white crests of the waves. It wouldn't be hard to spend a few more days in California, he thought, for all his longing to get home.

Home. Florence's letter had been funny. It had been waiting for him when he got in to port; he took it out again now and read it over. His father was due for retirement in six months, and the brewery was sending him the magazine *Harvest Years*. Florence said he grew furious when it arrived in the mail, and flung it across the room. She wanted him to come and stay with herself and Ralph. Jim doubted the father would go for that. The last time Jim was home, fourteen months before, the father had told Jim that Florence and Ralph's children got on his nerves.

Florence wrote that she was saying night prayers with the children and, in listing the family, they had come to Uncle Jim. "Who's that?" Lawrence, aged three, had asked. "So you see," wrote Florence, "You had better come home, as your niece and nephew don't even know who you are."

Jim smiled and folded over the letter. God, it would be good to get home.

He got off at San Clemente and followed Cricket's directions. Sure enough, he came to a red-and-white house on a bluff. It was built in Spanish Mediterranean style, with red, rounded terra-cotta tiles on the roof and white-washed walls. There was a note tacked to the door: "Make yourself at home. Back at 4:30. C."

Cricket had told Jim the key would be over the ledge. Jim let himself in, and found himself in a courtyard open to the sky that had trees and a swimming pool. He went into the house proper by sliding a glass panel door. The living room was big enough so that a couch and several chairs could be grouped in the center of the room and large areas of free space left around the furniture. There were more glass windows on the other side of the room, looking out on the Pacific. In one corner stood a life-size plaster nude, and the arms of the girl were raised over her head. A coffee table held a stack of Playboy magazines. Over in another corner was a bar, with the bottles set out in a row on top: scotch, gin, bourbon, vodka, the works. There was a sign: "help yourself."

In three years and four months of wandering the country and the world with the Navy, Jim had seen a lot of bachelor setups, but none to match this.

He went to the bar and smiled at the collection of gadgets: Cricket had always been mad for gadgets. There was a porcelain toilet two inches high with a sign: Park Your Butts here. There was a Busch Bavarian Beer scene with a light behind it. The corkscrew had a huge-busted girl for a handle.

There were even some familiar ones: the two-foot pipe with the long broken stem, and the white woolen hat with the pom pom. He had held onto them in his travels.

Jim went into the bedroom, changed into his bathing suit and took a towel and went out to the pool area. He looked around more carefully. There was a barbecue setup at one end of the pool, with a grill, a row of beer mugs, and the long-handled utensils. Suddenly a huge dog came bounding out of nowhere and gave a ferocious low-pitched bark. Jim's hair stood on end as he ran. The dog was on a chain, he soon realized, and it couldn't reach him. It was a Saint Bernard and it was three or four feet high. It continued to bark; heavy-throated basso barks. It had baggy eyes with red, low-hanging rims. It was leaning forward toward Jim with the chain pulling at its neck. The chain was a heavy one, and it was attached to a firm iron stake. Jim was relieved to see that. Cricket hadn't mentioned the dog. He'd laugh if he knew what a scare Jim got.

Jim studied the dog. It had a noble look, with its heavy down-turned mouth. It reminded Jim of some senator's picture that he had seen a lot; maybe it was Everett Dirksen. The dog continued to bark. Imagine something like that, Jim thought, coming at you in the Swiss Alps. It would be better to freeze to death. He decided to go down to the beach to swim.

It was a long way to the water even after he reached the beach, for it was low tide and the ocean approach was very gradual. The water was icy cold. He walked and walked. It numbed his feet, his calves, his thighs. Finally he got out far enough for a wave to break over him if he ducked low. One was enough. He ran back in and threw himself down on the towel. The sun was wonderfully warm and his body felt great from the shock of the cold water.

He looked around after he had luxuriated for a while in the warmth of the air. No one on the beach at all. It didn't matter. He didn't mind being alone. He had become something of a loner in the Navy; towards the end he even preferred to room alone. He had spent long hours in the Mediterranean or the Pacific on his tours, up near the bow of the ship watching the stars in the dark night, thinking or just dreaming.

What was he going to do for a career? He wasn't sure. All the thinking had led only to the non-decision to go back to New York and play it by ear. The newspaper business again? The wire service job would be open, he thought. It wasn't unattractive, but it wasn't that attractive either. He remembered the many, many nights in Newark during summers in college after coming off duty when the stories were buzzing through his head like cutting, whining machinery, and how long it took to relax. Was it worth it? Well, it was. But the stories were so much the same, and each day was a repetition of the one before, and he wanted something more.

Stay in the Navy? He had already decided against that. R.O.T.C. had helped pay for college, and he was glad for the experiences of the past few years, but he knew he wasn't meant for life as a naval officer.

To create something. That is what he wanted. Plays? The theater? But what kind of a business was that? Guys with silvery hair that had grown too long and curled over their ears. Well, he'd play it by ear in New York.

A lot of the hours at sea he had spent in dreaming of Alaco. He resolved to stop that. Six years later, it didn't make any sense. Yet there hadn't been any other girl really since. There had not been again the same feeling, the same intensity, the knowledge that there was just no happiness without this particular girl.

A collie dog came racing along the surf, a nice picture with the flowing hair. It was running full speed. It had come so far its owner was a speck way down the beach. Jim sat up to watch it; it was a civilized looking dog compared to the monster chained above. He saw why it was running; the sand birds were flying a foot over the water and the dog was trying to catch them. They were so swift they hardly seemed aware of his pursuit. The dog would run a hundred yards in one direction, then the birds would suddenly wheel and go the other direction, and the dog would gallop after them a couple of hundred yards in that direction. Occasionally a sand bird would land and run out after a receding wave, and then take off just before the arrival of the yapping collie.

Even the sand birds reminded him of Alaco, and the first night he met her in Mallard Lake. Here I go again, off thinking about her, Jim thought, and his resolution was broken, as it always was.

By four-thirty Jim was up in the house again. He got dressed, mixed himself a Manhattan and sat on the couch. Cricket arrived. Jim was surprised to see his hair "high and tight," in the crew-cut style of a Marine grunt. The Saint Bernard gave off his basso barks. Jim went to the sliding door. Cricket, in his Marine officer's khakis, was fondling the dog's head. Jim slid the door open and went out and they greeted each other enthusiastically, pumping each other's hand. They hadn't seen each other in over two years. "Come on in," said Cricket. Jim followed him back into the living room, taking a look back at the dog, who watched him passively, his red pouches hanging from his eyeballs like wounds. Cricket looked back. "Have you met Neil?"

"Have I met him? He almost had me for lunch."

Cricket laughed but not his old crazy giggle laugh, a more mature one.

"Have you got a drink?" Cricket asked, when they got in the living room.

"I fixed a Manhattan."

"Outstanding," said Cricket, going to the bar and fixing himself some scotch and fizzing a little soda into it, like the movies. "You're out, eh?"

"I'm out."

"You'll stay for a while?"

"Sure."

"Outstanding."

"How'd you ever get a layout like this?" Jim asked.

"It's a reward from my country, for service."

"Do you pay for it by yourself?"

"I had two other guys but they shipped out to Okinawa. I didn't replace them right away because Mom and Dad and Harold were out."

"Florence wrote me that."

"I couldn't find a thing in the house after my mother left. She rearranged everything."

"I presume you hid the magazines and the statue," Jim laughed.

"What do you think?"

"They liked it, eh?"

"Ah, yeah. My father kept asking for you. Wants to know if you're going back to the wire service. I told him I didn't know."

"I don't know myself," said Jim. "I'm just going back to New York and play it by ear."

"What did it do for him?" Cricket asked. "I told him: there's no money in it."

"He must have had a good time with his old newspaper buddies up in L.A."

"He boozed it up," said Cricket. "Half the time he was in L.A. and the rest of the time down in Del Mar at the track."

They talked about the family. Cricket had a lot of news from Nora. Harold, Cricket's brother, was starting in a month as a violinist with the Chicago Symphony. They talked about that.

"What are your plans?" Jim asked him.

"I signed up for another tour. I'll probably stay with it," said Cricket.

While Cricket talked, Jim watched for changes in him. He was stronger than college days but that wasn't so striking; it was something noted after Cricket returned after his first year in the Marines. His face was fuller, and he was, consequently, better looking. The most striking change was in his air. He was much more composed and sure of himself, not like the old silly days.

Two other Marine lieutenants arrived, with the close-cropped haircuts, and from the easy way they made a drink and settled themselves in the living room, it was apparent that the house was a social headquarters.

Jim wasn't too happy to see them; he was enjoying talk of the family, after so long. But a couple of drinks mellowed the atmosphere, and it turned out that one of them was from New York. His name was Dolan, and still had a New York accent; he called the ocean "the worter."

"The difference," Dolan told Jim, "between the girls in California and the ones back in the Bronx is that out here you can give a girl five drinks and it has an effect on her, but back in the Bronx you give a girl five drinks and she's just waiting for five more."

Jim laughed. "They start off with five highballs on Saturday night before they even leave the house, and they don't even smile."

"That's right," said Dolan. "Did you ever see anything like the capacity of a B.I.C.?"

"What's a B.I.C.?" asked Roach, the other officer.

"Bronx Irish Catholic," said Dolan. "Did you ever hear the ditty about the B.I.C.s?"

"Let's hear it," Jim said.

"My name is Mary Flanagan
My school is IHM
I drink like I do it;
I dance like I do it;
But I don't."

All four of them laughed.

"They'd dance like they do it, but they don't, eh?" asked Roach.

"Naw," said Dolan. "All they do is drink. They all got wooden legs."

"They're our B.I.C.s," said Cricket, meditatively, looking at his drink.

"Ninety percent of the girls around here are the same way," ventured Roach, who was not as forward as Dolan.

"The hell they are," said Cricket.

They left the two officers and drove to Laguna Beach to eat, about ten miles, and stopped at a place called The Lamplighter. "The steaks are a buck seventy five," said Cricket, as he walked through, waving to the bartender and several girls, "And you cook them yourself."

They grilled the steaks over an open hearth and brought them to a table. The place was dimly lit, with red lights hung on fishnets from the ceiling. There was a small dance floor, not too active, for there was a preponderance of men. "Boys town tonight," said Cricket, looking around.

"You going to get a hop back to New York for Christmas?" Jim asked.

"I'm not going to bother," said Cricket, with an expression of distaste. "It doesn't interest me anymore. Last time I was home I went downtown a lot; I met the type of girls you meet down there. But hell, I can find the same thing here, and it costs me a hotel in New York."

The bluntness of this was a shock to Jim.

When they left The Lamplighter, Cricket debated whether they should go up to Balboa—"lots of girls up there"—but decided to go to a club down on the next street called The Dipper. There was a piano there and the pianist sang, with much gusto, to his own accompaniment. They ordered drinks and sat at the regular bar. Jim felt good after the steaks and the drinks. He joined in the singing of "You're a Grand Old Flag." Cricket hushed him.

"Why?" asked Jim.

"Listen to the words."

Jim listened. The pianist was singing, "You're a grand old fag."

"Town's full of queers," said Cricket.

They drank and talked. For the first time in all the years they had been together, Jim found himself trying to impress Cricket.

"I really got around the world. That's one thing I'll say about the Navy," Jim told him.

"Been to 'Frisco?" Cricket asked.

"Not yet."

"'Frisco's the town. I never had it like I had it up there. The thing to do is go down to Paoli's or a place like that around the time the office girls are getting out, four-thirty, five. You get yourself a seat at the bar with an empty place next to you. The girls come up and ask you to order drinks for them. When you talk to each one, and you got one picked out—take your time, make sure she'll put out—then you ask her to sit down. Man, did I have it made in that city. Outstanding!"

Jim looked at Cricket without saying anything. Cricket's time in the Marines, Jim thought, had changed him.

"The night clerk in the hotel I was staying at," Cricket continued, unabashed, "told me I should have been charged for a double."

They looked at their drinks for a few moments. "How'd you like Japan?" asked Cricket. "Pick yourself up a mama-san?"

"Well, you know," said Jim equivocally. What am I supposed to say, he thought? Make an announcement in the bar that he'd been all around the world, three years and four months, and was coming out with his virginity intact? It wasn't the kind of thing a sailor made announcements about.

"I miss the old crowd in New York," said Jim.

"I've had it with New York," said Cricket. "I almost got hooked just before I left."

"To who?"

"Rosemary Lane."

Jim didn't know her. "You were away," said Cricket. "I really wanted her body. I kind of liked her too. I had her down on the seat of the car one night and I was really working for it. She said it wouldn't be so bad if we were engaged, anyway. And I almost said all right. Then I lit a cigarette and thought it over and said, 'The hell with this.' I told her to get up and put her clothes on."

Jim laughed. "You're full of stories," he said.

They left The Dipper and continued down the street. The noise of the surf could be heard. The ocean was only a block away. "Where we going now?"

"Place called The Tropics," said Cricket. "I got a waitress there."

The Tropics was decorated with palm trees and fronds and coconuts. Most of the patrons were dressed in beach clothes. Many of the men wore artist's beards. A large proportion of the girls were blonde. Cricket's waitress was a blonde, an attractive woman in her thirties. Cricket introduced her as Sue. She kept on about her duties; once in a while she would come over to Cricket and say something to him in a low voice that Jim couldn't overhear. He learned from Cricket that she was divorced and had a seven-year-old son.

They stayed in The Tropics for two hours. It wasn't enjoyable to Jim. In the old days, when he was zany and irresponsible, Cricket had been a good deal more entertaining, Jim thought.

A young man got up from a table near the bar and left a girl sitting alone. He didn't return. Jim looked the girl over. She was very homely, but had a good figure. He asked her to dance.

"Do you swing?" she asked.

"Yes."

They did a Lindy.

"You do it Eastern style," she said.

"I'm from New York."

"Oh." She didn't pursue it.

The next dance was slow, and he didn't have to look at her, and that was better.

He sat at her table. There was a perfume bottle there, next to a bottle of beer. She squeezed the atomizer and sprayed him with perfume.

"What did you do that for?"

"I don't know."

A hell of a thing, to be sprayed with perfume in Laguna, he thought. Some guy was liable to leap on you. Maybe it was her insurance. If she sprayed the guy with perfume, none of the other girls would want to dance with him, figuring he was not interested in women.

"Don't worry about it," she said. "You can't tell the men's perfumes from the women's perfumes these days."

Maybe not in Laguna, Jim thought.

He drifted back to the bar. At closing time, he left with Cricket.

Cricket brought Sue.

"Bring that girl you were with," said Cricket.

"No thanks," Jim replied.

They walked to the car and drove back to Cricket's place. Sue sat between them. Once or twice she turned her nose in Jim's direction and sniffed, but she didn't say anything. She talked about her son. "He's more observant than you think," she said to Cricket. "That's the way kids are. Silent. You think they don't know anything. But they see a lot more than you think they do. He was asking me about you," she said to Cricket. "He asked me, 'Is Eddie your friend?' 'Yes,' I told him. 'Eddie is my friend.' 'But he's not a daddy, is he?'"

Cricket laughed.

"No," she continued, "he's not a daddy."

"He watches everybody who comes in the house," she continued. "Christ, I don't know what I'm going to do with him when the summer vacation comes."

When they got to Cricket's place, Roach and Dolan were still there drinking, and there was a Marine captain there now too. Cricket and Sue went to the bedroom after they'd had a quick drink. Jim stayed with the three officers. They were discussing how much they'd won and lost playing cards in the officers' club. After a few minutes, Jim went outside and down the path to the beach. The fresh air was pleasant and clean.

Chapter 32

Jim took off the next day on a military flight for the East. He landed at McGuire Air Force in southern New Jersey. On the approach to the airfield, he passed over Fort Dix, the army base where he had done basic training. He could see soldiers marching across the sandy flats. Once on the ground, he collected his single bag and took the bus to New York. He got in the Port Authority terminal on 42nd Street at six in the evening. He went out to the corner of 42nd street and Eighth Avenue and looked up the long street of movie marquees stretching from Eighth to Seventh Avenue.

It was a pleasure to see the lights of downtown New York again, even though he had to clutch his coat collar around him in the bitter cold wind. He hailed a taxi and gave the Riverdale address, and all the way up the West Side Highway he sat on the front of the seat, anticipating home. The cab driver was a woman, big, in a zipper jacket, with straight matted hair down to her shoulders. She had a voice as deep as Jim's own. All she needed was a cigar. She made him really feel he was home—she was someone you couldn't find anywhere else except New York City.

They passed the George Washington Bridge and the span was lit with thousands of lights. A few minutes later they were crossing the Henry Hudson Bridge into Riverdale, and soon they turned the corner onto Brush Avenue. At last, there was the house, and there was a light in the living room. That had been his last fear; that when he got to Riverdale, there might be nobody home.

He paid and tipped her and grabbed his bag and went up to the window. His father was sitting in his chair, reading the paper. Jim went to the door, turned the knob—it was unlocked—and went in. His father turned in the chair and peered out. Jim put down the suitcase. He stood in the doorway. "Pop."

"James!" His father jumped up out of the chair. "You're home."

Jim hurried across the room. His father put out his arms and then put them right down again. They stood facing each other, caught between the rush of emotion and the habit of reserve.

They shook hands. "Are you well?" asked the father.

"I'm fine."

"That's good."

"How are you?" Jim asked.

"Sure I'm the same as always."

He wasn't though. He was a whole lot older. He hadn't looked sixty-two when Jim had seen him last. But he looked sixty-four now. His hair was whiter; it was really all white now, and thinning.

"It's good to be home," said Jim, and he looked around fondly at the room.

"Are you finished with the service?"

"Yep. I'm a civilian."

"Goddammit, why couldn't you tell me you were coming home so I could have something ready for you?"

"To tell you the truth, Pop I wasn't sure what day it was going to be. We can go out and eat anyway."

"If you want."

They went out to the kitchen as Jim kept up a stream of questions about the family, and got back mostly monosyllabic answers from his father, who was not at all inclined to gossip. Jim would have to wait to see Florence before he would get any details.

Jim took a can of beer. His father took down the Old Overholt bottle. "Would you care for a shot of whiskey?" It was the first time he had ever offered it to Jim.

"No thanks, Pop. You have one though."

The father put the bottle back on the shelf. "Sure they won't let me have anything."

"Have you been feeling all right, Pop?"

"Fine."

"How's the stomach?"

"Now and again it gives a kick-up. No worse than usual."

They talked for an hour at home, and went to the Riverdale Inn and talked for another hour. His father never once mentioned his impending retirement.

Later in the evening, Florence and Ralph came over to the house, and Jim got Florence aside in the living room.

"He's only working four hours a day," Florence whispered about their father. "He came home early from work one day with numbness in his cheek and down his side, and when they finally got him to a doctor, they found out he had suffered a slight stroke. You talk to him, Jimmy, so he'll stay with us. He shouldn't be working at all."

Florence was in her seventh month of pregnancy with her third child. During dinner, with one of his rare smiles, the father had said of herself and Ralph: "They're a pair of rabbits, the two of them." Florence had a lot of little wrinkles around her eyes now, but in the eyes themselves there was contentment. She and Ralph would go from one small discussion to another small discussion, and almost always, Florence was the aggressor and Ralph the patient resistor.

"As long as there's no linen on the bed," said Florence, "he best thing would be for Jimmy to come up and stay with us tonight."

"Honey," said Ralph, "he probably wants to get unpacked and get settled."

"As long as the bag isn't unpacked, it's just a simple thing to put it right in the car."

"He probably wants some time to see the guys."

"Ralph, Christina is over a year old now, and he hasn't even had a chance to see her yet."

"Give the guy a chance. He's just home."

"Ralph, he wants to see the children."

"Honey, let him make his own decision. He has plenty of time."

Jim never did have to enter the discussion.

Ralph was wearing a toupee. He was embarrassed about it; he told Jim in the kitchen he wouldn't be wearing it except for Florence. In this case, though, Florence was right. It brought his hairline two inches forward, and it was matched so well with his own hair that it was not distinguishable, and it aided his appearance. He was with a midtown law firm. The way he talked of his work, it seemed he was doing well.

"Tell me about the Navy," Ralph urged Jim. Jim told him of his travels and adventures and Ralph listened eagerly. Jim could see a trace of long-ing in his eyes: it was the look the footloose bachelor could draw from the settled married man with any recital of bachelor adventures. It made the telling doubly enjoyable.

"I don't know what your plans are, Jim," Ralph eventually said. "If you're planning to stay at home or not. . ."

"I'm not even sure yet, Ralph."

"Well, in case it ever comes up, if he should ever mention it, tell your father he'd really be welcome with us. No kidding. I think the world of him."

"He knows that, Ralph. And it's nice of you."

"Nora is working as a nurse's aide at Saint Elizabeth's Hospital," Ralph mentioned, "and your Uncle Arthur is on the evening shift at the paper, so you won't see either of them until tomorrow."

Just then the doorbell rang. It was Jill South from next door.

"I saw your car, Florence," she said, and then her eyes lit up. "Jim!"

She stayed even after Florence and Ralph left. She and Jim found they had much to talk about. About herself and what she was doing: she had gotten her M.A. at Hunter College and was going for her Ph.D at Fordham. She was teaching at Molloy College, a school for well-to-do Catholic girls, located in Nassau County, Long Island. She had news of the boys from Jim's class at Fordham, especially of Popeye Morrissey, who was doing graduate work in history at Fordham, and was also going to teach at Molloy the next September. Red and D'Arcy had married, and she told Jim that D'Arcy Harrigan was expecting. And of course she spoke at length of her brother Jack, who had stunned everyone four years before by entering the seminary and was now only a year and a half away from ordination.

Mr. Meagher had been about to go to bed when Jill arrived, but he stayed around. Finally, he went upstairs. At that point, Jim was standing on one side of the room and Jill on the other. "It really is good to see you Jill," he told her. He was amazed at what happened next.

She ran across the room into his arms. She searched out his lips to kiss him. He kissed her back. He led her over to the couch and sat down.

He held her, but he didn't feel right about it at all. He did feel emotion, but it wasn't what she felt. She felt something more. When he took her home, he kissed her again at the door. She stayed at the door as he went across the lawn; she had a sad expression on her face. She waved. He wished the father had stayed downstairs until she had left.

The next morning, Jim was up early. His father left for the brewery at nine. Jim had breakfast with Aunt Nora and Uncle Arthur. "Isn't it a lovely place that Edward has?" Aunt Nora repeated a few times. She always had crowed about Cricket and Harold, turning trifles into triumphs, but this time Jim agreed wholeheartedly; there was no denying that Cricket really did have a beautiful spot in San Clemente. He mentioned it several times during the breakfast. By the end, Aunt Nora had changed her attitude entirely: "That California, you can have it as far as I'm concerned, nothing but brown hills and the fog rolling in." She didn't like the idea of him settling down three thousand miles away. "Crazy place."

Uncle Arthur was the same as ever, so far as Jim could see. He was still having his bad weekends but he was in fine fettle this morning, and when

he was like that, he was a very interesting conversationalist. He had the reporter's eye. He talked about the extraordinary arm muscles that he had
noted the young boys had in San Clemente, from carrying the surf boards.
He had noted that the boys wore their hair long—Jim had noticed the same,
and assumed it was just youthful aversion to the barber. "Not at all," said
Uncle Arthur. "It's a reaction to the Marines in the area. The town boys don't
want to be identified with them, so the easiest way not to be is to let their
hair grow." He had gone to the trouble to investigate. "They call the Marines
'Js' for 'Jugheads,'" said Uncle Arthur.

He's a better reporter, thought Jim, than I am.

When Harold came in, he talked of his music. He had studied for several years at Juilliard, and would soon start the Chicago Symphony tour. His
success in his career had buoyed him and changed him. He was not nearly
so supercilious in manner. He wore a vest, which was not entirely unstylish,
but it matched his suit, so that gave him an old-mannish look. And he was
still very precise. He prepared his own egg because he wanted it "just so." He
had a thin, floorwalker's moustache which served to cut the length of skin
from his nose to his upper lip and lessened the somewhat monkeyish look
which had plagued his growing years.

How much did they know about Cricket, Jim wondered, and how he'd
changed? Harold was the only one who said anything. "Edward," he said, as
he was putting his violin away in the basement after playing Mozart for Jim,
"is typical of the young military officer class in any civilization. I told him
that too. He didn't even know he had been insulted."

The first week home Jim spent seeing relatives, but by the second week
the family pressure was off and his life was his own. On Wednesday morning, he realized he was completely free. He woke up at nine o'clock but there
was no place to go, so he went back to bed. He awoke again at eleven, with a
clear-headed exuberant feeling. He lay in the warm bed and thought about
going back to sleep again. Eventually he got up and wandered downstairs
and made a pot of coffee, and had a cup and walked into the living room,
and then walked out to the kitchen again and had another cup.

It was great. He couldn't do it all day, though, so he got dressed, put
on his windbreaker and walked down to the 242nd Street IRT subway stop
and got on the train, not even sure where he was going. He got off at Times
Square.

As he walked through Times Square, he noticed crowds standing under the marquees of the theaters on the side streets. Wednesday was matinee
day. He walked down to the first box office. The show was "The Disenchanted," by Budd Schulberg. He got a single ticket for the first balcony for $3.80.
When he got to his seat, he found himself between two matronly women

in fur jackets. As he looked around, it seemed that most of the theater was filled with matronly women in fur jackets.

When the curtain went up it was obvious, too, they were a poor audience. They laughed at all the cute things and they even had the actors playing for cheap laughs, but it was only a distraction, really, Jim thought, from the real drama. The play was wonderful. It was the story of a weekend in the twilight years of a talented author who had become an alcoholic and had turned to screenwriting for a living. The actor was good. He put over the pathos of a talented man who feels he is debasing his talent and, at the same time, can't help himself. By the end of the first act Jim was so caught up in the current that was being generated from the stage that he was sitting with his mouth open.

At intermission, Jim went down to the men's room and sat in one of the plush chairs in the gilded anteroom to smoke. He was still in a trance. What a power the author had! He could take a whole audience of people and introduce them into his world and make them react as one. He could take the human feelings of those in the theater and make electric moments out of them. He could recreate a part of the world and make people feel about it as he did.

After the show he decided he'd stay down for an evening show, too. He went to Gilhooley's on 46th Street and Eighth Avenue and had corned beef and cabbage, with beer to wash it down. He hardly paid attention to what he was eating. He had the feeling he'd like to go right home and write a play. He wished he had something to write about.

The second show he saw was "The Quare Fellow," by Brendan Behan, a wild, boisterous, shocking play set in a bawdy house in Dublin. In the middle of the confusion on stage, the author himself, Behan, appeared. A toothless, stout man, he sang his own lyrics to a song. The show swirled around him and went right on. It was such a wild river of confused vitality no interruption could have made any difference.

Jim went afterwards to Downey's, a bar on Eighty-Sixth Street, and he had a beer in there. He was caught under the spell of the show by this point. He tried to piece it all together. He wasn't sure what it had all meant. He wasn't sure either that the whole thing wasn't immoral. But it had certainly been electric and full of life.

He had to talk to someone. He had all these ideas running through his head, and his whole life's work was taking shape in his mind.

I will be a playwright, Jim thought.

He had to talk to someone, tell someone, discuss it. He needed someone who would understand it all.

He wanted to talk to Jill.

Chapter 33

He took a taxi to Riverdale. He had resolved after the kiss on the first night home that he would stay away from Jill, in fairness to her. She was serious about him, he thought, and he didn't want to be serious, so he didn't have any right to visit her and encourage her. He felt guilty in the taxi. He told himself, I'll make it clear from the very beginning. "Jill, I don't want to be serious now, but I want you for my friend."

Somehow the line had a silly ring to it.

It was after midnight when he stood in the alleyway between his own house and Jill's. No lights were on in either house. He threw a handful of dirt and light gravel at Jill's window. He waited a moment, then the window went up. She leaned out; she had six or seven metal rollers at the bottom of bunches of hair, so they hung below her face; she had a sleepy expression.

"Jim?"

"Hi, Jill." He had a sudden urge to laugh. I should have a ladder, he thought.

She didn't even make him explain. "I'll be down," she said and she shut the window. He went around to the front door. There was a cold winter wind blowing, and when she unlatched the door and opened it, it whooshed into the house. He had a heavy windbreaker on, whereas she was only in pajamas with a housecoat over them, but she stayed in the doorway anyway, and put her arms around him, just under his shoulders and rested her head against him.

I'm a Grade A bastard, he said to himself. A real Grade A bastard.

But he felt great at the same time. He put his arms around her, and where he touched her at the small of her back, the cloth yielded and slid under his hand up her back. It was a very enticing thing.

"Come on in," she said.

He went into the living room and she snapped on the lamp. He grinned at her. She didn't smile so much as look pleased, pleased and sleepy.

"What'll your mother and father say?" he asked.

"I'll tell them it's you."

She went upstairs. When she came down, she said, "They said to say hello."

"Good."

"I'll make some coffee." She went to the kitchen. She stayed out there a few minutes until the coffee was ready. He walked to the dining room, to the big table. She had obviously been working there, for it was covered with students' papers and stacks of books. He picked the top book off one of the stacks: *Wise Blood,* by Flannery O'Connor. A novel. She was always reading novels. She must have read every novel that was written since *Tom Jones,* Jim thought.

He went back to the living room and sat down again. She came in with the coffee. He took it, and she went and sat down on the overstuffed chair. There was a spoon on the saucer next to the cup, and there was a strawberry on the spoon, and the strawberry was coated with sugar. He looked up at her and she gave a slow smile. It was a nice touch; feminine, and subtle, and very like Jill.

He was starting to get the Grade A bastard feeling again.

There was a long moment. But she broke it. She was sitting there with the curlers pulling her hair down, no makeup, no lipstick, powder or eye shadow, and she had facial cream patches around her mouth. She said to him, "I'm so glad you picked just now to visit. I feel so prepared."

He laughed out loud.

She shushed him. "Jim, it's one in the morning."

"You look fine."

"I know."

She just sat there. She really was great. No interrogation even. She didn't demand any explanations. If he wanted to come visit at one in the morning, well, that was all right too.

"I saw two terrific plays today, Jill."

"Which?"

"'The Disenchanted' and 'The Quare Fellow'."

"Oh, that one by Behan."

"Do you know anything about him?"

"He's drunk all the time," said Jill. "He's always in the papers."

"He appeared in the play himself."

"I hear he does that," said Jill. "He's very funny. They wouldn't let him march in the Saint Patrick's Day parade because they were afraid he'd come staggering up the avenue, so he got mad and he issued a statement to the reporters and he said that when Saint Patrick drove the snakes out of Ireland he sent them to New York to run the Saint Patrick's Day parade."

"What a play," said Jim. "It was mad."

"He wrote a book," said Jill, "Called *The Borstal Boy* about his time in prison in England. He was arrested for an I.R.A. bomb throwing."

"He's a rebel all right," said Jim.

She had the book. "Here it is. Take it. You'd enjoy it. It's a real man's book."

"Thanks Jill. I got plenty of time for reading."

They talked about the two plays for a while. "You know, I'm really thinking of studying playwriting," he said.

She nodded. "You wrote good dialog in high school shows."

"I'd give my life to be able to move a whole audience of people, so that they're all right there." He held up his palm.

"It's the hardest of all the writing fields," she said. "You can go for years and get nothing produced. Even someone like Tennessee Williams, with all the talent he has. He had to wait until he was thirty-five."

"I wouldn't mind waiting," he said.

"If you hit, though, you really hit."

"I wouldn't even care about the money," he said.

"Well, you have to live. Did you read Moss Hart's biography?"

"What's that?" he asked.

"*Act One.* Here." She took it off the shelf. "He tells how he started out. It's interesting."

They talked until three in the morning, and when Jim finally left, he was loaded with books. She even knew about drama schools. Iowa and Yale were supposed to be fine, she said. The best of the Catholic ones was at Catholic University in Washington, D.C.

He spent the rest of the week reading the books she had given him and, in the evenings, he kept going to plays.

He thought of asking her. But that would be a date, different from evening chats. Also, he thought, single tickets could be gotten without reservations.

Saturday night after supper, he was getting dressed to go downtown when the doorbell rang. It was Popeye Morissey. Jim was glad to see him, if somewhat surprised. He had come to think that none of the old gang were left in the city. Several times he had thought of getting in touch with Popeye, but they hadn't been that close in school and had kept no contact afterwards. But he was genuinely glad to see him. He opened two cans of beer and they talked. Jim found out then that Popeye hadn't come over to Riverdale to see him, but was merely stopping in on his way to take Jill out.

This was certainly a new development.

There were changes in Popeye after three and a half years. He seemed, for one thing, much more mature. After two or three times calling him Popeye, Jim stopped it and called him Dan. He had about four cowlicks in his hair, front and back, which gave him a disordered look. At the same time his glasses and his serious jowly face gave him a scholarly appearance. A briar pipe wouldn't have been out of place, had he had one, which he didn't. He still had the big broad stomach and Jim noted that the under part of the stuffing of the chair he was sitting in was right down on the floor.

One thing which hadn't changed was his jaundiced view of the world. Jim asked him of the appointment to teach at Molloy the following September.

"The money's good, but that's about all," said Morissey. "They start instructors at five thousand."

"Boy, that's good pay, with summers off."

"Yeah, yeah," said Morissey, "But they got crazy ideas."

"What?"

"I had an interview with the dean last week. She tells me how happy she and all the other sisters are that I'm going to be there in September. Then she gives me this big line that Molloy is a special kind of school. They don't have any division between the administration and the faculty, and the faculty and the students. The dean says it's all one big happy family; we're all just older brothers and sisters of the girls, just showing them the way."

He said the last sentence in such a sarcastic way that Jim had to laugh. "What it comes down to," said Morissey, "is no discipline."

"Jill likes it."

"Jill likes everything," said Morissey. "You can't judge by a woman."

"Maybe the dean was just talking for effect. You know."

"No," said Morissey. "They have a different concept entirely from the European system. In a university in Europe, the teacher is the master, and the students come to him as a privilege to learn from him. They don't have any crap about older brother and sister. I know how it works out in practice too. I talked to guys who have been through it. As soon as the teacher starts to tighten the screws on the girls, some hard-nosed little class officer goes skipping to the dean's office and then the dean comes to see the teacher and puts a bug in his ear. What it comes down to is the girls run the school. Helluva system."

When Morissey left shortly afterwards, Jim sat in the chair in the living room for a long time, thinking. He couldn't remember Morissey ever going out with a girl in college—he didn't go to any of the dances—not even at the shore. He usually stuck by himself or with some of the guys. Now he was going out with Jill. Morissey and Jill. Maybe it was a match though, Jim thought. They were both scholars. They were both going for their Ph.D. Why not?

Chapter 34

The Christmas holidays came. Jim and his father spent Christmas Eve with Florence, Ralph, and the children. They went to Midnight Mass, then came home to a special supper of champagne and lasagna that Florence had prepared. They woke the children. "Santa Claus was here! Santa Claus was here!" they could hear Florence telling them in the bedroom. The two children, Larry and Christina, came out, rubbing their fists in sleepy eyes.

"Look what you got from Santa Claus!" Ralph cried, and snapped on the lights of the movie camera and started to whir away. The children, blinded and unable to see the toys, started to cry.

Florence came in front of them, clapping her hands, and cried, "Smile! Smile! It's Christmas! What's the matter? Larry! Oh, Ralph, they're scared of the lights."

When the children settled down and started to enjoy their toys, Mr. Meagher got down on the floor with them and played with them. It seemed strange to Jim whenever he heard one of the little ones call out, "Grandpa."

Start of a new era, he thought.

Ralph and Florence gave Mr. Meagher a special room upstairs, and he commented on it the next day at Christmas dinner at Aunt Nora's. "The grandest room you ever saw. Not drafty at all, like the one next door here. I'm beginning to think this place next door is too big and drafty anyway."

Jim and Florence and Ralph exchanged glances.

Christmas was on a Friday. The first of the holiday gatherings came Saturday night, when Red and D'Arcy gave a party. All the boys were there, fifteen in all, almost all from the one Fordham class. Most brought girls. Jim didn't, but of course Jack South didn't either—he even wore his black suit, which was unusual. Nor did Tom Power. He was engaged to a girl from Washington, D.C., Connie Corcoran.

D'Arcy was pregnant—she was expecting the following May—and the way Red hovered around her he gave the impression she might be expecting any minute. She told him to relax. They were a happy couple, and they gave the best laugh of the party when D'Arcy wondered how Red had ever found a hatmaker who could make one big enough to cover Red's ears.

"I haven't got big ears," said Red.

"No, dear," D'Arcy replied sweetly. "It's just that your head is small."

Jim Meagher and Jack South had some moments of nostalgia, for they rode to the party and rode home again in the Black Seducer. When they got home, at two in the morning, Jack presented Jim with the car.

"You're kidding."

"Why? It runs all right." Jack was miffed. He had expected it to be accepted with enthusiasm.

"I don't mean it that way. I didn't think you'd ever part with it."

"I have no use for it. Jill said you might be going to Washington. You're going to study drama?"

"I was thinking of it."

"It'll save you buying another heap."

They inspected the motor. It was very clean. Jack had always been very careful of his possessions. With the rumble seat, thought Jim, the car might even have antique value. Jim laughed at the loving way Jack put the hood down and patted it. "Take good care of her in her old age."

"Is this the official break with the past?"

"I guess so. Remember where you got it from," said Jack. "Just for propriety's sake, don't undress anybody in it."

"You know what you should do? You should have it mounted and polished. You could keep it in your bedroom in the rectory then."

Jack laughed. "I'd like to. I really would."

"I appreciate it."

They went in the back door to the Meagher kitchen and opened two cans of beer, and Jack signed over the car registration.

"Do you remember Alaco Armstrong?" Jack asked suddenly.

Jim stared at him. He had the urge to laugh. Did he remember Alaco Armstrong? "Are you pulling my leg?"

"No."

"Of course I do."

"I know you went out with her once or twice but you never mentioned her again."

"We almost got married that summer. The one after Freshman year."

"Oh yeah?"

"You know she's in the convent?" said Jack.

"Yes."

"I didn't know you two got serious," said Jack.

"We did," said Jim. "It was short and sweet."

"She never mentioned it," said Jack.

Jim felt a wave of annoyance. But maybe it wasn't a dig. "Why do you ask?"

"Her mother had an operation and they're looking for blood donors."

"Oh."

"Did you ever give?"

"In the Navy," said Jim. "Yeah. I'll give."

"I'm going over to the hospital tomorrow," said Jack. "I'll pick you up. Eleven."

"Okay. How is the mother?"

"She had some kind of a lung operation," said Jack. "I think she's pulling through. But they had to give her a lot of blood and if that's not replaced they have to pay for it, and they haven't got that kind of money."

"There are eleven children, aren't there?" Jim asked.

"Yes," said Jack. "I was over their house this morning with D'Arcy. It's a mess."

"Oh?"

"The grandmother is taking care of them, but she's too old. D'Arcy's been going down a couple of times a week but that's going to have to stop. D'Arcy has to take care of herself."

The two of them went to the hospital the next day. Jim gave a pint of blood. Jack didn't; he said he had a cold. "Dangerous to give unless you're up to par."

"You look all right to me."

"You know your old pal Jack wouldn't back out unless he had to."

"You're a big Samaritan," said Jim, "on my blood."

"Have a steak tonight," said Jack. "You'll have it back by dessert."

"You know," said Jim, "Every time I get involved in something with you, I always have the feeling at the end I got taken somehow. Tom Power used to say that all the time too."

Jack just laughed. "You want to go over to the house?"

"Her house?"

"Yeah. You ever been there?"

"No."

"I thought you had a big romance with her."

"Down at the shore."

"Oh." Jack had a wise look.

"Jack, do you mind if I say something to you?"

"Sure."

"You're not going to stand on your clerical dignity?"

"Naw. Go on. Say it."

"Fuck you."

Jack slapped his leg and laughed so loud it echoed up and down the hospital corridor.

They drove to the neighborhood of 149th Street in the Bronx. Jack was driving his brother Charley's car, a brand new Oldsmobile, and he locked it carefully when they got out. They stood under the El and Jack pointed out the apartment on the third floor, just at the level of the train tracks. Down at street level, the main doorway was dingy and chalk-marked. There were a few tough-looking youths standing beside the entrance.

The grandmother answered the door, and she was a tiny size: only about four and a half feet tall. Both Jack and Jim had to bow down to shake hands with her. She was all white: white hair, white wrinkled face. Her dress went right to her shoe tops. She gave Jack a happy welcome, repeating his name several times, nodding her head up and down. Jack introduced Jim, and then Jack asked how the mother was, and the grandmother said she was better. She led them down a long, long hallway. In the rooms on either side, through closed doors, they could hear children.

They apartment was laid out in an L shape and when they got to the end of the long hallway, they turned left, which brought them to a living room. There were five girls there, the oldest about fourteen. Jack gave them a hearty welcome, and two came over to him. Three hung shyly back, the older ones. One giggled.

It seemed to Jim that Alaco was everywhere in the room. She was in three of the girls at least, with the black hair and the fair complexion and the blue eyes. One had Alaco's exact smile. In just Alaco's way, she smiled a little then caught it as if she was trying to stop it, and then let the smile unfold entirely. He could feel his stomach moving. There were three pictures of her in the room. One was a high school picture; she had long hair, with the curls resting right on her shoulders. In the second picture, her hair was cut to the level Jim knew and she was posing formally, probably a college picture. The third was a snapshot, framed, a color photo of her in the convent, or rather the novitiate. The camera caught her just at the moment of the suppression of the smile, and her face was all aglow as if she were keeping back something just too good to tell. She was beautiful. Even the convent outfit became her: the dress, not quite black, oxford gray, set off her skin tones.

Jim felt a feverish excitement; at the same time the voice of common sense was telling him that he couldn't spend much more time dreaming of this girl who was beyond recall. She should long since have faded into a happy memory. He shouldn't have come over here.

More of the children had come in. Jack flicked jabs at the boys, and made them flinch and laugh. He teased the girls. The children climbed all over him.

They stayed for an hour. Jim tried to imitate Jack's easy style with the children but failed. The children wouldn't warm to him. Then Jack completed his conquest by passing out Hershey bars he had bought just before coming up. Jim tried to talk to the fourteen-year-old girl, the one who smiled like Alaco—her name was Stephanie—but he only made her more shy with his stilted questions: Where do you go to school? What grade are you in? So he gave up and studied the three pictures again, and looked around at the furniture and the surroundings. The rug had a split in it. The walls needed painting; the door jambs were discolored with finger marks. He could see what Jack meant when he said the place was a mess.

On the car ride home Jack explained there was a boy of nineteen and another boy of sixteen in the family, but the next girl after Alaco was Stephanie. "The kids could do more," said Jack, "especially the girls, but the grandmother doesn't know how to discipline them."

"Aren't there any aunts or uncles they could parcel the kids out to for a while?"

"I guess not," said Jack, "or maybe the father won't let them split up. You can't blame him. He's a cop. My father knows him." Jim remembered Alaco saying her father was a policeman.

"Maybe they'll send Alaco home."

"Only as a last resort," said Jack. He looked over at Jim and smiled. "They don't like to let nuns out. There are too many horny guys running around."

"You should know."

Chapter 35

Red Harrigan called Sunday night with the plans for New Year's Eve. A celebration was being organized by the Ancient Order of Hibernians, Division 3, to be held at the Trocadero Ballroom on Dyckman Street in Manhattan, ten dollars a couple. That included turkey dinner and drinks. Jim said it sounded good. When he hung up, he tried to think of someone to call for a date. He couldn't think of anyone. He was on the point of calling Red back to see if his sister Peggy were free, when suddenly he thought of Jill. He certainly owed her a date, for all the favors she had done for him. The latest was the Black Seducer; undoubtedly it had been her pressure on Jack which induced him to turn it over.

He went to see her.

"I'm sorry Jim," she told him. "Dan Morissey asked me already."

So that was that.

He called Red back and asked about Peggy. Red laughed. Peggy had been the Fordham homecoming queen in the fall. She had about ten guys beating the door down.

He found his old telephone book. But three and a half years had ended its usefulness. All the girls listed were married, or moved, or else he couldn't bring himself to call them. None had been exceptional even four years ago. They didn't ignite any flames now.

Tom Power was going to Washington on Wednesday morning. Jim decided he might as well leave for Washington at the same time, and forget about the New Year's party. He talked about it with his father. "Go on. What is there to keep you here?" the father told him.

"You don't mind being alone?"

"What have I been for the last couple of years?"

"It's all right then?"

"Of course. Don't worry about me."

So Jim called up Tom and offered him a ride to Washington in the Black Seducer. "Thanks," Tom replied. "I'll take the Greyhound."

"What do you want to take the bus for, when you got a car ride?"

"That heap won't make Washington."

Jim had to argue with him for an hour. When he did accept the ride, it was only reluctantly.

On Wednesday, December 30th, they set out from New York over the George Washington Bridge and down the New Jersey Turnpike. They had to stay in the slow lane, for the car bucked when pushed over fifty; but at fifty it was steady, if noisy.

"What did South stick you for it?"

"He gave it to me for nothing."

"There must be something wrong." Tom looked the car over again. "Tires must be about to blow."

"No, they've got tread. Relax, will you?"

There wasn't a leaf on a tree, and down in South Jersey the ground was just stubble covered with hoarfrost, so it wasn't very picturesque, but Jim was in an exuberant mood and it colored the landscape. He was starting his career; he was on his way to Broadway via Washington. "Beautiful day, eh?"

Tom roused himself, and leaned forward to look up through the windshield. "Huh?"

They stopped for lunch at the last Howard Johnson's restaurant on the turnpike before reaching Delaware. By that time Jim had talked for an hour about the Navy; Tom had told him stories about medical school and was talking about his fiancée, Connie Corcoran. "We should be married now," said Tom. "I wanted to get married last summer."

Jim tried to form a mental picture of Connie. He couldn't. She had been a college girl waitress at the shore but in the years since the summer at Mallard Lake she had become a blur.

"Have you set a date?"

"This June."

"That's better, isn't it? You'll be finished medical school then."

"It wouldn't have been that hard. We could have got through."

Jim had heard the story from Red and D'Arcy, but Tom seemed to think Jim didn't know anything about it, so Jim let him go on.

"She wants to finish nursing school," said Tom.

"They can't get married in nursing school?"

"Naw. But what does she need the nursing degree for? I'm not going to let her work anyway."

"It doesn't seem unreasonable to want to finish after putting in two years."

"That wasn't it," said Tom. "She figured she had to wait four years for me, so I could wait a year for her. That's the way women figure. That's the way they are."

They got to Washington about three in the afternoon. It was a thrill for Jim when they finally got into the city and he could see the United States Capitol building at the end of the long wide avenue. They drove out to Tom's place in Georgetown. "There shouldn't be anybody else back," said Tom. "You can stay for a couple of days." His apartment was on M Street near the Key Bridge, a dumpy second floor flat that he shared with two other medical students. It was located over an appliance store. Tom called Connie right away. Jim thought they would have a long conversation after the separation. Instead, the entire conversation on Tom's part consisted of "Ten minutes. Okay?" Then he hung up. There were advantages in going with a girl for years, Jim thought. No time wasted in superfluous greetings.

They drove up Wisconsin Avenue through the heart of Georgetown. Jim was anxious to see the section after hearing so much about it over the years. But Tom was the worst possible guide. "Phonies," he commented once or twice as he looked over the people on the street. They turned on Reservoir Road and drove past the Ursuline School and pulled into the driveway of the Georgetown Nursing School. Connie was waiting for them and she came bounding down the steps. As soon as he saw her, she came right back into focus for Jim, and he was surprised how little she had changed. Only the hair was different; it was cut short. She was only a little over five feet, but curvy and pretty. Tom kissed her and then she came over and kissed Jim. "How *are* you? It's so good to *see* you." She had a nice girlish enthusiasm, accented by a college girl outfit of a blue denim skirt and a madras blouse. "How was the Navy?"

"Well, you know."

"You look very good."

"Thank you. You look terrific."

She got in the front seat between them. "Did you have a nice vacation?" she asked Tom.

"Yeah," Tom replied, with a New York "Yeah." "But I had to study."

She put her hand on the back of his neck and she turned to Jim and said, "He's so persecuted."

"If I hadn't gone into training, I never would have found out what a racket the medical students have," said Connie.

"Come on."

"Where are we going?" Connie asked.

"Get something to eat, I guess."

"Chat 'n' Nibble?" she asked.

"I don't care."

"It's a cheap place where the medical students go," Connie explained to Jim.

"That's for me."

In the Chat 'n' Nibble, they joined a crowd of medical students who were giving the proprietor a difficult time. They sat at the tables in front of the delicatessen counters and shouted, "What've you got tonight?"

"Toikey," said the owner, a stout, red-faced man.

"Let's have it."

"It's not ready yet."

"You got soup?"

"Toikey soup."

"Let's have it."

"Come up and get it," he shouted. "You want I should serve you?"

"The prices you charge, Luke, you should give service."

"You don't know what you're talking about," yelled Luke. "I'm losing money."

They lined up for the soup. "You want kow-tow service, go to the Hot Shoppe," Luke cried as he ladled it out.

One student asked, "What kind of soup is this?"

"Toikey," replied another student, imitating Luke.

"See, I told you it was toikey soup," said a third. "I thought I saw a piece of toikey."

"Where? Where? I don't believe it," cried the other students.

Luke's face was beet-red. "Lissen, there's more toikey in that soup than anything you get in the Hot Shoppe. You don't like it, go to the Hot Shoppe."

"Easy there, Luke. Easy."

"Watch that ulcer."

"You should get that ulcer operated on."

"Get it cut out, Luke babe."

"That's what you want!" Luke shouted, his finger in the air, his eyes bulging. "You want to get me on a table and start sticking knives in me."

"We'll carve you cheap."

"That's right," Luke yelled. "Carve! Carve! Carve! That's all the doctors want to do." He hammered the counter.

The boys sat back and laughed.

Connie had her hands up, cradling her cheeks, and she was shaking her head. "It's terrible the way they tease the poor man."

"Stella!" Luke shouted to the back. "Come out here."

"I can't," a woman answered. "My hair is up."

"Come out whichever way you are," Luke yelled.

His wife came out. She was also stout. She had her hair in huge rollers and a bandana on her head. To cover her embarrassment, she did a dance step and cried out to the students, "I'm the Queen of Sheba!"

"Forget the Queen of Sheba," Luke yelled. "Bring some soup to Tom over there and Connie and their friend. They didn't even get soup yet."

"We'll come up and get it, Luke," Tom shouted.

"Sit there and shut up. She'll bring it to you."

A youth called for a hamburger.

Another warned him. "Don't eat the hamburger. Not 'till the milkman finds his horse."

"Hey Luke, what happened to the milkman's horse?"

"French fries, Luke."

"Carve me a thick piece of toikey, eh? That last one you almost missed."

"What are you giving me there, just gristle?"

"Green beans."

I recognize that pie. That's the same one you had in the case last week."

"This toikey wasn't killed. It died."

"All right!" Luke cried. He slammed down the carving knife. He left the counter and went to a pinball machine and began to play it. The machine sounded with a metallic "ping, ping" as the balls bounced off the markers, and the lights flashed on the backboard. When he had played once through, Luke put another nickel in and continued to play.

Stella came over with the bowls of soup and put them down in front of Connie and Tom. "He's crazy," she confided to them. "Punch drunk."

The boys had quieted down. They selected one student as spokesman. His voice carried across the restaurant. "Hey Luke, we're sorry. Come back and tell us all is forgiven."

Luke gave his answer in a voice loud enough to be heard across the street. He didn't turn around, however. He spoke to the pinball machine. "When the jokers decide they'd rather have dinner than tell jokes, and when the wise guys want to keep their mouths shut, then we serve."

"Okay Luke. Whatever you say."

"I'm on duty in half an hour," came a plaintive voice.

Luke returned to his post.

In a minute, the noise was as loud as it was before.

Connie and Tom and Jim got their turkey dinner. When they were finished, Tom went behind the counter to talk to Luke.

Connie said to Jim, "Tom always says he would have lost his mind in medical school without Luke. He says when he was about ready to crack a lot of times, he'd just come over here and laugh at Luke for an hour."

"A lot of the guys crack, eh?" Jim asked.

"Oh yes," said Connie. "They study like mad for weeks and then they go drinking. Then they study like mad. Then they go drinking. It's like a cycle. Tom doesn't drink but he felt the pressure. He's very thin, isn't he?"

"No. He looks good."

"He's very thin. He needs a regular life." The air tensed for a moment. "Do you think I'm doing the wrong thing?"

"What do you mean?" Jim asked.

"Am I doing the wrong thing by finishing my nursing degree? Should I just quit now?"

"No," said Jim honestly. "I can't see any sense in going for two years and not finishing."

They drove downtown to a place called the Bavarian on Eleventh Street which was a swing-your-stein-and-sing-your-college-song tavern. It wasn't too crowded—"The college kids are all home," said Tom—but the patrons who were there were in New Year's spirits. A three-man band dressed in Alpine shorts and knee socks cut away at the shins played Viennese waltzes and "Drink, Drink, Drink."

Connie and Tom were engrossed in each other, holding hands, singing, looking into each other's eyes. Jim felt out of things, and he looked around for a single girl, but there were only couples in the place.

It was only 9:30 when Connie and Tom called it an evening. Jim drove them to the nurses' residence. Tom got out there too and said he would walk to his apartment when he left Connie. "Go on down to a place on 13th Street," he told Jim, "called O'Malley's Irish Heaven. You'll have a good time down there."

Chapter 36

Jim headed back downtown and at 10:30 arrived at O'Malley's Irish Heaven.

He could hear the accordion music from the street. Up a long flight of stairs was a sign which proclaimed "The Only Authentic Irish Pub in America." Jim went in and was met with a blast of accordion music and singing. There were rebel yells and shouts all around him as he shouldered his way through the jam-packed crowd to the bar. He got a beer. He turned around. There was a girl on her hands and knees foraging under the table directly behind him. A beefy man with a size 17 neck was patting her on the backside, saying, "There's a grand heifer. There's a grand heifer." The bartender came out from his post and got down on his hands and knees and asked her, "What are you doing under there, sweetheart?"

"I lost my hat," she said, wrinkling her nose at him.

They searched around until she found it. She stood up and smoothed out the wrinkles in her skirt. Then she pointed out the man who had been patting her backside and she said to the bartender, "That man was annoying me."

The bartender grabbed the man by the seat of the pants and the back of the collar and hustled him at a half-trot right out the door. The girl put the hat on her head with a satisfied look, gave it a push down with the flat of her hand and walked to the back.

There could be no doubt, thought Jim as he looked around, of the authenticity of the Irish Celtic faces. On one side of him at the bar there was a man with a brick-red complexion singing as loud as he could with his face turned up toward the ceiling and his eyes shut. On the other side, there was a little man with a burly chin set at an angle, and as he sang he held his shoulders self-consciously squared and he bit off the words of the song with a pugnacious look on his face.

Two strong Irish fellows nearby were trying to impress two pretty greenhorn girls sitting at a table a few feet away. They were arguing with each other to attract the girls' attention. One of the boys had on a tweed suit with creaseless trousers, and he had his finger in the air and he was proclaiming to his friend: "Ai do not shrink from this ress-pons-a-bill-a-tee. Ai welcome it." He glanced at the girls to see if they were paying attention.

Jim went back to the back of the bar and the accordion medley was still going on. He found himself next to a wizened old man whose face was a mass of wrinkles. The lines on the sides of his temples were like the tributaries of a river leading into his eye sockets. He held a shot of whisky with a trembling hand. Turning to Jim, he smiled and said, "Ah, the dirty drink," and he poured the whisky into a glass of beer and drank it.

Jim saw another fascinated spectator of this operation, a young man about the same age as himself. "Powerful," Jim commented to this fellow, who had a mass of freckles on a big face, and laughing brown eyes, and a grin that showed big, firm-rooted teeth.

"Set you out of your mind," he answered Jim.

"Boilermaker."

"Is that what they call it?"

"That's what they call it in New York."

"Is that where you're from, New York?" he asked Jim.

"Yes. How about yourself?" Jim knew already from his lack of a brogue that he wasn't Irish-born.

"I'm from D.C. here."

"Jim Meagher." He put out his hand.

"Neil Cleary."

They got to talking. Cleary was very genial. Jim bought him a beer and Cleary bought him one back. He told Jim he went to George Washington law school. During the conversation, Cleary said hello to a dozen persons who passed. He seemed to know everyone in the place. "Where are you staying?"

"I'm staying with medical students for tonight and maybe tomorrow night. I have to find a place."

"Well, you can stay at our house," said Cleary.

"Where's that?"

"Georgetown. Canal Street. The basement is open. I lived there for a year. It's not bad. Thirty a month."

"I was thinking of registering at Catholic U. next semester. That's pretty far from Georgetown."

"It's not that far," said Cleary, "And Georgetown is the only place to live."

One of the men Cleary had greeted earlier stopped to talk. Cleary introduced him as Conor O'Hara; this new arrival did have a brogue, a deep, rich one.

"I just heard a good story," said O'Hara. "It's about this lady who was over in London in a hotel there. She was walking down the corridor of the hotel and she gets into the elevator, the lift as they call it. The operator shuts the door. He no sooner starts the elevator down than the woman begins hitting him on the arm, and shouting, "My husband! My husband! My husband is up there. You shut the door right in his face. Stop the elevator! My husband!"

The operator turns to her and says very calmly, "Madam, this is a lift. Not the Titanic."

The boys laughed. Conor was in his mid-twenties, scholarly looking. He had a gentleness in his manner that was immediately appealing.

"Do you know who used to tell that joke?" O'Hara went on. "Fred Allen, when he was on the radio. He had a grand, sly wit, that man."

Conor asked Jim his plans in Washington and Jim told him. Then Conor was pulled away to another group by someone who wanted to make an introduction. Jim was sorry to see him go. "He's a nice guy, isn't he?"

"Great guy," said Cleary. "His father's the Irish Ambassador."

A girl passed just then and Cleary called her, "Hey Barbara."

"Oh, hello Neil."

She was a slim, clean-looking blonde. She was the best Jim had seen all evening.

"How you doing?" Cleary asked.

Jim tried to get a look at her legs but it was difficult in the close quarters.

"I'm fine," she said. "You still going to parties?"

"Make 'em all," said Cleary. "Make 'em all."

It was apparent after a few minutes that Cleary wasn't going out of his way to make an introduction, so Jim introduced himself. "Would you care for a drink?" he asked Barbara.

"No, no thanks."

After a minute or two of conversation it was obvious she was out of place in O'Malley's. She might have wandered in from a cocktail party. She had a straight, level gaze.

"Do you go to New York much?" Jim asked.

"No, not much. What brought you down here?"

"I'm going to study playwriting."

"Well, good luck," she said and she walked off.

Jim was left with his next sentence hanging in his mouth. He watched her go and got a look at her legs and decided, in his annoyance, they had as much shape as Parker pens.

"Who's she?" he asked Cleary.

"She lives next door to us in Georgetown. With four other girls. Well, three now. One just got married."

The next round he bought, Jim brought a beer over to Conor. "Thank you," said Conor. "Down the jolly old hatch," he toasted. He took a long draught.

"You're the Ambassador's son?"

"So t'is said."

"Would my father love to meet you."

"As the girl said to the tinker. Come on over to the bar and let me buy you a drink too. Ah, that New York is a lovely city."

Conor knew the bartender of course. He was a curly-haired youth named Desmond.

"Sing us an old song," Conor urged Desmond.

Others took up the plea.

"Come on, Des."

"Give out, man."

"If I had a voice like you, Des, they'd be no quieting me."

But Desmond refused. "I'm too busy." Though, at the moment, he was doing nothing.

"Come on man."

"He has a lovely voice."

"Clear as a bugle."

"Turn around and pay no attention to him," Conor said to Jim. "He'll sing in a minute." So they turned their backs to the bar. Sure enough, in a minute's time, Des began to sing.

"He's a bit shy," Conor said in a low voice.

Des' tenor had real clarity of tone and it was a pleasure to listen to him. He sang a standard tune, "Galway Bay." Then he sang poetry called "The Lark in the Clear Air." A hush came over the crowd, then silence, to listen to him. It was an amazing thing in that raucous mass of people. When the song was ended, Des reached beneath the bar and pulled out several bottles of beer and started opening them with furious activity. He paid no heed to the applause.

Conor had been called to the telephone. He came back and said to Cleary, "A game. Are you for it?"

"Sure."

"Get Black Tom," said Conor. Cleary went to the back.

While they waited for Cleary, Conor asked Jim, "Would you care to play a game of poker?"

"Sure."

"Grand."

Cleary came back with Black Tom, a tiny, thin Irishman in a baggy suit in his fifties. He was fair-skinned but his nickname was apt, for he hadn't shaved in a day or two, and he had a shock of dark, unkempt hair hanging down over his forehead. He was making comments to Cleary as they advanced through the bar and, even though Tom had a deadpan expression, Cleary was laughing. Tom blinked his eyes as if he couldn't get used to the light.

"Ah, you Tom Potts," Conor cried.

Black Tom lifted one eyebrow. "Is it at Lahiff's?"

"Aye."

"That old divil," said Tom. "He's crazy for the cards."

Jim was introduced. Just before they left, Tom Potts filled his flask at the bar. Outside, they all got into Conor's car, and Conor roared the car up Massachusetts Avenue. He was a wild driver. "Bejaysus," cried Tom, who was sitting next to him in the front seat, "Let me out and take a taxi. When it comes to driving an au-to-mo-bile, you haven't a clue."

In between taking sips on his flask, he lectured them. "What are three young fellows like you doing looking for a card game. When I was your age, I was up in the hayloft where I belonged, slapping the saddle on some lass."

"Be off with you," Conor answered.

"I'm not much of a poker player," said Jim. He was getting nervous.

"None of us is any good," said Conor reassuringly.

"We'd blush at the sight of a card," said Black Tom.

Cleary nudged Jim in the back seat. "I live down that street," he said, pointing off the avenue.

Black Tom turned around. "Have you a home, Cleary? Sure and me thinking you did nothing but go from party to party and sleep on other people's couches."

"Where are we now?" Jim asked.

"We're going out Massachusetts Avenue," said Conor. "We'll be passing the embassy in a moment. There it is, over there. The home of saints and scholars."

"Sharpies and tinkers," cried Tom Potts. "Kitty Barry would find a welcome there. They'd pick your drawers and leave your pants."

"You old rogue," said Conor. "Be quiet."

Shortly after they passed the embassy, Conor turned into a long driveway and rode up to a white Georgian mansion.

"Is this where we're going to play cards?" Jim asked.

"It is," said Conor.

"Who is this Lahiff?"

"Senator Lahiff."

Jim hadn't made the connection at all between the name Lahiff and United States Senator Clinton Lahiff. Even as he stood there in front of the mansion, he suspected that maybe they were pulling his leg. Playing cards with a United States Senator?

They went up the steps and Conor touched the button and chimes sounded inside. The light came on in the foyer and the door opened and there was a white-haired, sweet-looking woman in a flowered dressing gown.

"Good evening, Mrs. Lahiff," said Conor.

"Good evening, Conor," she said softly. "Come in. He's expecting you."

She brought them in. She greeted them all in turn. "Go make yourselves at home. He's working upstairs. I'll tell him you're here."

Conor led them down to a game room in the basement. In the middle of the room was a felt-covered card table. In back of it was a leather couch and two chairs and a coffee table set out with cocktail frankfurters and cheese wedges and peanuts and potato chips. At the far end of the room was a bar with several high stools. Black Tom perched himself up on a bar stool. Cleary headed for the cocktail frankfurters and the cheese wedges. "What did I tell you?" cried Tom. "Look at him go for the food. That's his dinner. When he's finished that, he'll go to sleep on the couch and tomorrow night it will be somewhere else."

Conor sat down at the card table and shuffled one of the decks. "Fix yourself a drink," he said to Jim.

"I'll wait a while," said Jim. He sat down at the table. "Do you know the Senator well?"

"He's a friend of the family," said Conor.

"Do you play here a lot?"

"Once in a while," said Conor. "He works hard, the poor old man. We come over and give him a bit of fun. Ah, you'll see. You'll like him. He's very decent."

"The old divil. He's crazy for the cards," said Black Tom. Tom's feet came down only to the rung of the chair. He had one leg crossed over the other and he looked like he owned the world. Conor hushed him, though he was grinning at the same time. "He'll be down any minute," Conor warned.

"I should never have come," said Tom. "What time is it?"

"Half-twelve," said Conor.

"I'll get home at four in the morning," said Tom, "and the wife will be raging. She'll rear up in the bed and demand me whereabouts. 'I've been having a con-sul-ta-tion with a Senator,' I'll tell her. 'The way it is in this country, it's not like the old country, they have an appreciation of your old Tom here. When there's a problem to be settled, the Senators call in old Tom for a bit of con-sul-ta-tion.'"

"It's only right," agreed Conor.

"The answer I get from her will be a bit of mockery. 'Sure there's such a shortage of cracked wits in this country they have to call you in.' 'Indeed 'n' that's true,' I'll tell her. 'Bejaysus, she'll answer, 'You're not worth tuppence.' 'A fine bit of treachery,' I'll tell her, 'from the woman who twenty years since went screaming the length of Ireland telling all who'd listen t'was Tom Potts or the convent.' God spare us, as it turned out, t'was Tom Potts."

"Pay no attention to the old cod," said Conor to Jim. "His wife's a lovely woman."

"I don't want to give the impression we haven't had our happy days," Tom continued. "There was a time during the war we were as happy as two jaybirds. I was working in a factory in England, and she was working on the farm in Ireland, and we had the Irish Sea between us. Do you know how much I was making in those days, Conor?"

"How much?"

"Twenty pounds a week."

"That was good money."

"Indeed 'n' I'm telling you it was good money. It would be equal to one hundred fifty dollars a week in this country now."

"It would, that," Conor agreed.

Tom looked over at Cleary, who was just finishing his repast. "Have you had enough?"

"That was all right," said Cleary. "Good cheese."

"Why don't you go over and give a holler upstairs," Tom advised, "and see if she won't bring you down a wedge of pie for dessert."

Suddenly they quieted. The Senator was coming down the stairs. "How are you boys!" He spoke so loud it made the hushed tones they had been using seem foolish. They all stood up. He was a long, rangy man, somewhat stooped, easily seventy years old, with a full head of snow-white hair. His face was long, something of a horse face, and his nose was prominent. His expression was kindly and he seemed genuinely delighted to see them. He took Conor's hand. "Now, wasn't that nice of you to come over?"

"The pleasure is ours, Senator."

"Tom," said the Senator, "how are you?"

"Fine, sir. Fine." There was an unwonted respect in Tom's tone and his stance was stiff and straight.

Cleary came striding across the room and shook hands with the Senator. Conor introduced Jim as his friend.

"Nice to see you, Jim," the Senator told him. "You should feel that you are at home."

When they all had a drink—the Senator got a bottle of beer—they sat down for the game. They played five card stud, nickel and dime, with a two raise limit, so the pots were small, usually only a dollar or two.

They told stories. Conor told of his university days in Cork City in Ireland. "We ran a candidate for mayor. A simple sort of fellow. He decided there was a situation in downtown Cork that would make an ideal campaign issue. There were public restrooms built for the men but none for the women. He got up on the platform in front of a mob of people, and he cried out to the women with his finger raised in the air: 'You vote for me as your number one and I'll take care of your number two!'"

The Senator told of Teddy Roosevelt's campaign for president. "When he came to our city, we walked into the rally with a moose head and we had teddy bears strung up on poles and we started yelling 'Bull Moose! Bull Moose!' and you should have heard that crowd!" The Senator sat back in the chair and laughed delightedly at the scene that was recreating itself in his mind. They laughed with him.

By one in the morning Jim was down seven dollars. Even though he told stories and enjoyed himself, he played seriously and very cautiously. If he didn't have a good card in the hole, he just dropped out. Black Tom played just the opposite; he would try to bluff with nothing and he was down at least twelve dollars. Conor O'Hara and Neil Cleary were both winning.

Black Tom decided that, if he was to recoup, he would have to get more money on the table. "We'll have a ten cent a man ante," he announced.

They looked at the Senator. "That's no way to play poker," said the Senator. So that was that. The question wasn't even brought up again.

Shortly after two in the morning the Senator got up. "An old man has to get his sleep. No! No! You fellows stay right there. Finish up the game." He shook hands with each man in turn. He thanked them for coming. Then he went up to bed.

They had all had enough of the game except for Black Tom. "Ten cents a man ante," said Tom.

"I think we have all had enough," said Conor.

"What are you talking about?" asked Black Tom.

"We'll go over to my place," suggested Conor. "We'll have a cup of tea."

"Piss on your tea!" said Black Tom. "Sit down here and deal the cards."

They laughed at him.

"Come on now," said Conor.

Tom was disgusted. He went to the bar and filled his flask with the Senator's bourbon. "Did I ever see the like of this group? Well, ask me no more for your ladies' games."

"You won the last time," said Conor. "Shut up with ye."

Tom put the bottle of bourbon in his side pocket.

"You're not going to take that?"

"Indeed I am. Him and his 'no ante.' Bull Moose! Bull Moose indeed."

Tom turned his face up toward the top of the stairs where the Senator had disappeared. "Bull Moose your ass!"

They took the bottle off him, laughing and hushing him at the same time, and replaced it on the shelf, and got him up the stairs and out to the car. He rolled down the window and cried, "Bull Moose! You and your no ante. Bull Moose!"

Conor raced the car down the driveway. Tom continued to rant: "It's a fine thing when the people of this country will send a man to Washington with no more thought in his head than to take the last tosser off Tom Potts. Bull Moose your ass, you old divil."

It only took them a few minutes to get to the Irish Embassy. Tea at the Irish Embassy, thought Jim. Wouldn't Florence and Aunt Nora preen their feathers and buy new clothes if they were invited to tea at the Irish Embassy? Though, to be sure, Jim thought, this wouldn't be a very formal tea.

Conor gave them a warning. "Care now not to wake Kathleen or Juanita or Graciela." Kathleen, Jim found out, was Conor's sister. The other two were the house staff. Earlier in the evening, Conor had told the Senator his mother and father were in Cleveland where the Ambassador had a speaking engagement.

Conor brought them to a large room in the rear with glass doors opening on the back lawn. There were potted palms and a piano. Cleary stretched out on the couch and shut his eyes and Black Tom stood over him. "What did I tell you? He's there for the night now."

"Be quiet," said Cleary, not opening his eyes.

"Make yourself at home, Cleary."

"He's relaxed," said Jim.

"You're liable to find him anywhere," said Tom. "Sure the president has to wait in the White House in the morning for Cleary to finish using the bathroom."

Conor came in from the kitchen. "The kettle is boiling."

The side door opened and Kathleen, Conor's sister, arrived. She had a bathrobe on. "What are you doing up?" Conor asked.

"I heard you come in."

She was a pretty girl of seventeen or eighteen, with bangs in her hair and a white bow in front. She got a high compliment from Cleary: he sat up on the couch.

"Hello boys." She knew them all except Jim. Conor introduced him. "This is Jim Meagher. He's from New York." She gave him a nod.

She looked at Black Tom and laughed. He himself laughed, and when Jim saw Tom's brown teeth for the first time, he realized that Black Tom hadn't smiled before this all evening long. "Come over here," cried Tom, "and sit on my lap." She did, too. She bounded across the room and plunked right down. But she bounced right back up again.

"What a smell of drink."

"Get off with your smelling. Come back here." He patted his leg. She bounced to the middle of the floor. Jim wished she'd sit in his lap, and wished he had enough courage to ask.

"Where have ye all been?"

"We've been attending to affairs of state," said Tom.

"Indeed. Drinking and carousing."

"We played a bit of cards with the Senator," said Conor.

"Did he take you again?"

"The old divil," said Tom. He got angry as he thought about it. "He's as tight as a crab's ass. And that's watertight."

"A nice way to be talking," said Kathleen.

"T'is true. Come over here now and sit down."

"I won't."

"Ah, you sassy little thing."

"Did you lose, Conor?"

"I won."

"Good."

"Give us an old jig," cried Tom.

"Yeah," said Cleary. He started to clap a rhythm. He hadn't shown such energy all night.

"Is there no one to play the piano?" asked Tom. "Meagher, you play?"

"I can play 'The Irish Washerwoman,'" said Jim.

"Good," said Conor. "I don't think Juanita would mind."

"Not too fast, now," Kathleen warned.

So Jim played and she danced, skillfully crossing her ankles and weaving them back and forth. When it was finished, she called out breathlessly, "That was good, Meagher from New York."

"Thank you."

Black Tom stood up and gave her a handclap. "What wouldn't I give? What wouldn't I give to be eighteen again?"

"Be off with you," said Kathleen, her face flushed with her success. "I'll get tea." She ran out to the kitchen and Conor followed her. They came back in and Kathleen was carrying a silver tray with tea and cookies. Jim and Neil Cleary and Conor and Kathleen drank the tea while Black Tom swigged from his flask and mocked them.

Conor drove them downtown then. It was a quarter to five. Jim fell asleep in the car. The next thing he knew, Conor was shaking him. "We're here now, Jim. Show me where your car is."

Jim thanked him.

"We'll meet again tomorrow night. Well, later tonight," said Conor. "There'll be New Year's parties all over the city."

"Swell," said Jim.

"We'll meet here at O'Malley's at nine."

Chapter 37

Jim got lost several times going back to Georgetown. He went around Dupont Circle three times. Finally he got to M Street and passed Wisconsin Avenue, which he recognized, and he drove on to Tom's place. He arrived just before 6 in the morning.

Tom was already up, dressed in his medical scrubs, sitting in the kitchen having breakfast. There was an English muffin on the table and he was spreading jelly on it.

"What a night," said Jim.

"What'd you do?"

"I met an Irish crew at O'Malley's."

"What else?"

"I met the son of the Irish ambassador."

"Oh yeah."

"A nice guy."

"I heard that," said Tom.

"That's only the start of it," said Jim. "I played cards with a Senator."

"Who?"

"Clinton Lahiff." Jim told him the story of the poker game.

"That was your chance," said Tom. "You should have asked him for a job. Those guys have all kinds of connections."

"It didn't seem like the thing to do."

"Call him up," said Tom.

"I couldn't do that."

"I would," said Tom, continuing with his breakfast.

"Well," Jim replied, doubtfully.

"It's a good thing you stayed out," said Tom. "Two guys came back last night. All the beds were full."

"There's no place to sleep?"

"You can use mine."

"I got a tip on a place here in Georgetown. On Canal Street."

"How much?"

"Thirty a month."

"That's good."

"I figured it was." Jim was trying to break one of the muffins. "How long has this been here?"

"Put it in the toaster. It'll get soft."

Tom was in great spirits. Jim remembered in the old days when they were down at the shore Tom was always happy in the morning and would get cranky in the evening, just the opposite of most of the guys.

Tom showed him the bed and Jim stripped to shorts and a tee shirt and climbed in and fell asleep in seconds.

When he awoke, the sun was shining bright and the windows were closed, and the room was stuffy and dry from the steam heating, and he had a terrible headache. He reached over for his watch. Just past noon. He counted back. Only six hours sleep. He tried to fall asleep again but he couldn't. He went out to get a drink of water to quench his thirst. In the living room he found a guy and a girl sitting together on the couch. "Oh, excuse me." He ducked back in the bedroom and started to get dressed. The guy came in. "Who are you?"

"I'm a friend of Tom Power. Jim Meagher."

"Howie." He held out his hand. "Howie Nugent."

"I'm sorry."

"She doesn't care. Come out and meet her. Her name's Martha."

"I better put my pants on."

Martha wore her hair in a bun and she looked very prim. The boy wore khakis and a white sports shirt. He had carrot-colored hair and freckles and looked, Jim thought, a little like the movie actor Van Johnson.

He introduced Jim to Martha and then Jim went to the kitchen. He was longing for some cold juice and bacon and eggs, but there was nothing in the refrigerator.

Howie said goodbye to Martha at the door and came to the kitchen. "Nothing much to eat."

"I could really go for some bacon and eggs," said Jim.

"Me too."

"Let's go down the drug store," Jim suggested.

"I'm broke. I'm waiting for a check."

"I'll buy," said Jim.

Howie felt one of the English muffins. He tossed it out the window. "Okay."

At People's Drug Store, they had two fifty-nine-cent specials: bacon, eggs, toast and coffee. Howie was a second year medical student and he told Jim about medical school. "The only way to beat it is with a schedule. You've got to pound the books right away. A third of the class got lopped off last year. They were trying to cram at the end. You just can't do it. I almost went down in Bio-chem. That was the rough one."

"Are you studying during the vacation?"

"Sure. I'm going to take a break tonight though. Maybe see a flick with Martha."

"You want some dough?"

"Naw. Martha'll pay."

"Does she work?"

"Naw. She's in my class."

"Oh."

"She's a good kid, Martha. We were on the same lab team last year. Working on the cadavers."

Jim laughed. "You cut up the bodies together?"

"Yeah."

"That must have been embarrassing."

"Naw. Martha's a good kid. That doesn't bother her. That's what I was trying to tell you when you came out to the living room that time. You don't have to worry about Martha."

When they got back to the apartment, Howie showed him albums of stamps. "I've been collecting them for years," said Howie, as Jim looked through them. "If things really get rough, I can always unload them. I wouldn't want to though."

It was now after one. "I better get going," said Jim. "I got to find a place to live." So he gathered his stuff in the bedroom and brought it down to the car.

He headed to Canal Street, following directions he got from Howie. The street was a pretty one, with red brick sidewalks, ancient trees, and Georgetown-style homes crowded together, each with its clapboard shutters and gaslight and black-painted iron grill fence. He took out the slip that Cleary had given him and found the house and walked up the three steps to the front door. There was no bell so he hammered with the knocker, an iron replica of the mocking-faced muse of comedy. He could hear someone coming inside. The door was pulled open with sudden force. A hand came out at him. "Blatt," said the face behind the outthrust hand. "Barney Blatt."

Jim stepped back in surprise. He shook the hand. "Jim Meagher."

"What can I do for you, Trigger?"

Blatt, a young man about Jim's age, was wearing a cowboy suit; blue denim pants, blue denim Eisenhower jacket, a wide leather belt with a huge buckle, and ankle-high, narrow-heeled boots. He had funny eyes, starey, and he had his face thrust right up against Jim's.

"I'm looking for a room."

"Mrs. Hug is out."

"Will she be back soon?"

"Well, I don't know. I don't think she has anything open though."

"Does a fellow named Cleary live here?"

"Yeah. Neil Cleary. He sent you?"

"He said something about the basement."

Blatt turned and yelled upstairs for Cleary but there was no response. "Come on in. I'll take you down there. It's a rat hole."

They went through the living room and down the stairway.

"Where you from, Trigger?"

"New York."

"I'm from Montana," said Blatt.

"Oh, cowboy country."

"Yeah. How old are you?"

"Twenty-four."

"Do you have any insurance?" Blatt asked.

"No."

"About time you got some, Trigger."

Was it possible Blatt was an insurance salesman? It was a strange thing to ask someone you've just met, Jim thought. But insurance salesman would have been the last profession Jim would have picked for him.

He was. "Now is the time to buy insurance, when you're young," Blatt continued. "We'll talk about it later. A guy like you is the kind of guy I like to write up, because I know I'm doing him a favor."

"I'm kind of low on finances right now."

"Listen, Trigger. Nobody's ever too poor for a good investment."

"I can wait a while, I guess."

"That's just the point. You can't wait."

Jim was glad when they got to the basement. There was a large boiler there and a bed next to it. There were empty soda and beer cans thrown around the floor. The place was really squalid.

"This is it?"

"I warned you."

Toward the front there was another room. It too was filled with cartons and junk, but it had two windows that opened out on the street, at sidewalk level. "Cleary wouldn't sleep in here," said Blatt. "Said it was too cold."

"Thanks for showing it to me anyway," said Jim.

"Come on upstairs. I want to talk to you."

Jim was spared the sales talk, because Mrs. Hug was now in the living room. She was a woman of sixty with fluttery hands and mobile eyebrows. Her clothes, however, were anything but those of an elderly woman; she was wearing a red and white striped cotton tee shirt and slacks. "Well, aren't you Randolph!"

"Excuse me?" said Jim.

"Randolph," she said again, and she smiled at him.

"Mrs. Hug," said Blatt, "This is Jim. . .uh. . .what was your name again?"

"Meagher."

"Meagher. Talk loud. She's a little deaf."

"You look just like my Randolph."

"I just showed him the basement!" he shouted.

"Forty five a month."

"No thanks," said Jim, shaking his head.

"You can't find anything cheaper in Georgetown," she said.

"Thanks for letting me see it anyway."

"He's a friend of Cleary's," Blatt shouted.

"Forty a month."

Jim shook his head no and started for the door.

"Thirty-five," she called, smiling winningly, and quoting the price like a daytime television emcee.

Jim was at the door.

"Thirty," she said. "That's what Cleary paid when he lived down there."

Jim stopped. It really was cheap. He didn't have too much money either. He had blown all his savings from the Navy going to Broadway plays in New York. Maybe she would accept a week's rent, Jim thought. "Would it be all right if I tried it for a week?"

She didn't hear. Blatt shouted it at her.

"Certainly."

Jim paid her seven and a half dollars. "No girls," she cried.

"No, ma'am."

"You're a lovely young man." She looked at him affectionately. Jim nodded.

She turned to Blatt. "You introduce him to Mr. Cleary and Mr. Bigelow and Mr. Palmer."

"He knows Cleary," Blatt shouted. "He's a friend of Cleary's."

"You introduce him to Mr. Cleary and Mr. Bigelow and Mr. Palmer."

"Let's go, Trigger," said Blatt. They ascended the stairs. "She should have a hearing aid. Crazy old lady."

"Why doesn't she?"

"Beats the shit out of me. Thinks she's Gloria Swanson, I guess."

Jim turned on the stairway. Mrs. Hug waved to him.

Blatt peered in a door on the second floor. "Bigelow's not in. Cleary's out too. That's his room." He pointed to the door opposite Bigelow's.

"Mine's here," said Blatt. "Come on in. I want to talk to you."

"I better take a rain check. I got a lot to do."

"Okay, Trigger. If you want to go up to the third floor, you can see Palmer up there. I wouldn't go near the bastard."

"Why?"

"The lover," said Blatt scornfully. "The big party boy."

Jim waited until Blatt was in his room with the door closed, and then climbed to the third floor. The door was open. He went in. He caught his breath. Compared to the rest of the house, Palmer's apartment was a palace. There was a thick white carpet wall-to-wall. The couch, Danish modern, had orange, red and yellow striped upholstery. In front of the couch was a coffee table of green marble. Over by the front window was an oak-paneled bar with three stools in front of it. Along the wall was a bookcase with elaborate stone supports at each end, and the bottom shelf was a tank of tropical fish, barely illumined. A stereo was playing soft strains of Chopin, and the music was coming from both ends of the room.

In the midst of the elegance, reclining on a leather chair talking on the telephone, was Palmer. He supported the telephone with his chin and shoulder to leave his hands free, one hand to hold a drink, the other a cigarette. He pointed the cigarette with two fingers at Jim in greeting. He put down the drink—it was tomato-colored and looked like a Bloody Mary—covered the mouthpiece, and said to Jim, "Be right with you. Sit down." Jim walked across the room and sat on one of the barstools.

"Don't say that. Ah, honey, don't *say* that. There aren't enough clothes in the world to bring her up to you. Nothing. Absolutely nothing. If she disappeared right now, it wouldn't mean *that* to me." He snapped his fingers into the mouthpiece. "No honey, it's not you. It's the times. Everybody's affected. I mean, just think of jet travel. You can't expect to have physical dislocation on a scale like we have it today without having emotional dislocation too. You just can't give in to emotional self-pity. You've got to fight it. Remember what I was telling you about that book *Love and Be Desired*? Here, wait a second. Hold on. I'll read it to you."

Palmer put the telephone down and started toward the bookcase. "Who are you?" he asked Jim, as he pulled out a slim volume.

"I just moved in downstairs."

"Oh. Fix yourself a drink."

"A little early, no?" Jim asked.

"Suit yourself," Palmer shrugged. He went back to the chair and balanced the telephone on his shoulder as he paged through the book. "Let me find it now. It's right here somewhere. Here it is.

> The most serious impediment to the natural outgoing tendency of the ego is the emotional imbalance which, when yielded to, throws the subject back upon insufficient inner resources. The natural outgoing affections, thus stifled, do not furnish the normal motives of desire, and the subject finds himself unable to relate.

Honey, when you get right down to it, that's the essence of Christianity."

Jim found two dozen glasses waiting to be washed behind the bar, and a half-dozen ashtrays filled with cigarette butts. Apparently there had been a party the night before. There was a good selection of alcohol. Jim took some ice and lemon peel and bourbon and sweet vermouth and mixed a Manhattan. He brought this back to the stool with him and sipped it contentedly while he listened with amusement to his host explain the essence of Christianity.

"Go on out and fun it up," said Palmer, and on his face was the eagerness that was in his voice. "Go to that place where they got that show with the female impersonators. How about the Hungry I? Everybody wants to go there. Take advantage of your chances. I do. All the time. I'm looking at your picture right now." Jim followed Palmer's gaze. He was looking at a figurine of a sailor with a huge belly and a gaping navel who was holding up one of the lamps on the side table. "I think about you. I do. Bye now." He made some kissing sounds into the telephone.

He put the phone down. "Christ," he said. He looked at his watch. "Fifteen minutes. You know where she was calling from?"

"Where?"

"San Francisco."

"Boy."

"It must have cost her ten bucks."

"I guess she likes you."

"She's got problems," said Palmer. "You should see this gal. I mean the construction is unbelievable." He closed his eyes and pursed his lips and moved his head in a slow arc of appreciation. "She's a stewardess. And I mean when she takes that first walk up the aisle after the takeoff the guys are straining at the seat straps. By the time they get across the country, every man in the plane is exhausted from just panting. But she doesn't talk to anybody. She just freezes everybody that comes along. So she's sitting in a hotel room. New Year's Eve. In San Francisco. And she's sitting in a hotel room. It's a shame. I mean, it really is a shame."

Palmer had a silk bathrobe on. He got up and pulled the belt tight. "I'm Floyd Palmer."

"Jim Meagher."

"Did Cleary move out? Probably no such luck."

"I moved in to the basement."

"How could anybody live down there?"

"I might only take it for a week."

"How long are you in Washington?"

"Just since yesterday."

"I got a headache." Floyd went behind the bar and pulled out a bottle of aspirin and shook two into his palm and popped them into his mouth. He followed the aspirin with the rest of the Bloody Mary.

"Seems like everybody is off today," said Jim.

"Why? Who else is around?"

"Barney Blatt?" said Jim.

"Oh yeah. Trigger. He usually works evenings. He leaves here every day around five o'clock and tracks cow shit around Georgetown."

"You got a nice place," said Jim.

"Thanks." Floyd sat on the couch and rubbed his hands over his eyes. "You got a job?"

"I was planning to enroll at Catholic University."

"Halfway through the year?"

"It's a master's program," Jim explained, "rolling admissions."

"For what?"

"Drama."

Floyd took his hands off his eyes. "Drama! Christ."

"What do you do?"

"I work for a Congressman. Farrow, from Wisconsin."

"You from Wisconsin?"

"Yes. How much did Mrs. Hug stick you for the basement?"

"Thirty a month."

"It'll cost you another thirty in cleaning bills."

"You might have a point there," said Jim, getting up to take his leave.

"I'm having a New Year's party tonight," said Floyd. "Stop in."

"Thanks."

He walked to the Riggs National Bank on the corner of Wisconsin and M and cashed a traveler's check for twenty dollars, then went back to the house and settled his bags in the basement. The place looked even worse now that he could compare it with Floyd's bachelor paradise three floors above. Still. As he picked his way through the debris, he could see possibilities of turning it into a decent dwelling. The boiler room itself was beyond redemption. But the front room might be fixed up if he cleaned it, got some kind of a rug, put up plasterboard to cover the pipes, got some drapes for the window wall. He even visualized a stag's head hanging on the back wall. He might get Mrs. Hug to give him rent credit for the improvements.

Jim went upstairs to use the bathroom off the living room. When he came out, Mrs. Hug was sitting on the couch. "How are you?"

"Excuse me?" she said.

"How are you?" he asked in a louder voice.

"Oh yes. Thank you. You're a lovely young man."

He pointed out the piano and asked her if she played.

"No," she replied. "But you go right ahead."

"The Yellow Rose of Texas" was open on the music stand. He played this. When he turned, she gave him a beaming, maternal smile. "Is there anything you'd like?" he called out.

"Anything you want," she said.

He played her an Irish medley. She really seemed to enjoy it. She was so motherly it gave him a warm feeling, even brought some longing for the maternal care he'd never had. Who could tell? Maybe if she took a shine to him she'd invite him in for a couple of dinners. He might wind up with some home cooking, Jim thought.

He was suddenly aware that she was standing beside him. He stopped playing and stood up. "You play something," he told her. "I'll bet you're a good player." But she didn't sit down. She grabbed him and threw her arms around him and kissed him on the mouth with such pressure that Jim felt a sudden pain as his lips were flattened against his teeth.

He took a step backward, but he was up against the piano and there was nowhere to go. There was nothing to do but bend backward until she decided to let go. It was the hardest kiss he had ever been given in his life, and there was nothing maternal about it.

When she was finished kissing him, she gave him an extra squeeze. He got loose and ran around the piano. She came after him, but Jim had almost forty years on her and was faster.

"You're a lovely young man."

He stopped at the head of the stairs and turned. "I'm sorry, Mrs. Hug. I have to go now."

She was still advancing with that beaming smile. He slammed the door and beat it down the stairs. She didn't follow.

He started to laugh. At her age she still wanted to make out. He should have figured there was something different about her when he came in first and saw her in that red and white tee shirt.

As he got dressed he paused every once in a while and laughed all over again. It was some house.

Wait'll Tom Power hears about this, Jim thought.

He combed his hair and navigated his way carefully to the door so as to get out without too much dust on his pants. Outside, it was a clear sunny day. He stood on the sidewalk in front of the house and pulled in a good breath of air. While he stood there a Volkswagen parked in the empty space directly in front of his own car. A pair of girl's legs came swinging out of the confined car into the street. The rest of the girl appeared, and she pulled the skirt down and glanced at Jim. It was Barbara, the blonde who had snubbed him the night before in O'Malley's. Her legs hadn't looked like much then but they looked all right today. She took a package from the seat. She gave Jim another glance.

"How are you?" he called.

She looked puzzled.

"You don't remember me?" he asked.

"Oh yes," she said. "With Cleary last night. What are you doing here?"

"I just moved in here." He pointed out Mrs. Hug's place.

"I live in this house next door," she said.

"I know," he replied. "Cleary told me. Let me help you with your packages." She had a bunch of them in the back seat.

"I was shopping," she explained. "Or exchanging, I should say." They carried them up the path together. When they got in the house, she took them inside and he stood in the foyer.

She came back. "Would you like a cup of coffee?"

"Sure."

He sat down at her dining room table. She went out to the kitchen and fixed two cups of coffee and brought them in and she took the seat opposite. She was a pretty girl with exceptionally fine blonde hair. He wondered if it was dyed. Probably lightened, he thought, though it seemed blonde all the way down. She wore it in a nice fashion too, short, and it was curly. Her eyes were brown and alert: they were her best feature. Her mouth was a trifle too big but it wasn't homely, and she had a sweet smile.

"You're the one who wants to write plays, right?" she asked.

He told her his plans and his past, but soon realized she was more interested in hearing about the Navy and his travels than his future plans. She told him of herself; she was 24, from Grand Rapids, Michigan, had studied at a Catholic girls' college there, Sacre Coeur, and was studying history at the Georgetown graduate school.

"My dream is to work on Capitol Hill," she told him. "It's the whole reason I came to D.C. and to Georgetown."

She attempted to explain the aloofness of the evening before. "I feel very uncomfortable in that place," she explained. "There are so few women."

"I can see that."

It was getting late in the afternoon and he was getting hungry, so he asked her to recommend a place to eat. "Martin's is good. It's on Wisconsin Avenue. The fellows like it. It's like an Old English chop house. Dinner is less than three dollars."

"Sounds good," said Jim.

"Sam Rayburn eats there once in a while," she said.

"The Speaker of the House?"

"Yes. That's what the fellows say anyway. I've never seen him. He's a bachelor and that's one of his eating places."

"Would you want to come too?" he asked her.

"I'm not sure what the plans are with the other girls. We're supposed to go to a New Year's party."

"I figured that," said Jim.

"It's over at your house. Floyd Palmer. Did you meet him?"

"Sure," said Jim. "He invited me to the party."

"All of the girls in the house are going there."

"We can go to dinner first, then," Jim tried again.

"All right."

Jim went back next door to his own house. He stripped down and put a bathrobe on and went up the stairs to take a shower. It struck him that it might be a mistake to arrive upstairs with a bathrobe on, with Mrs. Hug on duty. He started to laugh. What a crazy house, between Barney and Mrs. Hug. On the first floor, he didn't meet Mrs. Hug, but he did meet Cleary.

"Hey!" Cleary came over with a big greeting. "You got here."

"I took the basement."

"Good. You can't beat the price. And it's warm in the winter."

"That's what I figured," said Jim, "But I don't love this running up and down the stairs to the can."

"You going to take a shower?"

"Yes."

"You got a shower down there," said Cleary.

Cleary went down with him and pointed out a small room near the back door which had a shower attachment hanging from the wall, and a sloping floor which led the water to a drain. "You'll freeze your ass off some mornings," said Cleary. "But most of the time it's all right." He showed him how he could also use the toilet in the basement if he filled the square tank behind it with a couple of buckets of water from the washing sink.

After Jim had a shower he went back upstairs. Cleary was still in the living room.

"Did you meet anyone else in the house yet?" Cleary asked.

"Barney Blatt and Floyd. And Mrs. Hug of course."

"Floyd's a pisser, isn't he?" asked Cleary.

"Yeah."

"Blatt's crazy," said Cleary. "He's after this airline hostess next door. If he thinks you got an eye on her, he'll go after you. He runs her back and forth to the airport. He thinks by running a taxi service he's going to make time."

"I was with Barbara this afternoon."

"Hey," said Cleary. "I've been after that."

"I already got a dinner date."

"Shit," said Cleary.

Jim laughed.

"She's all right," said Cleary.

"I think she's a little shy," said Jim.

"Good kid. Want to come up for a drink?"

Most of the room was taken up by a double bed. There was a kitchen table and a small refrigerator and a desk and bookshelves. Clothes were scattered on the unmade bed and the rest of he room was in similar disarray.

"It's a mess," said Cleary. "Mrs. Hug says she won't make it up until I pay the rent. That'll be a while."

Cleary fixed two bourbon and waters. "What's the story," Jim asked, "on Mrs. Hug?"

"Why?"

"She grabbed me this afternoon and really planted one on me."

"That's good," said Cleary. "You're in."

"She's an old lady."

Cleary laughed. "She'd probably had a few drinks."

"Is she an alky?"

"All old ladies drink," said Cleary. "She gets bitchy sometimes in the morning, but you get her in the afternoon and she's all right. Floyd leaves her a drink every day when he goes out and she really cleans that place up there. He's got a layout, hasn't he?"

"Yea," said Jim. "Nice place."

"I should leave her a drink too," said Cleary, "But hell, I can't afford it."

Jim started to put his drink on the table, then stopped. Every available portion of the table top was littered with papers.

"Sweep that shit off onto the deck," said Cleary.

Cleary proceeded to do so himself, clearing the papers off the table onto the floor with one sweep of his hand. "Floyd's having a party tonight," said Cleary.

"I know," said Jim.

"That's only one of them," said Cleary. He leaned over and picked one of the papers off the floor. He handed Jim a list. Jim scanned it. It was a list of parties and addresses. There were nine.

"You mean you plan to go to nine parties tonight?"

"Those are only the ones I took on the phone last night," said Cleary. "There'll be more tonight. I got a tip on one just this afternoon."

"How do you find out about them?"

"One guy gets the word and he spreads it."

"Don't people get sore?"

"Once in a while. But nobody knows who's invited and who isn't."

Jim laughed. "Can I join you?"

"Hell, yeah."

"Were you in the Navy?" Jim asked.

"Why?"

"You called the floor the deck."

"Marines," Cleary laughed. "How about you?"

"Navy."

They got to talking about the night before. Cleary was annoyed with Black Tom. "He loses one night in a year and he raises a big fuss."

"That Conor is a nice guy," said Jim.

"Great guy," said Cleary. "His sister's a good-looking head too."

Jim agreed. He had suspected Cleary liked Kathleen from the way he had perked up when she had entered the room the night before.

Chapter 38

Jim went down then to his basement and shaved and got dressed. As he polished his shoes, he kept thinking of Cleary and his nine parties. How could a guy *go* to nine parties in one night? Was there any *point* in going to nine parties in one night? Well, whether there was or there wasn't, there was something grandiose about the whole thing.

He went next door and rang the bell. The girl who answered the door had her eyes crossed. She brought her eyes back into focus then. "Hi. Do you want somebody or are you up for grabs?"

"I don't know if I should commit myself. Are you available?"

"Available!" she asked in a high-pitched voice that was almost a scream. "I'm eager."

She was wearing a blouse and cut-off dungarees and no shoes. She had a large bust and that gave a forward projection to her body, but her face was somehow projected forward too, so that her pointy nose was coming forward while her chin was receding slightly. She wrinkled her nose. "Well, introduce yourself."

"Jim Meagher."

"Come in, Meagher."

"I'm calling for Barbara."

She turned and called upstairs. "Bob-bruh! Bob-bruh!" She called the name several times but each time she gave it a different tone, switching from a soprano to a falsetto to an alto. She turned to him again and crossed and uncrossed her eyes. "Did you hear what the grape said when the elephant stepped on it?"

"No. What did the grape say when the elephant stepped on it?"

"It didn't say anything. It gave out with a little wine."

Jim laughed.

"That's very good. You didn't tell me your name yet though."

She adopted the pose of a girl called on in school and answered in a high-pitched, sing-song voice: "My name is Bonnie Beck."

Jim laughed. A chubby, jolly girl wearing a muumuu came out now from the kitchen. "Don't pay any attention to Bonnie," the chubby girl said. "She's a nut."

"I am not a nut."

"Barbara will be right down," said the chubby girl. "I'm Edna."

"I'm Jim. From next door."

He went into the living room with the two girls. Edna sat on the couch with him, though not close.

Bonnie clawed her hands like a witch and she shrieked dramatically at Edna, "Now you leave him alone, Edna Kirby. He belongs to Barbara."

"Stop it, Bonnie."

Bonnie shrieked again, "You leave that boy alone, Edna."

Jim couldn't imagine a more unlikely siren than Edna. So far as could be judged from the muumuu, she had the shape of a beer barrel.

"Stop it, Bonnie," said Edna, now with less humor in her voice.

"Edna knows all about you," said Bonnie.

"Bonnie, I'm going to get mad."

"Edna and Barbara were watching at the window today when you came in with your suitcase," Bonnie said to Jim. "They watch all the boys come in."

"Barbara's going to be mad," Edna warned.

Bonnie started doing knee bends.

"What are you doing?" Jim asked.

"My ski exercises," she started to chant: "M-i-c-k-e-y M-o-u-s-e. Mickey Mouse. Mickey Mouse."

"She's a nut," said Edna.

"Edna," said Bonnie, "wants to know why you only paid a week's rent."

Edna must have got that information from Mrs. Hug, thought Jim.

Edna was angry. "Barbara's going to be mad."

Jim was thinking: if Barbara and Edna saw him first arrive, then that whole scene of Barbara not recognizing him in the street when she got out of the car was just an act, probably.

Edna said sharply to Bonnie, "I don't think you're *one bit* funny."

"Have you girls been talking to Mrs. Hug?" Jim asked.

"Mrs. Hug thinks you're cute," said Bonnie. "So do I."

"Barbara's going to be mad."

Bonnie did a wicked imitation of Edna in a voice one octave higher: "Barbara's going to be mad."

"Stop it, Bonnie."

Bonnie sprang up. "I have to get my drink."

Edna was very embarrassed. "I hope you don't think we were spying on you."

"Oh, no."

"I'm very embarrassed."

"Don't be silly," said Jim.

Bonnie came traipsing back into the room. She was holding aloft a cocktail glass that was filled with a pinkish-colored frosted drink, probably a daiquiri. She came across the room and sat right in Jim's lap and put her face up close to him and asked, "What kind of a drink would you like?"

Edna jumped up and said, "Bonnie, if Barbara comes down, she's going to be mad."

"Fooey on Barbara. I'm just asking him what kind of a drink he wants."

"Anything's all right," he stammered, flustered by Bonnie's forward approach. "A cocktail? A Manhattan?"

"How do you make a Manhattan?" she asked, wrinkling up her nose.

"A beer is OK," he said.

"Come on out to the kitchen," she said, tugging Jim by the hand so that he got up from the chair. "You make yourself a Manhattan."

Edna went out to the foyer. "I don't know what's keeping Barbara."

Jim went out to the kitchen with Bonnie. There was a girl there with a red airline hostess uniform on—Alice, undoubtedly. She had her shoes off and she had her stockinged feet up on the oven door, resting them on the handle. "Y'all'll have to pardon me," she said to Jim in a thick Southern accent. "But ah just cain't get mah feet wahm. Ah think they's something wrong with mah circulation."

Jim started to laugh. They were all smashed. Bonnie and Alice anyway. Alice had a cocktail too. She was very cute, with a figure as well-developed as Bonnie's and that was about as good as could be found. Jim almost regretted the dinner invitation to Barbara; he wouldn't mind staying and joining the party right here.

"This is the new boy," said Bonnie. She still had Jim's hand.

"You the new bo' moved into Mrs. Hug's?" asked Alice.

"Yes."

"Po' thing. Y'ain't got no money. Y'only paid a week's rent."

"It's not that bad."

"Don't you worry 'bout it honey. You give Mrs. Hug a big kiss and you won' have to pay no rent at all." Alice, when she said this, ended with a wicked laugh.

"How do we make a Manhattan?" asked Bonnie.

"I can make it," said Jim. He saw a bottle of bourbon on the refrigerator. "Do you have any vermouth?"

Bonnie produced a bottle of sweet vermouth from the cupboard, and Jim mixed the drink. Bonnie climbed up on the table and sat there yoga-style, holding her cocktail glass at arm's length over her head, and pouring the drink two feet down into her mouth. She was, Jim thought, just about the craziest girl he'd ever met.

Alice had a lot of makeup on her face, with eye shadow and heavy lipstick, but she had nice features and a sweet look. She had honey-colored curly hair with lighter streaks in it, and she had curls arranged carefully along her forehead. She was balancing her cocktail glass in the cleavage of her bosom, which seemed to Jim rather an attractive way to hold a drink. She saw him looking at her. "D'y' meet Triggah yet?" she asked.

"Yes. Barney Blatt?"

"The million dollah sellah."

"He was trying to sell me some insurance."

"Did you buy?"

"I haven't got the money."

"Oh yes. Y'only paid a week's rent. Well, that won't stop Triggah."

"He was talking about you," said Jim.

She gave Jim a sharp look. "Ah hate him."

"Oh?"

"He comes to the aihport and annoys the life out o' me with his silly old talk. He wants me to be Mrs. Triggah. Then we can move to Noo Yohk, and he'll be a million-dollah-sellah. Well, shit on Noo Yohk, and shit on Triggah too. Ah hate 'im. Ah'm sohhy fo' being vulgah, but Ah'm annoyed at him. I hate people that hang around whah they ain't wanted. And that's Triggah. Everybody's Triggah. Hello there, Triggah."

She was looped, Jim thought. Was her accent even real?

"What's cooking?" Jim asked. "Whatever's in the oven smells good."

"That's Edna's ham," said Alice. "She's cooking it for a picnic tomorrow. She's going to feed it to her boyfriend Paul."

"A picnic in the winter?"

"They eat in the cah."

"A whole ham?"

His answer was a laugh from the two girls.

Edna came into the kitchen. "Barbara says she'll be right down."

"Thanks," Jim replied.

Alice took her feet down as Edna went to the oven. "Edna honah, sit down and have a drink. For New Yeah's."

"Later," said Edna. "I'm busier than a one-armed paper hanger with the seven year itch." She gave out with a rich laugh at her own humor that made her whole body shake. She pulled the ham out and ladled juice over it.

"Men have it made in the world," she said. "Men have it made."

"Paul has it made anyway," said Jim.

"He doesn't appreciate it," Edna commented sadly. "He's probably out tonight drinking the club treasury."

"Edna belongs to a social club," Alice explained. "Paul is the treasurer but he drinks all the dues." She laughed.

"Men have it made in this world," said Edna again. "I wish I'd been born a man." She closed the oven door and Alice put her feet up again.

"Ah think they's somethin' wrong with mah circulation."

"We'll have you over for dinner sometime," Edna said to Jim.

"Sure. Thanks," said Jim. She opened the oven again, sliced a piece off the ham and she gave it to him.

"How did you girls all get together?" Jim asked.

"Maggie brought us all together," said Alice.

"Who's Maggie?"

"She ran off with the postman."

"What?"

"Last Saturday," said Bonnie.

"You're kidding me?"

"She was always complaining that the mailman was annoying her in the mohnin'" said Alice. "She was going to complain to the post office. Then last Saturday she and the mailman just ran off and got married."

"Come on, will you," said Jim.

"No, it's true," said Edna, with big eyes. "They got married last Saturday."

Jim could hear Barbara coming down the stairs. He finished off the Manhattan quickly and went out to meet her. She gave him her red coat to hold while she slipped it on. The color was a nice contrast to her blonde hair. They said goodbye to the other girls.

Jim was sorry to leave. But they'd be back for the party later.

He was thinking as they started out that Bonnie and Alice hadn't given any indication that they had dates. In fact, the way they were casually drinking, it seemed that they probably didn't. And, of course, Barbara hadn't had a date until he met her this afternoon. It was an odd situation, three pretty girls going to a party stag on New Year's Eve.

"You've got a funny group in the house," he said to Barbara.

"It's usually entertaining. I heard all the laughing. What were you doing?"

"Just talking and joking. That Bonnie is a wild girl," he said.

"She's a good mimic," said Barbara. "She's been acting crazy the last day or two though. She just broke up with her boyfriend."

"Oh."

"Alice got so mad at her this morning. Bonnie got up at four in the morning and she went downstairs to the kitchen and I guess she was making a drink. She dropped ice cubes all over the floor and that woke Alice up, and she couldn't get back to sleep and she had a flight this morning. I don't blame her really for getting mad. It's hard work and she needs her sleep."

"Especially if she's going out tonight."

"She's just going to the party for a while," said Barbara. "It's awkward for her with that Barney Blatt. Did you meet him?"

"Yes," said Jim.

"Well, he's always annoying her. I think she'd like to be with Floyd Palmer but that Blatt acts so crazy."

"She should just cut him off."

"She does. But he's always around."

"The girls were telling me a funny story just before you came down: about a girl in the house who ran off with the mailman?"

"That's an exaggeration," said Barbara, annoyance in her voice. "My girlfriend Maggie got married last week to the boy who was working the mail route as Christmas help. But he's not just a mailman. He's a law student."

"Oh."

"They wanted to get married," she went on, "and they felt the best way to save family complications would be just to elope. He has to be back next week to start classes at George Washington, so they didn't have much time."

"Alice said that Maggie brought you all together."

"She was in the house the longest," said Barbara. "And the boy she married, Dan, is a very nice boy. I don't think it's fair to be calling him a mailman. He's doing very well in law school."

"There's nothing wrong with being a mailman."

"He is *not* a mailman," she said. "He's a law student."

She was really put out. "And I don't think it's right for Bonnie and Alice to be going around saying she ran off with the mailman."

He had to pacify her. "That's a nice coat."

"Thank you," she replied, holding it out a little with her hands, which she had in her pockets though she was wearing white gloves. "I made it myself."

"It's really a nice color."

"I love red," she said.

"Me too," he agreed. "You must be pretty versatile if you can make your own clothes."

Was he pouring it on too thick? Jim wondered. He was afraid maybe he was.

But she was pleased. "I like to make clothes."

"It's a nice evening," said Jim. "Would you mind if we walked to the restaurant?"

"All right."

The Manhattan had taken effect and he felt very good. He was walking through picturesque old Georgetown with a pretty girl, on a crisp New Year's Eve on his way to dinner and a good night of parties. He was so happy he felt like doing a jig step and letting out with a yell. But he felt that antics like that would be all right if his date were a girl like Bonnie; there was an air about Barbara, however which indicated such exuberance would be out of place.

He did feel like holding her hand. He reached out and tried to take it from her pocket. She deliberately frustrated him by switching her purse from her arm to the hand. So that was that.

Jim got the impression she was feeling cranky. Perhaps a drink and some more flattery in the restaurant, he thought, would take care of that.

They got to Wisconsin Avenue and crossed over to Martin's on the corner. Inside it was crowded, mostly with young men. Most of them turned to look Barbara over. This made Jim feel good, and he didn't mind at all the ten-minute wait for a table. They were seated finally in a side booth made of plain boards, no cushions. He liked the place. Most of the guys were drinking steins of beer with their dinners and there was a masculine atmosphere.

She had a daiquiri; he had another Manhattan. To make her feel good he asked her about her studies. She perked up. She went into a long discussion of her thesis paper, which was about the Yalta and Tehran Conferences, and the problems President Truman had dealing with the consequences of both after only a few months on the job. Jim had a difficult time concentrating on what she was saying, but she got so excited about the whole business that she really looked cute. He tried to play a little kneesies with her but she wasn't having anything of that either: she sat up straight on the bench and pulled her legs back.

Jim excused himself after a while and telephoned Tom Power to get his plans for the evening. Tom said he and Connie were going to spend their New Year's quietly; he had to be on duty in the morning.

After the meal, Jim and Barbara went for a walk. It was her suggestion. He thought she wanted to look in shop windows. But it developed she wanted to show him homes. They passed a corner house and she said, "That's where Senator Pell of Rhode Island lives." Then she pointed out Senator Symington's home and Senator Kennedy's.

He told her of his visit to Senator Lahiff's home, but she wasn't as impressed as he thought she'd be.

"They expect him to retire after this term," was her only comment.

On the way back, she talked about the house and the girls. The rent for their house was $200 a month, which they split, along with the utility and telephone bills. Originally the cooking duties were divided, but gradually the whole task fell on good-natured Edna. The girls did their shopping together, usually on Saturday morning. Jim was really impressed when he found out they only spent $6 apiece for food per week and apparently ate well. It was costing him more than that a day.

They talked in serious conversation for several blocks. Jim, in a New Year's mood, couldn't take the solemnity any more. On an impulse, he put one arm behind her legs and the other behind her back and lifted her up.

"What are you doing?" she cried.

"I'm going to carry you."

"You put me down this instant," she yelled at him.

"Don't worry."

"What will people think?"

"Who cares?"

She squirmed for a few steps. Then she got quiet. She even relaxed. She twined her arms around his neck.

"Am I heavy?" she asked him.

"A feather."

"I'm like a ten pound sack of potatoes," she said coyly.

"No, you're not. You're like a little doll."

After a few more steps she asked, "Are you going to carry me all the way home?"

"Yes."

"All right."

He started to sing: "Should auld acquaintance be forgot. . ."

"Don't sing that. It's a sad song."

"Happy New Year."

"Happy New Year."

"Barbara?"

"Yes."

"You know something? Last year on New Year's Eve, I was on a tanker off Durban, South Africa, and I couldn't even get ashore. And I promised myself that this year when I was a civilian, and I had the chance, I'd have a crazy New Year's Eve. Do you want to go out and have a crazy New Year's Eve?"

She laughed, then nodded her head. "Well all right."

"I know you don't like O'Malley's, but I told a friend of mine that I'd meet him there," Jim said. "Would it be all right if we went there first? Then we can come back here later."

"Sure." Barbara was suddenly much more agreeable.

He let her down in front of her house. "Just let me tell the girls," she said.

Alice had gone upstairs. But Bonnie was still in the kitchen. She was sitting by herself, sad-faced now and quiet. Barbara told her of the plan.

"Fine."

Jim felt sorry for her. "Why don't you get dressed?" he suggested. "We'll take you downtown to a place where there's a thousand guys and no girls."

Bonnie's face lit. "Would it be all right?" she asked Barbara.

"Sure," said Barbara. "Come on. Hurry up."

Bonnie went tearing up the stairs. In less than five minutes, she was down again, transformed by an evening dress and makeup. She was full of energy. "What's the name of this place?"

"O'Malley's," said Jim. "Ask Barbara if there's a lot of bachelors there."

"Oh, they got plenty, all right," said Barbara.

Bonnie clapped her hands and let out a squeal of delight and did a couple of leaps on the sidewalk, even though she was in high heels now.

Jim was ashamed of the Black Seducer. It looked like such an old junk wagon. But he didn't have time to think about it. The two girls were in the front seat with him and Bonnie made him a member of the Mickey Mouse Club. They sang all the way downtown. Barbara even started to get affectionate. She sat close to him and once she even let her hand trail across his knee.

They parked half a block from O'Malley's. Even from that distance they could hear the accordion music and the singing. They went up the steps and in the door and, in the midst of the smoke, confusion and noise, Jim spotted Black Tom sitting at the near end of the bar. He was perched on a stool, looking about him with his lidded eyes as he traded banter with some companions. He saw Jim at the door and cried out, "Bull Moose, y'ould divil! Bull Moose!"

"Bull Moose!" Jim yelled back.

"Bring those two lovely girls over here, that I meet them."

Jim brought them over. "This is Barbara Field and Bonnie Beck. Tom Potts."

Black Tom leaped off the stool. He shook hands with them. "Lovely, lovely," he cried.

Bonnie, game for anything, gave him a kiss. Tom nearly went out of his mind. "Ha-ha," he cried. "Ha-*ha*, ha-ha, ha-*ha*." He did a jig in a circle. "Sure they're still mad for old Tom." The men hooted him. Black Tom showed his brown teeth in a huge grin and he stood in front of the girls nodding his head up and down.

"The loveliest two lassies ever came into this old hole. Hold on now. Hold now. Let me get Conor. He's in the back room."

He went scooting back through the crowd to the other room.

"Conor is the son of the Irish Ambassador," Jim told Barbara.

Bonnie was looking around at the groups of men singing, drinking, listening to the accordion music or over at the side throwing darts at the board. Her eyes were shining. "There are so many men," she said.

Black Tom came back, pulling Conor after him. "Come up here. Come up here," he was saying to Conor. "I have the girl for you. One kiss and she took the ache out of my bones. Here you, lassie, come over here." He grabbed Bonnie's arm.

Conor saw Jim and waved. Conor tried to get over to talk to Jim, but Black Tom was determined to match him up with Bonnie.

"Is that the ambassador's son?" Barbara asked Jim.

"Yes, that's him."

Barbara looked at the slim, bespectacled Conor and said, "He's a nice-looking fellow."

Black Tom said to Bonnie, "Here, lassie. Here's the lad you want to give a kiss," gesturing at Conor. "Sure he needs someone to give him something."

Jim had thought Bonnie one of the few persons he had met who was without social fear. He was surprised now to see the wild girl he had met at the house turn shy. Her cheeks got pink and her ready tongue deserted her.

Conor was as red as a beet.

"Sure now put your arm around her," said Tom and he took Conor's arm and tried to force him. But Conor wouldn't.

"Come on, lassie. Give him a little hug. He needs encouragement." Bonnie wouldn't move.

Black Tom got annoyed. "Will you, for God's sakes," he said to Conor, "step forward and take the initiative. It's for you to be kissing her and not her to be chasing you."

Bonnie looked shyly at Conor. Conor, who seemed to be really in pain, said sincerely, "I'm sorry, ma'am. I'm not much for that kind of shtuff."

A whoop of laughter came from the men who were gathered around. One man repeated it to another all the way down the bar, and there was a succession of loud guffaws.

Black Tom was disgusted. "To tell with ye. Ye can match yourselves up." He went to the bar for his whiskey. The men were tormenting Conor. Jim had to steer the girls away for fear they'd hear some of the comments.

He could hear one of them saying to Conor, "Not much for that shtuff, my eye. Him that hasn't been out of the saddle since he came to this country."

"Sure," said another. "If she turns her back he'll have the clothes torn off her."

From the table where he took the girls, Jim could hear the shouts of merriment from the men, and he could see Conor getting redder and redder at the same time he was laughing. The two girls were looking at Conor sympathetically. Barbara squeezed Jim's hand and asked, "What are they saying to him?"

"Just teasing him," said Jim.

"How red he is," said Barbara.

Bonnie, still wrapped in silence, didn't take her eyes off Conor.

Black Tom came over with four drinks grouped in his two hands. Jim jumped up. "I wanted to buy the first round."

"Nonsense, lad. Sit down."

Tom put the drinks down on the table. "I bought Tom Collinses for the girls," he said, "For I know the ladies does be liking Tom Collinses. Is that all right now?"

"That's fine," said the girls.

Tom somewhat slyly made his way over next to Bonnie. She turned and looked at him sitting next to her with his dark turtle head and his hooded eyes and she laughed.

"You wouldn't be doing it again, would you?" he asked Bonnie.

"Sure," she said. And she gave him another big kiss.

Tom leaped up and cried, "A-*ha*!" He did a two-step. "Honest to Peter," he said to her, "you're making a teenager out of me!"

Conor had escaped his tormentors and he came to the table. "Have you all a drink?" he asked.

"We have," said Jim. "Sit down."

"Get out of here, O'Hara," Black Tom said to him. "You're not worth a nose blow. I have more go at my age than you'll ever have."

"Be quiet, you old divil," said Conor.

The accordionist came over, an elderly man in a tweed suit, stooped with the weight of his instrument. "What would you like, ladies?"

"Paris in the Spring Time," Barbara said right away.

He played it; they hummed the song, moving their heads with the beat. Conor looked down at the table. Jim watched him and Bonnie. Bonnie looked at Conor through the whole song. Conor looked up at her at the end and their eyes met. Jim noted that both their faces flushed. Well, Jim thought, Happy New Year.

He squeezed Barbara's hand. "You having a good time?"

"I am," she said. "Much better than last night."

The waiter stopped at their table. He had no uniform but was distinguishable because he carried a tray. "Des the bartender," he said to Jim, "would sing a song for the lady, if she'd like it." Jim looked over to the bar. Little Des was standing there eager-faced and bright-eyed, watching them.

"Ask him to sing 'Danny Boy'," said Barbara.

The waiter brought the request to Des. Des straightened and shut his eyes and, with no announcement, began to sing. But the same phenomenon happened as the night before. From the second note the raucous crowd fell to hushed silence. He seemed even better tonight.

Barbara, of course, was immensely flattered; the rest of the bar didn't know that Des was singing the song for her. When Des was finished they sent him up a drink. Black Tom rushed over to get the accordionist and he dragged the old man to the table. "What would you like now, for *your* song?" Tom asked Bonnie.

"'Hey There'," Bonnie requested.

"Hey there what?" asked Black Tom.

"That's the song: Hey There."

"I never heard of that before. Can you play that?" he asked the accordionist. The old man shook his head yes. "Play then."

The accordion started. But the noise of talk at the bar was too loud for the instrument to carry. Black Tom yelled to the men at the bar, "Hush! Or you'll hear from me."

This caused more disturbance as the men laughed at him. Tom stuck his chest out and cried: "Have ye not enough culture to keep your mouths shut when the man is playing music for the young ladies?"

The nearest patron at the bar, a brick-faced man with a stevedore's body, looked at Tom as if he were something that just crawled out from under a stone. "Jaysus," he said to his companions, "will you look at what's lecturing us on culture?"

Tom flew at him like a cock across a barnyard. The big guy stuck his fist out and Tom ran his jaw right into it, and it buckled his knees. It didn't stop him though. He came right back up and started throwing punches.

There was a roar of approval down the bar. The big guy took the punches on his forearms and laughed at the attack.

Conor jumped to his feet and pulled Tom back.

"Get him out of here," cried the big guy, "before I shpill my drink on him and dhrown him."

Tom lunged to get free. "You overgrown ox," he shouted. "Your fist is big and your mouth is bigger."

The big guy hit Tom square in the nose and there was a spurt of blood as Tom went reeling. Then Conor went after Tom's attacker. Conor hit him an ineffectual blow on the cheek, and got a glancing blow on the shoulder in return that spun him half around. Des the bartender came up quietly behind the big guy, and, taking a bottle of beer by the neck, smashed him across the back of the head. The big guy went down like a tree.

Des hauled himself up to take a look over the bar at the sprawled body. "The crust of that," he said quietly, "striking out at the ambassador's son." He gave a signal to the bouncer, who hauled the body out the door. Des then quieted the uproar very simply: he sang again.

During the song, Black Tom went to the men's room, and when he came back, apart from a pinkish nose, he looked fine. He even gave a speech at the end of the song.

"I have friends here from New York," he announced to the patrons at the bar, "who are people of culture and breeding. And when there's somebody playing the accordion music, they don't want to be interrupted by your old gaff."

They gave him a cheer and then they roared laughing.

Tom sat down pugnaciously on the edge of the chair with his knees spread wide. "I'm sorry," he said after he had turned to the girls and Jim, "that we haven't the culture here in Washington that you have in New York."

Jim tried to explain that the girls were residents of Washington, but Black Tom was concerned with getting the accordion music started again. When he had accomplished that, he turned to the group and apologized again as a spokesman for Washington. "You people from New York probably think you're down here among barbarians."

"Don't be silly," said Jim.

"That's a grand city, New York," said Conor. "Whenever I've gone there I've enjoyed it. The people are very hospitable."

"I've never seen New York," said Bonnie.

"You haven't? Really?" Jim asked, surprised.

"I thought you were from New York," said Black Tom.

"I'm from Pennsylvania," said Bonnie. "Pottsville."

"You have to see New York," said Conor.

"It's only an hour by plane," said Jim.

"You could leave here now," said Conor, looking at his watch. "At nine o'clock, and you'd be there by eleven."

"Tonight would be the night to be in New York," said Jim. "Times Square on New Year's Eve."

"That must be something to see," said Conor.

"Don't they televise it all over the country?" said Black Tom.

"Why don't we go tonight?" asked Jim, on a whim.

"Do you think we could?" questioned Conor.

"Why not?"

'Are you serious?" cried Bonnie.

"It's been a while since I've seen New York," said Black Tom.

"I'm serious," said Jim. "If we didn't want to come back tonight, you could all stay at my house. There's no one there now but my father."

"Would you go?" Bonnie asked Barbara.

"Sure."

"I'd love to," Bonnie squealed.

"I think the air shuttle fare is ten dollars," said Jim. "I'll pay Barbara's."

"I'll pay Bonnie's," Conor offered.

"I'll pay my own," said Tom.

"Indeed ' n' you will," Conor affirmed.

As quickly as that, it was settled. They all went outside and piled into Conor's car to head for the airport. He was pulling out of the parking space when a car drove up behind them and waited to take the space. The car horn sounded. "Is it Cleary's car?" Conor asked, peering into the rear view mirror.

"It is," said Tom, looking out the back.

Jim turned. He could see Cleary's moon face grinning at them from behind the windshield.

"Ask him if he wants to come," said Conor.

Black Tom leaned out the window and yelled, "Cleary, do you want to go to New York?"

Cleary, without hesitation, yelled back, "All right."

He parked his car in Conor's space and got in with the others. "Where we going? New York, you said?"

"Yes," said Conor. "Times Square next stop."

"Good," said Cleary.

"I knew we wouldn't have the good fortune to get away without you, Cleary," said Tom.

"Do you want to call your wife?" Conor asked Black Tom.

"When she sees me, she'll expect me," said Black Tom.

"We can call from the airport anyway," said Conor. With that he hit the gas pedal and the car leaped toward the Fourteenth Street Bridge and National Airport. They had their tickets bought for the ten o'clock plane by twenty minutes to ten. Then they made their telephone calls.

They did a do-si-do step across the marble lobby to the airport bar to have a glass of champagne to start the trip. Inside, Bonnie toasted Black Tom and he returned it. "Up Pottsville! Up Fermanagh! Up New York!"

Jim turned around and got the definite sense that Cleary was making a play for Barbara, talking to her with excitement. When Cleary let go with that much conversation, Jim was learning, it was motivated by desire. Conor was shaking hands with the bar patrons. "You must know half of Washington," Jim said to him.

"I never met a stranger," Conor replied.

The New York flight was announced over the loudspeaker and Bonnie got so excited, she started people laughing all over the bar. Jim got nervous when they got on the boarding line that they wouldn't even be let on the plane, for Black Tom had his flask out and between swigs he called out, "Bull Moose," at Bonnie and she answered "Bull Moose," in her crazy high falsetto with her eyes crossed. Even Barbara seemed to have lost her senses with the last drink. She was skittering around and skipping here and there. But it was New Year's Eve and few of the persons on the line were altogether sober, and they were laughing at Bonnie.

They got through the gate and onto the plane. Jim and Barbara sat together, and Bonnie and Conor also. Black Tom had to sit with Cleary and he complained bitterly. With each insult though, Cleary only turned to the others and smiled wider. When it came to abuse, he was impregnable.

Bonnie could be heard all over the plane when the motors revved for the takeoff, to the delight of the men around her. Conor greeted everyone, shaking hands, talking. Barbara put her head on Jim's shoulder and fell asleep.

After the takeoff, the stewardess went up the aisle and Black Tom gave her a brown-toothed leer. "Will you be coming by again, sweetheart?" Jim followed her progress back down the aisle, as much as he could without turning his head too far and waking up Barbara. He saw the stewardess point out Tom to the other stewardess and the two of them giggled back at the pantry. Bonnie was squealing again, sure that she could see the lights of Pottsville below.

It seemed only minutes when they landed in New York. By eleven they were in the terminal at LaGuardia. The girls went to the ladies' room to get fixed up. The four men went to the bar. While they talked, Jim got on the subject of Mrs. Hug, and he told them about the scene in the living room.

"Jaysus," cried Tom Potts. "It wouldn't be down to the basement I'd run if she wanted a kiss or two."

Conor's eyes were wide. "Did she really do that?"

"She did."

"Look under your bed from now on," said Black Tom.

"You don't know what they do be thinking, do you?" said Conor, with a puzzled expression.

The girls came out, freshly made up, with their hair combed. They got a taxi into Manhattan and Jim routed the driver along Central Park South to Fifth Avenue. They turned the corner at the St. Moritz and The Plaza. "That's the Pulitzer Fountain over there," said Jim. "F. Scott Fitzgerald swam there one night when he was drunk."

"We'll do that later," said Bonnie.

The taxi turned at Saint Patrick's Cathedral. They stopped and got out at the ice rink in Rockefeller Center and watched the skaters, then walked a handful of blocks to Times Square. They got there at ten minutes to twelve. They stood there with the thousands and thousands of people amidst the wonderland of lights, and counted off the minutes and then the seconds.

Then the round ball on top of the Times Building fell and the roar from the crowd announced that it was the new year.

Jim kissed Barbara.

Conor kissed Bonnie.

Black Tom and Cleary glared at each other, then shook hands.

They got in another taxi and Jim gave the address of the Ancient Order of Hibernians' party on Dyckman Street.

"Where on earth are we going?" Bonnie asked. The others chorused their questions as well.

"A place I know," said Jim cryptically. With a surge of excitement he looked forward to the surprise of Red and D'Arcy and all the crowd. He was getting to the New Year's party after all. It was crazy how things turned out.

"Happy New Year!"

Chapter 39

arch 1960

M   The bad thing with borrowing money from Floyd was that it would create a poor impression, Jim knew. And he wanted to use Floyd. He had all the contacts. He travelled in the good circles. He went to the best parties. In the natural course of events he would get around to inviting Jim to them, and Jim wanted those invitations. That's why he was in Georgetown.

Jim went back to the house and met Floyd coming down the stairs. He was wearing a good chalk-striped suit and carrying his town topcoat. Off to a Saturday afternoon cocktail party, undoubtedly.

"Floyd."

"Jim babe."

"Floyd, do you mind if I ask a favor?"

Jim could see the refusal all over his face but he charged on. "I'm a little short, and I was wondering if you could lend me a five or so until I get straightened away. I hate to ask you."

"Aw, gee Jim, I'd like to help you. Honest, I really would. But I can't hack it right now."

"That's all right," said Jim, embarrassed, anxious to get away. "Don't worry about it."

"I have so many people in to me already," said Floyd, "That I'll be lucky to get through to my next paycheck."

"Don't worry about it. Hey, don't let me hold you up."

"That Alice next door here hit me for fifty during the week," Floyd went on. "I just can't afford that kind of thing."

"I understand," said Jim.

Floyd left. Jim went downstairs wondering how Alice could ask a guy for fifty bucks. Or why. He was a great guy to borrow from, Floyd. He announced it to the neighborhood.

What now? Even if Jim got a job, he wouldn't get paid for a week. He looked around the room and begrudged every dollar he had spent fixing it up. There was a plaque on the wall, a silver eagle, that had cost him twelve-fifty. I must have been out of my mind that day, Jim thought.

He went to work on an assignment for his playwriting class, just to get his mind off his problems. It was to be a scene of five pages, with two characters, that involved conflict. His two characters bore a strong resemblance to his father and his Aunt Nora. Instead of brother and sister, though, he made them man and wife. He had no trouble writing the dialogue. The two of them had been arguing in real life for as long as he could remember, and all he had to do was listen to them in his mind. He enjoyed it, once he got to work, and stayed at it until the middle of the afternoon.

Eventually he had to face the problem of dinner. He went to see the girls next door. He had never gone there at dinner time when they hadn't asked him to stay. Bonnie Beck answered. "Hi, Jim. Come in. I was working on some clothes upstairs. I'll be down in a minute."

"I just stopped in to say hello."

She settled him in the living room and told him she'd be right back. Edna came in from the kitchen. Edna assumed he was coming to see Barbara, and explained that Barbara was out for the afternoon. When it came to socializing, Jim thought, women always had to have reasons. Of course, he was there in the hopes of scrounging some dinner himself.

He hadn't even asked Barbara to as much as a movie for weeks, nor did she seem especially disappointed. She was working as a volunteer for Senator Kennedy in his campaign to get the Democratic presidential nomination in July. All her interests were centered on that.

But Jim talked about her with Edna. When Bonnie came back, she wanted to know how Conor O'Hara was. This was another awkward situation. She had been stuck on him since New Year's but he'd never asked her out.

Jim had asked him about Bonnie now and again, but always got some version of the same reply.

"Do you know, Jim," Conor would reply, "I've been thinking about asking her out. She's a lovely girl. I'm going to ask her out one of these days." But one of these days never came.

"Jim, why don't you stay for dinner?" Edna asked. "Barbara should be in."

He accepted, of course.

Bonnie made the cocktails, then the three of them sat to the table. Alice wasn't going to be there; she had a flight. The food was good and plentiful. It always was. He ate a huge meal, feeling guilty throughout. He tried to soothe his conscience by assuring himself that he would take them all out to a restaurant as soon as he got some money. That, however, was anything but an immediate prospect.

He got back to his own place at six. Since it was Saturday, he cleaned. This involved sweeping the floor and wiping the bar and polishing the eagle.

Cleary came in. "Do you have a date?" he asked Jim.

"No. I'm broke."

"Come on. We'll hit a few parties."

"I couldn't even bring a bottle," said Jim.

"You don't need one."

So he went out with Cleary. Cleary took a half-pint of bourbon in his pocket. The first stop was a church hall in the neighborhood where a candidate for President of the Young Democrats was having an affair to win votes. The beer, band music, baloney sandwiches and speeches were free. Jim went out for several of the dances while Cleary made his dinner on the beer and sandwiches. But the girls were only the Saturday night leftovers.

The second party was in Glover Park. When Jim arrived behind Cleary and saw the bartender in a white uniform, and a table full of fancy hors d'oeuvres, he was afraid they might get thrown out. As it developed, there was no need for fear. The party was given by three girls, all in their thirties, and they welcomed stray males. "We only have a party once a year," one of the hostesses told them, "so we go all out and hire everything. We think it's the only way to give a party." Cleary was annoyed because his belly was full and there was real food—turkey and ham—being served. The bourbon and scotch were also of the best.

"They deserve better guests," Jim commented to Cleary on the way out.

"We'll stop back," said Cleary, "If nothing better develops."

For two hours, it seemed nothing better was going to develop. The next two parties that Cleary had lined up were all bring-your-own-bottle affairs. Jim had to beg Cleary for drinks. When the half-pint ran out at the second party, Cleary motioned at Jim to follow him into the kitchen, where he foraged in the pot closet. "You can always find a bottle in the pot closet at one of these affairs," he said, and he was right. Cleary filled his own bottle from the bigger one.

At one in the morning, they got to an apartment in the Westchester Towers. The party here was the first affair during the evening to which Cleary had actually been invited; it was given by a law school classmate. There were two attractive girls dancing to a Victrola in a foyer off the main room. Jim got one to teach him the step; he was glad to get up and dance after the political chit-chat of the three previous parties. The girl was from Guatemala and she had dramatic coloring, with fair skin and black hair and dark eyes.

The host broke up the party. He had been passing a notebook around to get the girls' names and addresses and telephone numbers. When he got the book back the pages with the names and numbers were torn out. He threw a tantrum.

Jim and Cleary gave the Latin girls a ride home. When Jim brought the Guatemalan girl from the car to her apartment, the other girlfriend, apparently under orders, came along. The mother was waiting at the door, and took her daughter in before there was even a chance to exchange goodbyes. Then he and Cleary took the other girl home. Apparently no one worried about her virtue. She let herself in at the door.

Back at the car, Jim turned to Cleary. "Let me have the Guatemalan girl's number," he said.

"Why would I know her number?"

"Because I'm sure you were the one who tore those pages out of that book," Jim replied.

"You're right," Cleary roared with laughter, and handed a piece of paper to Jim. They both laughed as they drove down toward town. Jim wondered if he'd ever have enough money to take the girl out.

The next stop was O'Malley's Irish Heaven. It was closed—all the bars closed Saturday at midnight—but they went up and rapped on the window and O'Malley himself let them in. Conor was there along with all the usuals, laughing, drinking, telling stories.

Jim hadn't wanted to go because he couldn't buy a round. But Cleary had insisted. As soon as Jim sat down at the table, he saw his round was the next one. Conor was next to him and he told Conor he was broke; Conor passed him a five. Jim got a dollar change back from the round and Conor told him to hold on to it. They stayed until five in the morning, and when Jim and Cleary got out of the car in front of Mrs. Hug's in Georgetown, they were both in a staggering silly mood.

Sunday morning Jim found the dollar in his pocket. It bought a cup of coffee and some typing paper, and the rest of it went for a can of Spam and a loaf of bread. It served for lunch and dinner and breakfast again on Monday morning. He spent the day quietly, prepared his scene for class, read the papers from upstairs, pored over the want ads, and then went to the Georgetown library to read. And to look at the girls.

Monday in class, the teacher, Father Lavin, called on students to read their scenes. First up was an unkempt bearded young man who wore old clothes and was known as Lou the Beat. Jim had formed a great respect for him without even knowing him, for he looked like a playwright. Lou had two characters on a park bench, Mr. Now and Mrs. Then, argue the meaning of life. The scene was a great disappointment to Jim, who thought it worked better as written language rather than spoken language. But the assignment had been to write a dialogue. Lou the Beat's images were abstract and the speech was too logical. The nun who followed was better. She had two peasants arguing outside Joan of Arc's court room on the question of whether she was guilty or not.

When Jim got his chance, he put all he had into the lines. He got a laugh right away with Harry's shout: "Don't get horsey with me, woman." And Nora's taunt in reply, one which Jim had actually heard her use on Harry before: "Born in Ireland. Pig-headed, and born in Ireland." Father Lavin had a good laugh. He was from an Irish family. He told Jim the scene was good and the dialogue was fine. It made Jim feel wonderful. In bed the night before, suffering from hunger pangs, Jim had really debated the wisdom of studying law, or maybe getting a business job. He remembered now there wasn't anything greater than writing a line which made people react, and directed their emotions.

Even Lou the Beat came up after class and told him it was a good scene, and invited Jim to come have a cup of coffee. As he shuffled along with Jim, Lou apparently decided that maybe he had praised the scene too much. "The whole class is more or less a Mickey Mouse group," he said. "But today they weren't bad. I got to admit it. I was a little impressed."

"Why don't you write lines like you speak, Lou?" Jim asked.

"What do you mean?"

"That expression you just used. 'Mickey Mouse group,' that's very funny."

"Didn't you like my scene?" Lou was aggressive.

"Well, the language was very philosophical."

"You probably didn't understand it," said Lou, his face coloring.

"No offense," said Jim. But Lou's feathers were ruffled and he didn't open up again until they got to the cafeteria. Jim said he had no money, so Lou bought.

"You flat?" Lou asked.

"Yes."

"Give a pint, man."

"What do you mean? Blood?" Jim asked.

"Sure." Lou told him where the blood donor center was downtown. "Four bucks a pint. Six if you got the right kind."

It was too good to be true, Jim thought. But he went anyway.

The blood bank was in a slum section downtown. Jim walked the whole way. When he found the entrance, there were a number of seedy-looking men around the door. One had a whiskey bottle and was swigging from it as the others jumped around him and clapped their palms in anticipation and frustration. Jim looked in the front door. There must have been at least a hundred men sitting on union hall-type benches, their shoulders hunched forward, looking up at the nurse. The nurse was a burly black woman, dressed in starched whites. The sign on the desk gave her name: Loretta.

She called the first row and fifteen men stood. Jim took a seat on the last bench. Each of the men had to put his hand under a fluorescent light and Loretta checked through a viewer. She stopped one of them. "Ain't been no eight weeks for you," she told him. "That mark on your nail ain' mo' 'n' fo' weeks old." The man quietly turned and walked out. Those who were accepted made a line on her side of the desk. They looked to Jim like a cross-section of all life's losers. Some of them were wearing clothes hardly better than rags.

Loretta knew many of them. "How you, Sam? How you, Roy?"

From his seat in the back bench, Jim watched. He got depressed and started to lose his courage.

Loretta took a sample of blood from Roy's earlobe and tested it in a green solution. He was an elderly man with no teeth and when he found out he passed, he showed both gums in a smile. The next fellow was in a dirty white shirt and an oversized pair of pants that bagged around his crotch and fell free in the areas between his belt notches. Loretta was happy to see him. "How you been, Lester?" She opened a packet with a new glass tube, and took the sample of blood from his earlobe. She dropped it in the green solution. The drop quivered. She shook her head sadly. "It jumpin' up and down, Lester. You ain't got no iron." She motioned him off the line.

Lester got angry. "Eff you Loretta if you say I got no iron."

Loretta's face grew wrathful. "Don' you talk to me like that."

Lester was suddenly repentant. He smiled at her with rotted teeth. "Ain' no call for you getting mad."

"Course I getting mad," she said, "when you talk that way."

"Ain' talkin' that way about you. I mad 'cause you ain' goin' let me sell my blood."

"You ain' got no iron. You go find yourself some raisins."

"I don' say nothing wrong about you," said Lester. "I think about you same as I think about my mother."

"You ain' giving no blood. You got no iron."

"You like a mother to me."

"No man talk like that to his mother."

Jim had moved forward as the men were taken. He wondered if he had enough iron in his blood.

A rather well-dressed young black man came in, a handsome youth of about twenty-five, and Loretta gave him a delighted smile. "Where you *been,* Norman?"

"Oh I been roun.' How you been?"

"Fine," said Loretta. "I ain't seen you in so long I thought you was doing all right."

"I ain' bad," said Norman. "Couple of times I almost croaked, but I been all right."

"Good to see you, Norman." Norman went back to wait his turn.

"How much you giving for blood?" a man asked Loretta.

"Four dollars, less'n youse O negative, like Norman back there. He gets six dollars."

Jim finally got to Loretta. She examined his hand under the light and took the drop of blood and passed him. He went down to a white nurse who took blood pressure and temperature and—if the man was accepted for the blood sale—put the mark on his fingernail. Jim found out he was worth only four dollars a pint. Finally he was on the table and the tube was extracting the blood from his arm. It seemed to him the nurse would never take it out. He was afraid that maybe they were taking a quart and paying him for a pint.

Finally he was finished. The girl gave him four new bills. On his way out, Norman was right behind him. He waved to Loretta. "Take care of yo'self. Hear?"

"Bye, Norman. Where you going now?"

"Get something to eat."

"Norman."

"Yes'm."

"You give a dollar to Lester. He ain' got no iron and he ain' got no money either."

Norman looked at the six new bills in his hand. He was reluctant. But he smiled and agreed. "Yes'm."

Jim watched him outside. He did give a dollar to Lester.

Jim stopped at Holy Trinity Church in Georgetown on his way home and said a prayer of thanks for the money. He made a resolution to go to Mass and Communion each day during Lent, which would start on Wednesday. He went to the store and got a pack of cigarettes, but when he lit one and inhaled the smoke, it made him dizzy because it had been a day since he'd had one. He stopped in the Wisconsin Avenue cafeteria and had the $1.25 roast beef special. He counted his money then. He would need a dollar for gas for the Black Seducer, and had spent 25 cents for a pack of cigarettes and dollar and a quarter for dinner. He had a dollar fifty left. He hated to spend it. Blood money, literally, he thought.

He made it last until Wednesday. After class he sought out Lou the Beat to inquire if he had any other suggestions for raising quick money. Lou suggested Workmen Inc. It was an outfit downtown that sent out day laborers upon request from employers. They paid the day following the work day.

Jim was at the Workmen Inc. office at six the next morning. He had to walk there, since once again there wasn't enough gas in the car. It was in the basement of a business building. There were about fifty men there waiting for possible jobs. They looked much like the group at the blood bank: drifters, alkies, some outright bums.

The men were all gathered in one large room on benches. At the front was a glass window and behind this was the dispatcher, a crew-cut young man about thirty. The men tried to get as close to this window as they could, with the exception of the few men who were stretched out asleep on the back benches. Each time the telephone rang, the men would lean forward. The dispatcher would single out the men he wanted, give each of them a dollar for carfare, and send them to the job. In between calls, the men would pick newspaper sheets off the floor to read them, or fish half-smoked cigarettes out of their pockets and light them for whatever drags were left in them, or lean forward in the benches and cough. It seemed everyone had a cough.

Some of the men would go forward to buddy with the dispatcher to better their chances. The dispatcher seemed pleasant, though slightly bored. He didn't seem aware of his power. A flick of his finger and a man ate that day. No flick of his finger, a man didn't eat.

Jim wondered what he'd do if he was left behind at the end of the selection process.

Beg on the street?

Go to the Franciscan monastery and get on the bread and soup line? Did they even have such things anymore?

The Salvation Army? "Put a nickel on the drum, save another drunken bum!"

Call his father?

He wasn't picked. The dispatcher took the men he knew. At nine o'clock Jim was still sitting there. He gave up. He went to Mass at Mary Star of the Sea nearby. Please, Lord, he prayed, I need a little help.

On an impulse, after Mass he went to the National Press building on 14th Street. He spent the day going from office to office, from floor to floor, repeating the same pitch. "I'm from New York. I worked for the wire service and I'm looking for a reporter's job down here."

Almost every time, he got the same answer: "Sorry, kid."

He found a few sympathetic ears. The head of the *New York Herald Tribune* bureau, a distinguished reporter Jim had heard of, took a quarter hour out from his work just to talk to him. In another office, a distinguished columnist, bylined all the way to California, stopped typing when Jim came in and offered him a cigarette and listened to his troubles. He told Jim there was nothing in Washington, but he gave a contact in New York if Jim wanted to go back.

Jim didn't. But he was grateful for the honor of the conversation. It was almost as good as food.

That's all he could think of all the way back to Georgetown. Food. He looked in all the restaurant windows. He stopped at the delicatessens. He would have danced for just a nickel for a candy bar.

There was one possibility, Jim thought. The girls next door. Go see Barbara? He'd have to have a purpose. Ask her for a date? But he couldn't afford it. Nor would he be able to, probably, when Saturday night came around. Then he remembered she told him once she didn't accept a date if the request were made after Wednesday. This was Thursday. It was safe. He'd ask her for Saturday night, and she'd refuse. She had also once refused a movie date on Saturday night. It was another strict regulation in her social life: Movies were only for during the week. So he would ask her for a movie for Saturday night.

She was home when he knocked, and she brought him into the living room. She was full of news of Senator Kennedy. She read him James Reston's column from the *New York Times*. Reston called Kennedy's campaign "The presidential debut of the Organization Men with their wide minds and narrow lapels and lovely wives in carelessly beautiful scarlet coats." The whole time she was reading the column, Jim listened to Edna working in the kitchen. He could smell the ham and cabbage. He felt close to fainting.

Barbara put the paper down and waited for him to come to the point. He made his request. She hesitated. For a moment he had a fear she was going to accept. But she stuck to her rules and turned him down.

"Some nice smells coming from the kitchen," he commented.

"Cabbage smells up the whole house," said Barbara. She stood up. The visit was over. He kept talking to stall her. She brought him to the front door. Finally Edna stuck her head out from the kitchen. "Hiya, Jim."

"Hello, Edna. Some nice smells you're making."

"Ham and cabbage. Why don't you stay? We have plenty."

"Sure!"

So it was Edna he had to thank. And with every mouthful he had at the table he fell a little more in love with her. She was homely as a kitchen pot, Jim thought, but she was worth ten of the good-looking girls. After dinner Barbara went upstairs. Bonnie and Alice had never showed at all. They weren't very regular, apparently, about meals. Jim washed the dishes for Edna. He did everything he could to please her. He told her how nice she looked. She accepted the flattery with the simplicity that was her nature, and laughed and laughed.

On the way to his own place after his goodbyes, Jim made the resolution he'd take Edna out to dinner some night. The deflating thought came to his mind that he had made the same resolution a few nights before.

He got up at four-thirty in the morning and walked downtown again to Workmen Inc. It meant he would miss class. He sat on the benches with the brigade of the lost. He eager-eyed the dispatcher each time the telephone rang. He reasoned that the dispatcher would pick him out, having seen him before. But the dispatcher ignored him again, so he had cut class in vain. Seven o'clock came. Eight o'clock. He was hungry and tired.

At nine o'clock he left and went to Mass. Each reference in the Mass to Lenten fasting seemed a personal thing. He was really keeping the fast this Lent, he thought, out of necessity more than will. The Epistle reading was from Isaiah: "Deal your bread to the hungry and bring the needy and harbor less into your house. . .Then shall your light break forth as the morning. . .And the glory of the Lord shall gather you up." Jim thought of Norman and Lester from the blood bank. Norman would get to the last judgment, and because he gave a dollar of his blood money to Lester he'd get a passport into paradise. That was the way it worked, Jim thought. Christ himself had said that. We'd be judged on kindness. Jim wished he were in a position to give a dollar to anybody. When he received the Host, he prayed for food. And he said a prayer for Edna.

He decided to go back to Workmen Inc. If there were fewer calls after 9:30, there would also be fewer men to choose from. Perseverance, he hoped. It sometimes paid off.

He waited until eleven o'clock. There were only half a dozen men left. But there weren't any telephone calls at all now. It was hopeless. Five minutes more, he told himself, then kept delaying five minutes at a time until it was eleven thirty. All he could think of was food. Just to have something to eat! If he were sent on a job he would be advanced a dollar. He could buy some food out of that, Jim thought. A donut and coffee anyway.

The telephone rang. The men who were awake straightened in their places. The dispatcher took the order and called out: "Anybody know how to work an electric saw?"

Jim's heart sank. Actually he had no experience as a workman. Next to him on the bench was a moronic-looking youth. This youth waved his arm in the air. The thought came to Jim: if this goofy-looking guy can operate one, I can. So Jim put his hand up too. But the dispatcher ignored them both and picked a man from the corner.

The moronic-looking youth bellowed out, "Hey! I had my hand up first."

The dispatcher ignored him.

"You cocksucker," the youth said, under his breath. He had beady eyes that were too small for his big face. His hair hung matted down over the dirty back collar of his overcoat. His nose had exposed nostrils: it looked as if someone had given it a yank up. There was spittle on his big, turned down mouth.

Jim got up and left. He was walking through the alley to the street when he saw that the moronic-looking youth was behind him. Jim stopped at the head of the alley, wondering where to go next. The youth came up next to him. "I know how to operate electric saws," he said.

"Yeah," said Jim.

"They don't want a guy to work," the youth went on.

"Well," said Jim, "he picks the guys he knows."

"I'd like to go down and kill him," said the youth. Jim looked at his shoulders. He was capable of it.

"This your first time here?" Jim asked.

"Why do you want to know?"

He asked the question with such hostility that Jim decided he'd better get away from him. "I'll see you. Good luck," he told him.

"You wanna go eat?" he asked Jim.

Jim paused.

"You wanna eat?" he asked again.

"I haven't got any money," Jim said.

"Who the fuck asked if you had any money?"

He started up the street. Three stores up there was a delicatessen. He stopped in front of it and turned to Jim who hadn't moved yet from the front of the alley. "Come on," he bellowed.

Jim walked up to the delicatessen and followed him in the door. "What do you want?" the youth asked him.

"A sandwich," said Jim. "Do you have any money?" He looked more than crazy enough to Jim to walk into a store without any money.

"I got money." He pulled a dollar out of his pocket.

"A tuna fish sandwich," said Jim. "And coffee. I'd really appreciate it."

"Give him a tuna fish sandwich!" the youth yelled at the proprietor.

"One?"

"I said one!"

The proprietor naturally got hostile. Jim wished he was out of there.

The youth ordered a Swiss cheese sandwich for himself, and he got a coffee too.

Back on the street, with the sandwich and coffee in a bag in his hand, Jim had an urge to run. But he couldn't do that in return for the act of kindness. "You want to eat in the park?" he asked the youth.

"Yeah."

"I really appreciate the sandwich," said Jim. "I haven't eaten all day. My name is Jim Meagher." He held out his hand.

"Clyde," replied the youth. He didn't bother to give a surname. They shook hands.

They sat on a bench in the park a block away. It was cold, but the sun was out. Jim got a newspaper and spread it out so the planks wouldn't be too cold. The sandwich was very good. And the coffee was warm and savory and sweet.

"Where you from, Clyde?"

"Nowhere."

"You been in Washington long?"

"No."

Clyde wolfed his sandwich. When he'd gotten it down, he took out his wallet and passed it over to Jim. "You want to look?" he asked. He had the wallet open to a picture in the plastic file. It was a snapshot of a girl in the nude. "Take it out," said Clyde. "You can see it better."

"That's all right," said Jim, closing the wallet and handing it back. "Where'd you get that?"

"Why do you want to know for?"

"No reason."

"A guy sold it to me."

Clyde looked at the picture. "I'd like to eat her."

"You'd better put it away," said Jim.

"My friend Jimmy gave it to me."

"Who's Jimmy?"

"He's my friend."

"Here in town?"

"Back home."

"Where's back home?"

"Michigan."

"Do you have a trade or anything that you can get a job at?"

"What's that?"

"What'd you do back in Michigan?"

"I didn't do nothin.'"

Jim stood up. "Well, thanks again. I wish you luck."

"Where you going?"

"I used to be a reporter one time. I'm going down to the National Press Building to see if maybe I can get a job."

"Oh."

Jim went up the street. He looked back. Clyde was staring at the ground. His mouth was hanging open.

Jim's efforts in the afternoon were as futile as those in the morning. He completed the full round of the National Press Building. He met foreign reporters, domestic reporters, lady reporters, male reporters, a full cross section of the world's newspaper people, but nobody had a job. At best he would be given an application.

He walked home in the late afternoon, discouraged, hungry again. All that evening he debated calling his father in New York. He couldn't bring himself to do it. He was twenty-five and if he couldn't support himself now without calling home for money, he would never would be able to. Besides, what if his father were to refuse?

He went to bed after long night prayers. Need gave ardor.

He got up at five o'clock again the next morning and walked downtown to Workmen Inc. He didn't know what else to do. He met Clyde on the street. Jim noticed that his topcoat was torn from the pocket halfway around the side. He looked even more unkempt than he had the day before.

"Hello, Clyde."

Clyde looked up. His face gathered into a smile. "Hey," he said, returning the greeting.

"How'd you do yesterday?"

"I didn't get no job."

"Me either," said Jim.

"You want a donut?" Clyde took out a bag from his pocket and there were two donuts in it. Jim reached in and took one and wolfed it down.

"You can have the other one too," said Clyde.

"No, that's all right."

Clyde insisted. So Jim ate that one too.

They went in and sat as close as they could to the front. The crowd was down from the previous day. Saturday apparently was slow. Each time the dispatcher passed them over, Clyde called him an obscenity, though not loud enough to be heard beyond the area. Jim realized that by sitting next to Clyde he was lessening his already slim chances. But he didn't care, not after the donuts. It was also somehow comforting to listen to Clyde's stream of invective. It was what Jim was thinking too. "Where'd you stay last night?" Jim asked.

"Nowhere."

"You don't have a place?"

"No."

"You mean you just walked around all night?"

"I slept in a hallway for a while." Jim could see the lines of fatigue in his face. It was a hell of a thing, not even to have a place to sleep. As bad as his own situation was, Jim thought, at least he had a roof over his head and a warm bed to sleep in. Jim thought guiltily of Cleary's old cot by the furnace that had lain empty the night before. Clyde could have slept there if Jim hadn't been so anxious to get away from him. But the thought was ridiculous. How could he bring Clyde to Georgetown? What would people say? What would Mrs. Hug say? What would anybody say who saw him? He was close to a moron.

After an hour or so, Jim began to smell Clyde. The room was steam-heated and warm. Clyde apparently hadn't changed his clothes in weeks. Or maybe months.

At five to nine, Jim got up. It was hopeless. He wanted to go to Mass, anyway.

Clyde got up also. "Where are you going?" he asked.

Jim didn't know what to answer. "I'm going for a walk. No use staying here."

"I'm goin' too. That sonofabitch ain't givin' nobody a job."

When they reached Star of the Sea, Jim said, "I'm going in here for a while."

"Can I come too?"

"Sure."

Jim genuflected and knelt in the pew. Clyde didn't genuflect. He just sat down. The priest started Mass. By the time the prayers at the foot of the altar were finished, Clyde was asleep, his head hanging forward, his mouth open.

The Epistle reading was again from Isaiah: "When you shall pour out your soul to the hungry and shall satisfy the afflicted soul, then shall your light rise up in darkness. . .And the Lord will give you rest continually, and will fill your soul with brightness. . .and you shall be like a watered garden, and like a fountain of water whose waters shall not fail. . ."

In the Gospel reading, Christ told the Apostles: "Take courage, it is I. Do not be afraid."

At the end of Mass, Jim shook Clyde. "Do you want to sleep for a while at my place?"

"Okay," said Clyde in a sleepy, dopey manner.

Canal Street was quiet when they got there. Jim was glad no one saw them arrive. Jim brought Clyde into the furnace room and showed him

Cleary's old cot. Clyde threw himself down on it and fell asleep immediately. Jim went into his own room in the front. He felt better for having brought Clyde back, but he still wondered if it hadn't been a crazy thing to do. He was very tired himself. His nerves were strained. He had a headache. He still had no money. He would have to borrow from someone.

It was either Conor O'Hara or call his father in New York. He decided to call Conor. It struck him then he didn't have a dime for a telephone call. If he used the telephone upstairs he would have to reverse charges.

Suddenly he realized he would have to call home anyway. He had no right to borrow more money off Conor. It would be an imposition. He went upstairs to the living room and took the phone and dialed the operator rapidly before there was any more time to think about it. His father answered with a gruff hello.

The operator asked if he'd accept the charges from James Meagher in Washington.

"I will. Is this you James?"

"Hi, Dad."

"Is anything wrong?"

"No, I'm fine."

There was a long pause. Jim realized he would have to talk first, or his father would never say anything at all.

"Dad, I need some money."

"How much?"

"What can you spare?"

"I can spare what you need. How much do you want?"

"Whatever you can send."

"I'll send you thirty dollars. More if you want. What do you need it for?"

"I'm just having trouble getting a job."

"You were working in a record store, you wrote."

"It didn't work out, Dad."

"Shall I send a check?"

"Wire it, will you? There's a Western Union office on 242nd Street. I'll wait for it in the office here."

"All right, son."

"Thank you very much, Dad."

His father grunted. "Are you going to school still?"

"Yes. It's a good course."

"God knows there's nothing in that playwriting."

"We'll see, Dad. Is everything well?"

"Everybody's well."

"How's Florence?"

"How would she be? She's fine. There's no need for more talk on the long distance. Goodbye. And take care you get work."

"Yes, Dad. Thanks again."

"Goodbye. I'll go now and send the money."

"Goodbye, Dad."

His father had already hung up.

On the way down the stairs to the basement, the tensions of the whole week broke. "Goddammit, I'm not going to cry," Jim said to the wall. He went into his room and put his face in his hands and cried.

It was a two-mile walk to 14th Street to the Western Union office. He made it in half an hour. The money order was already there. And it was forty dollars, not thirty. "You'll have to answer two code questions first," the clerk told him.

"What do you mean?" Jim asked nervously, afraid of something going wrong.

"You have to give the same answers as the person who sent the money."

"Okay."

The clerk read: "How old are you?"

"Twenty-five."

"What college did you go to?"

"Fordham."

"Okay. Sign here." The clerk gave him the money. Jim put the four tens in his wallet and went out elated. Why had his father chosen "How old are you" as one of the questions? Was it a stock question suggested by the clerk at the other end? Or was it a barb? It didn't matter. If it was a barb, Jim thought, he had it coming. He couldn't think any thoughts against his father at the moment.

The fastest way home would have been a taxicab, but it would have been at least fifty cents more than the bus. He couldn't throw away fifty cents. He even thought of walking back again. But he didn't have enough strength. He went in to a deli and got a cup of coffee. Then he caught a bus.

When he got to Georgetown, he had to decide whether to get Clyde and go out and eat, or buy some food and bring it in. He went to the Safeway and bought a barbecued chicken, a quart of potato salad, a quart of cole slaw, a chocolate cake, and a six-pack of beer. He told himself as he pushed the cart around the store that he was buying the food because it was cheaper that way, and not because he didn't want to appear in a restaurant with Clyde. All the way home he anticipated eating. He enjoyed too the feeling of bringing home the groceries, of feeding the hungry, even if the hungry were only himself and Clyde. He found Clyde still sprawled out asleep, so he went into the front room and tore a leg off the chicken and ate it, and drank a can of beer. He realized he would have to borrow some utensils to eat the potato salad and cole slaw, so he went upstairs.

He listened at the door of Mrs. Hug's rooms. Mr. Bigelow was talking inside. He and Mrs. Hug ate together on Saturday. Mrs. Hug had told Jim they always had the same meal: martinis, steak and red wine, salad and shortcake. What happened after that she didn't say, though it caused ribald speculation among the boys in the house, and the girls next door. Jim decided not to knock. It would be a bad time to interrupt. The only other person in the house who had a kitchen was Floyd Palmer. Jim didn't relish having to borrow even two forks off Floyd. But there wasn't much choice.

On his way up, he passed Barney Blatt's door on the second floor, and the door opened slightly. He saw Blatt peering through the crack. What a crazy house, thought Jim. What was Blatt spying for?

"Hey, Trigger," Blatt called, opening his door.

"What do you want, Barney?"

"You going up to Palmer's room?"

"Yes."

"If Alice is up there, come back and tell me."

Jim didn't even answer him but kept on going. It was so ridiculous. He was peering through a crack in the door, spying on a girl who didn't have the slightest interest in him. He was a nut.

Jim got no answer for a long while at Palmer's door. He started to turn away when it opened.

"Jim! How are you?" asked Floyd. He had his bathrobe on.

"Fine, Floyd. I'm sorry to bother you. I got some food down there and I'm trying to scout up a couple of forks."

"Sure," said Floyd. He put one hand on Jim's arm. "You need anything else? Dishes?"

"I don't want to bother you."

"No trouble."

"I guess I could use two plates too, then."

Floyd headed for his kitchen. "Catching up on some paperwork," he commented as he passed the coffee table, which was littered with papers.

Jim took the dishes and forks from him. "I'll bring them back in an hour." Then he noted a girl's pocketbook. It was on the side table next to the couch. And there was a blue airline hostess cap next to it.

Floyd followed Jim's gaze and saw them too.

"Alice is taking a nap inside," he explained.

Jim didn't know what to say.

"She said there was too much noise over at the house, so I told her she could take a nap inside there. It's quiet," Floyd continued. "She just came off two straight shifts. She's really bushed, the poor kid."

"It's tough, I guess."

"Hey, you still need that five?" Floyd asked.

"No, it's all right. I got some money."

"Jeez," said Floyd. "I felt bad about that. You just hit me at a bad time. I had just put money in the bank."

"No sweat."

"Any time. Remember that."

"Okay. Thanks for this stuff."

Jim went downstairs, moving with extra speed past Barney Blatt's room. The door didn't open.

Clyde was up. He was tearing the chicken apart, fingering it all over.

"Hey Clyde. Wash your hands, eh?"

"Somebody left a chicken here," said Clyde.

"Nobody left it, I bought it."

"Where did you get the money?" Clyde asked.

"My father wired it."

Jim set down the plates and looked with distaste at the torn-apart chicken. "Go wash your hands," he told Clyde again.

When Clyde came back, they both had a beer and ate. Jim found a part of the chicken that looked like it hadn't been touched. Clyde ate the rest. Jim thought he himself would have a ravenous appetite but he didn't. Clyde had to eat almost all the food. When he had finished, he looked around the room. His gaze settled on the bull's horns over the bar. "Did you shoot that?"

"No. I bought it."

"I shot a cat once."

"That's good. Hope it didn't belong to anyone."

"Naw."

"The chicken is good, eh?" Jim asked.

"Shit, yeah."

Jim had a small piece of the chocolate cake. While he was picking at his piece, Clyde ate almost half of the rest of the cake around investigating the rest of the room. He stopped in front of the bookcase. "You read all these books?"

"Yes."

"Wow."

Clyde went around the back of the bar. He found the beer tap. It was an authentic tavern tap, though not connected. Clyde pushed it down and let it swing back. He pushed it down again. He was delighted. "How do you like that?" He pushed it down again. "Where's the beer?" He peered underneath the counter.

Jim laughed. "I don't know where my next meal is coming from, and you think I can afford barrels of beer?"

"What the fuck you got a tap for with no beer?" He reappeared. He pushed the tap down again and he laughed uproariously. "I'm a bartender, a fuckin' bartender. Hey, eh!"

Jim tried to hush him, afraid Mrs. Hug would come down. But it was no use. He was having the time of his life. "One time I was in a bar," said Clyde.

"Once?"

"Yeah. I had a beer too."

"How old are you, Clyde?"

"Twenty."

This was a surprise. Jim thought him older than that.

There was a knock on the door.

Mrs. Hug, thought Jim. This is it.

But it was Alice.

"Y'all must think I'm terrible," she said to Jim.

"Why?"

"Floyd said you were in the apartment. I just wanted to explain."

"That's all right, Alice."

She saw Clyde. Jim could see the startled expression on her face. He should have introduced him, but he didn't. He could tell Alice was waiting to be introduced, or for Jim to explain Clyde's presence.

Jim stood in front of Clyde to try to block him out.

"I was just taking a nap," said Alice. "But I know it must have look jus' awful. I jus' know it."

"Don't be silly."

"I'm embarrassed, Jim. I am."

"Don't be silly."

"I just wanted to explain." She explained several times before she left.

When the door closed on her, Clyde asked in his tuba voice, "Who's that?"

"She lives next door. Don't talk so loud, eh?"

"What she say she's embarrassed for?"

"Nothing. Something that happened."

Jim cleaned up the rest of the food while Clyde continued his inspection of the room. "I wish I had a cup of coffee," said Jim.

"Me too," said Clyde. "Let's go get one."

Jim didn't want to insult Clyde by backing out after suggesting it, so the two of them went down to People's Drug Store. Every person in the place turned to look at Clyde. The waitress served him warily. He made things worse by booming his conversation all over the store.

"You got a good place back there," he said.

"It's not bad for a basement."

"Nobody's using that bed next to the furnace, eh?"

"The landlady's kind of strict about having visitors," said Jim.

"Screw her," Clyde replied.

"I got to live alone like that," said Jim. "I can't do any writing when there's anyone else around. That's why I don't want anybody living with me."

"If I was living there," said Clyde, "I wouldn't bother you."

Of all the characters to have for a roommate, Jim thought. And in Georgetown. Clyde.

"Can I stay with you?" Clyde asked. The waitress heard him and looked at them both sharply.

"Don't talk so loud."

"Why?"

"People are listening."

"Screw them," said Clyde, looking around.

Jim decided he'd had enough of Clyde. "Here's five dollars," he said to him.

"What are you giving me five dollars for?"

The waitress was watching them again.

"Take it and shut up, will you?"

"I don't want no five dollars." He pushed it back at Jim.

"Take it."

"Naw. I don't want any five dollars."

Well, to hell with you then, Jim said to himself. You survived up to now by yourself. You can survive the rest of the way too. Why am I responsible for you?

Jim got up and put on his coat. He looked down at Clyde, who seemed genuinely unconcerned about the way the conversation was going.

What would happen to him, Jim thought, if I just left him now? He didn't have any money. He had no place to sleep. He couldn't get a day's work until Monday at least. Jim was starting to hate him. He sat down again.

On the way back to the house, Jim decided to compromise. "You can sleep next to the furnace until Monday morning. But that's it. Then you go."

"Okay."

Jim left him at the basement. He warned him not to go upstairs and not to answer the door. Jim went for a walk. He hated the situation and he hated himself for hating it. One thing was sure: Clyde wasn't all the simpleton that he looked. He was shrewd somehow. What was Jim going to do now?

It was Saturday night. He could hook up with Cleary, especially now that he had some money in his pocket. But could he just leave Clyde? He didn't even consider the possibility of taking Clyde along on a round of parties. It would have been ridiculous. Jim wished now that he had made the date with Barbara. If he had asked her to go dancing, she would have accepted, Jim knew. It would have been a legitimate excuse to just leave Clyde for the evening.

I must be going nuts, he said. Why am I responsible for him?

When Jim got back, he asked Clyde to take a shower. He was surprised when Clyde agreed. While he was showering, Jim threw out his clothes. They made a rag-tag outfit of the clothes that Cleary and other former inhabitants had left in the back of the furnace room. It didn't look like much, but at least Clyde didn't smell anymore. His hair was too long, but it was too late in the day for a barber.

Clyde played with the bar tap for a while. When he got tired of being a bartender, Jim tried to teach him gin rummy. After two hours, Clyde was still showing his hand of cards to Jim every time. Jim gave up.

"Tell me about your past," he encouraged Clyde, and bit by bit some information emerged. Clyde had tried to get into the Navy but didn't pass the test. He spoke bitterly of his parents, from whom he was estranged. From the look of things, Jim thought, Clyde's anger with them was probably justified. He had run away the year before and had been on the road ever since.

They talked for hours that way, in bursts and snippets. At midnight, Jim decided he had to get out of the house. He told himself it was necessary to go to O'Malley's and pay Conor O'Hara the five dollars he owed him.

"Clyde, I'm going to see a guy to pay some money I borrowed."

"Okay, let's go."

"No, you better go to bed. You must be tired."

"I ain't tired."

"You must be. You only slept a couple of hours today and you didn't sleep at all last night."

"Don't you want me to come?"

"It's not that. It's just that you should get a decent sleep. I got an extra pair of pajamas you can use tonight." The end of those pajamas, thought Jim.

"I don't wear no pajamas."

"Suit yourself. Don't go out though. And don't go upstairs. I won't be long."

"Don't worry about me. What do you think I am? A kid?"

At O'Malley's, Jim found Conor and Black Tom and Des the bartender and Phil the accordionist. He paid Conor the five and then he sat down. They sang and joked and drank until three in the morning. Several times he thought of Clyde and it made him feel guilty. He'd given him food and clothes, but he wouldn't give him what he really wanted, which was simple friendship. Clyde would love to be down here now, Jim thought, amid the accordion music and the laughter, and the camaraderie. And was it so certain they wouldn't accept the poor ox? Conor certainly would. And, following his lead, the others would too. Or maybe just following their own lead.

I'm a bastard, thought Jim. Well, to hell with it then. I'm a bastard. That was maybe Clyde's one talent. That he could make a person feel like a bastard.

Sunday morning, Jim slept very late. When he awoke, Clyde was sitting up on the barstool, looking at him.

"Good morning," said Jim.

"Mornin'." Clyde was munching on a piece of chocolate cake.

"Have you been up long?" Jim asked.

"I been up since six o'clock."

"What have you been doing?" It was eleven thirty.

"I walked around outside."

"Did you meet anybody?"

"No."

That's good, thought Jim. "You should have had breakfast. You should have taken that five I gave you last night. I'll give it to you now." Jim reached for his wallet. He looked in the flap. He only had twenty four dollars. How much had he spent last night? He couldn't even remember. He'd bought more than one round though. Stupid. "I'll give you three dollars," said Jim.

"Okay." Jim handed it over.

"I'll pay you tomorrow when I get a job," said Clyde. "For the clothes too."

"That's all right," said Jim. "Boy, I feel great. That's the best sleep I've had since I can remember."

"You went to see a girl last night, didn't you?" Clyde asked.

Jim laughed. If that's what Clyde wanted to think, what harm, he thought. It explained why Jim couldn't take him, anyway.

When Jim laughed, Clyde's face creased in a smile. "You cocksucker. You go leave me and you go see your girl."

"You can go get your own girls," said Jim.

"I had a girl back home," said Clyde. "I'm going to have another girl friend too."

"That's good. Hope she can put up with you."

"She'll be a nice girl," said Clyde. "She won't be a fool like me."

It was very embarrassing. Jim didn't say anything; he didn't know what to say. He went to the back and showered and dressed. Clyde came with him to Sunday Mass. They sat in the choir loft; it was Jim's idea so they wouldn't be seen. They ate at People's Drug Store. Then Jim read the *Washington Post* back at the house while Clyde continued his investigations, crawling under the bar, fingering the eagle, taking books out of the bookcase. Jim watched him eat another piece of the chocolate cake. It made Jim hungry, and he got up to have a piece. There were ants crawling on the cake. "Clyde, did you eat this with ants on it?"

"Couple of bugs don't hurt nobody."

"You're going to get sick."

"Naw."

Jim felt sick. He threw the rest of the cake in the trash barrel out back.

They had dinner at the Wisconsin Avenue cafeteria. Clyde tried his loud humor on the girls on the serving line, but all he did was scare them. He hit Jim in the ribs once, spilling soup and coffee on his tray. "Look at all the meat they give!" Jim got away from him as fast as he could and he sat in a corner of the cafeteria in the hope Clyde might not find him.

In the evening, Jim read Ibsen's *Ghosts*, the play assigned for next class, while Clyde played with the beer tap. In the morning, Clyde kept to his agreement and left. He was up at 5:30 to go down to Workmen Inc. Jim gave him another three dollars and offered to drive him downtown, but Clyde said he'd take the bus. They shook hands and parted.

After class, Jim checked the bulletin board at the student union, but there were no new job offers. He checked the want ads in the paper next, and followed up two leads but nothing came of them. He did his laundry, put gas and oil in the car, bought food, supplies, cigarettes. His money was growing short again already.

He job-hunted all day Tuesday. In vain. Try as he did to conserve money he still spent three dollars that day. He seemed to have holes in his pockets. With a panic he changed his last dollar in buying breakfast on Wednesday morning. He redoubled his prayers at Mass that morning. He had gone through forty dollars in five days. How had he done it? Would he ever learn to save?

He went to class Wednesday because he couldn't skip again without the professor noticing. He was frightened. He couldn't ask his father for more money. Even if he got a job immediately, he would have to wait for a paycheck. He didn't even have any money to buy a meal. Panicked thoughts stampeded through his head.

What will I eat tonight?

Jim was surprised to find Clyde sitting on the basement steps when he got home. The big youth looked as unkempt as when Jim had first seen him. "You've been sleeping outdoors?" Jim asked.

"Yeah."

"You might as well stay here tonight."

"I got a lead on a job for tomorrow," said Clyde. "You can come too. They need two guys. That's what I came to tell you."

"I haven't got any money, Clyde. So I can't give you any food."

Clyde took out his wallet. He had two dollars. He also had two quarters. "I didn't want to spend all the money you gave me," he said to Jim.

"You still have all that left?"

"I didn't want to spend it," said Clyde, "because I didn't know if I'd be able to pay it all back because I didn't have no job. And I don't like to take no money from a guy if I don't pay it back. I didn't spend hardly anything."

They used the money to buy a barbecued chicken in the Safeway. The job Clyde had heard of was a landscaping one in Rockville, Maryland. They used the remainder of the two-fifty to buy gas and drive up there early the next morning. Sure enough, the landscaper hired them for a day's work. They worked eight hours and got paid twelve dollars apiece, and the landscaper asked them to come back again.

"You might as well stay here," Jim told Clyde that evening.

"Okay. Sure. I'll pay part of the rent."

And just like that, Jim had a roommate.

Chapter 40

January 1961

In three hours on the bus, Jim Meagher moved from 13th Street to the block before Dupont Circle—a total of five blocks. It was incredible. He'd left the florist shop at two and it was five-thirty now and he wasn't even out of downtown Washington. The snow howled around the bus. Car tires whined on ice patches. People complained, muttered, talked about President-elect Kennedy's inauguration the next day. Jim had given up his seat on the bus two hours before. Most of the men were standing. The air was stifling. He sweated in his winter clothes.

"We're not going to get home at all tonight," said the lady sitting facing where Jim was standing.

"All night on a bus!" cried an eighteen- or nineteen-year-old girl in a seat faced toward the front.

"No parade tomorrow. They'll call everything off," said the girl next to her.

"Naw. They'll clear it off tonight," said a man beside Jim.

"I doubt it," said the man next to him.

Was there anything to be gained by trying to walk it to Georgetown? Jim had seen men get off, then get back on after the bus had gone a block or so. Besides, the orchid he had bought earlier would surely freeze and die. He lifted the flower box and opened it. The flower still had color and texture. He had waited in the snow for the bus though and then sat in the heat. The sudden temperature changes wouldn't do it any good. Five bucks shot to hell. And where would he get another orchid tomorrow, on Inauguration Day itself?

"Could I see it?" asked the lady in front of him.

He handed it down to her and she opened it eagerly. "It's going to die," he said.

"It's beautiful. Are you going to the Ball?" she asked.

"Yes."

"I hope she'll wear it in luck," said the lady. "You never know. Put it in the refrigerator when you get home. It might be all right."

"Can I see it?" asked a teenaged girl.

Jim gave it to her reluctantly. She took it out of the box and held it above her breast and called out: "I'm Jackie Kennedy!" She tilted her head in a picture pose. She got laughs.

"Don't handle it," said Jim.

"Don't worry about it, Jack," said the man next to him. "There ain't going to be no ball."

Jim got the flower back and put it in the box and put the box under the coat on his arm.

"You want your seat back, Mister?" the girl asked him.

"No, it's all right."

She stood up anyway. "Take a rest for a few minutes." So he sat down. Most of the people in the bus were taking turns. Jim was next to one of the young girls. The lady was sitting in profile in front of him.

"I'm so hungry," said the girl next to him.

The lady turned and looked at Jim's wan expression. "Don't worry. We'll make it."

"Sometime."

He looked at his watch. Twenty to six.

All the old gang had come down for the Inaugural Ball. The whole crowd would be at Mrs. Hug's by now. He could just see them, Red and D'Arcy, and Morissey and Jill. Even Alaco. Alaco, seeing his life in Washington. He imagined them knocking on the door, and Clyde coming out and telling them, "I don't know where the hell he is." Clyde was sure to come out with something stupid. As if it wasn't bad enough for him just to be there. They'd be shocked just to meet him.

The arrangements had been wrong from the beginning. He should have followed Tom and Connie's plans to have everyone come from the train station to their house, since Red and D'Arcy and Alaco and Jill were going to stay there anyway. But he wanted his place to be the first one that Alaco would see. A champagne party at his place. It would be a great champagne party now, he thought, with Clyde as the host. What would they think of Clyde? He should have given them some preparation.

The bus moved a few yards, then stopped again. Passengers cleared circles in the steam on the windows to check the progress. Chances were, he hoped, the whole group got stranded at Union Station. But if they were lucky enough to get a cab, they might get through. A cab would make it where a bus wouldn't. He should get out and walk. It was senseless to sit for hours. But they were almost into Dupont Circle. It would be a straight run after that. By foot, it would be an hour or more in the snow.

That would be the end of Alaco's orchid, Jim thought glumly. How could he take her to the Ball without an orchid?

Donuts were passed back. A good Samaritan up front. The girls ate them. Jim gave the girl standing next to him the seat back. He watched a man in the back row nibble a chocolate bar furtively and slip it back in his pocket. It was like a concentration camp, Jim thought wildly. People hoarding food.

He was overemphasizing his own troubles, Jim knew. After all, the whole city was tied up. How about poor Kennedy? He'd have to be inaugurated in the snow. Maybe Clyde had found work and was stuck somewhere. Better nobody home than Clyde.

The bus moved a full half block and the passengers cheered. Word came back from someone with a portable radio that soldiers were being brought in to clear Pennsylvania Avenue. Would the New York train even get to Washington? The trains always got through. Jim had prepared so long to make everything go right this weekend. Everything had built up to it. That's what made it so disappointing.

He thought back to Thanksgiving, when he had first seen Alaco again. Her mother was back in the hospital, probably the third time in as many years. The nuns had taken pity on Mr. Armstrong, caring for the huge unruly brood himself while still working as a policeman. Alaco was the oldest daughter. They had sent her home, a work of mercy; come back, they had said, when your family can spare you.

She'd blushed when he saw her at Red and D'Arcy's apartment over Thanksgiving weekend, just as she had blushed at Mallard Lake that first time. At that moment, a hope he had thought dead was born again in his heart.

When he was home for Christmas, it took root deeper. In a still moment during conversation after dinner at Red's, Jim had asked Alaco the question that had been hanging in the air. "When your mother gets back, will you enter again?"

"I don't know," she had replied. "I'm not sure. Father said to just lead an ordinary life and let things take their course."

Trapped in the bus, he ran over in his mind all the things he'd tell her once he got her alone. How there had never been anyone else, not over all the years. All those hours in the Mediterranean that he'd thought about her.

He didn't want to stop her if she wanted to go back to the convent. He couldn't anyway, of course. But maybe God didn't want her to go back, he thought. Maybe God wanted her to marry *him*. Should he say that? Maybe not. Maybe overdramatizing.

The play is in New York, Jim thought. It won't make me rich, but even if it gets just an option, it will be money coming in. And a part-time job would supplement that. We won't starve. Not as long as I have two hands, we won't starve.

The bus hadn't moved at all in at least ten minutes. He got off. The snow and wind were welcome for a brief moment, after the heat of the bus, but soon his face began to sting. He walked for an hour and a half, slipping and sliding along the sidewalks. He was blue by the time he got to Canal Street.

They were all there, celebrating. As soon as he opened the door, he saw Cleary's big meat face at the bar. He was pouring the champagne. Jim got a shout when he came in. He greeted them all, but he saw only Alaco. She was talking to Clyde. She had a sweater and skirt on; a yellow sweater, and a brown-checked skirt. Her cheeks were apple-red from the weather. She was as beautiful as ever. She came over with a big smile. "You have a nice place, Jim."

"Thanks, Al."

"I was talking to your roommate."

"Oh yeah, Clyde."

Clyde gave him a whack on the back. "What a girlfriend. Wow!"

Alaco blushed. Good old Clyde. Always said the right thing.

He shook hands with Red, who was looking for the beer. "It's out back. I'll get it." He kissed D'Arcy and Connie and waved to Tom. Where was Jill? Dan Morissey brought over a girl with red-gold hair and a beaming smile. He introduced her as Jeannine, Jeannine Clark.

"Nice to meet you, Jeannine." She was a beautiful girl. And Morissey, fat old Popeye, had his arm around her.

Out back, getting the beer, Jim asked Red, "What happened to Jill?"

Red shrugged. "I figured Popeye would bring her. I gave him the two tickets. Then he showed up with this gal."

"Where'd he find her?" Jim asked.

"She's one of his students. He told me he had to arrange it with a nun to get her out of the dormitory for the weekend. She's some head, isn't she?" asked Red, grinning.

"A knockout. What's her name? Jeannine?"

"Yeah. I was sure he was going to ask Jill. I guess he's not going with her anymore."

"What's this gal bothering with Morissey for?"

"Let me tell you," said Red. "You can never figure women."

"Morissey is full of surprises, no kidding."

But Jim found himself disappointed that Jill was going to miss the weekend. "It would have been fun to see Jill," he said aloud. "What conversations we used to have. And I wanted to tell her about my play."

"That's right!" Red shouted, and clapped him on the back. "You sold a play! Who would have thought it, a successful playwright!"

Jim was embarrassed. "It's not sold yet," he protested. "They're taking an option on it. Let's talk about something else."

"Who's that guy, Clyde?" Red asked.

"I met him last year on a job. He helped me out when I was really low, and he had no place to stay, so I let him stay on here."

"He's noisy, isn't he?"

"He's just a kid."

Then Red told Jim some more surprising news. Red was going to run for the Democratic Council in Yonkers. He was in an exuberant mood. He thanked Jim twice for the tickets. They had cost $50 a pair, but apparently Red didn't mind the expense. He was doing good in the law now. "D'Arcy," Red said, "hasn't been so happy about anything in months. You really did me a favor."

"You should thank Conor O'Hara, really, for the tickets," said Jim. "He arranged for them."

"I will," said Red.

Jim went back inside. He really had no duties as a host, since everyone but him was high already. He was longing to talk to Alaco with none of her brothers and sisters or their mutual friends around her. But he couldn't get rid of Clyde. Clyde was delighted with Alaco. Clyde told her everything that happened over the year, and started every story with "Me and Jim," until Jim was fearful she'd think Clyde was the only friend Jim had in Washington.

"The Irish Ambassador's son was going to come tonight and a lot of other people," Jim finally interrupted. "But I guess no one will make it in the snow."

"That's too bad," Alaco said. "Jim, is this where you wrote the play?"

"Yes, on that typewriter." He pointed to the manual in the corner.

"I type," said Clyde.

"Yeah, Clyde. Why don't you go type?" Jim suggested.

"Naw. I want to talk to your girlfriend. She's nice."

Alaco laughed.

"The play is in New York now," Jim told her.

"I hope it's a success," she said. "Really I do." She said it with such meaning his heart turned over.

"I gave him the good parts of his play," said Clyde.

"Why don't you go get some ice?" Jim asked sharply.

"We don't need no ice. Cleary got the ice."

"Go up and ask Mrs. Hug if she'll come down to the party, then."

"Okay," said Clyde. He was devoted to Mrs. Hug because of an incident that had occurred months before. Floyd Palmer, who had grown weary of Clyde's presence in the house, had issued an ultimatum to her, "Either that half-wit leaves or I leave." Palmer had been shocked when Mrs. Hug came to a quick decision; she had told Palmer that *he* could leave.

Clyde went to get Mrs. Hug.

D'Arcy asked after Bonnie and Barbara, both of whom Jim had mentioned when they saw each other over the holidays.

"Bonnie went back to Pottsville," Jim said. "That whole house of girls split up. And I don't know what happened to Barbara." Barbara was living in another house in Georgetown.

Mrs. Hug did come down eventually. The party went on until midnight. Then all except Mrs. Hug and Cleary went to Tom and Connie's house, where Red and D'Arcy and the girls would stay. Morissey would stay with Jim and Clyde.

The snow had stopped. Clyde wanted to come along on the walk to Tom and Connie's house, and Jim got annoyed. Clyde had agreed he wouldn't tag along for the weekend.

"Let him come," said Alaco.

So he came. There was a snowball fight of course, and Clyde joined in with delight.

Jim walked ahead with Alaco. "I don't know what you think of Clyde," he started to say.

She interrupted. "He's Christ to you."

Jim stopped cold. "What?"

She smiled at Jim. "I figured that out right away, Jim Meagher. I'm not so bad at figuring things, you know."

Jim looked back at the rest of the gang. Morissey and Red were arguing about Kennedy, with Red defending him and Morissey attacking him. Jeannine and Connie and Tom and Clyde were frolicking in the snow. D'Arcy was the wildest of all, running like a colt and throwing snowballs.

Jim looked down at Alaco, at the white face in the fur hood, and the twinkling eyes. "I've looked forward so much to this weekend," he told her.

"I have, too," she said. "I'm glad you asked me. You promised once to take me to a ball, you know."

"I remembered, don't worry."

She laughed. He took her hand, and they all made their way to Tom and Connie's.

When Jim got back again to the basement with Morissey and Clyde, it was two in the morning. Clyde went to his bed by the furnace, and Jim pulled out the bed couch in his room to accommodate Morissey. Clyde started to sing in the furnace room. "What's he doing?" Morissey asked.

"He likes folk music. He sings himself to sleep."

Morissey shut the door. He turned. "Where did you find that fool?"

Jim explained.

"I thought he came to Washington with Kennedy," said Morissey. "I had him figured for Secretary of State." Jim lay back on the couch and laughed.

"What? He'd fit right in with this administration," Popeye Morissey continued. Jim laughed again. It had been a long time since he'd heard Morissey sound off.

"Who's that Jeannine?" Jim asked.

"She's mad for me," said Morissey.

"What did you do: promise her all A's if she came to Washington?"

"I told you. She's mad for me. She came up to me at Thanksgiving and asked for a date. What am I going to do? Fight it?"

"She's beautiful," said Jim.

"She's not bad," said Morissey, pleased.

"Seems like a lot of fun."

"Did you think I'd pay twenty five dollars for her ticket otherwise?"

"She's young though."

"Old enough."

In bed at last, Jim couldn't sleep. What did it mean, he wondered, when Alaco let him take her hand? Did it mean what he hoped it meant?

Red was going into politics. Jim had expected that. It was funny about Red and D'Arcy: they seemed much older than the rest of the group. D'Arcy looked thirty and she was twenty-five. Red looked even older.

Alaco hadn't aged a month in five years. It was the convent, Jim thought. The clock stopped there. And Morissey was going out with a girl who wasn't any older than Alaco was in that one summer long ago. That one unforgotten summer. All the others were forgotten, except that one. Because she held his hand against her on the beach and gave him the happiest moment of his life.

Did he really have a chance? If he did have a chance—it was ironic—it would be because of Clyde. "He's Christ to you. I figured that out." She always gave the highest of motives.

He had set the alarm for seven. The whole group was going to Mass before the inaugural ceremony. It seemed that barely a moment had passed before it was ringing loudly through the room.

Morissey sat up, enraged. "Where are we going at this hour of the morning?"

"The girls want to go to Mass."

"Let them go."

"I told Alaco I'd take her."

"The hell with them."

"Get up, you heap," Jim told Morissey. "You want that kid to find out what an old bastard you are? She'll leave you and go back to school."

"Let her."

"It's a hell of a thing," said Jim. "You're teaching in a Catholic college, and you wouldn't get up to say a prayer for the first Catholic president."

"Don't give me any lectures on religion," Morissey raged. "You seducer of nuns. You convent hawk."

"Popeye, what are you talking about?"

"You snake in the holy water font, you fox in the wimple, you—"

"You should talk," Jim replied. "Jill was a fellow professor, at least. Now you're a lecher in the dormitory, wolf in the nursery."

"At least I'm not crawling on my belly behind the altar rail."

"Yeah? What did you give your girlfriend for Christmas? A rattle?"

"I gave her a rattle, all right," said Morissey with a leer in his voice.

"You're so full of bull," said Jim. "That kid knows more than you'll know when you're thirty-five."

"She knows what I taught her and that's all she knows," said Morissey.

"She doesn't even know the facts of life then."

This stung Morissey. "Lecher in the vestibule, hawk in the choir loft, seducer in a surplice."

Jim laughed. But he worried about it later at Saint Matthew's Cathedral. Maybe he was doing wrong even in just chasing Alaco. But it didn't seem so. She said she wasn't sure she was going back. It was her decision to make. Not his to worry about.

There was cold bright sunshine on Pennsylvania Avenue as they listened to the inaugural address. The ruddy-faced president seemed young, younger even than his forty-three years. The day seemed young, and they felt young again. It was an atmosphere full of hope. They stayed for as much of the parade as they could stand in the cold. Everyone went back then to Tom and Connie's for dinner. Then they got dressed for the ball. Jim and Morissey went back to the basement. Popeye fixed Jim's stud amid a new series of epithets: "Wolf in the nunnery, lecher in the beeswax. . ."

"You're a real tiger when you're with me, Popeye," Jim laughed. "But when that little Jeannine is around you're like a lamb. You haven't got two words to say."

"I say what I want, when I want."

"She clears her throat and you apologize."

"I run the show," Popeye yelled. "No woman runs me." He was so vehement that Jim was surprised.

Back at Tom's, the girls came down in their ball gowns. Again, Alaco was the only one Jim really saw. She wore a simple white dress, with no frills besides gold slippers. Nor did she need any. Even the orchid—it had survived—seemed superfluous.

They went to the Sheraton Park Hotel. The ballroom was jammed when they got there, and the champagne was already gone. The president came just before midnight. The crowd flocked to the end of the ballroom where he stood behind a barrier, shaking hands. There was no chance for Jim and Alaco to get near. He held her up so that she could see him close anyway. "He's so handsome," she said. "He's so handsome."

They danced to the jazz band downstairs, and to the formal band upstairs. It was the best night for Jim in years. Five years.

They went back to Tom and Connie's for more champagne and sandwiches. It was time to be alone. Morissey and Jeannine disappeared. Jim went to the kitchen, and over near the patio, he saw Red and D'Arcy with their backs to him. D'Arcy had her arm around Red's waist. When Jim went back into the living room, Tom and Connie were gone too. Alaco was alone, sitting on the couch.

"Would you like a sandwich?"

"No, thanks Jim. I'm too excited."

"Did you have a good time?"

"One of the best nights I ever had," she said.

He sat down near her, but not too close. He wanted to leave the initiative to her. If she was ever going to come to him, she'd come right then, Jim thought. Without coyness. Of her own volition. It was her way. His heart felt like it had stopped beating.

He waited for her to come over.

She didn't.

He wanted to cry but didn't. They sat in silence for a long minute.

"You're going back, aren't you?"

"Yes."

"I wanted to marry you."

"I'm a bride already, Jim. A bride of Christ. That's where I belong. I know that now."

"I understand."

It was as simple as that.

She did kiss him good night. But it was not I Love You. It was Thank You.

Chapter 41

June 1962

It was a cloudy day, the first Saturday in June. Rain was in the air. That was a delight to Jim's aunts, uncles and cousins, for it was part of Irish folklore—rain on one's wedding day was a promise of many children.

Jim was sure he was very calm as he stood outside St. Margaret's Church, greeting family and friends arriving for the ceremony. But then his father came over to him and said abruptly, "You belong inside. The bridal car will be along any moment."

Jim went into the church. All the heads in the pews were turned to the vestibule. He walked up the side aisle to the pew where his best man, Red Harrigan, and the ushers, Cricket and Harold Connolly, were already seated. They pushed in to make room for him. Cricket had something in his hand, which he revealed slyly to Jim. It was his ridiculous old white woolen cap with the pom-pom. Where had he found it after all these years, Jim wondered? They shared a muted laugh.

Five minutes passed. There was stirring and activity in the vestibule. Altar boys came and went in preparation; Jim smiled at the youngest of the bunch, Florence's oldest boy Lawrence. As Lawrence passed by one of the pews, Jim saw Aunt Nora shoot out a hand and fix the cincture he wore askew atop his cassock. Uncle Arthur sat upright next to her, incongruously barbered and well-scrubbed for the occasion.

Suddenly a buzzer sounded upstairs in the choir loft and the organ pealed out the first notes of the wedding march. The crowd rose to its feet as one. And now there was no time to be nervous. The ceremony was on.

Red guided Jim to the head of the aisle. They looked toward the rear door. She was coming, looking radiant behind the diaphanous covering of the veil, grinning to family and friends on both sides of the long aisle.

The church was crowded. All Riverdale, it seemed, from the Hudson River to Van Cortlandt Park, from Marble Hill to Yonkers, was there in attendance. But Jim had no eyes for anyone else in church but the bride, now halfway up the aisle. Was she as frightened as he was, the thought sprung to his mind? She didn't seem frightened at all.

And then she was his. Her father had kissed her. She turned to him with a shy, yet blooming smile. There was no need to say anything.

So all he said was, "Jill."

Then they turned toward Father Jack South and started up the steps.